THE
JEEVES OMNIBUS

Volume 4

Books by P. G. Wodehouse

Fiction
Aunts Aren't Gentlemen
The Adventures of Sally
Bachelors Anonymous
Barmy in Wonderland
Big Money
Bill the Conqueror
Blandings Castle and
  Elsewhere
Carry On, Jeeves
The Clicking of Cuthbert
Cocktail Time
The Code of the Woosters
The Coming of Bill
Company for Henry
A Damsel in Distress
Do Butlers Burgle Banks
Doctor Sally
Eggs, Beans and Crumpets
A Few Quick Ones
French Leave
Frozen Assets
Full Moon
Galahad at Blandings
A Gentleman of Leisure
The Girl in Blue
The Girl on the Boat
The Gold Bat
The Head of Kay's
The Heart of a Goof
Heavy Weather
Ice in the Bedroom
If I Were You
Indiscretions of Archie
The Inimitable Jeeves
Jeeves and the Feudal Spirit
Jeeves in the Offing
Jill the Reckless
Joy in the Morning
Laughing Gas
Leave it to Psmith
The Little Nugget
Lord Emsworth and Others
Louder and Funnier
Love Among the Chickens
The Luck of Bodkins
The Man Upstairs
The Man with Two Left Feet
The Mating Season
Meet Mr Mulliner
Mike and Psmith
Mike at Wrykyn
Money for Nothing
Money in the Bank
Mr Mulliner Speaking
Much Obliged, Jeeves
Mulliner Nights
Not George Washington
Nothing Serious
The Old Reliable
Pearls, Girls and Monty Bodkin
A Pelican at Blandings
Piccadilly Jim
Pigs Have Wings

Plum Pie
The Pothunters
A Prefect's Uncle
The Prince and Betty
Psmith, Journalist
Psmith in the City
Quick Service
Right Ho, Jeeves
Ring for Jeeves
Sam the Sudden
Service with a Smile
The Small Bachelor
Something Fishy
Something Fresh
Spring Fever
Stiff Upper Lip, Jeeves
Summer Lightning
Summer Moonshine
Sunset at Blandings
The Swoop
Tales of St Austin's
Thank You, Jeeves
Ukridge
Uncle Dynamite
Uncle Fred in the Springtime
Uneasy Money
Very Good, Jeeves
The White Feather
William Tell Told Again
Young Men in Spats

Omnibuses
The World of Blandings
The World of Jeeves
The World of Mr Mulliner
The World of Psmith
The World of Ukridge
The World of Uncle Fred
Wodehouse Nuggets
  (edited by Richard Usborne)
The World of Wodehouse Clergy
The Hollywood Omnibus
Weekend Wodehouse

Paperback Omnibuses
The Golf Omnibus
The Aunts Omnibus
The Drones Omnibus
The Clergy Omnibus
The Jeeves Omnibus 1
The Jeeves Omnibus 2
The Jeeves Omnibus 3
The Jeeves Omnibus 4
The Jeeves Omnibus 5
The Mulliner Omnibus

Poems
The Parrot and Other Poems

Autobiographical
Wodehouse on Wodehouse
  (comprising Bring on the Girls,
  Over Seventy, Performing Flea)

Letters
Yours, Plum

THE
JEEVES OMNIBUS

Volume 4

P. G. Wodehouse

Hutchinson

London

First published in this collection 1992
© in this collection the Trustees of the P.G. Wodehouse Estate 1992
Jeeves and the Feudal Spirit © P.G.Wodehouse 1954
Jeeves in the Offing © P.G.Wodehouse 1960
Stiff Upper Lip Jeeves © P.G.Wodehouse 1963

24

Hutchinson
The Random House Group Ltd
20 Vauxhall Bridge Road,
London SW1V 2SA

www.rbooks.co.uk

Addresses for companies within The Random House Group Limited
can be found at: www.randomhouse.co.uk/offices.htm

The Random House Group Limited Reg. No. 954009

A CIP catalogue record for this book
is available from the British Library

ISBN 9780091753405

The Random House Group Limited supports The Forest Stewardship Council (FSC®),
the leading international forest certification organisation. Our books carrying the FSC
label are printed on FSC® certified paper. FSC is the only forest certification scheme
endorsed by the leading environmental organisations, including Greenpeace. Our
paper procurement policy can be found at www.randomhouse.co.uk/environment

Typeset by Pure Tech Corporation, Pondicherry, India
Printed and bound by
CPI Group (UK) Ltd, Croydon, CR0 4YY

Contents

JEEVES AND THE FEUDAL SPIRIT

1

As I sat in the bath tub, soaping a meditative foot and singing, if I remember correctly, 'Pale Hands I Loved Beside the Shalimar', it would be deceiving my public to say that I was feeling boomps-a-daisy. The evening that lay before me promised to be one of those sticky evenings, no good to man or beast. My Aunt Dahlia, writing from her country residence, Brinkley Court down in Worcestershire, had asked me as a personal favour to take some acquaintances of hers out to dinner, a couple of the name of Trotter.

They were, she said, creeps of the first water and would bore the pants off me, but it was imperative that they be given the old oil, because she was in the middle of a very tricky business deal with the male half of the sketch and at such times every little helps. 'Don't fail me, my beautiful bountiful Bertie', her letter had concluded, on a note of poignant appeal.

Well, this Dahlia is my good and deserving aunt, not to be confused with Aunt Agatha, the one who kills rats with her teeth and devours her young, so when she says Don't fail me, I don't fail her. But, as I say, I was in no sense looking forward to the binge. The view I took of it was that the curse had come upon me.

It had done so, moreover, at a moment when I was already lowered spiritually by the fact that for the last couple of weeks or so Jeeves had been away on his summer holiday. Round about the beginning of July each year he downs tools, the slacker, and goes off to Bognor Regis for the shrimping, leaving me in much the same position as those poets one used to have to read at school who were always beefing about losing gazelles. For without this right-hand man at his side Bertram Wooster becomes a mere shadow of his former self and in no condition to cope with any ruddy Trotters.

Brooding darkly on these Trotters, whoever they might be, I was starting to scour the left elbow and had switched to 'Ah, Sweet Mystery of Life', when my reverie was interrupted by the sound of a soft footstep in the bedroom, and I sat up, alert and, as you might say, agog, the soap frozen in my grasp. If feet were stepping softly in my sleeping quarters, it could only mean, I felt, unless of course a burglar had happened to drop in, that the prop of the establishment had returned from his vacation, no doubt looking bronzed and fit.

A quiet cough told me that I had reasoned astutely, and I gave tongue.

'Is that you, Jeeves?'

'Yes, sir.'

'Home again, what?'

'Yes, sir.'

'Welcome to 3a Berkeley Mansions, London, W.1,' I said, feeling like a shepherd when a strayed sheep comes trickling back to the fold. 'Did you have a good time?'

'Most agreeable, thank you, sir.'

'You must tell me all about it.'

'Certainly, sir, at your convenience.'

'I'll bet you hold me spellbound. What are you doing in there?'

'A letter has just arrived for you, sir. I was placing it on the dressing-table. Will you be dining in, sir?'

'No, out, blast it! A blind date with some slabs of gorgonzola sponsored by Aunt Dahlia. So if you want to go to the club, carry on.'

As I have mentioned elsewhere in these memoirs of mine, Jeeves belongs to a rather posh club for butlers and valets called the Junior Ganymede, situated somewhere in Curzon Street, and I knew that after his absence from the metropolis he would be all eagerness to buzz round there and hobnob with the boys, picking up the threads and all that sort of thing. When I've been away for a week or two, my first move is always to make a beeline for the Drones.

'I can see you getting a rousing welcome from the members, with a hey-nonny-nonny and a hot cha-cha,' I said. 'Did I hear you say something about there being a letter for me?'

'Yes, sir. It was delivered a moment ago by special messenger.'

'Important, do you think?'

'One can only conjecture, sir.'

'Better open it and read contents.'

'Very good, sir.'

There was a stage wait of about a minute and a half, during which, my moodiness now much lightened, I rendered 'Roll Out the Barrel', 'I Love a Lassie', and 'Every Day I Bring Thee Violets', in the order named. In due season his voice filtered through the woodwork.

'The letter is of considerable length, sir. Perhaps if I were to give you its substance?'

'Do so, Jeeves. All ready at this end.'

'It is from a Mr. Percy Gorringe, sir. Omitting extraneous matter and concentrating on essentials, Mr. Gorringe wishes to borrow a thousand pounds from you.'

I started sharply, causing the soap to shoot from my hand and fall with a dull thud on the bath mat. With no preliminary warning to soften the shock, his words had momentarily unmanned me. It is not often that one is confronted with ear-biting on so majestic a scale, a fiver till next Wednesday being about the normal tariff.

'You said . . . *what*, Jeeves? A thousand pounds? But who is this hound of hell? I don't know any Gorringes.'

'I gather from his communication that you and the gentleman have not met, sir. But he mentions that he is the stepson of a Mr. L.G. Trotter, with whom Mrs. Travers appears to be acquainted.'

I nodded. Not much use, of course, as he couldn't see me.

'Yes, he's on solid ground there,' I admitted. 'Aunt Dahlia does know Trotter. He's the bloke she has asked me to put the nosebag on with tonight. So far, so good. But I don't see that being Trotter's stepson entitles this Gorringe to think he can sit on my lap and help himself to the contents of my wallet. I mean, it isn't a case of "Any stepson of yours, L.G. Trotter, is a stepson of mine". Dash it, Jeeves, once start letting yourself be touched by stepsons, and where are you? The word flies round the family circle that you're a good provider, and up roll all the sisters and cousins and aunts and nephews and uncles to stake out their claims, several being injured in the crush. The place becomes a shambles.'

'There is much in what you say, sir, but it appears to be not so much a loan as an investment that the gentleman is seeking. He wishes to give you the opportunity of contributing the money to the production of his dramatization of Lady Florence Craye's novel *Spindrift*.'

'Oh, that's it, is it? I see. Yes, one begins to follow the trend of thought.'

This Florence Craye is . . . well, I suppose you would call her a sort of step-cousin of mine or cousin once removed or something of that nature. She is Lord Worplesdon's daughter, and old W. in a moment of temporary insanity recently married my Aunt Agatha *en secondes noces*, as I believe the expression is. She is one of those intellectual girls, her bean crammed to bursting point with the little grey cells, and about a year ago, possibly because she was full of the divine fire but more probably because she wanted something to take her mind off Aunt Agatha, she wrote this novel and it was well received by the intelligentsia, who notoriously enjoy the most frightful bilge.

'Did you ever read *Spindrift*?' I asked, retrieving the soap.

'I skimmed through it, sir.'

'What did you think of it? Go on, Jeeves, don't be coy. The word begins with an I.'

'Well, sir, I would not go so far as to apply to it the adjective which I fancy you have in mind, but it seemed to me a somewhat immature production, lacking in significant form. My personal tastes lie more in the direction of Dostoevsky and the great Russians. Nevertheless, the story was not wholly devoid of interest and might quite possibly have its appeal for the theatregoing public.'

I mused awhile. I was trying to remember something, but couldn't think what. Then I got it.

'But I don't understand this,' I said. 'I distinctly recall Aunt Dahlia telling me that Florence had told her that some manager had taken the play and was going to put it on. Poor misguided sap, I recollect saying. Well, if that is so, why is Percy dashing about trying to get into people's ribs like this? What does he want a thousand quid for? These are deep waters, Jeeves.'

'That is explained in the gentleman's letter, sir. It appears that one of the syndicate financing the venture, who had promised the sum in question, finds himself unable to fulfil his obligations. This, I believe, frequently happens in the world of the theatre.'

I mused again, letting the moisture from the sponge slide over the torso. Another point presented itself.

'But why didn't Florence tell Percy to go and have a pop at Stilton Cheesewright? She being engaged to him, I mean. One would have thought that Stilton, linked to her by bonds of love, would have been the people's choice.'

'Possibly Mr. Cheesewright has not a thousand pounds at his disposal, sir.'

'That's true. I see what you're driving at. Whereas I have, you mean?'

'Precisely, sir.'

The situation had clarified somewhat. Now that I had the facts, I could discern that Percy's move had been based on sound principles. When you are trying to raise a thousand quid, the first essential, of course, is to go to someone who has got a thousand quid, and no doubt he had learned from Florence that I was stagnant with the stuff. But where he had made his error was in supposing that I was the king of the mugs and in the habit of scattering vast sums like birdseed to all and sundry.

'Would you back a play, Jeeves?'

'No, sir.'

'Nor would I. I meet him with a firm *nolle prosequi*, I think, don't you, and keep the money in the old oak chest?'

'I would certainly advocate such a move, sir.'

'Right. Percy gets the bird. Let him eat cake. And now to a more urgent matter. While I'm dressing, will you be mixing me a strengthening cocktail?'

'Certainly, sir. A martini or one of my specials?'

'The latter.'

I spoke in no uncertain voice. It was not merely the fact that I was up against an evening with a couple whom Aunt Dahlia, always a good judge, had described as creeps that influenced this decision on my part. I needed fortifying for another reason.

These last few days, with Jeeves apt to return at any moment, it had been borne in upon me quite a good deal that when the time came for us to stand face to face I should require something pretty authoritative in the way of bracers to nerve me for what would inevitably be a testing encounter, calling for all that I had of determination and the will to win. If I was to emerge from it triumphant, no stone must be left unturned and no avenue unexplored.

You know how it is when two strong men live in close juxtaposition, if juxtaposition is the word I want. Differences arise. Wills clash. Bones of contention pop up and start turning handsprings. No one was more keenly alive than I to the fact that one such bone was scheduled to make its début the instant I swam into his ken, and mere martinis, I felt, despite their numerous merits, would not be enough to see me through the ordeal that confronted me.

It was in quite fairly tense mood that I dried and clothed the person, and while it would perhaps be too much to say that as I entered the sitting-room some quarter of an hour later I was a-twitter, I was unquestionably conscious of a certain jumpiness. When Jeeves came in with the shaker, I dived at it like a seal going after a slice of fish and drained a quick one, scarcely pausing to say 'Skin off your nose'.

The effect was magical. That apprehensive feeling left me, to be succeeded by a quiet sense of power. I cannot put it better than by saying that, as the fire coursed through my veins, Wooster the timid fawn became in a flash Wooster the man of iron will, ready for anything. What Jeeves inserts in these specials of his I have never ascertained, but their morale-building force is extraordinary. They wake the sleeping tiger in a chap. Well, to give you some idea, I remember once after a single one of them striking the table with clenched fist and telling my Aunt Agatha to stop talking rot. And I'm not sure it wasn't 'bally rot'.

'One of your best and brightest, Jeeves,' I said, refilling the glass. 'The weeks among the shrimps have not robbed your hand of its cunning.'

He did not reply. Speech seemed to have been wiped from his lips, and I saw, as I had foreseen would happen, that his gaze was riveted on the upper slopes of my mouth. It was a cold, disapproving gaze, such as a fastidious luncher who was not fond of caterpillars might have directed at one which he had discovered in his portion of salad, and I knew that the clash of wills for which I had been bracing myself was about to raise its ugly head.

I spoke suavely but firmly. You can't beat suave firmness on these occasions, and thanks to that life-giving special I was able to be as firmly suave as billy-o. There was no mirror in the sitting-room, but had there been, and had I caught a glimpse of myself in it, I have no doubt I should have seen something closely resembling a haughty seigneur of the old régime about to tell the domestic staff just where it got off.

'Something appears to be arresting your attention, Jeeves. Is there a smut on my nose?'

His manner continued frosty. There are moments when he looks just like a governess, one of which was this one.

'No, sir. It is on the upper lip. A dark stain like mulligatawny soup.'

I gave a careless nod.

'Ah, yes,' I said. 'The moustache. That is what you are alluding to, is it not? I grew it while you were away. Rather natty, don't you think?'

'No, sir, I do not.'

I moistened my lips with the special, still suave to the gills. I felt strong and masterful.

'You dislike the little thing?'

'Yes, sir.'

'You don't feel it gives me a sort of air? A . . . how shall I put it? . . . A kind of diablerie?'

'No, sir.'

'You hurt and disappoint me, Jeeves,' I said, sipping a couple of sips and getting suaver all the time. 'I could understand your attitude if the object under advisement were something bushy and waxed at the ends like a sergeant-major's, but it is merely the delicate wisp of vegetation with which David Niven has for years been winning the applause of millions. When you see David Niven on the screen, you don't recoil in horror, do you?'

'No, sir. His moustache is very becoming to Mr. Niven.'

'But mine isn't to me?'

'No, sir.'

It is at moments like this that a man realizes that the only course for him to pursue, if he is to retain his self-respect, is to unship the velvet hand in the iron glove, or, rather, the other way about. Weakness at such a time is fatal.

There are limits, I mean to say, and sharply defined limits at that, and these limits I felt that he had passed by about a mile and a quarter. I yield to nobody in my respect for Jeeves's judgment in the matter of socks, shoes, shirts, hats and cravats, but I was dashed if I was going to have him muscling in and trying to edit the Wooster face. I finished my special and spoke in a quiet, level voice.

'I am sorry, Jeeves. I had hoped for your sympathy and co-operation, but if you are unable to see your way to sympathizing and co-operating, so be it. Come what may, however, I shall maintain the *status quo*. It is *status quos* that people maintain, isn't it? I have been put to considerable trouble and anxiety growing this moustache, and I do not propose to hew it off just because certain prejudiced parties, whom I will not specify, don't know a good thing when they see one. *J'y suis, j'y reste*, Jeeves,' I said, becoming a bit Parisian.

Well, after this splendid exhibition of resolution on my part I suppose there was nothing much the chap could have said except 'Very good, sir' or something of that sort, but, as it happened, he hadn't time to say even that, for the final word had scarcely left my lips when the front-door bell tootled. He shimmered out, and a moment later shimmered in again.

'Mr. Cheesewright,' he announced.

And in clumped the massive form of the bird to whom he alluded. The last person I had expected to see, and, for the matter of that, about the last one I wanted to.

2

I don't know if you have had the same experience, but I have always found that there are certain blokes whose mere presence tends to make me ill at ease, inducing the nervous laugh, the fiddling with the tie and the embarrassed shuffling of the feet. Sir Roderick Glossop, the eminent loony doctor, until circumstances so arranged themselves that I was enabled to pierce the forbidding exterior and see his better, softer side, was one of these. J. Washburn Stoker, with his habit of kidnapping people on his yacht and throwing his weight about like a pirate of the Spanish Main, was another. And a third is this G. D'Arcy ('Stilton') Cheesewright. Catch Bertram Wooster *vis-à-vis* with him, and you do not catch him at his best.

Considering that he and I have known each other since, as you might say, we were so high, having been at private school, Eton and Oxford together, we ought, I suppose, to be like Damon and what's-his-name, but we aren't by any means. I generally refer to him in conversation as 'that blighter Stilton', while he, I have been informed by usually reliable sources, makes no secret of his surprise and concern that I am still on the right side of the walls of Colney Hatch or some similar institution. When we meet, there is always a certain stiffness and what Jeeves would call an imperfect fusion of soul.

One of the reasons for this is, I think, that Stilton used to be a policeman. He joined the Force on coming down from Oxford with the idea of rising to a position of eminence at Scotland Yard, a thing you find a lot of the fellows you know doing these days. True, he turned in his truncheon and whistle shortly afterwards because his uncle wanted him to take up another walk in life, but these rozzers, even when retired, never quite shake off that 'Where were you on the night of June the fifteenth?' manner, and he seldom fails, when we run into one another, to make me feel like a rat of the Underworld detained for questioning in connection with some recent smash-and-grab raid.

Add the fact that this uncle of his wins his bread as a magistrate at one of the London police courts, and you will understand why I avoid him as much as possible and greatly prefer him elsewhere. The man of sensibility shrinks from being closeted with an ex-bluebottle with magistrate blood in him.

In my demeanour, accordingly, as I rose to greet him, a close observer would have noted more than a touch of that To-what-am-I-indebted-for-the-honour-of-this-visit stuff. I was at a loss to imagine what he was doing invading my privacy like this, and another thing that had fogged me was why, having invaded it, he was standing staring at me in a stern, censorious sort of way, as if the sight of me had got right in amongst him, revolting his finest feelings. I might have been some dreg of society whom he had caught in the act of slipping a couple of ounces of cocaine to some other dreg.

'Ho!' he said, and this alone would have been enough to tell an intelligent bystander, had there been one, that he had spent some time in the ranks of the Force. One of the first things the Big Four teach the young recruit is to say 'Ho!' 'I thought as much,' he went on, knitting the brow. 'Swilling cocktails, eh?'

This was the moment when, had conditions been normal, I would no doubt have laughed nervously, fingered the tie and shuffled the feet, but with two of Jeeves's specials under my belt, still exercising their powerful spell, I not only remained intrepid but retorted with considerable spirit, putting him right in his place.

'I fail to understand you, officer,' I said coldly. 'Correct me if I am wrong, but I believe this is the hour when it is customary for an English gentleman to partake of a short snifter. Will you join me?'

His lip curled. Most unpleasant. These coppers are bad enough when they leave their lips *in statu quo*.

'No, I won't,' he replied, curtly and offensively. '*I* don't want to ruin my constitution. What do you suppose those things are going to do to your eye and your power of control? How can you expect to throw doubles if you persist in stupefying yourself with strong drink? It's heart-breaking.'

I saw all. He was thinking of the Darts sweep.

The annual Darts sweep is one of the high spots of life at the Drones Club. It never fails to stir the sporting instincts of the members, causing them to roll up in dense crowds and purchase tickets at ten bob a go, with the result that the sum in the kitty is always colossal. This time my name had been drawn by Stilton, and as Horace Pendlebury-Davenport, last year's winner, had gone and got married and at his wife's suggestion resigned his membership, the thing was pretty generally recognized as a sitter for me, last year's runner-up. 'Wooster,' the word flew to and fro, 'is the deadest of snips. He throws a beautiful dart.'

So I suppose it was only natural in a way that, standing, if all went well, to scoop in a matter of fifty-six pounds ten shillings, Stilton should feel that it was his mission in life to see that I kept at the peak of my form. But that didn't make this incessant surveillance of his easier to endure. Ever since he had glanced at his ticket, seen that it bore the name Wooster, and learned that I was a red-hot favourite for the tourney, his attitude towards me had been that of an official at Borstal told off to keep an eye on a more than ordinarily up-and-coming juvenile delinquent. He had a way of looming up beside me at the club, sniffing quickly at my glass and giving me an accusing look, coupled with a sharp whistling intake of the breath, and here he was now doing the same thing in my very home. It was worse than being back in a Little Lord Fauntleroy suit and ringlets and having a keen-eyed nurse always at one's elbow, watching one's every move like a bally hawk.

I was about to say how deeply I resented being tailed up in this manner, when he resumed.

'I have come here tonight to talk seriously to you, Wooster,' he said, frowning in a most unpleasant manner. 'I am shocked at the casual, frivolous way in which you are treating this Darts tournament. You seem not to be taking the most elementary precautions to ensure victory on the big day. It's the old, old story. Over-confidence. All these fatheads keep telling you you're sure to win, and you suck it down like one of your beastly cocktails. Well, let me tell you you're living in a fool's paradise. I happened to look in at the Drones this afternoon, and Freddie Widgeon was at the Darts board, stunning all beholders with a performance that took the breath away. His accuracy was sensational.'

I waved a hand and tossed the head. In fact, I suppose you might say I bridled. He had wounded my amour propre.

'Tchah!' I said, registering scorn.

'Eh?'

'I said "Tchah!" With ref. to F. Widgeon. I know his form backwards. Flashy, but no staying power. The man will be less than the dust beneath my chariot wheels.'

'That's what you think. As I said before, over-confidence. You can take it from me that Freddie is a very dangerous competitor. I happen to know that he has been in strict training for weeks. He's knocked off smoking and has a cold bath every morning. Did you have a cold bath this morning?'

'Certainly not. What do you suppose the hot tap's for?'

'Do you do Swedish exercises before breakfast?'

'I wouldn't dream of such a thing. Leave these excesses to the Swedes, I say.'

'No,' said Stilton bitterly. 'All you do is riot and revel and carouse. I am told that you were at that party of Catsmeat Potter-Pirbright's last night. You probably reeled home at three in the morning, rousing the neighbourhood with drunken shouts.'

I raised a haughty eyebrow. This police persecution was intolerable.

'You would scarcely expect me, constable,' I said coldly, 'to absent myself from the farewell supper of a boyhood friend who is leaving for Hollywood in a day or two and may be away from civilization for years. Catsmeat would have been pained to his foundations if I had oiled out. And it wasn't three in the morning, it was two-thirty.'

'Did you drink anything?'

'The merest sip.'

'And smoke?'

'The merest cigar.'

'I don't believe you. I'll bet, if the truth was known,' said Stilton morosely, intensifying the darkness of his frown, 'you lowered yourself to the level of the beasts of the field. I'll bet you whooped it up like a sailor in a Marseilles bistro. And from the fact that there is a white tie round your neck and a white waistcoat attached to your foul stomach at this moment I gather that you are planning to be off shortly to some other nameless orgy.'

I laughed one of my quiet laughs. The word amused me.

'Orgy, eh? I'm giving dinner to some friends of my Aunt Dahlia's, and she strictly warned me to lay off the old Falernian because my guests are teetotallers. When the landlord fills the flowing bowl, it will be with lemonade, barley water, or possibly lime juice. So much for your nameless orgies.'

This, as I had expected, had a mollifying effect on his acerbity, if acerbity is the word I want. He did not become genial, because he couldn't, but he became as nearly genial as it was in his power to be. He practically smiled.

'Capital,' he said. 'Capital. Most satisfactory.'

'I'm glad you're pleased. Well, good night.'

'Teetotallers, eh? Yes, that's excellent. But avoid all rich foods and sauces and be sure to get to bed early. What was that you said?'

'I said good night. You'll be wanting to run along, no doubt.'

'I'm not running along.' He looked at his watch. 'Why the devil are women always late?' he said peevishly. 'She ought to have been here long ago. I've told her over and over again that if there's one thing that makes Uncle Joe furious, it's being kept waiting for his soup.'

This introduction of the sex motif puzzled me.

'She?'

'Florence. She is meeting me here. We're dining with my uncle.'

'Oh, I see. Well, well. So Florence will be with us ere long, will she? Splendid, splendid, splendid.'

I spoke with quite a bit of warmth and animation, trying to infuse a cheery note into the proceedings, and immediately wished I hadn't, because he quivered like a palsy patient and gave me a keen glance, and I saw that we had got on to dangerous ground. A situation of considerable delicacy had been precipitated.

One of the things which make it difficult to bring about a beautiful friendship between G. D'Arcy Cheesewright and self is the fact that not long ago I unfortunately got tangled up in his love life. Incensed by some crack he had made about modern enlightened thought, modern enlightened thought being practically a personal buddy of hers, Florence gave him the swift heave-ho and – much against my will, but she seemed to wish it – became betrothed to me. And this had led Stilton, a man of volcanic passions, to express a desire to tear me limb from limb and dance buck-and-wing dances on my remains. He also spoke of stirring up my face like an omelette and buttering me over the West End of London.

Fortunately before matters could proceed to this awful extreme love resumed work at the old stand, with the result that my nomination was cancelled and the peril passed, but he has never really got over the distressing episode. Ever since then the green-eyed monster has always been more or less round and about, ready to snap into action at the drop of the hat, and he has tended to docket me as a snake in the grass that can do with a lot of watching.

So, though disturbed, I was not surprised that he now gave me that keen glance and spoke in a throaty growl, like a Bengal tiger snarling over its breakfast coolie.

'What do you mean, splendid? Are you so anxious to see her?'

I saw that tact would be required.

'Not anxious, exactly,' I said smoothly. 'The word is too strong. It's just that I would like to have her opinion of this moustache of mine. She is a girl of taste, and I would be prepared to accept her verdict. Shortly before you arrived, Jeeves was subjecting the growth to some destructive criticism, and it shook me a little. What do you think of it, by the way?'

'I think it's ghastly.'

'Ghastly?'

'Revolting. You look like something in the chorus line of a touring revue. But you say Jeeves doesn't like it?'

'He didn't seem to.'

'Ah, so you'll have to shave it. Thank God for that!'

I stiffened. I resent the view, so widely held in my circle of acquaintances, that I am a mere Hey-you in the home, bowing to Jeeves's behests like a Hollywood yes-man.

'Over my dead body I'll shave it! It stays just where it is, rooted to the spot. A fig for Jeeves, if I may use the expression.'

He shrugged his shoulders.

'Well, it's up to you, I suppose. If you don't mind making yourself an eyesore –'

I stiffened a bit further.

'Did you say eyesore?'

'Eyesore was what I said.'

'Oh, it was, was it?' I riposted, and it is possible that, had we not been interrupted, the exchanges would have become heated, for I was still under the stimulating influence of those specials and in no mood to brook back-chat. But before I could tell him that he was a fatheaded ass, incapable of recognizing the rare and the beautiful if handed to him on a skewer, the door bell rang again and Jeeves announced Florence.

3

It's just occurred to me, thinking back, that in that passage where I gave a brief pen portrait of her – fairly near the start of this narrative, if you remember – I may have made a bloomer and left you with a wrong impression of Florence Craye. Informed that she was an intellectual girl who wrote novels and was like ham and eggs with the boys with the bulging foreheads out Bloomsbury way, it is possible that you conjured up in your mind's eye the picture of something short and dumpy with ink spots on the chin, as worn by so many of the female intelligentsia.

Such is far from being the truth. She is tall and willowy and handsome, with a terrific profile and luxuriant platinum-blond hair, and might, so far as looks are concerned, be the star unit of the harem of one of the better-class Sultans. I have known strong men to be bowled over by her at first sight, and it is seldom that she takes her walks abroad without being whistled at by visiting Americans.

She came breezing in, dressed up to the nines, and Stilton received her with a cold eye on his wrist-watch.

'So there you are at last,' he said churlishly. 'About time, dash it. I suppose you had forgotten that Uncle Joe has a nervous breakdown if he's kept waiting for his soup.'

I was expecting some haughty response to this crack, for I knew her to be a girl of spirit, but she ignored the rebuke, and I saw that her eyes, which are bright and hazel in colour, were resting on me with a strange light in them. I don't know if you have ever seen a female of what they call teen-age gazing raptly at Humphrey Bogart in a cinema, but her deportment was much along those lines. More than a touch of the Soul's Awakening, if I make my meaning clear.

'Bertie!' she yipped, shaking from stem to stern. 'The moustache! It's *lovely*! Why have you kept this from us all these years? It's wonderful. It gives you such a dashing look. It alters your whole appearance.'

Well, after the bad Press the old fungus had been getting of late, you might have thought that a rave notice like this would have been right up my street. I mean, while one lives for one's Art, so to speak, and cares little for the public's praise or blame and all that sort of thing, one can always do with something to paste into one's scrapbook, can one not? But it left me cold, particularly in the vicinity of the feet. I found my eye swivelling round to Stilton, to see how he was taking it, and was concerned to note that he was taking it extremely big.

Pique. That's the word I was trying to think of. He was looking definitely piqued, like a diner in a restaurant who has bitten into a bad oyster, and I wasn't sure I altogether blamed him, for his loved one had not only patted my cheek with an affectionate hand but was drinking me in with such wide-eyed admiration that any fiancé, witnessing the spectacle, might well have been excused for growing a bit hot under the collar. And Stilton, of course, as I have already indicated, is a chap who could give Othello a couple of bisques and be dormy one at the eighteenth.

It seemed to me that unless prompt steps were taken through the proper channels, raw passions might be unchained, so I hastened to change the subject.

'Tell me all about your uncle, Stilton,' I said. 'Fond of soup, is he? Quite a boy for the bouillon, yes?'

He merely gave a grunt like a pig dissatisfied with its ration for the day, so I changed the subject again.

'How is *Spindrift* going?' I asked Florence. 'Still selling pretty copiously?'

I had said the right thing. She beamed.

'Yes, it's doing splendidly. It has just gone into another edition.'

'That's good.'

'You knew it had been made into a play?'

'Eh? Oh, yes. Yes, I heard about that.'

'Do you know Percy Gorringe?'

I winced a trifle. Proposing, as I did, to expunge the joy from Percy's life by giving him the uncompromising miss-in-baulk before tomorrow's sun had set, I would have preferred to keep him out of the conversation. I said the name seemed somehow familiar, as if I had heard it somewhere in some connection.

'He did the dramatization. He has made a splendid job of it.'

Here Stilton, who appeared to be allergic to Gorringes, snorted in his uncouth way. There are two things I particularly dislike about G. D'Arcy Cheesewright – one, his habit of saying 'Ho!', the other his tendency, when moved, to make a sound like a buffalo pulling its foot out of a swamp.

'We have a manager who is going to put it on and he's got the cast and all that, but there has been an unfortunate hitch.'

'You don't say?'

'Yes. One of the backers has failed us, and we need another thousand pounds. Still, it's going to be all right. Percy assures me he can raise the money.'

Again I winced, and once more Stilton snorted. It is always difficult to weigh snorts in the balance, but I think this second one had it over the first in offensiveness by a small margin.

'That louse?' he said. 'He couldn't raise tuppence.'

These, of course, were fighting words. Florence's eyes flashed.

'I won't have you calling Percy a louse. He is very attractive and very clever.'

'Who says so?'

'I say so.'

'Ho!' said Stilton. 'Attractive, eh? Who does he attract?'

'Never mind whom he attracts.'

'Name three people he ever attracted. And clever? He may have just about enough intelligence to open his mouth when he wants to eat, but no more. He's a half-witted gargoyle.'

'He is not a gargoyle.'

'Of course he's a gargoyle. Are you going to look me in the face and deny that he wears short side-whiskers?'

'Why shouldn't he wear short side-whiskers?'

'I suppose he has to, being a louse.'

'Let me tell you –'

'Oh, come on,' said Stilton brusquely, and hustled her out. As they wended their way, he was reminding her once more of his Uncle Joseph's reluctance to be kept waiting for his soup.

It was a pensive Bertram Wooster, with more than a few furrows in his forehead, who returned to his chair and put match to cigarette. And I'll tell you why I was pensive and furrowed. The recent slab of dialogue between the young couple had left me extremely uneasy.

Love is a delicate plant that needs constant tending and nurturing, and this cannot be done by snorting at the adored object like a gas explosion and calling her friends lice. I had the disquieting impression that it wouldn't take too much to make the Stilton-Florence axis go p'fft again, and who could say that in this event, the latter, back in circulation, would not decide to hitch on to me once more? I remembered what had happened that other time and, as the fellow said, the burned child fears the spilled milk.

You see, the trouble with Florence was that though, as I have stated, indubitably comely and well equipped to take office as a pin-up girl, she was, as I have also stressed, intellectual to the core, and the ordinary sort of bloke like myself does well to give this type of female as wide a miss as he can manage.

You know how it is with these earnest, brainy beasels of what is called strong character. They can't let the male soul alone. They want to get behind it and start shoving. Scarcely have they shaken the rice from their hair in the car driving off for the honeymoon than they pull up their socks and begin moulding the partner of joys and sorrows, and if there is one thing that gives me the pip, it is being moulded. Despite adverse criticism from many quarters – the name of my Aunt Agatha is one that springs to the lips – I like B. Wooster the way he is. Lay off him, I say. Don't try to change him, or you may lose the flavour.

Even when we were merely affianced, I recalled, this woman had dashed the mystery thriller from my hand, instructing me to read instead a perfectly frightful thing by a bird called Tolstoy. At the thought of what horrors might ensue after the clergyman had done his stuff and she had a legal right to bring my grey hairs in sorrow to the grave, the imagination boggled. It was a subdued and apprehensive Bertram Wooster who some moments later reached for the hat and light overcoat and went off to the Savoy to shove food into the Trotters.

The binge, as I had anticipated, did little or nothing to raise the spirits. Aunt Dahlia had not erred in stating that my guests would prove to be creeps of no common order. L.G. Trotter was a little man with a face like a weasel, who scarcely uttered during the meal because, whenever he tried to, the moon of his delight shut him up, and Mrs. Trotter a burly heavyweight with a beaked nose who talked all the time, principally about some woman she disliked named Blenkinsop. And nothing to help me through the grim proceedings except the faint, far-off echo of those specials of Jeeves's. It was a profound relief when they finally called it a day and I was at liberty to totter off to the Drones for the restorative I so sorely needed.

The almost universal practice of the inmates being to attend some form of musical entertainment after dinner, the smoking-room was empty when I arrived, and it would not be too much to say that five minutes later, a cigarette between my lips and a brimming flagon at my side, I was enveloped in a deep peace. The strained nerves had relaxed. The snootered soul was at rest.

It couldn't last, of course. These lulls in life's battle never do. Came a moment when I had that eerie feeling that I was not alone and, looking round, found myself gazing at G. D'Arcy Cheesewright.

4

This Cheesewright, I should perhaps have mentioned earlier, is a bimbo who from the cradle up has devoted himself sedulously to aquatic exercise. He was Captain of Boats at Eton. He rowed four years for Oxford. He sneaks off each summer at the time of Henley Regatta and sweats lustily with his shipmates on behalf of the Leander Club. And if he ever goes to New York, I have no doubt he will squander a fortune sculling about the lake in Central Park at twenty-five cents a throw. It is only rarely that the oar is out of his hand.

Well, you can't do that sort of thing without developing the thews and sinews, and all this galley-slave stuff has left him extraordinarily robust. His chest is broad and barrel-like and the muscles of his brawny arms strong as iron bands. I remember Jeeves once speaking of someone of his acquaintance whose strength was as the strength of ten, and the description would have fitted Stilton nicely. He looks like an all-in wrestler.

Being a pretty broad-minded chap and realizing that it takes all sorts to make a world, I had always till now regarded this beefiness of his with kindly toleration. The way I look at it is, if blighters want to be beefy, let them be beefy. Good luck to them, say I. What I did not like at the moment of going to press was the fact that in addition to bulging in all directions with muscle he was glaring at me in a highly sinister manner, his air that of one of those Fiends with Hatchet who are always going about the place Slaying Six. He was plainly much stirred about something, and it would not be going too far to say that, as I caught his eye, I wilted where I sat.

Thinking that it must be the circumstance of his having found me restoring the tissues with a spot of the right stuff that was causing his chagrin, I was about to say that the elixir in my hand was purely medicinal and had been recommended by a prominent Harley Street physician when he spoke.

'If only I could make up my mind!'

'About what, Stilton?'

'About whether to break your foul neck or not.'

I did a bit more wilting. It seemed to me that I was alone in a deserted smoking-room with a homicidal loony. It is a type of loony I particularly bar, and the homicidal loony I like least is one with a forty-four chest and biceps in proportion. His fingers, I noticed, were twitching, always a bad sign. 'Oh, for the wings of a dove' about summed up my feelings as I tried not to look at them.

'Break my foul neck?' I said, hoping for further information. 'Why?'

'You don't know?'

'I haven't the foggiest.'

'Ho!'

He paused at this point to dislodge a fly which had sauntered in through the open window and become mixed up with his vocal cords. Having achieved his object, he resumed.

'Wooster!'

'Still here, old man.'

'Wooster,' said Stilton, and if he wasn't grinding his teeth, I don't know a ground tooth when I see one, 'what was the thought behind that moustache of yours? Why did you grow it?'

'Well, rather difficult to say, of course. One gets these whims.' I scratched the chin a moment.

'I suppose I felt it might brighten things up,' I hazarded.

'Or had you an ulterior motive? Was it part of a subtle plot for stealing Florence from me?'

'My dear Stilton!'

'It all looks very fishy to me. Do you know what happened just now, when we left my uncle's?'

'I'm sorry, no. I'm a stranger in these parts myself.'

He ground a few more teeth.

'I will tell you. I saw Florence home in a cab, and all the way there she was raving about that moustache of yours. It made me sick to listen to her.'

I weighed the idea of saying something to the effect that girls would be girls and must be expected to have their simple enthusiasms, but decided better not.

'When we got off at her door and I turned after paying the driver, I found she was looking at me intently, examining me from every angle, her eyes fixed on my face.'

'You enjoyed that, of course?'

'Shut up. Don't interrupt me.'

'Right ho. I only meant it must have been pretty gratifying.'

He brooded for a space. Whatever had happened at that lovers' get-together, one could see that the memory of it was stirring him like a dose of salts.

'A moment later,' he said, and paused, wrestling with his feelings. 'A moment later,' he went on, finding speech again, 'she announced that she wished me to grow a moustache, too. She said – I quote her words – that when a man has a large pink face and a head like a pumpkin, a little something around the upper lip often does wonders in the way of easing the strain. Would you say my head was like a pumpkin, Wooster?'

'Not a bit, old man.'

'Not like a pumpkin?'

'No, not like a pumpkin. A touch of the dome of St. Paul's, perhaps.'

'Well, that is what she compared it to, and she said that if I split it in the middle with a spot of hair, the relief to pedestrians and traffic would be enormous. She's crazy. I wore a moustache my last year at Oxford, and it looked frightful. Nearly as loathsome as yours. Moustache forsooth!' said Stilton, which surprised me, for I hadn't supposed he knew words like "forsooth". ' "I wouldn't grow a moustache to please a dying grandfather," I told her. "A nice fool I'd look with a moustache," I said. "It's how you look without one," she said. "Is that so?" I said. "Yes, it is," she said. "Oh?" I said. "Yes," she said. "Ho!" I said, and she said "Ho to you!" '

If she had added 'With knobs on', it would, of course, have made it stronger, but I must say I was rather impressed by Florence's work as described in this slice of dialogue. It seemed to me snappy and forceful. I suppose girls learn this sort of cut-and-thrust stuff at their finishing schools. And Florence, one must remember, had been moving a good deal of late in Bohemian circles – Chelsea studios and the rooms of the intelligentsia in Bloomsbury and places like that – where the repartee is always of a high order.

'So that was that,' proceeded Stilton, having brooded for a space. 'One thing led to another, hot words passed to and fro, and it was not long before she was returning the ring and saying she would be glad to have her letters back at my earliest convenience.'

I tut-tutted. He asked me rather abruptly not to tut-tut, so I stopped tut-tutting, explaining that my reason for having done so was that his tragic tale had moved me deeply.

'My heart aches for you,' I said.

'It does, does it?'

'Profusely.'

'Ho!'

'You doubt my sympathy?'

'You bet I doubt your ruddy sympathy. I told you just now that I was trying to make up my mind, and what I'm trying to make it up about is this. Had you foreseen that that would happen? Did your cunning fiend's brain spot what was bound to occur if you grew a moustache and flashed it on Florence?'

I tried to laugh lightly, but you know how it is with these light laughs, they don't always come out just the way you would wish. Even to me it sounded more like a gargle.

'Am I right? Was that the thought that came into your cunning fiend's brain?'

'Certainly not. As a matter of fact, I haven't got a cunning fiend's brain.'

'Jeeves has. The plot could have been his. Was it Jeeves who wove this snare for my feet?'

'My dear chap! Jeeves doesn't weave snares for feet. He would consider it a liberty. Besides, I told you he is the spearhead of the movement which disapproves of my moustache.'

'I see what you mean. Yes, on second thoughts I am inclined to acquit Jeeves of complicity. The evidence points to your having thought up the scheme yourself.'

'Evidence? How do you mean, evidence?'

'When we were at your flat and I said I was expecting Florence, I noticed a very significant thing – your face lit up.'

'It didn't.'

'Pardon me. I know when a face lights up and when it doesn't. I could read you like a book. You were saying to yourself, "This is the moment! This is where I spring it on her!"'

'Nothing of the sort. If my face lit up – which I gravely doubt – it was merely because I reasoned that as soon as she arrived you would be leaving.'

'You wanted me to leave?'

'I did. You were taking up space which I required for other purposes.'

It was plausible, of course, and I could see it shook him. He passed a hamlike hand, gnarled with toiling at the oar, across his brow.

'Well, I shall have to think it over. Yes, yes, I shall have to think it over.'

'Go away and start now, is what I would suggest.'

'I will. I shall be scrupulously fair. I shall weigh this and that. But if I find my suspicions are correct, I shall know what to do about it.'

And with these ominous words he withdrew, leaving me not a little bowed down with weight of woe. For apart from the fact that when a bird of Stilton's impulsive temperament gets it into his nut that you have woven snares for his feet, practically anything can happen in the way of violence and mayhem, it gave me goose pimples to think of Florence being at large once more. It was with heavy heart that I finished my whisky and splash and tottered home. 'Wooster,' a voice seemed to be whispering in my ear, 'things are getting hot, old sport.'

Jeeves was at the telephone when I reached the sitting-room.

'I am sorry,' he was saying, and I noticed that he was just as suave and firm as I had been at our recent get-together. 'No, please, further discussion is useless. I am afraid you must accept my decision as final. Good night.'

From the fact that he had not chucked in a lot of 'sirs' I presumed that he had been talking to some pal of his, though from the curtness of his tone probably not the one whose strength was as the strength of ten.

'What was that, Jeeves?' I asked. 'A little tiff with one of the boys at the club?'

'No, sir. I was speaking to Mr. Percy Gorringe, who rang up shortly before you entered. Affecting to be yourself, I informed him that his request for a thousand pounds could not be entertained. I thought that this might spare you discomfort and embarrassment.'

I must say I was touched. After being worsted in that clash of wills of ours, one might have expected him to show dudgeon and be loath to do the feudal thing by the young master. But Jeeves and I, though we may have our differences – as it might be on the subject of lip-joy – do not allow them to rankle.

'Thank you, Jeeves.'

'Not at all, sir.'

'Lucky you came back in time to do the needful. Did you enjoy yourself at the club?'

'Very much, sir.'

'More than I did at mine.'

'Sir?'

'I ran into Stilton Cheesewright there and found him in difficult mood. Tell me, Jeeves, what do you do at this Junior Ganymede of yours?'

'Well, sir, many of the members play a sound game of bridge. The conversation, too, rarely fails to touch a high level of interest. And should one desire more frivolous entertainment, there are the club books.'

'The . . . Oh, yes, I remember.'

Perhaps you do, too, if you happened to be around when I was relating the doings at Totleigh Towers, the country seat of Sir Watkyn Bassett, when this club book had enabled me to put it so crushingly across the powers of darkness in the shape of Roderick Spode. Under Rule Eleven at the Junior Ganymede, you may recall, members are required to supply intimate details concerning their employers for inclusion in the volume, and its pages revealed that Spode, who was an amateur Dictator of sorts, running a gang called the Black Shorts, who went about in black footer bags shouting 'Heil, Spode!', also secretly designed ladies' underclothing under the trade name of Eulalie Sœurs. Armed with this knowledge, I had had, of course, little difficulty in reducing him to the level of a third-class power. These Dictators don't want a thing like that to get spread about.

But though the club book had served me well on that occasion, I was far from approving of it. Mine has been in many ways a chequered career, and it was not pleasant to think that full details of episodes I would prefer to be buried in oblivion were giving a big laugh daily to a bunch of valets and butlers.

'You couldn't tear the Wooster material out of that club book, could you, Jeeves?'

'I fear not, sir.'

'It contains matter that can fairly be described as dynamite.'

'Very true, sir.'

'Suppose the contents were bruited about and reached the ears of my Aunt Agatha?'

'You need have no concern on that point, sir. Each member fully understands that perfect discretion is a *sine qua non*.'

'All the same I'd feel happier if that page –'

'Those eleven pages, sir.'

'– if those eleven pages were consigned to the flames.' A sudden thought struck me. 'Is there anything about Stilton Cheesewright in the book?'

'A certain amount, sir.'

'Damaging?'

'Not in the real sense of the word, sir. His personal attendant merely reports that he has a habit, when moved, of saying "Ho!" and does Swedish exercises in the nude each morning before breakfast.'

I sighed. I hadn't really hoped, and yet it had been a disappointment. I have always held – rightly, I think – that nothing eases the tension of a difficult situation like a well-spotted bit of blackmail, and it would have been agreeable to have been in a position to go to Stilton and say 'Cheesewright, I know your secret!' and watch him wilt. But you can't fulfil yourself to any real extent in that direction if all the party of the second part does is say 'Ho!' and tie himself into knots before sailing into the eggs and b. It was plain that with Stilton there could be no such moral triumph as I had achieved in the case of Roderick Spode.

'Ah, well,' I said resignedly, 'if that's that, that's that, what?'

'So it would appear, sir.'

'Nothing to do but keep the chin up and the upper lip as stiff as can be managed. I think I'll go to bed with an improving book. Have you read *The Mystery of the Pink Crayfish* by Rex West?'

'No, sir, I have not enjoyed that experience. Oh, pardon me, sir, I was forgetting. Lady Florence Craye spoke to me on the telephone shortly before you came in. Her ladyship would be glad if you would ring her up. I will get the number, sir.'

I was puzzled. I could make nothing of this. No reason, of course, why she shouldn't want me to give her a buzz, but on the other hand no reason that I could see why she should.

'She didn't say what she wanted?'

'No, sir.'

'Odd, Jeeves.'

'Yes, sir . . . One moment, m'lady. Here is Mr. Wooster.'

I took the instrument from him and hullo-ed.

'Bertie?'

'On the spot.'

'I hope you weren't in bed?'

'No, no.'

'I thought you wouldn't be. Bertie, will you do something for me? I want you to take me to a night club tonight.'

'Eh?'

'A night club. Rather a low one. I mean garish and all that sort of thing. It's for the book I'm writing. Atmosphere.'

'Oh, ah,' I said, enlightened. I knew all about this atmosphere thing. Bingo Little's wife, the well-known novelist Rosie M. Banks, is as hot as a pistol on it, Bingo has often told me. She frequently sends him off to take notes of this and that so that she shall have plenty of ammunition for her next chapter. If you're a novelist, apparently, you have to get your atmosphere correct, or your public starts writing you stinkers beginning 'Dear Madam, are you aware . . . ?' 'You're doing something about a night club?'

'Yes, I'm just coming to the part where my hero goes to one, and I've never been to any except the respectable ones where everybody goes, which aren't the sort of thing I want. What I need is something more –'

'Garish?'

'Yes, garish.'

'You want to go tonight?'

'It must be tonight, because I'm off tomorrow afternoon to Brinkley.'

'Oh, you're going to stay with Aunt Dahlia?'

'Yes. Well, can you manage it?'

'Oh, rather. Delighted.'

'Good. D'Arcy Cheesewright,' said Florence, and I noted the steely what-d'you-call-it in her voice, 'was to have taken me, but he finds himself unable to. So I've had to fall back on you.'

This might, I thought, have been more tactfully put, but I let it go.

'Right ho,' I said. 'I'll call for you at about half-past eleven.'

You are surprised? You are saying to yourself 'Come, come, Wooster, what's all this?' – wondering why I was letting myself in for a beano from which I might well have shrunk? The matter is susceptible of a ready explanation.

My quick mind, you see, had spotted instantly that this was where I might quite conceivably do myself a bit of good. Having mellowed this girl with food and drink, who knew but that I might succeed in effecting a reconciliation between her and the piece of cheese with whom until tonight she had been headed for the altar rails, thus averting the peril which must always loom on the Wooster horizon while she remained unattached and at a loose end? It needed, I was convinced, only a few kindly words from a sympathetic man of the world, and these I was prepared to supply in full measure.

'Jeeves,' I said, 'I shall be going out again. This will mean having to postpone finishing *The Mystery of the Pink Crayfish* to a later date, but that can't be helped. As a matter of fact, I rather fancy I have already wrested its secret from it. Unless I am very much mistaken, the man who bumped off Sir Eustace Willoughby, Bart, was the butler.'

'Indeed, sir?'

'That is what I think, having sifted the clues. All that stuff throwing suspicion on the vicar doesn't fool me for an instant. Will you ring up The Mottled Oyster and book a table in my name.'

'Not too near the band, sir?'

'How right you are, Jeeves. Not too near the band.'

5

I don't know why it is, but I'm not much of a lad for night clubs these days. Age creeping on me, I suppose. But I still retain my membership in about half a dozen, including this Mottled Oyster at which I had directed Jeeves to book me a table.

The old spot has passed a somewhat restless existence since I first joined, and from time to time I get a civil note from its proprietors saying that it has changed its name and address once more. When it was raided as The Feverish Cheese, it became The Frozen Limit, and when it was raided as The Frozen Limit, it bore for awhile mid snow and ice the banner with the strange device The Startled Shrimp. From that to The Mottled Oyster was, of course, but a step. In my hot youth I had passed not a few quite pleasant evenings beneath its roof in its various incarnations, and I thought that, if it preserved anything approaching the old form, it ought to be garish enough to suit Florence. As I remembered, it rather prided itself on its garishness. That was why the rozzers were always raiding it.

I picked her up at her flat at eleven-thirty, and found her in sombre mood, the lips compressed, the eyes inclined to gaze into space with a sort of hard glow in them. No doubt something along these lines is always the aftermath of a brisk dust-up with the heart-throb. During the taxi drive she remained about as silent as the tomb, and from the way her foot kept tapping on the floor of the vehicle I knew that she was thinking of Stilton, whether or not in agony of spirit I was, of course, unable to say, but I thought it probable. Following her into the joint, I was on the whole optimistic. It seemed to me that with any luck I ought to be successful in the task that lay before me – viz. softening her with well-chosen words and jerking her better self back to the surface.

When we took our seats and I looked about me, I must confess that, having this object in mind, I could have done with dimmer lights and a more romantic *tout ensemble*, if *tout ensemble* is the expression I want. I could also have dispensed with the rather strong smell of kippered herrings which hung over the establishment like a fog. But against these drawbacks could be set the fact that up on the platform, where the band was, a man with adenoids was singing through a megaphone and, like all men who sing through megaphones nowadays, ladling out stuff well calculated to melt the hardest heart.

It's an odd thing. I know one or two song writers and have found them among the most cheery of my acquaintances, ready of smile and full of merry quips and so forth. But directly they put pen to paper they never fail to take the dark view. All that 'We're-drifting-apart-you're-breaking-my-heart' stuff, I mean to say. The thing this bird was putting across per megaphone at the moment was about a chap crying into his pillow because the girl he loved was getting married next day, but – and this was the point or nub – not to him. He didn't like it. He viewed the situation with concern. And the megaphonist was extracting every ounce of juice from the set-up.

Some fellows, no doubt, would have taken advantage of this out-standing goo to plunge without delay into what Jeeves calls *medias res*, but I, being shrewd, knew that you have to give these things time to work. So, having ordered kippers and a bottle of what would probably turn out to be rat poison, I opened the conversation on a more restrained note, asking her how the new novel was coming along. Authors, especially when female, like to keep you posted about this.

She said it was coming very well but not quickly, because she was a slow, careful worker who mused a good bit in between paragraphs and spared no pains to find the exact word with which to express what she wished to say. Like Flaubert, she said, and I said I thought she was on the right lines.

'Those,' I said, 'were more or less my methods when I wrote that thing of mine for the *Boudoir*.'

I was alluding to the weekly paper for the delicately nurtured, *Milady's Boudoir*, of which Aunt Dahlia is the courteous and popular proprietor or proprietress. She has been running it now for about three years, a good deal to the annoyance of Uncle Tom, her husband, who has to foot the bills. At her request I had once contributed an article – or 'piece', as we journalists call it – on What The Well-Dressed Man Is Wearing.

'So you're off to Brinkley tomorrow,' I went on. 'You'll like that. Fresh air, gravel soil, company's own water, Anatole's cooking and so forth.'

'Yes. And of course it will be wonderful meeting Daphne Dolores Morehead.'

The name was new to me.

'Daphne Dolores Morehead?'

'The novelist. She is going to be there. I admire her work so much. I see, by the way, she is doing a serial for the *Boudoir*.'

'Oh, yes?' I said, intrigued. One always likes to hear about the activities of one's fellow-writers.

'It must have cost your aunt a fortune. Daphne Dolores Morehead is frightfully expensive. I can't remember what it is she gets a thousand words, but it's something enormous.'

'The old sheet must be doing well.'

'I suppose so.'

She spoke listlessly, seeming to have lost interest in *Milady's Boudoir*. Her thoughts, no doubt, had returned to Stilton. She cast a dull eye hither and thither about the room. It had begun to fill up now, and the dance floor was congested with frightful bounders of both sexes.

'What horrible people!' she said. 'I must say I am surprised that you should be familiar with such places, Bertie. Are they all like this?'

I weighed the question.

'Well, some are better and some worse. I would call this one about average. Garish, of course, but then you said you wanted something garish.'

'Oh, I'm not complaining. I shall make some useful notes. It is just the sort of place to which I pictured Rollo going that night.'

'Rollo?'

'The hero of my novel. Rollo Beaminster.'

'Oh, I see. Yes, of course. Out on the tiles, was he?'

'He was in wild mood. Reckless. Desperate. He had lost the girl he loved.'

'What ho!' I said. 'Tell me more.'

I spoke with animation and vim, for whatever you may say of Bertram Wooster, you cannot say that he does not know a cue when he hears one. Throw him the line, and he will do the rest. I hitched up the larynx. The kippers and the bot had arrived by now, and I took a mouthful of the former and a sip of the latter. It tasted like hair-oil.

'You interest me strangely,' I said. 'Lost the girl he loved, had he?'

'She had told him she never wished to see or speak to him again.'

'Well, well. Always a nasty knock for a chap, that.'

'So he comes to this low night club. He is trying to forget.'

'But I'll bet he doesn't.'

'No, it is useless. He looks about him at the glitter and garishness and feels how hollow it all is. I think I can use that waiter over there in the night club scene, the one with the watery eyes and the pimple on his nose,' she said, jotting down a note on the back of the bill of fare.

I fortified myself with a swig of whatever the stuff was in the bottle and prepared to give her the works.

'Always a mistake,' I said, starting to do the sympathetic man of the world, 'fellows losing girls and – conversely, if that's the word I want – girls losing fellows. I don't know how you feel about it, but the way it seems to me is that it's a silly idea giving the dream man the raspberry just because of some trifling tiff. Kiss and make up, I always say. I saw Stilton at the Drones tonight,' I said, getting down to it.

She stiffened and took a reserved mouthful of kipper. Her voice, when the consignment had passed down the hatch and she was able to speak, was cold and metallic.

'Oh, yes?'

'He was in wild mood.'

'Oh, yes?'

'Reckless. Desperate. He looked about him at the Drones smoking-room, and I could see he was feeling what a hollow smoking-room it was.'

'Oh, yes?'

Well, I suppose if someone had come along at this moment and said to me 'Hullo there, Wooster, how's it going? Are you making headway?' I should have had to reply in the negative. 'Not perceptibly, Wilkinson' – or Banks or Smith or Knatchbull-Huguessen or whatever the name might have been, I would have said. I had the uncomfortable feeling of having been laid a stymie. However, I persevered.

'Yes, he was in quite a state of mind. He gave me the impression that it wouldn't take much to make him go off to the Rocky Mountains and shoot grizzly bears. Not a pleasant thought.'

'You mean if one is fond of grizzly bears?'

'I was thinking more if one was fond of Stiltons.'

'I'm not.'

'Oh? Well, suppose he joined the Foreign Legion?'

'It would have my sympathy.'

'You wouldn't like to think of him tramping through the hot sand without a pub in sight, with Riffs or whatever they're called potting at him from all directions.'

'Yes, I would. If I saw a Riff trying to shoot D'Arcy Cheesewright, I would hold his hat for him and egg him on.'

Once more I had that sense of not making progress. Her face, I observed, was cold and hard, like my kipper, which of course during these exchanges I had been neglecting, and I began to understand how these birds in Holy Writ must have felt after their session with the deaf adder. I can't recall all the details, though at my private school I once won a prize for Scripture Knowledge, but I remember that they had the dickens of an uphill job trying to charm it, and after they had sweated themselves to a frazzle no business resulted. It is often this way, I believe, with deaf adders.

'Do you know Horace Pendlebury-Davenport?' I said, after a longish pause during which we worked away at our respective kippers.

'The man who married Valerie Twistleton?'

'That's the chap. Formerly the Drones Club Darts champion.'

'I've met him. But why bring him up?'

'Because he points the moral and adorns the tale. During the period of their betrothal he and Valerie had a row similar in calibre to that which has occurred between you and Stilton and pretty nearly parted for ever.'

She gave me the frosty eye.

'Must we talk about Mr. Cheesewright?'

'I see him as tonight's big topic.'

'I don't, and I think I'll go home.'

'Oh, not yet. I want to tell you about Horace and Valerie. They had this row of which I speak and might, as I say, have parted for ever, had they not been reconciled by a woman who, so Horace says, looked as if she bred cocker spaniels. She told them a touching story, which melted their hearts. She said she had once loved a bloke and quarrelled with him about some trifle, and he turned on his heel and went off to the Federated Malay States and married the widow of a rubber planter. And each year from then on there arrived at her address a simple posy of white violets, together with a slip of paper bearing the words "It might have been". You wouldn't like that to happen with you and Stilton, would you?'

'I'd love it.'

'It doesn't give you a pang to think that at this very moment he may be going the rounds of the shipping offices, inquiring about sailings to the Malay States?'

'They'd be shut at this time of night.'

'Well, first thing tomorrow morning, then.'

She laid down her knife and fork and gave me an odd look.

'Bertie, you're extraordinary,' she said.

'Eh? How do you mean, extraordinary?'

'All this nonsense you have been talking, trying to reconcile me and D'Arcy. Not that I don't admire you for it. I think it's rather wonderful of you. But then everybody says that, though you have a brain like a peahen, you're the soul of kindness and generosity.'

Well, I was handicapped here by the fact that, never having met a peahen, I was unable to estimate the quality of these fowls' intelligence, but she had spoken as if they were a bit short of the grey matter, and I was about to ask her who the hell she meant by 'everybody', when she resumed.

'You want to marry me yourself, don't you?'

I had to take another mouthful of the substance in the bottle before I could speak. One of those difficult questions to answer.

'Oh, rather,' I said, for I was anxious to make the evening a success. 'Of course. Who wouldn't?'

'And yet you —'

She did not proceed further than the word 'you', for at this juncture, with the abruptness with which these things always happen, the joint was pinched. The band stopped in the middle of a bar. A sudden hush fell upon the room. Square-jawed men shot up through the flooring, and one, who seemed to be skippering the team, stood out in the middle and in a voice like a foghorn told everybody to keep their seats. I remember thinking how nicely timed the whole thing was — breaking loose, I mean, at a moment when the conversation had taken a distasteful turn and threatened to become fraught with embarrassment. I have heard hard things said about the London police force — notably by Catsmeat Potter-Pirbright and others on the morning after the annual Oxford and Cambridge boat race — but a fairminded man had to admit that there were occasions when they showed tact of no slight order.

I wasn't alarmed, of course. I had been through this sort of thing many a time and oft, as the expression is, and I knew what happened. So, noting that my guest was giving a rather close imitation of a cat on hot bricks, I hastened to dispel her alarm.

'No need to get the breeze up,' I said. 'Nothing is here for tears, nothing to wail or knock the breast,' I added, using one of Jeeves's gags which I chanced to remember. 'Everything is quite in order.'

'But won't they arrest us?'

I laughed lightly. These novices!

'Absurd. No danger of that whatsoever.'

'How do you know?'

'All this is old stuff to me. Here in a nutshell is the procedure. They round us up, and we push off in an orderly manner to the police station in plain vans. There we assemble in the waiting-room and give our names and addresses, exercising a certain latitude as regards the details. I, for example, generally call myself Ephraim Gadsby of The Nasturtiums, Jubilee Road, Streatham Common. I don't know why. Just a whim. You, if you will be guided by me, will be Matilda Bott of 365 Churchill Avenue, East Dulwich. These formalities concluded, we shall be free to depart, leaving the proprietor to face the awful majesty of Justice.'

She refused to be consoled. The resemblance to a cat on hot bricks became more marked. Though instructed by the foghorn chap to keep her seat, she shot up as if a spike had come through it.

'I'm sure that's not what happens.'

'It is, unless they've changed the rules.'

'You have to appear in court.'

'No, no.'

'Well, I'm not going to risk it. Good night.'

And getting smoothly off the mark she made a dash for the service door, which was not far from where we sat. And an adjacent constable, baying like a bloodhound, started off in hot pursuit.

Whether I acted judiciously at this point is a question which I have never been able to decide. Sometimes I think yes, reflecting that the Chevalier Bayard in my place would have done the same, sometimes no. Briefly what occurred was that as the gendarme came galloping by, I shoved out a foot, causing him to take the toss of a lifetime. Florence withdrew, and the guardian of the peace, having removed his left boot from his right ear, with which it had become temporarily entangled, rose and informed me that I was in custody.

As at the moment he was grasping the scruff of my neck with one hand and the seat of my trousers with the other, I saw no reason to doubt the honest fellow.

6

I spent the night in what is called durance vile, and bright and early next day was haled before the beak at Vinton Street police court, charged with assaulting an officer of the Law and impeding him in the execution of his duties, which I suppose was a fairly neat way of putting it. I was extremely hungry and needed a shave.

It was the first time I had met the Vinton Street chap, always hitherto having patronized his trade rival at Bosher Street, but Barmy Fotheringay-Phipps, who was introduced to him on the morning of January the first one year, had told me he was a man to avoid, and the truth of this was now borne in upon me in no uncertain manner. It seemed to me, as I stood listening to the cop running through the story sequence, that Barmy, in describing this Solon as a twenty-minute egg with many of the less lovable qualities of some high-up official of the Spanish Inquisition, had understated rather than exaggerated the facts.

I didn't like the look of the old blister at all. His manner was austere, and as the tale proceeded his face, such as it was, grew hard and dark with menace. He kept shooting quick glances at me through his pince-nez, and the dullest eye could see that the constable was getting all the sympathy of the audience and that the citizen cast for the role of Heavy in this treatment was the prisoner Gadsby. More and more the feeling stole over me that the prisoner Gadsby was about to get it in the gizzard and would be lucky if he didn't fetch up on Devil's Island.

However, when the *J'accuse* stuff was over and I was asked if I had anything to say, I did my best. I admitted that on the occasion about which we had been chatting I had extended a foot causing the officer to go base over apex, but protested that it had been a pure accident without any *arrière-pensée* on my part. I said I had been feeling cramped after a longish sojourn at the table and had merely desired to unlimber the leg muscles.

'You know how sometimes you want a stretch,' I said.

'I am strongly inclined,' responded the beak, 'to give you one. A good long stretch.'

Rightly recognizing this as comedy, I uttered a cordial guffaw to show that my heart was in the right place, and an officious blighter in the well of the court shouted 'Silence!' I tried to explain that I was convulsed by His Worship's ready wit, but he shushed me again, and His Worship came to the surface once more.

'However,' he went on, adjusting his pince-nez, 'in consideration of your youth I will exercise clemency.'

'Oh, fine!' I said.

'Fine,' replied the other half of the cross-talk act, who seemed to know all the answers, 'is right. Ten pounds. Next case.'

I paid my debt to Society, and pushed off.

Jeeves was earning the weekly envelope by busying himself at some domestic task when I reached the old home. He cocked an inquiring eye at me, and I felt that an explanation was due to him. It would have surprised him, of course, to discover that my room was empty and my bed had not been slept in.

'A little trouble last night with the minions of the Law, Jeeves,' I said. 'Quite a bit of that Eugene-Aram-walked-between-with-gyves-upon-his-wrists stuff.'

'Indeed, sir? Most vexing.'

'Yes, I didn't like it very much, but the magistrate – with whom I have just been threshing the thing out – had a wonderful time. I brought a ray of sunshine into his drab life all right. Did you know that these magistrates were expert comedians?'

'No, sir. The fact had not been drawn to my attention.'

'Think of Groucho Marx and you will get the idea. One gag after another, and all at my expense. I was just the straight man, and I found the experience most unpleasant, particularly as I had had no breakfast that any conscientious gourmet could call breakfast. Have you ever passed the night in chokey, Jeeves?'

'No, sir. I have been fortunate in that respect.'

'It renders the appetite unusually keen. So rally round, if you don't mind, and busy yourself with the skillet. We have eggs on the premises, I presume?'

'Yes, sir.'

'I shall need about fifty, fried, with perhaps the same number of pounds of bacon. Toast, also. Four loaves will probably be sufficient, but stand by to weigh in with more if necessary. And don't forget the coffee – say sixteen pots.'

'Very good, sir.'

'And after that,' I said with a touch of bitterness, 'I suppose you will go racing round to the Junior Ganymede to enter this spot of bother of mine in the club book.'

'I fear I have no alternative, sir. Rule Eleven is very strict.'

'Well, if you must, you must, I suppose. I wouldn't want you to be hauled up in a hollow square of butlers and have your buttons snipped off. That club book, Jeeves. You're absolutely sure there's nothing in it in the C's under "Cheesewright"?'

'Nothing but what I outlined last night, sir.'

'And a lot of help that is!' I said moodily. 'I don't mind telling you, Jeeves, that this Cheesewright has become a menace.'

'Indeed, sir?'

'And I had hoped that you might have found something in the club book which would have enabled me to spike his guns. Still, if you can't, you can't, of course. All right, rush along and dish up that breakfast.'

I had slept but fitfully on the plank bed which was all that Vinton Street Gestapo had seen their way to provide for the use of clients, so after partaking of a hearty meal I turned in between the sheets. Like Rollo Beaminster, I wanted to forget. It must have been well after the luncheon hour when the sound of the telephone jerked me out of the dreamless. Feeling a good deal refreshed, I shoved on a dressing-gown and went to the instrument.

It was Florence.

'Bertie?' she yipped.

'Hullo? I thought you said you were going to Brinkley today.'

'I'm just starting. I rang up to ask how you got on after I left last night.'

I laughed a mirthless laugh.

'Not so frightfully well,' I replied. 'I was scooped in by the constabulary.'

'What! You told me they didn't arrest you.'

'They don't. But they did.'

'Are you all right now?'

'Well, I have a pinched look.'

'But I don't understand. Why did they arrest you?'

'It's a long story. Cutting it down to the gist, I noticed that you were anxious to leave, so, observing that a rozzer was after you hell for leather, I put a foot out, tripping him up and causing him to lose interest in the chase.'

'Good gracious!'

'It seemed to me the prudent policy to pursue. Another moment and he would have had you by the seat of the pants, and of course we can't have that sort of thing going on. The upshot of the affair was that I spent the night in a prison cell and had rather a testing morning with the magistrate at Vinton Street police court. However, I'm pulling round all right.'

'Oh, Bertie!' Seeming deeply moved, she thanked me brokenly, and I said Don't mention it. Then she gasped a sudden gasp, as if she had received a punch on the third waistcoat button. 'Did you say Vinton Street?'

'That's right.'

'Oh, my goodness! Do you know who that magistrate was?'

'I couldn't tell you. No cards were exchanged. We boys in court called him Your Worship.'

'He's D'Arcy's uncle!'

I goshed. It had startled me not a little.

'You don't mean that?'

'Yes.'

'What, the one who likes soup?'

'Yes. Just imagine if after having dinner with him last night I had appeared before him in the dock this morning!'

'Embarrassing. Difficult to know what to say.'

'D'Arcy would never have forgiven me.'

'Eh?'

'He would have broken the engagement.'

I didn't get this.

'How do you mean?'

'How do I mean what?'

'How do you mean he would have broken the engagement? I thought it was off already.'

She gave what I believe is usually called a rippling laugh.

'Oh, no. He rang me up this morning and climbed down. And I forgave him. He's starting to grow a moustache today.'

I was profoundly relieved.

'Well, that's splendid,' I said, and when she Oh-Bertied and I asked her what she was Oh-Bertying about, she explained that what she had had in mind was the fact that I was so chivalrous and generous.

'Not many men in your place, feeling as you do about me, would behave like this.'

'Quite all right.'

'I'm very touched.'

'Don't give it another thought. It's really all on again, is it?'

'Yes. So mind you don't breathe a word to him about my being at that place with you.'

'Of course not.'

'D'Arcy is so jealous.'

'Exactly. He must never know.'

'Never. Why, if he even found out I was telephoning to you now, he would have a fit.'

I was about to laugh indulgently and say that this was what Jeeves calls a remote contingency, because how the dickens could he ever learn that we had been chewing the fat, when my eye was attracted by a large object just within my range of vision. Slewing the old bean round a couple of inches, I was enabled to perceive that this large O was the bulging form of G. D'Arcy Cheesewright. I hadn't heard the door bell ring, and I hadn't seen him come in, but there unquestionably he was, haunting the place once more like a resident spectre.

7

It was a moment for quick thinking. One doesn't want fellows having fits all over one's sitting-room. I was extremely dubious, moreover, as to whether, should he ascertain who was at the other end of the wire, he would confine himself to fits.

'Certainly, Catsmeat,' I said. 'Of course, Catsmeat. I quite understand, Catsmeat. But I'll have to ring off now, Catsmeat, as our mutual friend Cheesewright has just come in. Good-bye, Catsmeat.' I hung up the receiver and turned to Stilton. 'That was Catsmeat,' I said.

He made no comment on this information, but stood glowering darkly. Now that I had been apprised of the ties of blood linking him with mine host of Vinton Street, I could see the family resemblance. Both uncle and nephew had the same way of narrowing their gaze and letting you have it from beneath the overhanging eyebrow. The only difference was that whereas the former pierced you to the roots of the soul through rimless pince-nez, with the latter you got the eye nude.

For a moment I was under the impression that my visitor's emotion was due to his having found me at this advanced hour in pyjamas and a dressing-gown, a costume which, if worn at three o'clock in the afternoon, is always liable to start a train of thought. But it seemed that this was not so. More serious matters were on the agenda paper.

'Wooster,' he said, in a rumbling voice like the Cornish express going through a tunnel, 'where were you last night?'

I own the question rattled me. For an instant, indeed, I rocked on my base. Then I reminded myself that nothing could be proved against me, and was strong again.

'Ah, Stilton,' I said cheerily, 'come in, come in. Oh, you are in, aren't you? Well, take a seat and tell me all your news. A lovely day, is it not? You'll find a lot of people who don't like July in London, but I am all for it myself. It always seems to me there's a certain sort of something about it.'

He appeared to be one of those fellows who are not interested in July in London, for he showed no disposition to pursue the subject, merely giving one of those snorts of his.

'Where were you last night, you blighted louse?' he said, and I noticed that the face was suffused, the cheek muscles twitching and the eyes, like stars, starting from their spheres.

I had a pop at being cool and nonchalant.

'Last night?' I said, musing. 'Let me see, that would be the night of July the twenty-second, would it not? H'm. Ha. The night of –'

He swallowed a couple of times.

'I see you have forgotten. Let me assist your memory. You were in a low night club with Florence Craye, my fiancée.'

'Who, me?'

'Yes, you. And this morning you were in the dock at Vinton Street police court.'

'You're sure you mean me?'

'Quite sure. I had the information from my uncle, who is the magistrate there. He came to lunch at my flat today, and as he was leaving he caught sight of your photograph on the wall.'

'I didn't know you kept my photograph on your wall, Stilton. I'm touched.'

He continued to ferment.

'It was a group photograph,' he said curtly, 'and you happened to be in it. He looked at it, sniffed sharply and said "Do you know this young man?" I explained that we belonged to the same club, so it was not always possible to avoid you, but that was the extent of our association. I was going on to say that, left to myself, I wouldn't touch you with a ten-foot pole, when he proceeded. Still sniffing, he said he was glad I was not a close friend of yours, because you weren't at all the sort of fellow he liked to think of any nephew of his being matey with. He said you had been up before him this morning, charged with assaulting a policeman, who stated that he had arrested you for tripping him up while he was chasing a girl with platinum hair in a night club.'

I pursed the lips. Or, rather, I tried to, but something seemed to have gone wrong with the machinery. Still, I spoke boldly and with spirit.

'Indeed?' I said. 'Personally I would be inclined to attach little credence to the word of the sort of policeman who spends his time chasing platinum-haired girls in night clubs. And as for this uncle of yours, with his wild stories of me having been up before him – well, you know what magistrates are. The lowest form of pond life. When a fellow hasn't the brains and initiative to sell jellied eels, they make him a magistrate.'

'You mean that when he said that about your photograph he was deceived by some slight resemblance?'

I waved a hand.

'Not necessarily a slight resemblance. London's full of chaps who look like me. I'm a very common type. People have told me that there is a fellow called Ephraim Gadsby – one of the Streatham Common Gadsbys – who is positively my double. I shall, of course, take this into consideration when weighing the question of bringing an action for slander and defamation of character against this uncle of yours, and shall probably decide to let justice be tempered with mercy. But it would be a kindly act to warn the old son of a bachelor to be more careful in future how he allows his tongue to run away with him. There are limits to one's forbearance.'

He brooded darkly for about forty-five seconds.

'Platinum hair, the policeman said,' he observed at the end of this lull. 'This girl had platinum hair.'

'No doubt very becoming.'

'I find it extremely significant that Florence has platinum hair.'

'I don't see why. Hundreds of girls have. My dear Stilton, ask yourself if it is likely that Florence would have been at a night club like the . . . what did you say the name was?'

'I didn't. But I believe it was called The Mottled Oyster.'

'Ah, yes, I have heard of it. Not a very nice place, I understand. Quite incredible that she would have gone to a joint like that. A fastidious, intellectual girl like Florence? No, no.'

He pondered. It seemed to me that I had him going.

'She wanted me to take her to a night club last night,' he said. 'Something to do with getting material for her new book.'

'But you very properly refused?'

'No, as a matter of fact, I said I would. Then we had that bit of trouble, so of course it was off.'

'And she, of course, went home to bed. What else would any pure, sweet English girl have done? It amazes me that you can suppose even for a moment that she would have gone to one of these dubious establishments without you. Especially a place where, as I understand your story, squads of policemen are incessantly chasing platinum-haired girls hither and thither, and probably even worse things happening as the long night wears on. No, Stilton, dismiss these thoughts – which, if you will allow me to say so, are unworthy of you – and . . . Ah, here is Jeeves,' I said, noting with relief that the sterling fellow, who had just oozed in, was carrying the old familiar shaker. 'What have you there, Jeeves? Some of your specials?'

'Yes, sir. I fancied that Mr. Cheesewright might possibly be glad of refreshment.'

'He's just in the vein for it. I won't join you, Stilton, because, as you know, with this Darts tournament coming on, I am in more or less strict training these days, but I must insist on your trying one of these superb mixtures of Jeeves's. You have been anxious . . . worried . . . disturbed . . . and it will pull you together. Oh, by the way, Jeeves.'

'Sir?'

'I wonder if you remember, when I came home last night after chatting with Mr. Cheesewright at the Drones, my saying to you that I was going straight to bed with an improving book?'

'Certainly, sir.'

'*The Mystery of the Pink Crayfish*, was it not?'

'Precisely, sir.'

'I think I said something to the effect that I could hardly wait till I could get at it?'

'As I recollect, those were your exact words, sir. You were, you said, counting the minutes until you could curl up with the volume in question.'

'Thank you, Jeeves.'

'Not at all, sir.'

He oozed off, and I turned to Stilton, throwing the arms out in a sort of wide gesture. I don't suppose I have ever come closer in my life to saying '*Voilà*'!

'You heard?' I said. 'If that doesn't leave me without a stain on my character, it is difficult to see what it does leave me without. But let me help you to your special. You will find it rare and refreshing.'

It's a curious thing about those specials of Jeeves's, and one on which many revellers have commented, that while, as I mentioned earlier, they wake the sleeping tiger in you, they also work the other way round. I mean, if the tiger in you isn't sleeping but on the contrary up and doing with a heart for any fate, they lull it. You come in like a lion, you take your snootful, and you go out like a lamb. Impossible to explain it, of course. One can merely state the facts.

It was so now with Stilton. In his pre-special phase he had been all steamed up and fit for treasons, stratagems and spoils, as the fellow said, and he became a better, kindlier man beneath my very gaze. Half-way through the initial snifter he was admitting in the friendliest way that he had wronged me. I might be the most consummate ass that ever eluded the vigilance of the talent scouts of Colney Hatch, he said, but it was obvious that I had not taken Florence to The Mottled Oyster. And dashed lucky for me I hadn't, he added, for had such been the case, he would have broken my spine in three places. In short, all very chummy and cordial.

'Harking back to the earlier portion of our conversation, Stilton,' I said, changing the subject after we had agreed that his Uncle Joseph was a cockeyed fathead who would do well to consult some good oculist, 'I noticed that when you spoke of Florence, you used the expression "My fiancée". Am I to infer from this that the dove of peace has pulled a quick one since I saw you last? That broken engagement, has it been soldered?'

He nodded.

'Yes,' he said. 'I made certain concessions and yielded certain points.' Here his hand strayed to his upper lip and a look of pain passed over his face. 'A reconciliation took place this morning.'

'Splendid!'

'You're pleased?'

'Of course.'

'Ho!'

'Eh?'

He eyed me fixedly.

'Wooster, come off it. You know you're in love with her yourself.'

'Absurd.'

'Absurd, my foot! You needn't think you can fool me. You worship that girl, and I am still inclined to believe that the whole of this moustache sequence was a vile plot on your part to steal her from me. Well, all I have to say is that if I ever catch you oiling round her and trying to alienate her affections, I shall break your spine in four places.'

'Three, I thought you said.'

'No, four. However, she will be out of your reach for some little time, I am glad to say. She goes today to visit your aunt, Mrs. Travers, in Worcestershire.'

Amazing how with a careless word you can land yourself in the soup. I was within the merest toucher of saying Yes, so she had told me, which would, of course, have been fatal. In the nick of time I contrived to substitute an 'Oh, really?'

'She's going to Brinkley, is she? You also?'

'I shall be following in a few days.'

'You aren't going with her?'

'Talk sense. You don't suppose I intend to appear in public during the early stages of growing that damned moustache she insists on. I shall remain confined to my room till the foul thing has started to sprout a bit. Good-bye, Wooster. You will remember what I was saying about your spine?'

I assured him that I would bear it in mind, and he finished his special and withdrew.

8

The days that followed saw me at the peak of my form, fizzy to an almost unbelievable extent and enchanting one and all with my bright smile and merry sallies. During this halcyon period, if halcyon is the word I want, it would not be too much to say that I revived like a watered flower.

It was as if a great weight had been rolled off the soul. Only those who have had to endure the ordeal of having G. D'Arcy Cheesewright constantly materialize from thin air and steal up behind them, breathing down the back of their necks as they took their ease in their smoking-room, can fully understand the relief of being able to sink into a chair and order a restorative, knowing that the place would be wholly free from this pre-eminent scourge. My feelings, I suppose, were roughly what those of Mary would have been, had she looked over her shoulder one morning and found the lamb no longer among those present.

And then – *bing* – just as I was saying to myself that this was the life, along came all those telegrams.

The first to arrive reached me at my residence just as I was lighting the after-breakfast cigarette, and I eyed it with something of the nervous discomfort of one confronted with a ticking bomb. Telegrams have so often been the heralds or harbingers or whatever they're called of sharp crises in my affairs that I have come to look on them askance, wondering if something is going to pop out of the envelope and bite me in the leg. It was with a telegram, it may be recalled, that Fate teed off in the sinister episode of Sir Watkyn Bassett, Roderick Spode and the silver cow-creamer which I was instructed by Aunt Dahlia to pinch from the first-named's collection at Totleigh Towers.

Little wonder, then, that as I brooded over this one – eyeing it, as I say, askance – I was asking myself if Hell's foundations were about to quiver again.

Still, there the thing was, and it seemed to me, weighing the pros and cons, that only one course lay before me – viz. to open it.

I did so. Handed in at Brinkley-cum-Snodsfield-in-the-Marsh, it was signed 'Travers', this revealing it as the handiwork either of Aunt Dahlia or Thomas P. Travers, her husband, a pleasant old bird whom she had married at her second pop some years earlier. From the fact that it started with the words 'Bertie, you worm' I deduced that it was the former who had taken post-office pen in hand. Uncle Tom is more guarded in his speech than the female of the species. He generally calls me 'Me boy'.

This was the substance of the communication:

> Bertie, you worm, your early presence
> desired. Drop everything and come
> down here pronto, prepared for lengthy
> visit. Urgently need you to buck up
> a blighter with whiskers. Love. Travers.

I brooded over this for the rest of the morning, and on my way to lunch at the Drones shot off my answer, a brief request for more light:

> Did you say whiskers or whisky? Love. Wooster.

I found another from her on returning:

> Whiskers, ass. The son of a what-not
> has short but distinct side-whiskers.
> Love. Travers.

It's an odd thing about memory, it so often just fails to spear the desired object. At the back of my mind there was dodging about a hazy impression that somewhere at some time I heard someone mention short side-whiskers in some connection, but I couldn't pin it down. It eluded me. So, pursuing the sound old policy of going to the fountain-head for information, I stepped out and dispatched the following:

> What short side-whiskered son of a what-not
> would this be, and why does he need bucking up?
> Wire full details, as at present fogged,
> bewildered and mystified. Love. Wooster.

She replied with the generous warmth which causes so many of her circle to hold on to their hats when she lets herself go:

Listen, you foul blot. What's the idea of making
me spend a fortune on telegrams like this?
Do you think I am made of money? Never you
mind what short side-whiskered son of a
what-not it is or why he needs bucking up.
You just come as I tell you and look slippy
about it. Oh, and by the way, go to Aspinall's in
Bond Street and get pearl necklace of mine they
have there and bring it down with you. Have
you got that? Aspinall's. Bond Street. Pearl
necklace. Shall expect you tomorrow. Love. Travers.

A little shaken but still keeping the flag flying, I responded with
the ensuing:

Fully grasp all that Aspinall's-Bond-Street-
pearl-necklace stuff, but what you are overlooking
is that coming to Brinkley at present juncture not
so jolly simple as you seem to think. There are
complications and what not. Wheels within
wheels, if you get what I mean. Whole thing calls
for deep thought. Will weigh matter carefully
and let you know decision. Love. Wooster.

You see, though Brinkley Court is a home from home and gets five
stars in Baedeker as the headquarters of Monsieur Anatole, Aunt
Dahlia's French cook – a place, in short, to which in ordinary circs I
race, when invited, with a whoop and a holler – it had taken me but
an instant to spot that under existing conditions there were grave
objections to going there. I need scarcely say that I allude to the fact
that Florence was on the premises and Stilton expected shortly.

It was this that was giving me pause. Who could say that the latter,
finding me in residence on his arrival, would not leap to the conclusion
that I had rolled up in pursuit of the former like young Lochinvar
coming out of the west? And should this thought flit into his mind,
what, I asked myself, would the harvest be? His parting words about
my spine were still green in my memory. I knew him to be a man
rather careful in his speech, on whose promises one could generally
rely, and if he said he was going to break spines in four places, you
could be quite sure that four places was precisely what he would break
them in.

I passed a restless and uneasy evening. In no mood for revelry at the Drones, I returned home early and was brushing up on my *Mystery of the Pink Crayfish* when the telephone rang, and so disordered was the nervous system that I shot ceilingwards at the sound. It was as much as I could do to totter across the room and unhook the receiver.

The voice that floated over the wire was that of Aunt Dahlia.

Well, when I say floated, possibly 'thundered' would be more the *mot juste*. A girlhood and early womanhood spent in chivvying the British fox in all weathers under the auspices of the Quorn and Pytchley have left this aunt brick-red in colour and lent amazing power to her vocal cords. I've never pursued foxes myself, but apparently, when you do, you put in a good bit of your time shouting across ploughed fields in a high wind, and this becomes a habit. If Aunt Dahlia has a fault, it is that she is inclined to talk to you when face to face in a small drawing-room as if she were addressing some crony a quarter of a mile away whom she had observed riding over hounds. For the rest, she is a large, jovial soul, built rather on the lines of Mae West, and is beloved by all including the undersigned. Our relations had always been chummy to the last drop.

'Hullo, hullo, hullo!' she boomed. The old hunting stuff coming to the surface, you notice. 'Is that you, Bertie, darling?'

I said it was none other.

'Then what's the idea, you half-witted Gadarene swine, of all this playing hard-to-get? You and your matter-weighing! I never heard such nonsense in my life. You've got to come here, and immediately, if you don't want an aunt's curse delivered on your doorstep by return of post. If I have to cope unaided with that ruddy Percy any longer, I shall crack beneath the strain.'

She paused to take in breath, and I put a question.

'Is Percy the whiskered bloke?'

'That's the one. He's casting a thick pall of gloom over the place. It's like living in a fog. Tom says if something isn't done soon, he will take steps.'

'But what's the matter with the chap?'

'He's madly in love with Florence Craye.'

'Oh, I see. And it depresses him to think that she's engaged to Stilton Cheesewright?'

'Exactly. He's as sick as mud about it. He moons broodingly to and fro, looking like Hamlet. I want you to come and divert him. Take him for walks, dance before him, tell him funny stories. Anything to bring a smile to that whiskered, tortoiseshell-rimmed face.'

I saw her point, of course. No hostess wants a Hamlet on the premises. But what I couldn't understand was how a chap like that came to be polluting the pure air of Brinkley. I knew the old relative to be quite choosey in the matter of guests. Cabinet Ministers have sometimes failed to crash the gate. I put this to her, and she said the explanation was perfectly simple.

'I told you I was in the middle of a spot of business with Trotter. I've got the whole family here – Percy's stepfather, L.G. Trotter, Percy's mother, Mrs. Trotter, and Percy in person. I only wanted Trotter, but Mrs. T. and Percy rang themselves in.'

'I see. What they call a package deal.' I broke off, aghast. Memory had returned to its throne, and I knew now why that stuff about short side-whiskers had seemed to have a familiar ring. 'Trotter?' I cried.

She whooped censoriously.

'Don't yell like that. You nearly broke my ear-drum.'

'But did you say Trotter?'

'Of course I said Trotter.'

'This Percy's name isn't Gorringe?'

'That's what it unquestionably is. He admits it.'

'Then I'm frightfully sorry, old thing, but I can't possibly come. It was only the other day that the above Gorringe was trying to nick me for a thousand quid to put into this play he's made of Florence's book, and I turned him down like a bedspread. You can readily see, then, how fraught with embarrassment a meeting in the flesh would be. I shouldn't know which way to look.'

'If that's all that's worrying you, forget it. Florence tells me he has raised that thousand elsewhere.'

'Well, I'm dashed. Where did he get it?'

'She doesn't know. He's secretive about it. He just said it was all right, he had got the stuff and they could go ahead. So you needn't be shy about meeting him. What if he does think you the world's premier louse? Don't we all?'

'Something in that.'

'Then you'll come?'

I chewed the lower lip dubiously. I was thinking of Stilton.

'Well, speak up, dumb-bell,' said the relative with asperity. 'What's all the silence about?'

'I was musing.'

'Then stop musing and give me the good word. If it will help to influence your decision, I may mention that Anatole is at the top of his form just now.'

I started. If this was so, it would clearly be madness not to be one of the company ranged around the festive board.

I have touched so far only lightly on this Anatole, and I take the opportunity now of saying that his was an output which had to be tasted to be believed, mere words being inadequate to convey the full facts with regard to his amazing virtuosity. After one of Anatole's lunches has melted in the mouth, you unbutton the waistcoat and loll back, breathing heavily and feeling that life has no more to offer, and then, before you know where you are, along comes one of his dinners, with even more on the ball, the whole lay-out constituting something about as near Heaven as any reasonable man could wish.

I felt, accordingly, that no matter how vehemently Stilton might express and fulfil himself on discovering me . . . well, not perhaps exactly cheek by jowl with the woman he loved but certainly hovering in her vicinity, the risk of rousing the fiend within him was one that must be taken. It cannot ever, of course, be agreeable to find yourself torn into a thousand pieces with a fourteen-stone Othello doing a 'Shuffle off to Buffalo' on the scattered fragments, but if you are full at the time of Anatole's *Timbale de ris de veau Toulousiane*, the discomfort unquestionably becomes modified.

'I'll come,' I said.

'Good boy. With you taking Percy off my neck, I shall be free to concentrate on Trotter. And every ounce of concentration will be needed, if I'm to put this deal through.'

'What is the deal? You never told me. Who is this Trotter, if any?'

'I met him at Agatha's. He's a friend of hers. He owns a lot of papers up in Liverpool and wants to establish a beach-head in London. So I'm trying to get him to buy the *Boudoir*.'

I was amazed. Absolutely the last thing I would have expected. I had always supposed *Milady's Boudoir* to be her ewe lamb. To learn that she contemplated selling it stunned me. It was like hearing that Rodgers had decided to sell Hammerstein.

'But why on earth? I thought you loved it like a son.'

'I do, but the strain of having to keep going to Tom and trying to get money out of him for its support has got me down. Every time I start pleading with him for another cheque, he says "But isn't it paying its way yet?" and I say "No, darling, it is not paying its way yet", and he says "H'm!", adding that if this sort of thing goes on, we shall all be on the dole by next Christmas. It's become too much for me. It makes me feel like one of those women who lug babies around in the streets and want you to buy white heather. So when I met Trotter at Agatha's, I decided that he was the man who was going to take over, if human ingenuity could work it. What did you say?'

'I said "Oh, ah". I was about to add that it was a pity.'

'Yes, quite a pity, but unavoidable. Tom gets more difficult to touch daily. He says he loves me dearly, but enough is sufficient. Well, I'll expect you tomorrow, then. Don't forget the necklace.'

'I'll send Jeeves over for it in the morning.'

'Right.'

I think she would have spoken further, but at this moment a female voice off-stage said 'Three-ee-ee minutes', and she hung up with the sharp cry of a woman who fears she is going to be soaked for another couple of bob or whatever it is.

Jeeves came trickling in.

'Oh, Jeeves,' I said, 'we shall be heading for Brinkley tomorrow.'

'Very good, sir.'

'Aunt Dahlia wants me there to infuse a bit of the party spirit into our old pal Percy Gorringe, who is at the moment infesting the joint.'

'Indeed, sir? I wonder, sir, if it would be possible for you to allow me to return to London next week for the afternoon?'

'Certainly, Jeeves, certainly. You have some beano in prospect?'

'It is the monthly luncheon of the Junior Ganymede Club, sir. I have been asked to take the chair.'

'Take it by all means, Jeeves. A well-deserved honour.'

'Thank you, sir. I shall of course return the same day.'

'You'll make a speech, no doubt?'

'Yes, sir. A speech from the chair is of the essence.'

'I'll bet you have them rolling in the aisles. Oh, Jeeves, I was nearly forgetting. Aunt Dahlia wants me to bring her necklace. It's at Aspinall's in Bond Street. Will you toddle over and get it in the morning?'

'Certainly, sir.'

'And another thing I almost forgot to mention. Percy has raised that thousand quid.'

'Indeed, sir?'

'He must have approached someone with a more biteable ear than mine. One wonders who the mug was.'

'Yes, sir.'

'Some half-wit, one presumes.'

'No doubt, sir.'

'Still, there it is. It just bears out what the late Barnum used to say about there being one born every minute.'

'Precisely, sir. Would that be all, sir?'

'Yes, that's all. Good night, Jeeves.'

'Good night, sir. I will attend to the packing in the morning.'

9

It was getting on for the quiet evenfall on the morrow when after a pleasant drive through the smiling countryside I steered the two-seater in at the gates of Brinkley Court and ankled along to inform my hostess that I had come aboard. I found her in her snuggery or den, taking it easy with a cup of tea and an Agatha Christie. As I presented myself, she gave the moustache a swift glance, but apart from starting like a nymph surprised while bathing and muttering something about 'Was this the face that stopped a thousand clocks?' made no comment. One received the impression that she was saving it up.

'Hullo, reptile,' she said. 'You're here, are you?'

'Here I am,' I responded, 'with my hair in a braid and ready to the last button. A very merry pip-pip to you, aged relative.'

'The same to you, fathead. I suppose you forgot to bring that necklace?'

'Far from it. Here it is. It's the one Uncle Tom gave you at Christmas, isn't it?'

'That's right. He likes to see me wearing it at dinner.'

'As who wouldn't?' I said courteously. I handed it over and helped myself to a slice of buttered toast. 'Well, nice to be in the old home once more. I'm in my usual room, I take it? And how is everything in and around Brinkley Court? Anatole all right?'

'Never better.'

'You look pretty roguish.'

'Oh, I'm fine.'

'And Uncle Tom?'

A cloud passed over her shining evening face.

'Tom's still a bit low, poor old buster.'

'Owing to Percy, you mean?'

'That's right.'

'There has been no change then in this Gorringe's gloom?'

'Naturally not. He's been worse than ever since Florence got here. Tom winces every time he sees him, especially at meals. He says that having to watch Percy push away untasted food cooked by Anatole gives him a rush of blood to the head, and that gives him indigestion. You know how sensitive his stomach is.'

I patted her hand.

'Be of good cheer,' I said. 'I'll buck Perce up. Freddie Widgeon was showing me a trick with two corks and a bit of string the other night which cannot fail to bring a smile to the most tortured face. It had the lads at the Drones in stitches. You will doubtless be able to provide a couple of corks?'

'Twenty, if you wish.'

'Good.' I took a cake with pink icing on it. 'So much for Percy. What of the rest of the personnel? Anybody here besides the Trotter gang and Florence?'

'Not yet. Tom said something about somebody named Lord Sidcup looking in for dinner tomorrow on his way to the brine baths at Droitwich. Do you know him?'

'Never heard of him. He's a sealed book to me.'

'He's some man Tom met in London. Apparently he's a bit of a nib on old silver, and Tom wants to show him his collection.'

I nodded. I knew this uncle to be greatly addicted to the collecting of old silver. His apartments both at Brinkley Court and at his house in Charles Street are full of things I wouldn't be seen dead in a ditch with.

'What they call a virtuoso this Lord Sidcup would be, I presume?'

'Something on those lines.'

'Ah well, it takes all sorts to make a world, does it not?'

'We shall also have with us tomorrow the boy friend Cheesewright, and the day after that Daphne Dolores Morehead. She's the novelist.'

'I know. Florence was telling me about her. You've bought a serial from her, I understand.'

'Yes. I thought it would be a shrewd move to salt the mine.'

I didn't get this. She seemed to me an aunt who was talking in riddles.

'How do you mean, salt the mine? What mine? This is the first I've heard of any mines.'

I think that if her mouth had not been full of buttered toast, she would have clicked her tongue, for as soon as she had cleared the gangway with a quick swallow she spoke impatiently, as if my slowness in the uptake had exasperated her.

'You really are an abysmal ass, young Bertie. Haven't you ever heard of salting mines? It's a recognized business precaution. When you've got a dud mine you want to sell to a mug, you sprinkle an ounce or two of gold over it and summon the mug to come along and inspect the property. He rolls up, sees the gold, feels that this is what the doctor ordered and reaches for his cheque book. I worked on the same principle.'

I was still at a loss, and said so, and this time she did click her tongue.

'Can't you grasp it, chump? I bought the serial to make the paper look good to Trotter. He sees the announcement that a Daphne Morehead opus is coming along and is terrifically impressed. "Gosh!" he says to himself. "Daphne Dolores Morehead and everything! *Milady's Boudoir* must be hot stuff".'

'But don't these blokes want to see books and figures and things before they brass up?'

'Not if they've been having Anatole's cooking for a week or more. That's why I asked him down here.'

I saw what she meant, and her reasoning struck me as sound. There is something about those lunches and dinners of Anatole's that mellows you and saps your cool judgment. After tucking into them all this time I presumed that L.G. Trotter was going about in a sort of rosy mist, wanting to do kind acts right and left like a Boy Scout. Continue the treatment a few more days, and he would probably beg her as a personal favour to accept twice what she was asking.

'Very shrewd,' I said. 'Yes, I think you're on the right lines. Has Anatole been giving you his *Rognons aux Montagnes*?'

'*And* his *Selle d'Agneau aux laitues à la Grecque*.'

'Then I would say the thing was in the bag. All over but the cheering. But here's a point that has been puzzling me,' I said. 'Florence tells me that La Morehead is one of the more costly of our female pen-pushers and has to have purses of gold flung to her in great profusion before she will consent to sign on the dotted line. Correct?'

'Quite correct.'

'Then how the dickens,' I said, getting down to it in my keen way, 'did you contrive to extract the necessary ore from Uncle Tom? Didn't he pay his income-tax this year?'

'You bet he did. I should have thought you would have heard his screams in London. Poor old boy, how he does suffer on these occasions.'

She spoke sooth. Uncle Tom, though abundantly provided with the chips, having been until his retirement one of those merchant princes who scoop it up in sackfuls out East, has a rooted objection to letting the hellhounds of the Inland Revenue dip in and get theirs. For weeks after they have separated him from his hard-earned he is inclined to go off into corners and sit with his head between his hands, muttering about ruin and the sinister trend of socialistic legislation and what is to become of us all if this continues.

'He certainly does,' I assented. 'Quite the soul in torment, what? And yet, despite this, you succeeded in nicking him for what must have been a small fortune. How did you do it? From what you were saying on the phone last night I got the impression that he was in more than usually non-parting mood these days. You conjured up in my mind's eye the picture of a man who was sticking his ears back and refusing to play ball, like Balaam's ass.'

'What do you know about Balaam's ass?'

'Me? I know Balaam's ass from soup to nuts. Have you forgotten that when a pupil at the Rev. Aubrey Upjohn's educational establishment at Bramley-on-Sea I once won a prize for Scripture Knowledge?'

'I'll bet you cribbed.'

'Not at all. My triumph was due to sheer merit. But, getting back to it, how did you induce Uncle Tom to scare the moths from his pocket-book? It must have required quite a scuttleful of wifely wiles on your part?'

I wouldn't like to say of a loved aunt that she giggled, but unquestionably the sound that proceeded from her lips closely resembled a giggle.

'Oh, I managed.'

'But how?'

'Never mind how, you pestilential young Nosy Parker. I managed.'

'I see,' I said, letting it go. Something told me she did not wish to spill the data. 'And how is the Trotter deal coming along?'

I seemed to have touched an exposed nerve. The giggle died on her lips, and her face – always, as I have said, on the reddish side – deepened in colour to a rich mauve.

'Blister his blighted insides!' she said, speaking with the explosive heat which had once made fellow-members of the Quorn and Pytchley leap convulsively in their saddles. 'I don't know what's the matter with the son of Belial. Here he is, with nine of Anatole's lunches and eight of Anatole's dinners tucked away among the gastric juices, and he refuses to get down to brass tacks. He hums –'

'What on earth does he do that for?'

'– and haws. He evades the issue. I strain every nerve to make him talk turkey, but I can't pin him down. He doesn't say Yes and he doesn't say No.'

'There's a song called that ... or, rather, "She didn't say Yes and she didn't say No". I sing it a good deal in my bath. It goes like this.'

I started to render the refrain in a pleasant light baritone, but desisted on receiving Agatha Christie abaft the frontal bone. The old relative seemed to have fired from the hip like somebody in a Western B. picture.

'Don't try me too high, Bertie dear,' she said gently, and fell into what looked like a reverie. 'Do you know what I think is the trouble?' she went on, coming out of it. 'I believe Ma Trotter is responsible for this non-co-operation of his. For some reason she doesn't want him to put the deal through, and has told him he mustn't. It's the only explanation I can think of. When I met him at Agatha's, he spoke as if it were just a matter of arranging terms, but these last few days he has come over all coy, as if acting under orders from up top. When you stood them dinner that night, did he strike you as being crushed beneath her heel?'

'Very much so. He wept with delight when she gave him a smile and trembled with fear at her frown. But why would she object to him buying the *Boudoir*?'

'Don't ask me. It's a complete mystery.'

'You haven't put her back up somehow since she got here?'

'Certainly not. I've been fascinating.'

'And yet there it is, what?'

'Exactly. There it blasted well is, curse it!'

I heaved a sympathetic sigh. Mine is a tender heart, easily wrung, and the spectacle of this good old egg mourning over what might have been had wrung it like a ton of bricks.

'Too bad,' I said. 'One had hoped for better things.'

'One had,' she assented. 'I was so sure that Morehead serial would have brought home the bacon.'

'Of course, he may be just thinking it over.'

'That's true.'

'A fellow thinking it over would naturally hum.'

'And haw?'

'And, possibly, also haw. You could scarcely expect him to do less.'

We would no doubt have proceeded to go more deeply into the matter, subjecting this humming and hawing of L.G. Trotter's to a close analysis, but at this moment the door opened and a careworn face peered in, a face disfigured on either side by short whiskers and in the middle by tortoiseshell-rimmed spectacles.

'I say,' said the face, contorted with anguish, 'have you seen Florence?'

Aunt Dahlia replied that she had not been privileged to do so since lunch.

'I thought she might be with you.'

'She isn't.'

'Oh,' said the face, still running the gamut of the emotions, and began to recede.

'Hey!' cried Aunt Dahlia, arresting it as it was about to disappear. She went to the desk and picked up a buff envelope. 'This telegram came for her just now. Will you give it to her if you see her. And while you're here, meet my nephew Bertie Wooster, the pride of Piccadilly.'

Well, I hadn't expected him on learning of my identity to dance about the room on the tips of his toes, and he didn't. He gave me a long, reproachful look, similar in its essentials to that which a black beetle gives a cook when the latter is sprinkling insect powder on it.

'I have corresponded with Mr. Wooster,' he said coldly. 'We have also spoken on the telephone.'

He turned and was gone, gazing at me reproachfully to the last. It was plain that the Gorringes did not lightly forget.

'That was Percy,' said Aunt Dahlia.

I replied that I had divined as much.

'Did you notice how he looked when he said "Florence"? Like a dying duck in a thunderstorm.'

'And did you notice,' I inquired in my turn, 'how he looked when you said "Bertie Wooster"? Like someone finding a dead mouse in his pint of beer. Not a bonhomous bird. Not my type.'

'No. You would scarcely suppose that even a mother could view him without nausea, would you? And yet he is the apple of Ma Trotter's eye. She loves him as much as she hates Mrs. Alderman Blenkinsop. Did she touch on Mrs. Alderman Blenkinsop at that dinner of yours?'

'At several points during the meal. Who is she?'

'Her bitterest social rival up in Liverpool.'

'Do they have social rivals up in Liverpool?'

'You bet they do, in droves. I gather that it is nip and tuck between the Trotter and the Blenkinsop as to who shall be the uncrowned queen of Liverpudlian society. Sometimes one gets her nose in front, sometimes the other. It's like what one used to read about the death struggles for supremacy in New York's Four Hundred in the old days. But why am I telling you all this? You ought to be out there in the sunset, racing after Percy and bucking him up with your off-colour stories. You have a fund of off-colour stories, I presume?'

'Oh, rather.'

'Then get going, laddie. Once more into the breach, dear friends, once more, or close the wall up with our English dead. Yoicks! Tally-ho! Hark for'ard!' she added, reverting to the argot of the hunting field.

Well, when Aunt Dahlia tells you to get going, you get going, if you know what's good for you. But I was in no cheery mood as I made my way into the great open spaces. That look of Percy's had told me he was going to be a hard audience. It had had in it much of the austerity which I had noticed in Stilton Cheesewright's Uncle Joseph during our get-together at Vinton Street police court.

It was with not a little satisfaction, accordingly, that I found on arriving in the open no signs of him. Relieved, I abandoned the chase and started to stroll hither and thither, taking the air. And I hadn't taken much of it, when there he was, rounding a rhododendron bush in my very path.

10

If it hadn't been for the whiskers, I don't believe I would have recognized him. It was only about ten minutes since he had shoved his face in at the door of Aunt Dahlia's lair, but in that brief interval his whole aspect had changed. No longer the downcast duck in a thunderstorm from whom I had so recently parted, he had become gay and bobbish. His air was jaunty, his smile bright, and there was in his demeanour more than a suggestion of a man who might at any moment break into a tap dance. It was as if he had spent a considerable time watching that trick of Freddie Widgeon's with the two corks and the bit of string.

'Hullo there, Wooster,' he cried buoyantly, and you would have supposed that finding Bertram in his midst had just about made his day. 'Taking a stroll, eh?'

I said Yes I was taking a stroll, and he beamed as though feeling that I could have pursued no wiser and more admirable course. 'Sensible chap, Wooster,' he seemed to be saying. 'He takes strolls.'

There was a short intermission here, during which he looked at me lovingly and slid his feet about a bit in the manner of one trying out dance steps. Then he said it was a beautiful evening, and I endorsed this.

'The sunset,' he said, indicating it.

'Very fruity,' I agreed, for the whole horizon was aflame with glorious Technicolor.

'Seeing it,' he said, 'I am reminded of a poem I wrote the other day for *Parnassus*. Just a little thing I dashed off. You might care to hear it.'

'Oh, rather.'

'It's called "Caliban at Sunset".'

'What at sunset?'

'Caliban.'

He cleared his throat, and began:

> I stood with a man
> Watching the sun go down.

The air was full of murmurous summer scents
And a brave breeze sang like a bugle
From a sky that smouldered in the west,
A sky of crimson, amethyst and gold and sepia
And blue as blue as were the eyes of Helen
When she sat
Gazing from some high tower in Ilium
Upon the Grecian tents darkling below.
And he,
This man who stood beside me,
Gaped like some dull, half-witted animal
And said,
'I say,
Doesn't that sunset remind you
Of a slice
Of underdone roast beef?'

He opened his eyes, which he had closed in order to render the *morceau* more effectively.

'Bitter, of course.'

'Oh, frightfully bitter.'

'I was feeling bitter when I wrote it. I think you know a man named Cheesewright. It was he I had in mind. Actually, we had never stood watching a sunset together, but I felt it was just the sort of thing he would have said if he had been watching a sunset, if you see what I mean. Am I right?'

'Quite right.'

'A soulless clod, don't you think?'

'Soulless to the core.'

'No finer feelings?'

'None.'

'Would I be correct in describing him as a pumpkin-headed oaf?'

'Quite correct.'

'Yes,' he said, 'she is well out of it.'

'She?'

'Florence.'

'Oh, ah. Well out of what?'

He eyed me speculatively, heaving gently like a saucepan of porridge about to reach the height of its fever. I am a man who can observe and deduce, and it was plain to me, watching him sizzle, that something had happened pretty recently in his affairs which had churned him up like a seidlitz powder, leaving him with but two alternatives – (*a*) to burst where he stood and (*b*) to decant his pent-up emotions on the first human being who came along. No doubt he would have preferred this human being to have been of a non-Wooster nature, but one imagines that he was saying to himself that you can't have everything and that he was in no position to pick and choose.

He decided on Alternative B.

'Wooster,' he said, placing a hand on my shoulder, 'may I ask you a question? Has your aunt told you that I love Florence Craye?'

'She did mention it, yes.'

'I thought she might have done. She is not what I would call a reticent woman, though of course with many excellent qualities. I was forced to take her into my confidence soon after my arrival here, because she asked me why the devil I was going about looking like a dead codfish.'

'Or like Hamlet?'

'Hamlet or a dead codfish. The point is immaterial. I confessed to her that it was because I loved Florence with a consuming passion and had discovered that she was engaged to the oaf Cheesewright. It had been, I explained, as if I had received a crushing blow on the head.'

'Like Sir Eustace Willoughby.'

'I beg your pardon?'

'In *The Mystery of the Pink Crayfish.* He was conked on the bean in his library one night, and if you ask me it was the butler who did it. But I interrupted you.'

'You did.'

'I'm sorry. You were saying it was as if you had received a crushing blow on the head.'

'Exactly. I reeled beneath the shock.'

'Must have been a nasty jar.'

'It was. I was stunned. But now . . . You remember that telegram your aunt gave me to give to Florence?'

'Ah, yes, the telegram.'

'It was from Cheesewright, breaking the engagement.'

I had no means of knowing, of course, what his form was when reeling beneath shocks, but I doubted whether he could have put up a performance topping mine as I heard these words. The sunset swayed before my eyes as if it were doing the shimmy, and a bird close by which was getting outside its evening worm looked for an instant like two birds, both flickering.

'What!' I gurgled, rocking on my base.

'Yes.'

'He's broken the engagement?'

'Precisely.'

'Oh, golly! Why?'

He shook his head.

'Ah, that I couldn't tell you. All I know is that I found Florence in the stable yard tickling a cat behind the ear, and I came up and said "Here's a telegram for you", and she said "Really? I suppose it's from D'Arcy". I shuddered at the name, and while I was shuddering, she opened the envelope. It was a long telegram, but she had not read more than the first words when she uttered a sharp cry. "Bad news?" I queried. Her eyes flashed, and a cold, proud look came into her face. "Not at all," she replied. "Splendid news. D'Arcy Cheesewright has broken the engagement." '

'Gosh!'

'You may well say "Gosh!" '

'She didn't tell you any more than that?'

'No. She said one or two incisive things about Cheesewright with which I thoroughly concurred and strode off in the direction of the kitchen garden. And I came away, walking, as you may well imagine, on air. I deprecate the modern tendency to use slang, but I am not ashamed to confess that what I was saying to myself was the word "Whoopee!" Excuse me, Wooster, I must now leave you. I can't keep still.'

And with these words he pranced off like a mustang, leaving me to face the changed conditions alone.

It was with a brooding sense of peril that I did so. And if you are saying 'But why, Wooster? Surely everything is pretty smooth? What matter if the girl's nuptials with Cheesewright have been cancelled, when here is Percy Gorringe all ready and eager to take up the white man's burden?' I reply 'Ah, but you've not seen Percy Gorringe'. I mean to say, I couldn't picture Florence, however much on the rebound, accepting the addresses of a man who voluntarily wore side-whiskers and wrote poems about sunsets. Far more likely, it seemed to me, that having a vacant date on her hands she would once again reach out for the old and tried – viz. poor old Bertram. It was what she had done before, and these things tend to become a habit.

I was completely at a loss to imagine what could have caused this in-and-out running on Stilton's part. The thing didn't make sense. When last seen, it will be remembered, he had had all the earmarks of one about whom Love had twined its silken fetters. His every word at that parting chat of ours had indicated this beyond peradventure and doubt. Dash it, I mean, you don't go telling people you will break their spines in four places if they come oiling round the adored object unless you have more than a passing fancy for the bally girl.

So what had occurred to dim the lamp of love and all that sort of thing?

Could it be, I asked myself, that the strain of growing that moustache had proved too much for him? Had he caught sight of himself in the mirror about the third day – the third day is always the danger spot – and felt that nothing in the way of wedded bliss could make the venture worth while? Called upon to choose between the woman he loved and a hairless upper lip, had he cracked, with the result that the lip had had it by a landslide?

With a view to getting the inside stuff straight from the horse's mouth, I hurried to the kitchen garden, where, if Percy was to be relied on, Florence would now be, probably pacing up and down with lowered head.

She was there with lowered head, though not actually pacing up and down. She was bending over a gooseberry bush, eating gooseberries in an overwrought sort of way. Seeing me, she straightened up, and I snapped into the *res* without preamble.

'What's all this I hear from Percy Gorringe?' I said.

She swallowed a gooseberry with a passionate gulp that spoke eloquently of the churned-up soul, and I saw, as Percy's words had led me to expect, that she was madder than a wet hen. Her whole aspect was that of a girl who would have given her year's dress allowance for the privilege of beating G. D'Arcy Cheesewright over the head with a parasol.

I continued.

'He says there has been a rift within the lute.'

'I beg your pardon?'

'You and Stilton. According to Percy, the lute is not the lute it was. Stilton has broken the engagement, he tells me.'

'He has. I'm delighted, of course.'

'Delighted? You like the set-up?'

'Of course I do. What girl would not be delighted who finds herself unexpectedly free from a man with a pink face and a head that looks as if it had been blown up with a bicycle pump?'

I clutched the brow. I am a pretty astute chap, and I could see that this was not the language of love. I mean, if you had heard Juliet saying a thing like that about Romeo, you would have raised the eyebrows in quick concern, wondering if all was well with the young couple.

'But when I saw him last, everything seemed perfectly okey-doke. I could have sworn that, however reluctantly, he had reconciled himself to growing that moustache.'

She stooped and took another gooseberry.

'It has nothing to do with moustaches,' she said, reappearing on the surface. 'The whole thing is due to the fact that D'Arcy Cheesewright is a low, mean, creeping, crawling, slinking, spying, despicable worm,' she proceeded, dishing out the words from between clenched teeth. 'Do you know what he did?'

'I haven't a notion.'

She refreshed herself with a further gooseberry and returned to the upper air, breathing a few puffs of flame through the nostrils.

'He sneaked round to that night club yesterday and made inquiries.'

'Oh, my gosh!'

'Yes. You wouldn't think a man could stoop so low, but he bribed people and was allowed to look at the head waiter's book and found that a table had been reserved that night in your name. This confirmed his degraded suspicions. He knew that I had been there with you. I suppose,' said Florence, diving at the gooseberry bush once more and starting to strip it of its contents, 'a man gets a rotten, spying mind like that from being a policeman.'

To say that I was appalled would not be putting it any too strongly. I was, moreover, astounded. It was a revelation to me that a puff-faced poop like Stilton could have been capable of detective work on this uncanny scale. I had always respected his physique, of course, but had supposed that the ability to fell an ox with a single blow more or less let him out. Not for an instant had I credited him with reasoning powers which might well have made Hercule Poirot himself draw the breath in with a startled 'What ho'. It just showed how one ought never to underestimate a man simply because he devotes his life to shoving oars into rivers and pulling them out again, this being about as silly a way of passing the time as could be hit upon.

No doubt, as Florence had said, this totally unforeseen snakiness was the result of his having been, if only briefly, a member of the police force. One presumes that when the neophyte has been issued his uniform and regulation boots, the men up top take him aside and teach him a few things likely to be of use to him in his chosen profession. Stilton, it was plain, had learned his lesson well and, if one did but know, was probably capable of measuring blood stains and collecting cigar ash.

However, it was only a fleeting attention that I gave to this facet of the situation. My thoughts were concentrated on something of far greater pith and moment, as Jeeves would say. I allude to the position – now that the man knew all – of B. Wooster, which seemed to me sticky to a degree. Florence, having sated herself with gooseberries, was starting to move off, and I arrested her with a sharp 'Hoy!'

'That telegram,' I said.

'I don't want to talk about it.'

'I do. Was there anything about me in it?'

'Oh, yes, quite a lot.'

I swallowed a couple of times and passed a finger round the inside of my collar. I had thought there might be.

'Did he hint at any plans he had with regard to me?'

'He said he was going to break your spine in five places.'

'*Five* places?'

'I think he said five. Don't you let him,' said Florence warmly, and it was nice, of course, to know that she disapproved. 'Breaking spines! I never heard of such a thing. He ought to be ashamed of himself.'

And she moved off in the direction of the house, walking like a tragedy queen on one of her bad mornings.

What I have heard Jeeves call the glimmering landscape was now fading on the sight, and it was getting on for the hour when dressing-gongs are beaten. But though I knew how rash it is ever to be late for one of Anatole's dinners, I could not bring myself to go in and don the soup-and-fish. I had so much to occupy the mind that I lingered on in a sort of stupor. Winged creatures of the night kept rolling up and taking a look at me and rolling off again, but I remained motionless, plunged in thought. A man pursued by a thug like D'Arcy Cheesewright has need of all the thought he can get hold of.

And then, quite suddenly, out of the night that covered me, black as a pit from pole to pole, there shone a gleam of light. It spread, illuminating the entire horizon, and I realized that, taken by and large, I was sitting pretty.

You see, what I had failed till now to spot was the fact that Stilton hadn't a notion that I was at Brinkley. Thinking me to be in the metropolis, it was there that he would be spreading his drag-net. He would call at the flat, ring bells, get no answer and withdraw, baffled. He would haunt the Drones, expecting me to drop in, and eventually, when I didn't so drop, would slink away, baffled again. 'He cometh not', he would say, no doubt grinding his teeth, and a fat lot of good that would do him.

And of course, after what had occurred, there was no chance of him visiting Brinkley. A man who has broken off his engagement doesn't go to the country house where he knows the girl to be. Well, I mean,

I ask you. Naturally he doesn't. If there was one spot on earth which could be counted on as of even date to be wholly free from Cheesewrights, it was Brinkley Court, Brinkley-cum-Snodsfield-in-the-Marsh, Worcestershire.

Profoundly relieved, I picked up the feet and hastened to my room with a song on my lips. Jeeves was there, not actually holding a stop-watch but obviously shaking his head a bit over the young master's tardiness. His left eyebrow quivered perceptibly as I entered.

'Yes, I know I'm late, Jeeves,' I said, starting to shed the upholstery. 'I went for a stroll.'

He accepted the explanation indulgently.

'I quite understand, sir. It had occurred to me that, the evening being so fine, you were probably enjoying a saunter in the grounds. I told Mr. Cheesewright that this was no doubt the reason for your absence.'

11

Half in and half out of the shirt, I froze like one of those fellows in the old fairy stories who used to talk out of turn to magicians and have spells cast upon them. My ears were sticking up like a wirehaired terrier's, and I could scarcely believe that they had heard aright.

'Mr. Chuch?' I quavered. 'What's that, Jeeves?'

'Sir?'

'I don't understand you. Are you saying . . . are you telling me . . . are you actually asserting that Stilton Cheesewright is on the premises?'

'Yes, sir. He arrived not long ago in his car. I found him waiting here. He expressed a desire to see you and appeared chagrined at your continued absence. Eventually, the dinner-hour becoming imminent, he took his departure. He is hoping, I gathered from his remarks, to establish contact with you at the conclusion of the meal.'

I slid dumbly into the shirt and started to tie the tie. I was quivering, partly with apprehension, but even more with justifiable indignation. To say that I felt that this was a bit thick would not be straining the facts unduly. I mean, I know D'Arcy Cheesewright to be of coarse fibre, the sort of bozo who, as Percy had said, would look at a sunset and see in it only a resemblance to a slice of under-done roast beef, but surely one is entitled to expect even bozos of coarse fibre to have a certain amount of delicacy and decent feeling and what not. This breaking off his engagement to Florence with one hand and coming thrusting his society on her with the other struck me, as it would have struck any fine-minded man, as about as near the outside rim as it was possible to go.

'It's monstrous, Jeeves!' I cried. 'Has this pumpkin-headed oaf no sense of what is fitting? Has he no tact, no discretion? Are you aware that this very evening, through the medium of a telegram which I have every reason to believe was a stinker, he severed his relations with Lady Florence?'

'No, sir, I had not been apprised. Mr. Cheesewright did not confide in me.'

'He must have stopped off *en route* to compose the communication, for it arrived not so very long before he did. Fancy doing the thing by telegram, thus giving some post-office clerk the laugh of a lifetime. And then actually having the crust to come barging in here! That, Jeeves, is serving it up with cream sauce. I don't want to be harsh, but there is only one word for D'Arcy Cheesewright – the word "uncouth". What are you goggling at?' I asked, noticing that his gaze was fixed upon me in a meaning manner.

He spoke with quiet severity.

'Your tie, sir. It will not, I fear, pass muster.'

'Is this a time to talk of ties?'

'Yes, sir. One aims at the perfect butterfly shape, and this you have not achieved. With your permission, I will adjust it.'

He did so, and I must say made a very fine job of it, but I continued to chafe.

'Do you realize, Jeeves, that my life is in peril?'

'Indeed, sir?'

'I assure you. That hunk of boloney . . . I allude to G. D'Arcy Cheesewright . . . has formally stated his intention of breaking my spine in five places.'

'Indeed, sir? Why is that?'

I gave him the facts, and he expressed the opinion that the position of affairs was disturbing.

I shot one of my looks at him.

'You would go so far as that, Jeeves?'

'Yes, sir. Most disturbing.'

'Ho!' I said, borrowing a bit of Stilton's stuff, and was about to tell him that if he couldn't think of a better word than that to describe what was probably the ghastliest imbroglio that had ever broken loose in the history of the human race, I would be glad to provide him with a Roget's *Thesaurus* at my personal expense, when the gong went and I had to leg it for the trough.

I do not look back to that first dinner at Brinkley Court as among the pleasantest functions which I have attended. Ironically, considering the circumstances, Anatole, that wizard of the pots and pans, had come through with one of his supremest efforts. He had provided the company with, if memory serves me correctly,

Le Caviar Frais
Le Consommé aux Pommes d'Amour
Les Sylphides à la crème d'Écrevisses

Les Fried Smelts
Le Bird of some kind with chipped potatoes
Le Ice Cream

and, of course, les fruits and le café, but for all its effect on the Wooster soul it might have been corned beef hash. I don't say I pushed it away untasted, as Aunt Dahlia had described Percy doing with his daily ration, but the successive courses turned to ashes in my mouth. The sight of Stilton across the table blunted appetite.

I suppose it was just imagination, but he seemed to have grown quite a good deal both upwards and sideways since I had last seen him, and the play of expression on his salmon-coloured face showed only too clearly the thoughts that were occupying his mind, if you could call it that. He gave me from eight to ten dirty looks in the course of the meal, but except for a remark at the outset to the effect that he was hoping to have a word with me later, did not address me.

Nor, for the matter of that, did he address anyone. His demeanour throughout was that of a homicidal deaf mute. The Trotter female, who sat on his right, endeavoured to entertain him with a saga about Mrs. Alderman Blenkinsop's questionable behaviour at a recent church bazaar, but he confined his response to gaping at her like some dull, half-witted animal, as Percy would have said, and digging silently into the foodstuffs.

Sitting next to Florence, who spoke little, merely looking cold and proud and making bread pills, I had ample leisure for thought during the festivities, and by the time the coffee came round I had formed my plans and perfected my strategy. When eventually Aunt Dahlia blew the whistle for the gentler sex to buzz off and leave the men to their port, I took advantage of their departure to execute a quiet sneak through the french windows into the garden, being well in the open before the first of the procession had crossed the threshold. Whether or not this clever move brought a hoarse cry to Stilton's lips, I cannot say for certain, but I fancied I heard something that sounded like the howl of a timber wolf that has stubbed its toe on a passing rock. Not bothering to go back and ask if he had spoken, I made my way into the spacious grounds.

Had circumstances been different from what they were – not, of course, that they ever are – I might have derived no little enjoyment from this after-dinner saunter, for the air was full of murmurous scents and a brave breeze sang like a bugle from a sky liberally studded with stars. But to appreciate a starlit garden one has to have a fairly tranquil mind, and mine was about as far from being tranquil as it could jolly well stick.

What to do? I was asking myself. It seemed to me that the prudent course, if I wished to preserve a valued spine intact, would be to climb aboard the two-seater first thing in the morning and ho for the open spaces. To remain *in statu quo* would, it was clear, involve a distasteful nippiness on my part, for only by the most unremitting activity could I hope to elude Stilton and foil his sinister aims. I would be compelled, I saw, to spend a substantial portion of my time flying like a youthful hart or roe over the hills where spices grow, as I remembered having heard Jeeves once put it, and the Woosters resent having to sink to the level of harts and roes, whether juvenile or getting on in years. We have our pride.

I had just reached the decision that on the morrow I would melt away like snow on the mountain-tops and go to America or Australia or the Fiji Islands or somewhere for awhile, when the murmurous summer scents were augmented by the aroma of a powerful cigar and I observed a dim figure approaching. After a tense moment when I supposed it to be Stilton and braced myself for a spot of that youthful-hart-or-roe stuff, I got it placed. It was only Uncle Tom, taking his nightly prowl.

Uncle Tom is a great lad for prowling in the garden. A man with greyish hair and a face like a walnut – not that that has anything to do with it, of course – I just mention it in passing – he likes to be among the shrubs and flowers early and late, particularly late, for he suffers a bit from insomnia and the tribal medicine man told him that a breath of fresh air before hitting the hay would bring relief.

Seeing me, he paused for station identification.

'Is that you, Bertie, me boy?'

I conceded this, and he hove alongside, puffing smoke.

'Why did you leave us?' he asked, alluding to that quick duck of mine from the dining-room.

'Oh, I thought I would.'

'Well, you didn't miss much. What a set! That man Trotter makes me sick.'

'Oh, yes?'

'His stepson Percy makes me sick.'

'Oh, yes?'

'And that fellow Cheesewright makes me sick. They all make me sick,' said Uncle Tom. He is not one of your jolly-innkeeper-with-entrance-number-in-act-one hosts. He looks with ill-concealed aversion on at least ninety-four per cent of the guests within his gates and spends most of his time dodging them. 'Who invited Cheesewright here? Dahlia, I suppose, though why we shall never know. A deleterious young slab of damnation, if ever I saw one. But she will do these things. I've even known her to invite her sister Agatha. Talking of Dahlia, Bertie, me boy, I'm worried about her.'

'Worried?'

'Exceedingly worried. I believe she's sickening for something. Has her manner struck you as strange since you got here?'

I mused.

'No, I don't think so,' I said. 'She seemed to be about the same as usual. How do you mean, strange?'

He waved a concerned cigar. He and the old relative are a fond and united couple.

'It was just now, when I looked in on her in her room to ask if she would care to come for a stroll. She said No, she didn't think she would, because if she went out at night she always swallowed moths and midges and things and she didn't believe it was good for her on top of a heavy dinner. And we were talking idly of this and that, when she suddenly seemed to come over all faint.'

'Swooned, do you mean?'

'No, I wouldn't say she actually swooned. She continued perpendicular. But she tottered, pressing her hand to the top of her head. Pale as a ghost she looked.'

'Odd.'

'Very. It worried me. I'm not at all easy in my mind about her.'

I pondered.

'It couldn't have been something you said that upset her?'

'Impossible. I was talking about this fellow Sidcup who's coming tomorrow to look at my silver collection. You've never met him, have you?'

'No.'

'Rather a fatheaded ass,' said Uncle Tom, who thinks most of his circle fatheaded asses, 'but apparently knows quite a bit about old silver and jewellery and all that sort of thing, and anyway he'll only be here for dinner, thank God,' he added in his hospitable way. 'But I was telling you about your aunt. As I was saying, she tottered and looked as pale as a ghost. The fact of the matter is, she's been overdoing it. This paper of hers, this Madame's Nightshirt or whatever it's called. It's wearing her to a shadow. Silly nonsense. What does she want with a weekly paper? I'll be thankful if she sells it to this man Trotter and gets rid of the damned thing, because apart from wearing her to a shadow it's costing me a fortune. Money, money, money, there's no end to it.'

He then spoke with considerable fervour for awhile of income-tax and surtax, and after making a tentative appointment to meet me in the breadline at an early date popped off and was lost in the night. And I, feeling that the hour being now advanced, it might be safe to retire to my room, made my way thither.

As I started to get into something loose, I continued to brood on what he had told me about Aunt Dahlia. I found myself mystified. At dinner I had, of course, been distrait and preoccupied, but even so I would, I thought, have noticed if she had shown any signs of being in the grip of a wasting sickness or anything of that kind. As far as I could recollect, she had appeared to be tucking into the various items on the menu with her customary zip and brio. Yet Uncle Tom had spoken of her as looking as pale as a ghost, a thing which took some doing with a face as red as hers.

Odd, not to say mysterious.

I was still musing on this and wondering what Osborne Cross, the sleuth in *The Mystery of the Pink Crayfish*, would have made of it, when I was jerked out of my meditations by the turning of the door handle. This was followed by a forceful bang on the panel, and I realized how prudent I had been in locking up before settling in for the night. For the voice that now spoke was that of Stilton Cheese-wright.

'Wooster!'

I rose, laying down my *Crayfish*, into which I had been about to dip, and put my lips to the keyhole.

'Wooster!'

'All right, my good fellow,' I said coldly. 'I heard you the first time. What do you want?'

'A word with you.'

'Well, you jolly well aren't going to have it. Leave me, Cheesewright. I would be alone. I have a slight headache.'

'It won't be slight, if I get at you.'

'Ah, but you can't get at me,' I riposted cleverly, and returning to my chair resumed my literary studies, pleasantly conscious of having worsted him in debate. He called me a few derogatory names through the woodwork, banged and handle-rattled a bit more, and finally shoved off, no doubt muttering horrid imprecations.

It was about five minutes later that there was another knock on the door, this time so soft and discreet that I had no difficulty in identifying it.

'Is that you, Jeeves?'

'Yes, sir.'

'Just a moment.'

As I crossed the room to admit him, I was surprised to find that the lower limbs were feeling a bit filleted. That verbal duel with my recent guest had shaken me more than I had suspected.

'I have just had a visit from Stilton Cheesewright, Jeeves,' I said.

'Indeed, sir? I trust the outcome was satisfactory.'

'Yes, I rather nonplussed the simple soul. He had imagined that he could penetrate into my sanctum without let or hindrance, and was struck all of a heap when he found the door locked. But the episode has left me a little weak, and I would be glad if you could dig me out a whisky-and-soda.'

'Certainly, sir.'

'It wants to be prepared in just the right way. Who was that pal of yours you were speaking about the other day whose strength was as the strength of ten?'

'A gentleman of the name of Galahad, sir. You err, however, in supposing him to have been a personal friend. He was the subject of a poem by the late Alfred, Lord Tennyson.'

'Immaterial, Jeeves. All I was going to say was that I would like the strength of this whisky-and-soda to be as that of ten. Don't flinch when pouring.'

'Very good, sir.'

He departed on his errand of mercy, and I buckled down to the *Crayfish* once more. But scarcely had I started to collect clues and interview suspects when I was interrupted again. A clenched fist had sloshed against the portal with a disturbing booming sound. Assuming that my visitor was Stilton, I was about to rise and rebuke him through the keyhole as before, when there penetrated from the outer spaces an ejaculation so fruity and full of vigour that it could have proceeded only from the lips of one who had learned her stuff among the hounds and foxes.

'Aunt Dahlia?'

'Open this door!'

I did so, and she came charging in.

'Where's Jeeves?' she asked, so plainly all of a-twitter that I eyed her in considerable alarm. After what Uncle Tom had been saying about her tottering I didn't like this febrile agitation.

'Is something the matter?' I asked.

'You bet something's the matter. Bertie,' said the old relative, sinking on to the chaise-longue and looking as if at any moment she might start blowing bubbles, 'I'm up against it, and only Jeeves can save my name in the home from becoming mud. Produce the blighter, and let him exercise that brain of his as never before.'

12

I endeavoured to soothe her with a kindly pat on the topknot. 'Jeeves will be back in a moment,' I said, 'and will doubtless put everything right with one wave of his magic wand. Tell me, my fluttering old aspen, what seems to be the trouble?'

She gulped like a stricken bull pup. I had rarely seen a more jittery aunt.

'It's Tom!'

'The uncle of that name?'

'How many Toms do you think there are in this joint, for goodness' sake?' she said, with a return of her normal forcefulness. 'Yes, Thomas Portarlington Travers, my husband.'

'Portarlington?' I said, a little shocked.

'He came pottering into my room just now.'

I nodded intelligently. I remembered that he had spoken of having done so. It was on that occasion, you recall, that he had observed her pressing her hand to the top of her head.

'I see. Yes, so far I follow you. Scene, your room. Discovered sitting, you. Enter Uncle Tom, pottering. What then?'

She was silent for a space. Then she spoke in what was for her a hushed voice. That is to say, while rattling the vases on the mantelpiece, it did not bring plaster down from the ceiling.

'I'd better tell you the whole thing.'

'Do, old ancestor. Nothing like getting it off the chest, whatever it is.'

She gulped like another stricken bull pup.

'It's not a long story.'

'Good,' I said, for the hour was late and I had had a busy day.

'You remember when we were talking after you got here this evening . . . Bertie, you revolting object,' she said, deviating momentarily from the main thread, 'that moustache of yours is the most obscene thing I ever saw outside a nightmare. It seems to take one straight into another and a dreadful world. What made you commit this rash act?'

I tut-tutted a bit austerely.

'Never mind my moustache, old flesh and blood. You leave it alone, and it'll leave you alone. When we were talking this evening, you were saying?'

She accepted the rebuke with a moody nod.

'Yes, I mustn't get side-tracked. I must stick to the point.'

'Like glue.'

'When we were talking this evening, you said you wondered how I had managed to get Tom to cough up the price of the Daphne Dolores Morehead serial. You remember?'

'I do. I'm still wondering.'

'Well, it's quite simple. I didn't.'

'Eh?'

'Tom didn't contribute a penny.'

'Then how –?'

'I'll tell you how. I pawned my pearl necklace.'

I gazed at her . . . well, I suppose 'awestruck' would be the word. Acquaintance with this woman dating from the days when I was an infant mewling and puking in my nurse's arms, if you will excuse the expression, had left me with the feeling that her guiding motto in life was 'Anything goes', but this seemed pretty advanced stuff even for one to whom the sky had always been the limit.

'Pawned it?' I said.

'Pawned it.'

'Hocked it, you mean? Popped it? Put it up the spout?'

'That's right. It was the only thing to do. I had to have that serial in order to salt the mine, and Tom absolutely refused to give me so much as a fiver to slake the thirst for gold of this blood-sucking Morehead. "Nonsense, nonsense", he kept saying. "Quite out of the question, quite out of the question." So I slipped up to London, took the necklace to Aspinall's, told them to make a replica, and then went along to the pawnbroker's. Well, when I say pawnbroker's, that's a figure of speech. My fellow was much higher class. More of a moneylender, you would call him.'

I whistled a bar or two.

'Then that thing I picked up for you this morning was a dud?'

'Cultured stuff.'

'Golly!' I said. 'You aunts do live!' I hesitated. I was loath to bruise that gentle spirit, especially at a moment when she was worried about something, but it seemed to me a nephew's duty to point out the snag. 'And when . . . I'm afraid this is going to spoil your day, but what happens when Uncle Tom finds out?'

'That's exactly the trouble.'

'I thought it might be.'

She gulped like a third stricken bull pup.

'If it hadn't been for a foul bit of bad luck, he wouldn't have found out in a million years. I don't suppose Tom, bless him, would know the difference between the Koh-i-noor and something from Woolworth's.'

I saw her point. Uncle Tom, as I have indicated, is a red-hot collector of old silver and there is nothing you can teach him about sconces, foliation, scrolls and ribbon wreaths, but jewellery is to him, as to most of the male sex, a sealed book.

'But he's going to find out tomorrow evening, and I'll tell you why. I told you he came to my room just now. Well, we had been kidding back and forth for a few moments, all very pleasant and matey, when he suddenly . . . Oh, my God!'

I administered another sympathetic pat on the bean.

'Pull yourself together, old relative. What did he suddenly do?'

'He suddenly told me that this Lord Sidcup who is coming tomorrow is not only an old-silver hound but an expert on jewellery, and he was going to ask him, while here, to take a look at my necklace.'

'Gosh!'

'He said he had often had a suspicion that the bandits who sold it to him had taken advantage of his innocence and charged him a lot too much. Sidcup, he said, would be able to put him straight about it.'

'Golly!'

' "Gosh!" is right, and so is "Golly!" '

'Then that's why you clutched the top of your head and tottered?'

'That's why. How long do you suppose it will take this fiend in human shape to see through that dud string of pearls and spill the beans? Just about ten seconds, if not less. And then what? Can you blame me for tottering?'

I certainly couldn't. In her place, I would have tottered myself and tottered like nobody's business. A far duller man than Bertram Wooster would have been able to appreciate that this aunt who sat before me clutching feverishly at her perm was an aunt who was in the dickens of a spot. A crisis had been precipitated in her affairs which threatened, unless some pretty adroit staff-work was pulled by her friends and well-wishers, to put the home right plumb spang in the melting-pot.

I have made a rather close study of the married state, and I know what happens when one turtle dove gets the goods on the other turtle dove. Bingo Little has often told me that if Mrs. Bingo had managed to get on him some of the things it seemed likely she was going to get, the moon would have been turned to blood and Civilization shaken to its foundations. I have heard much the same thing from other husbands of my acquaintance, and of course similar upheavals occur when it is the little woman who is caught bending.

Always up to now Aunt Dahlia had been the boss of Brinkley Court, maintaining a strong centralized government, but let Uncle Tom discover that she had pawned her pearl necklace in order to buy a serial story for what for some reason he always alluded to as Madame's Nightshirt, a periodical which from the very start he had never liked, and she would be in much the same position as one of those monarchs or dictators who wake up one morning to find that the populace has risen against them and is saying it with bombs. Uncle Tom is a kindly old bimbo, but even kindly old bimbos can make themselves dashed unpleasant when the conditions are right.

'Egad!' I said, fingering the chin. 'This is not so good.'

'It's the end of all things.'

'You say this Sidcup bird will be here tomorrow? It doesn't give you much time to put your affairs in order. No wonder you're sending out S O S's for Jeeves.'

'Only he can save me from the fate that is worse than death.'

'But can even Jeeves adjust matters?'

'I'm banking on him. After all, he's a hell of an adjuster.'

'True.'

'He's got you out of some deepish holes in his time.'

'Quite. I often say there is none like him, none. He should be with us at any moment now. He stepped out to get me a tankard of the old familiar juice.'

Her eyes gleamed with a strange light.

'Bags I first go at it!'

I patted her hand.

'Of course,' I said, 'of course. You may take that as read. You don't find Bertram Wooster hogging the drink supply when a suffering aunt is at his side with her tongue hanging out. Your need is greater than mine, as whoever-it-was said to the stretcher case. Ah!'

Jeeves had come in bearing the elixir, not a split second before we were ready for it. I took the beaker from him and offered it to the aged relative with a courteous gesture. With a brief 'Mud in your eye' she drank deeply. I then finished what was left at a gulp.

'Oh, Jeeves,' I said.

'Sir?'

'Lend me your ears.'

'Very good, sir.'

It had needed but a glance at my late father's sister to tell me that if there was going to be any lucid exposition of the *res*, I was the one who would have to attend to it. After moistening her clay she had relapsed into a sort of frozen coma, staring before her with unseeing eyes and showing a disposition to pant like a hart when heated in the chase. Nor was this to be wondered at. Few women would have been in vivacious mood, had Fate touched off beneath them a similar stick of trinitrotoluol. I imagine her emotions after Uncle Tom had said his say must have been of much the same nature as those which she had no doubt frequently experienced in her hunting days when her steed, having bucked her from the saddle, had proceeded to roll on her. And while the blushful Hippocrene of which she had just imbibed her share had been robust and full of inner meaning, it had obviously merely scratched the surface.

'A rather tight place has popped up out of a trap, Jeeves, and we should be glad of your counsel and advice. This is the posish. Aunt Dahlia has a pearl necklace, the Christmas gift of Uncle Tom, whose second name, I'll bet you didn't know, is Portarlington. The one you picked up at Aspinall's this morning. Are you with me?'

'Yes, sir.'

'Well, this is where the plot thickens. It isn't a pearl necklace, if I make my meaning clear. For reasons into which we need not go, she put the Uncle-Tom-Merry-Christmas one up the spout. What is now in her possession is an imitation of little or no intrinsic value.'

'Yes, sir.'

'You don't seem amazed.'

'No, sir. I became aware of the fact when I saw the necklace this morning. I perceived at once that what had been given to me was a cultured replica.'

'Good Lord! Was it as easy to spot as that?'

'Oh, no, sir. I have no doubt that it would deceive the untutored eye. But I spent some months at one time studying jewellery under the auspices of a cousin of mine who is in the trade. The genuine pearl has no core.'

'No what?'

'Core, sir. In its interior. The cultured pearl has. A cultured pearl differs from a real one in this respect, that it is the result of introducing into the oyster a foreign substance designed to irritate it and induce it to coat the substance with layer upon layer of nacre. Nature's own irritant is invariably so small as to be invisible, but the core in the cultured imitation can be discerned, as a rule merely by holding the cultured pearl up before a strong light. This was what I did in the matter of Mrs. Travers's necklace. I had no need of the endoscope.'

'The what?'

'Endoscope, sir. An instrument which enables one to peer into the cultured pearl's interior and discern the core.'

I was conscious of a passing pang for the oyster world, feeling – and I think correctly – that life for these unfortunate bivalves must be one damn thing after another, but my principal emotion was one of astonishment.

'Great Scot, Jeeves! Do you know everything?'

'Oh, no, sir. It just happens that jewellery is something of a hobby of mine. With diamonds, of course, the test would be different. To ascertain the genuineness of a diamond it would be necessary to take a sapphire-point gramophone needle – which is, as you are no doubt aware, corundum having a hardness of 9 – and make a small test scratch on the underside of the suspect stone. A genuine diamond, I need scarcely remind you, is the only substance with a hardness of 10 – Moh's scale of hardness. Most of the hard objects we see about us are approximately 7 in the hardness scale. But you were saying, sir?'

I was still blinking a bit. When Jeeves gets going nicely, he often has this effect on me. With a strong effort I pulled myself together and was able to continue.

'Well, that's the nub of the story,' I said. 'Aunt Dahlia's necklace, the one now in her possession, is, as your trained senses told you, a seething mass of cores and not worth the paper it's written on. Right. Well, here's the point. If no complications had been introduced into the scenario, all would be well, because Uncle Tom couldn't tell the difference between a real necklace and an imitation one if he tried for months. But a whale of a complication has been introduced. A pal of his is coming tomorrow to look at the thing, and this pal, like you, is an expert on jewellery. You see what will happen the moment he cocks an eye at the worthless substitute. Exposure, ruin, desolation and despair. Uncle Tom, learning the truth, will blow his top, and Aunt Dahlia's prestige will be down among the wines and spirits. You get me, Jeeves?'

'Yes, sir.'

'Then let us have your views.'

'It is disturbing, sir.'

I wouldn't have thought that anything would have been able to rouse that crushed aunt from her trance, but this did the trick. She came up like a rocketing pheasant from the chair into which she had slumped.

'Disturbing! What a word to use!'

I sympathized with her distress, but checked her with an upraised hand.

'Please, old relative! Yes, Jeeves, it is, as you say, a bit on the disturbing side, but one feels that you will probably have something constructive to place before the board. We shall be glad to hear your solution.'

He allowed a muscle at the side of his mouth to twitch regretfully.

'With a problem of such magnitude, sir, I fear I am not able to provide a solution off-hand, if I may use the expression. I should require to give the matter thought. Perhaps if I might be permitted to pace the corridor for awhile?'

'Certainly, Jeeves. Pace all the corridors you wish.'

'Thank you, sir. I shall hope to return shortly with some suggestion which will give satisfaction.'

I closed the door behind him and turned to the aged r., who, her face bright purple, was still muttering 'Disturbing'.

'I know just how you feel, old flesh and blood,' I said. 'I ought to have warned you that Jeeves never leaps about and rolls the eyes when you spring something sensational on him, preferring to preserve the calm impassivity of a stuffed frog.'

' "Disturbing"! '

'I have grown not to mind this much myself, though occasionally, as I was about to do tonight, administering a rather stern rebuke, for experience has taught me —'

' "Disturbing", for God's sake! *Disturbing*! '

'I know, I know. That manner of his does afflict the nerve centres quite a bit, does it not? But, as I was saying, experience has taught me that there always follows some ripe solution of whatever the problem may be. As the fellow said, if stuffed frogs come, can ripe solutions be far behind?'

She sat up. I could see the light of hope dawning in her eyes.

'You really think he will find the way?'

'I am convinced of it. He always finds the way. I wish I had a quid for every way he has found since first he started to serve under the Wooster banner. Remember how he enabled me to put it across Roderick Spode at Totleigh Towers.'

'He did, didn't he?'

'He certainly did. One moment, Spode was a dark menace, the next a mere blob of jelly with all his fangs removed, grovelling at my feet.

You can rely implicitly on Jeeves. Ah,' I said, as the door opened. 'Here he comes, his head sticking out at the back and his eyes shining with intelligence and what not. You have thought of something, Jeeves?'

'Yes, sir.'

'I knew it. I was saying a moment ago that you always find the way. Well, let us have it.'

'There is a method by means of which Mrs. Travers can be extricated from her sea of troubles. Shakespeare.'

I didn't know why he was addressing me as Shakespeare, but I motioned him to continue.

'Proceed, Jeeves.'

He did so, turning now to Aunt Dahlia, who was gazing at him like a bear about to receive a bun.

'If, as Mr. Wooster has told me, madam, this jewellery expert is to be with us shortly, it would seem that your best plan is to cause the necklace to disappear before he arrives. If I may make my meaning clearer, madam,' he went on in response to a query from the sizzling woman as to whether he supposed her to be a bally conjuror. 'What I had in mind was something in the nature of a burglarious entry, as the result of which the piece of jewellery would be abstracted. You will readily see, madam, that if the gentleman, coming to examine the necklace, finds that there is no necklace for him to examine –'

'He won't be able to examine it?'

'Precisely, madam. *Rem acu tetigisti.*'

I shook the lemon. I had expected something better than this. It seemed to me that that great brain had at last come unglued, and this saddened me.

'But, Jeeves,' I said gently, 'where do you get your burglar? From the Army and Navy Stores?'

'I was thinking that you might consent to undertake the task, sir.'

'Me?'

'Gosh, yes,' said Aunt Dahlia, her dial lighting up like a stage moon. 'How right you are, Jeeves! You wouldn't mind doing a little thing like that for me, would you, Bertie? Of course you wouldn't. You've grasped the idea? You get a ladder, prop it up against my window, pop in, pinch the necklace and streak off with it. And tomorrow I go to Tom in floods of tears and say, "Tom! My pearls! They've gone! Some low bounder sneaked in last night and snitched them as I slept." That's the idea, isn't it, Jeeves?'

'Precisely, madam. It would be a simple task for Mr. Wooster. I notice that since my last visit to Brinkley Court the bars which protected the windows have been removed.'

'Yes, I had that done after that time when we were all locked out. You remember?'

'Very vividly, madam.'

'So there's nothing to stop you, Bertie.'

'Nothing but –'

I paused. I had been about to say 'Nothing but my total and absolute refusal to take on the assignment in any shape or form', but I checked the words before they could pass the lips. I saw that I was exaggerating what I had supposed to be the dangers and difficulties of the enterprise.

After all, I felt, there was nothing so very hazardous about it. A ludicrously simple feat for one of my agility and lissomness. A nuisance, of course, having to turn out at this time of night, but I was quite prepared to do so in order to bring the roses back to the cheeks of a woman who in my bib-and-cradle days had frequently dandled me on her knee, not to mention saving my life on one occasion when I had half-swallowed a rubber comforter.

'Nothing at all,' I replied cordially. 'Nothing whatever. You provide the necklace, and I will do the rest. Which is your room?'

'That last one on the left.'

'Right.'

'Left, fool. I'll be going there now, so as to be in readiness. Golly, Jeeves, you've taken a weight off my mind. I feel a new woman. You won't mind if you hear me singing about the house?'

'Not at all, madam.'

'I shall probably start first thing tomorrow.'

'Any time that suits you, madam.'

He closed the door behind her with an indulgent smile, or something as nearly resembling a smile as he ever allows to appear on his map.

'One is glad to see Mrs. Travers so happy, sir.'

'Yes, you certainly bucked her up like a tonic. No difficulty about finding a ladder, I take it?'

'Oh, no, sir. I chanced to observe one outside the tool-shed by the kitchen garden.'

'So did I, now you mention it. No doubt it's still there, so let's go. If it were . . . what's that expression of yours?'

'If it were done when 'tis done, then 'twere well it were done quickly, sir.'

'That's right. No sense in standing humming and hawing.'

'No, sir. There is a tide in the affairs of men which, taken at the flood, leads on to fortune.'

'Exactly,' I said.

I couldn't have put it better myself.

The venture went with gratifying smoothness. I found the ladder, by the tool-shed as foreshadowed, and lugged it across country to the desired spot. I propped it up. I climbed it. In next to no time I was through the window and moving silently across the floor.

Well, not so dashed silently, as a matter of fact, because I collided with a table which happened to be in the fairway and upset it with quite a bit of noise.

'Who's there?' asked a voice from the darkness in a startled sort of way.

This tickled me. 'Ah,' I said to myself amusedly, 'Aunt Dahlia throwing herself into her part and giving the thing just the touch it needed to make it box-office.' What an artist, I felt.

Then it said 'Who's there?' again, and it was as though a well-iced hand had been laid upon my heart.

Because the voice was not the voice of any ruddy aunt, it was the voice of Florence Craye. The next moment light flooded the apartment and there she was, sitting up in bed in a pink boudoir cap.

13

I don't know if you happen to be familiar with a poem called 'The Charge of the Light Brigade' by the bird Tennyson whom Jeeves had mentioned when speaking of the fellow whose strength was as the strength of ten. It is, I believe, fairly well known, and I used to have to recite it at the age of seven or thereabouts when summoned to the drawing-room to give visitors a glimpse of the young Wooster. 'Bertie recites so nicely,' my mother used to say – getting her facts twisted, I may mention, because I practically always fluffed my lines – and after trying to duck for safety and being hauled back I would snap into it. And very unpleasant the whole thing was, so people have told me.

Well, what I was about to say, when I rambled off a bit on the subject of the dear old days, was that though in the course of the years most of the poem of which I speak has slid from the memory, I still recall its punch line. The thing goes, as you probably know,

> Tum tiddle umpty-pum
> Tum tiddle umpty-pum
> Tum tiddle umpty-pum

and this brought you to the snapperoo or pay-off, which was

Someone had blundered.

I always remember that bit, and the reason I bring it up now is that, as I stood blinking at this pink-boudoir-capped girl, I was feeling just as those Light Brigade fellows must have felt. Obviously someone had blundered here, and that someone was Aunt Dahlia. Why she should have told me that her window was the last one on the left, when the last one on the left was what it was anything but, was more than I could imagine. One sought in vain for what Stilton Cheesewright would have called the ulterior motive.

However, it is hopeless to try to fathom the mental processes of aunts, and anyway this was no time for idle speculation. The first thing the man of sensibility has to do on arriving like a sack of coals in a girl's bedroom in the small hours is to get the conversation going, and it was to this that I now addressed myself. Nothing is worse on these occasions than the awkward pause and the embarrassed silence.

'Oh, hullo,' I said, as brightly and cheerily as I could manage. 'I say, I'm most frightfully sorry to pop in like this at a moment when you were doubtless knitting up the ravelled sleave of care, but I went for a breather in the garden and found I was locked out, so I thought my best plan was not to rouse the house but to nip in through the first open window. You know how it is when you rouse houses. They don't like it.'

I would have spoken further, developing the theme, for it seemed to me that I was on the right lines . . . so much better, I mean to say, than affecting to be walking in my sleep. All that 'Where am I?' stuff, I mean. Too damn silly . . . but she suddenly gave one of those rippling laughs of hers.

'Oh, Bertie!' she said, and not, mark you, with that sort of weary fed-up-ness with which girls generally say 'Oh, Bertie!' to me. 'What a romantic you are!'

'Eh?'

She rippled again. It was a relief, of course, to find that she did not propose to yell for help and all that sort of thing, but I must say I found this mirth a bit difficult to cope with. You've probably had the same experience yourself – listening to people guffawing like hyenas and not having the foggiest what the joke is. It makes you feel at a disadvantage.

She was looking at me in an odd kind of way, as if at some child for whom, while conceding that it had water on the brain, she felt a fondness.

'Isn't this just the sort of thing you would do!' she said. 'I told you I was no longer engaged to D'Arcy Cheesewright, and you had to fly to me. You couldn't wait till the morning, could you? I suppose you had some sort of idea of kissing me softly while I slept?'

I leaped perhaps six inches in the direction of the ceiling. I was appalled, and I think not unjustifiably so. I mean, dash it, a fellow who has always prided himself on the scrupulous delicacy of his relations with the other sex doesn't like to have it supposed that he deliberately shins up ladders at one in the morning in order to kiss girls while they sleep.

'Good Lord, no!' I said, replacing the chair which I had knocked over in my agitation. 'Nothing further from my thoughts. I take it your attention happened to wander for a moment when I was outlining the facts, just now. What I was saying, only you weren't listening, was that I went for a breather in the garden and found I was locked out –'

She rippled once more. That looking-fondly-at-idiot-child expression on her face had become intensified.

'You don't think I'm angry, do you? Of course I'm not. I'm very touched. Kiss me, Bertie.'

Well, one has to be civil. I did as directed, but with an uneasy feeling that this was a bit above the odds. I didn't at all like the general trend of affairs, the whole thing seeming to me to be becoming far too French. When I broke out of the clinch and stepped back, I found the expression on her face had changed. She was now regarding me in a sort of speculative way, if you know what I mean, rather like a governess taking a gander at the new pupil.

'Mother's quite wrong,' she said.

'Mother?'

'Your Aunt Agatha.'

This surprised me.

'You call her Mother? Oh, well, okay, if you like it. Up to you, of course. What was she wrong about?'

'You. She keeps insisting that you are a vapid and irreflective nitwit who ought years ago to have been put in some good mental home.'

I drew myself up haughtily, cut more or less to the quick. So this was how the woman was accustomed to shoot off her bally head about me in my absence, was it! A pretty state of affairs. The woman, I'll trouble you, whose repulsive son Thos I had for years practically nursed in my bosom. That is to say, when he passed through London on his way back to school, I put him up at my residence and not only fed him luxuriously but with no thought of self took him to the Old Vic and Madame Tussaud's. Was there no gratitude in the world?

'She does, does she?'

'She's awfully amusing about you.'

'Amusing, eh?'

'It was she who said that you had a brain like a peahen.'

Here, of course, if I had wished to take it, was an admirable opportunity to go into this matter of peahens and ascertain just where they stood in the roster of our feathered friends as regarded the I.Q., but I let it go.

She adjusted the boudoir cap, which the recent embrace had tilted a bit to one side. She was still looking at me in that speculative way.

'She says you are a guffin.'

'A what?'

'A guffin.'

'I don't understand you.'

'It's one of those old-fashioned expressions. What she meant, I think, was that she considered you a wet smack and a total loss. But I told her she was quite mistaken and that there is a lot more in you than people suspect. I realized that when I found you in that bookshop that day buying *Spindrift*. Do you remember?'

I had not forgotten the incident. The whole thing had been one of those unfortunate misunderstandings. I had promised Jeeves to buy him the works of a cove of the name of Spinoza – some kind of philosopher or something, I gathered – and the chap at the bookshop, expressing the opinion that there was no such person as Spinoza, had handed me *Spindrift* as being more probably what I was after, and scarcely had I grasped it when Florence came in. To assume that I had purchased the thing and to autograph it for me in green ink with her fountain-pen had been with her the work of an instant.

'I knew then that you were groping dimly for the light and trying to educate yourself by reading good literature, that there was something lying hidden deep down in you that only needed bringing out. It would be a fascinating task, I told myself, fostering the latent potentialities of your budding mind. Like watching over some timid, backward flower.'

I bridled pretty considerably. Timid, backward flower, my left eyeball, I was thinking. I was on the point of saying something stinging like 'Oh, yes?' when she proceeded.

'I know I can mould you, Bertie. You want to improve yourself, and that is half the battle. What have you been reading lately?'

'Well, what with one thing and another, my reading has been a bit cut into these last days, but I am in the process of plugging away at a thing called *The Mystery of the Pink Crayfish*.'

Her slender frame was more or less hidden beneath the bedclothes, but I got the impression that a shudder had run through it.

'Oh, Bertie!' she said, this time with something more nearly approaching the normal intonation.

'Well, it's dashed good,' I insisted stoutly. 'This baronet, this Sir Eustace Willoughby, is discovered in his library with his head bashed in –'

A look of pain came into her face.

'Please!' she sighed. 'Oh, dear,' she said, 'I'm afraid it's going to be uphill work fostering the latent potentialities of your budding mind.'

'I wouldn't try, if I were you. Give it a miss, is my advice.'

'But I hate to think of leaving you in the darkness, doing nothing but smoke and drink at the Drones Club.'

I put her straight about this. She had her facts wrong.

'I also play Darts.'

'Darts!'

'As a matter of fact, I shall very soon be this year's club champion. The event is a snip for me. Ask anybody.'

'How can you fritter away your time like that, when you might be reading T.S. Eliot? I would like to see you –'

What it was she would have liked to see me doing she did not say, though I presumed it was something foul and educational, for at this juncture someone knocked on the door.

It was the last contingency I had been anticipating, and it caused my heart to leap like a salmon in the spawning season and become entangled with my front teeth. I looked at the door with what I have heard Jeeves call a wild surmise, the persp. breaking out on my brow.

Florence, I noticed, seemed a bit startled, too. One gathered that she hadn't expected, when setting out for Brinkley Court, that her bedroom was going to be such a social centre. There's a song I used to sing a good deal at one time, the refrain or burthen of which began with the words 'Let's all go round to Maud's'. Much the same sentiment appeared to be animating the guests beneath Aunt Dahlia's roof, and it was, of course, upsetting for the poor child. At one in the morning girls like a bit of privacy, and she couldn't have had much less privacy if she had been running a snack bar on a racecourse.

'Who's that?' she cried.

'Me,' responded a deep, resonant voice, and Florence clapped a hand to her throat, a thing I didn't know anybody ever did off the stage.

For the d.r.v. was that of G. D'Arcy Cheesewright. To cut a long story short, the man was in again.

It was with a distinctly fevered hand that Florence reached out for a dressing-gown, and in her deportment, as she hopped from between the sheets, I noted a marked suggestion of a pea on a hot shovel. She is one of those cool, calm, well-poised modern girls from whom as a rule you can seldom get more than a raised eyebrow, but I could see that this thing of having Stilton a pleasant visitor at a moment when her room was all cluttered up with Woosters had rattled her more than slightly.

'What do you want?'

'I have brought your letters.'

'Leave them on the mat.'

'I will not leave them on the mat. I wish to confront you in person.'

'At this time of night! You aren't coming in here!'

'That,' said Stilton crisply, 'is where you make your ruddy error. I *am* coming in there.'

I remember Jeeves saying something once about the poet's eye in a fine frenzy rolling and glancing from heaven to earth, from earth to heaven. It was in much the same manner that Florence's eye now rolled and glanced. I could see what was disturbing her, of course. It was that old problem which always bothers chaps in mystery thrillers – viz. how to get rid of the body – in this case, that of Bertram. If Stilton proposed to enter, it was essential that Bertram be placed in storage somewhere for the time being, but the question that arose was where.

There was a cupboard on the other side of the room, and she nipped across and flung open the door.

'Quick!' she hissed, and it's all rot to say you can't hiss a word that hasn't an 's' in it. She did it on her head.

'In here!'

The suggestion struck me as a good one. I popped in and she closed the door behind me.

Well, actually, the fingers being, I suppose, nerveless, she didn't, but left it ajar. I was able, consequently, to follow the ensuing conversation as clearly as if it had been coming over the wireless.

Stilton began it.

'Here are your letters,' he said stiffly.

'Thank you,' she said stiffly.

'Don't mention it,' he said stiffly.

'Put them on the dressing-table,' she said stiffly.

'Right ho!' he said stiffly.

I don't know when I've known a bigger night for stiff speakers.

After a brief interval, during which I presumed that he was depositing the correspondence as directed, Stilton resumed.

'You got my telegram?'

'Of course I got your telegram.'

'You notice I have shaved my moustache?'

'I do.'

'It was my first move on finding out about your underhanded skulduggery.'

'What do you mean, my underhanded skulduggery?'

'If you don't call it underhanded skulduggery, sneaking off to night clubs with the louse Wooster, it would be extremely entertaining to be informed how you would describe it.'

'You know perfectly well that I wanted atmosphere for my book.'

'Ho!'

'And don't say "Ho".'

'I will say "Ho"!' retorted Stilton with spirit. 'Your book, my foot! I don't believe there is any book. I don't believe you've ever written a book.'

'Indeed? How about *Spindrift*, now in its fifth edition and soon to be translated into the Scandinavian?'

'Probably the work of the louse Gorringe.'

I imagine that at this coarse insult Florence's eyes flashed fire. The voice in which she spoke certainly suggested it.

'Mr. Cheesewright, you have had a couple!'

'Nothing of the kind.'

'Then you must be insane, and I wish you would have the courtesy to take that pumpkin head of yours out of here.'

I rather think, though I can't be sure, that at these words Stilton ground his teeth. Certainly there was a peculiar sound, as if a coffee mill had sprung into action. The voice that filtered through to my cosy retreat quivered hoarsely.

'My head is not like a pumpkin!'

'It is, too, like a pumpkin.'

'It is not like a pumpkin at all. I have this on the authority of Bertie Wooster, who says it is more like the dome of St. Paul's.' He broke off, and there was a smacking sound. He had apparently smitten his brow. 'Wooster!' he cried, emitting an animal snarl. 'I didn't come here to talk about my head, I came to talk about Wooster, the slithery serpent who slinks behind chaps' backs, stealing fellows' girls from them. Wooster the home-wrecker! Wooster the snake in the grass from whom no woman is safe! Wooster the modern Don what's-his-name! You've been conducting a clandestine intrigue with him right along. You thought you were fooling me, didn't you? You thought I didn't see through your pitiful . . . your pitiful . . . Dammit, what's the word? . . . your pitiful . . . No, it's gone.'

'I wish you would follow its excellent example.'

'Subterfuges! I knew I'd get it. Do you think I didn't see through your pitiful subterfuges? All that bilge about wanting me to grow a moustache. Do you think I'm not on to it that the whole of that moustache sequence was just a ruse to enable you to break it off with me and switch over to the grass snake Wooster? "How can I get rid of this Cheesewright?" you said to yourself. "Ha, I have it!" you said to yourself. "I'll tell him he's got to grow a moustache. He'll say like hell he'll grow any bally moustache. And then I'll say Ho! You won't, won't you? All right, then all is over between us. That'll fix it." It must have been a nasty shock to you when I yielded to your request. Upset your plans quite a bit, I imagine? You hadn't bargained for that, had you?'

Florence spoke in a voice that would have frozen an Eskimo.

'The door is just behind you, Mr. Cheesewright. It opens if you turn the handle.'

He came right back at her.

'Never mind the door. I'm talking about you and the leper Wooster. I suppose you will now hitch on to him, or what's left of him after I've finished stepping on his face. Am I right?'

'You are.'

'It is your intention to marry this human gumboil?'

'It is.'

'Ho!'

Well, I don't know how you would have behaved in my place, hearing these words and realizing for the first time that the evil had spread as far as this. You would probably have started violently, as I did. No doubt I ought to have spotted the impending doom, but for some reason or other, possibly because I had been devoting so much thought to Stilton, I hadn't. This abrupt announcement of my betrothal to a girl of whom I took the gravest view shook me to my depths, with the result, as I say, that I started violently.

And, of course, the one place where it is unwise to start violently, if you wish to remain unobserved and incognito, is a cupboard in a female's bedroom. What exactly it was that now rained down on me, dislodged by my sudden movement, I cannot say, but I think it was hat-boxes. Whatever it was, it sounded in the stilly night like coal being lowered down a chute into a cellar, and I heard a sharp exclamation. A moment later a hand wrenched open the door and a suffused face glared in on me as I brushed the hat-boxes, if they were hat-boxes, from my hair.

'Ho!' said Stilton, speaking with difficulty like a cat with a fishbone in its throat. 'Come on out of there, serpent,' he added, attaching himself to my left ear and pulling vigorously.

I emerged like a cork out of a bottle.

14

It is always a bit difficult to know just what to say on occasions like this. I said, 'Oh, there you are, Stilton. Nice evening', but it seemed to be the wrong thing, for he merely quivered as if he had got a beetle down his back and increased the incandescence of his gaze. I saw that it was going to require quite a good deal of suavity and tact on my part to put us all at our ease.

'You are doubtless surprised –' I began, but he held up a hand as if he had been back in the Force directing the traffic. He then spoke in a quiet, if rumbling, voice.

'You will find me waiting in the corridor, Wooster,' he said, and strode out.

I understood the spirit which had prompted the words. It was the *preux chevalier* in him coming to the surface. You can stir up a Cheesewright till he froths at the mouth, but you cannot make him forget that he is an Old Etonian and a pukka Sahib. Old Etonians do not brawl in the presence of the other sex. Nor do pukka Sahibs. They wait till they are alone with the party of the second part in some secluded nook.

I thoroughly approved of this fineness of feeling, for it had left me sitting on top of the world. It would now, I saw, be possible for me to avoid anything in the nature of unpleasantness by executing one of those subtle rearward movements which great Generals keep up their sleeves for moments when things are beginning to get too hot. You think you have got one of these Generals cornered and are all ready to swoop on him, and it is with surprise and chagrin that, just as you are pulling up your socks and putting a final polish on your weapons, you observe that he isn't there. He has withdrawn on his strategic railway, taking his troops with him.

With that ladder waiting in readiness for me, I was in a similarly agreeable position. Corridors meant nothing to me. I didn't need to go into any corridors. All I had to do was slide through the window, place my foot on the top rung and carry on with a light heart to terra firma.

But there is one circumstance which can dish the greatest of Generals – viz. if, toddling along to the station to buy his ticket, he finds that since he last saw it the strategic railway has been blown up. That is the time when you will find him scratching his head and chewing the lower lip. And it was a disaster of this nature that now dished me. Approaching the window and glancing out, I saw that the ladder was no longer there. At some point in the course of the recent conversations it had vanished, leaving not a wrack behind.

What had become of it was a mystery I found myself unable to solve, but that was a thing that could be gone into later. At the moment it was plain that the cream of the Wooster brain must be given to a more urgent matter – to wit, the question of how I was to get out of the room without passing through the door and finding myself alone in a confined space with Stilton, the last person in his present frame of mind with whom a man of slender physique would wish to be alone in confined spaces. I put this to Florence, and she agreed, like Sherlock Holmes, that the problem was one which undoubtedly presented certain points of interest.

'You can't stay here all night,' she said.

I admitted the justice of this, but added that I didn't at the moment see what the dickens else I could do.

'You wouldn't care to knot your sheets and lower me to the ground with them?'

'No, I wouldn't. Why don't you jump?'

'And smash myself to hash?'

'You might not.'

'On the other hand, I might.'

'Well, you can't make an omelette without breaking eggs.'

I gave her a look. It seemed to me the silliest thing I had ever heard a girl say, and I have heard girls say some pretty silly things in my time. I was on the point of saying 'You and your bally omelettes!' when something seemed to go off with a pop in my brain and it was as though I had swallowed a brimming dose of some invigorating tonic, the sort of pick-me-up that makes a bedridden invalid rise from his couch and dance the Carioca. Bertram was himself again. With a steady hand I opened the door. And when Stilton advanced on me like a mass murderer about to do his stuff, I quelled him with the power of the human eye.

'Just a moment, Stilton,' I said suavely. 'Before you give rein, if that's the expression I want, to your angry passions, don't forget you've drawn me in the Drones Club Darts sweep.'

It was enough. Halting abruptly, as if he had walked into a lamp-post, he stood goggling like a cat in an adage. Cats in adages, Jeeves tells me, let 'I dare not' wait upon 'I would', and I could see with the naked eye that this was what Stilton was doing.

Flicking a speck of dust from my sleeve and smiling a quiet smile, I proceeded to rub it in.

'You appreciate the position of affairs?' I said. 'By drawing my name, you have set yourself apart from ordinary men. To make it clear to the meanest intelligence . . . I allude to yours, my dear Cheesewright . . . where the ordinary man, seeing me strolling along Piccadilly, merely says "Ah, there goes Bertie Wooster", you, having drawn me in the sweep, say "There goes my fifty-six pounds ten shillings", and you probably run after me to tell me to be very careful when crossing the street because the traffic nowadays is so dangerous.'

He raised a hand and fingered his chin. I could see that my words were not being wasted. Shooting my cuffs, I resumed.

'In what sort of condition shall I be to win that Darts tourney and put nearly sixty quid in your pocket, if you pull the strong-arm stuff you are contemplating? Try that one on your bazooka, my dear Cheesewright.'

It was a tense struggle, of course, but it didn't last long. Reason prevailed. With a low grunt which spoke eloquently of the overwrought soul, he stepped back, and with a cheery 'Well, good night, old man' and a benevolent wave of the hand I left him and made my way to my room.

As I entered it, Aunt Dahlia in a maroon dressing-gown rose from the chair in which she had been sitting and fixed me with a blazing eye, struggling for utterance.

'Well!' she said, choking on the word like a Pekingese on a chump chop too large for its frail strength. After which, speech failing her, she merely stood and gargled.

I must say that this struck me as in the circs a bit thick. I mean, if anyone was entitled to have blazing eyes and trouble with the vocal cords, it was, as I saw it, me. I mean, consider the facts. Owing to this woman's cloth-headed blundering when issuing divisional orders, I was slated to walk down the aisle with Florence Craye and had been subjected to an ordeal which might well have done permanent damage to the delicate nerve centres. I was strongly of the opinion that so far from being glared and gargled at I was in a position to demand a categorical explanation and to see that I got it.

As I cleared my throat in order to put this to her, she mastered her emotion sufficiently to be able to speak.

'Well!' she said, looking like a female minor prophet about to curse the sins of the people. 'May I trespass on your valuable time long enough to ask you what in the name of everything bloodsome you think you're playing at, young piefaced Bertie? It is now some twenty minutes past one o'clock in the morning, and not a spot of action on your part. Do you expect me to sit up all night waiting for you to get around to a simple, easy task which a crippled child of six could have had all done and washed up in a quarter of an hour? I suppose this is just the shank of the evening to you dissipated Londoners, but we rustics like to get our sleep. What's the idea? Why the delay? What on earth have you been doing all this while, you revolting young piece of cheese?'

I laughed a hollow, mirthless laugh. Getting quite the wrong angle on it, she begged me to postpone my farmyard imitations to a more suitable moment. I told myself that I must be calm . . . calm.

'Before replying to your questions, aged relative,' I said, holding myself in with a strong effort, 'let me put one to you. Would you mind informing me in a few simple words why you told me that your window was the end one on the left?'

'It is the end one on the left.'

'Pardon me.'

'Looking from the house.'

'Oh, looking *from* the house?' A great light dawned on me. 'I thought you meant looking *at* the house.'

'Looking at the house it would of course be . . . ' She broke off with a startled yowl, staring at me with quite a good deal of that wild surmise stuff. 'Don't tell me you got into the wrong room?'

'It could scarcely have been wronger.'

'Whose was it?'

'Florence Craye's.'

She whistled. It was plain that the drama of the situation had not escaped her.

'Was she in bed?'

'With a pink boudoir cap on.'

'And she woke up and found you there?'

'Almost immediately. I knocked over a table or something.' She whistled again.

'You'll have to marry the girl.'

'Quite.'

'Though I doubt if she would have you.'

'I have positive inside information to the contrary.'

'You fixed it up?'

'She fixed it up. We are affianced.'

'In spite of that moustache?'

'She likes the moustache.'

'She does? Morbid. But what about Cheesewright? I thought he and she were affianced, as you call it?'

'No longer. It's off.'

'They've bust up?'

'Completely.'

'And now she's taken you on?'

'That's right.'

A look of concern came into her face. Despite the occasional brusqueness of her manner, and the fruity names she sees fit to call me from time to time, she loves me dearly and my well-being is very near her heart.

'She's pretty highbrow for you, isn't she? If I know her, she'll have you reading W.H. Auden before you can say "What ho".'

'She rather hinted at some such contingency, though, if I recollect, T.S. Eliot was the name that was mentioned.'

'She proposes to mould you?'

'I gathered so.'

'You won't like that.'

'No.'

She nodded understandingly.

'Men don't. I attribute my own happy marriage to the fact that I have never so much as laid a finger on old Tom. Agatha is trying to mould Worplesdon, and I believe his agonies are frightful. She made him knock off smoking the other day, and he behaved like a cinnamon bear with its foot in a trap. Has Florence told you to knock off smoking?'

'Not yet.'

'She will. And after that it'll be cocktails.' She gazed at me with a good deal of what-do-you-call-it. You could see that remorse had her in its grip. 'I'm afraid I've got you into a bit of a jam, my poppet.'

'Don't give it a thought, old blood relation,' I said. 'These things happen. It is your predicament, not mine, that is exercising me. We've got to get you out of your sea of troubles, as Jeeves calls it. Everything else is relatively unimportant. My thoughts of self are merely in about the proportion of the vermouth to the gin in a strongish dry martini.'

She was plainly touched. Unless I am very much mistaken, her eyes were wet with unshed tears.

'That's very altruistic of you, Bertie dear.'

'Not at all, not at all.'

'One wouldn't think it, to look at you, but you have a noble soul.'

'*Who* wouldn't think it, to look at me?'

'And if that's the way you feel, all I can say is that it does you credit and let's get going. You'd better go and shift that ladder to the right window.'

'You mean the left window.'

'Well, let's call it the correct window.'

I braced myself to break the bad news.

'Ah,' I said, 'but what you're overlooking – possibly because I forgot to tell you – is that a snag has arisen which threatens to do our aims and objects a bit of no good. The ladder isn't there.'

'Where?'

'Under the right window, or perhaps I should say the wrong window. When I looked out, it was gone.'

'Nonsense. Ladders don't melt into thin air.'

'They do, I assure you, at Brinkley Court, Brinkley-cum-Snodsfield-in-the-Marsh. I don't know what conditions prevail elsewhere, but at Brinkley Court they vanish if you take your eye off them for so much as an instant.'

'You mean the ladder's disappeared?'

'That is precisely the point I was endeavouring to establish. It has folded its tents like the Arabs and silently stolen away.'

She turned bright mauve, and I think was about to rap out something in the nature of a Quorn-and-Pytchley expletive, for she is a woman who seldom minces her words when stirred, but at this juncture the door opened and Uncle Tom came in. I was too distrait to be able to discern whether or not he was pottering, but a glance was enough to show me that he was definitely all of a doodah.

'Dahlia!' he exclaimed. 'I thought I heard your voice. What are you doing up at this hour?'

'Bertie had a headache,' replied the old relative, a quick thinker. 'I have been giving him an aspirin. The head a little better now, Bertie?'

'One notes a slight improvement,' I assured her, being a quick thinker myself. 'You're out and about a bit late, aren't you, Uncle Tom?'

'Yes,' said Aunt Dahlia. 'What are *you* doing up at this hour, my old for-better-or-for-worser? You ought to have been asleep ages ago.'

Uncle Tom shook his head. His air was grave.

'Asleep, old girl? I shan't get any sleep tonight. Far too worried. The place is alive with burglars.'

'Burglars? What gives you that idea? I haven't seen any burglars. Have you, Bertie?'

'Not one. I remember thinking how odd it was.'

'You probably saw an owl or something, Tom.'

'I saw a ladder. When I was taking my stroll in the garden before going to bed. Propped up against one of the windows. I took it away in the nick of time. A minute later, and burglars would have been streaming up it in their thousands.'

Aunt Dahlia and I exchanged a glance. I think we were both feeling happier now that the mystery of the vanishing l. had been solved. It's an odd thing, but however much of an *aficionado* one may be of mysteries in book form, when they pop up in real life they seldom fail to give one the pip.

She endeavoured to soothe his agitation.

'Probably just a ladder one of the gardeners was using and forgot to put back where it belonged. Though, of course,' she went on thoughtfully, feeling no doubt that a spot of paving the way would do no harm, 'I suppose there is always a chance of a cracksman having a try for that valuable pearl necklace of mine. I had forgotten that.'

'I hadn't,' said Uncle Tom. 'It was the first thing I thought of. I went straight to your room and got it and locked it up in the safe in the hall. A burglar will have to be pretty smart to get it out of there,' he added with modest pride, and pushed off, leaving behind him what I have sometimes heard called a pregnant silence.

Aunt looked at nephew, nephew looked at aunt.

'Hell's whiskers!' said the former, starting the conversation going again. 'Now what do we do?'

I agreed that the situation was sticky. Indeed, off-hand it was difficult to see how it could have been more glutinous.

'What are the chances of finding out the combination?'

'Not a hope.'

'I wonder if Jeeves can crack a safe.'

She brightened.

'I'll bet he can. There's nothing Jeeves can't do. Go and fetch him.'

I Lord-love-a-duck-ed impatiently.

'How the dickens can I fetch him? I don't know which his room is. Do you?'

'No.'

'Well, I can't go from door to door, rousing the whole domestic staff. Who do you think I am? Paul Revere?'

I paused for a reply, and as I did so who should come in but Jeeves in person. Late though it was, the hour had produced the man.

'Excuse me, sir,' he said. 'I am happy to find that I have not interrupted your slumbers. I ventured to come to inquire whether matters had developed satisfactorily. Were you successful in your enterprise, sir?'

I shook the coconut.

'No, Jeeves. I moved in a mysterious way my wonders to perform, but was impeded by a number of Acts of God,' I said, and in a few crisp words put him abreast. 'So the necklace is now in the safe,' I concluded, 'and the problem as I see it, and as Aunt Dahlia sees it, is how the dickens to get it out. You grasp the position?'

'Yes, sir. It is disturbing.'

Aunt Dahlia uttered a passionate cry.

'Don't *do* it!' she boomed with extraordinary vehemence. 'If I hear that word "disturbing" once more . . . Can you bust a safe, Jeeves?'

'No, madam.'

'Don't say "No, madam" in that casual way. How do you know you can't?'

'It requires a specialized education and upbringing, madam.'

'Then I'm for it,' said Aunt Dahlia, making for the door. Her face was grim and set. She might have been a marquise about to hop into the tumbril at the time when there was all that unpleasantness over in France. 'You weren't through the San Francisco earthquake, were you, Jeeves?'

'No, madam. I have never visited the western coastal towns of the United States.'

'I was only thinking that if you had been, what's going to happen tomorrow when this Lord Sidcup arrives and tells Tom the awful truth would have reminded you of old times. Well, good night, all. I'll be running along and getting my beauty sleep.'

She buzzed off, a gallant figure. The Quorn trains its daughters well. No weakness there. In the fell clutch of circumstance, as I remember Jeeves putting it once, they do not wince or cry aloud. I mentioned this to him as the door closed, and he agreed that it was substantially so.

'Under the tiddly-poms of whatever-it-is . . . How does the rest of it go?'

'Under the bludgeonings of chance their heads are . . . pardon me . . . bloody but unbowed, sir.'

'That's right. Your own?'

'No, sir. The late William Ernest Henley, 1849–1903.'

'Ah?'

'The title of the poem is "Invictus". But did I understand Mrs. Travers to say that Lord Sidcup was expected, sir?'

'He arrives tomorrow.'

'Would he be the gentleman of whom you were speaking, who is to examine Mrs. Travers's necklace?'

'That's the chap.'

'Then I fancy that all is well, sir.'

I started. It seemed to me that I must have misunderstood him. Either that, or he was talking through his hat.

'All is *well*, did you say, Jeeves?'

'Yes, sir. You are not aware who Lord Sidcup is, sir?'

'I never heard of him in my life.'

'You will possibly remember him, sir, as Mr. Roderick Spode.'

I stared at him. You could have knocked me down with a toothpick.

'Roderick Spode?'

'Yes, sir.'

'You mean the Roderick Spode of Totleigh Towers?'

'Precisely, sir. He recently succeeded to the title on the demise of the late Lord Sidcup, his uncle.'

'Great Scot, Jeeves!'

'Yes, sir. I think you will agree with me, sir, that in these circumstances the problem confronting Mrs. Travers is susceptible of a ready solution. A word to his lordship, reminding him of the fact that he sells ladies' underclothing under the trade name of Eulalie Sœurs, should go far towards inducing him to preserve a tactful silence with regard to the spurious nature of the necklace. At the time of our visit to Totleigh Towers you will recollect that Mr. Spode, as he then was, showed unmistakably his reluctance to let the matter become generally known.'

'Egad, Jeeves!'

'Yes, sir. I thought I would mention it, sir. Good night, sir.'

He oozed off.

15

We Woosters are never very early risers, and the sun was highish in the heavens next morning when I woke to greet a new day. And I had just finished tucking away a refreshing scrambled eggs and coffee, when the door opened as if a hurricane had hit it and Aunt Dahlia came pirouetting in.

I use the word 'pirouetting' advisedly, for there was an elasticity in her bearing which impressed itself immediately upon the eye. Of the drooping mourner of last night there remained no trace. The woman was plainly right above herself.

'Bertie,' she said, after a brief opening speech in the course of which she described me as a lazy young hound who ought to be ashamed to be wallowing in bed on what, if you asked her, was the maddest merriest day of all the glad new year, 'I've just been talking to Jeeves, and if ever a life-saving friend in need drew breath, it is he. Hats off to Jeeves is the way I look at it.'

Pausing for a moment to voice the view that my moustache was an offence against God and man but that she saw in it nothing that a good weed-killer couldn't cure, she resumed.

'He tells me this Lord Sidcup who's coming here today is none other than our old pal Roderick Spode.'

I nodded. I had divined from her exuberance that he must have been spilling the big news.

'Correct,' I said. 'Apparently, all unknown to us, Spode was right from the start the secret nephew of the holder of the title, and since that sojourn of ours at Totleigh Towers the latter has gone to reside with the morning stars, giving him a step up. Jeeves has also, I take it, told you about Eulalie Sœurs?'

'The whole thing. Why didn't you ever let me in on that? You know how I enjoy a good laugh.'

I spread the hands in a dignified gesture, upsetting the coffee-pot, which was fortunately empty.

'My lips were sealed.'

'You and your lips!'

'All right, me and my lips. But I repeat. The information was imparted to me in confidence.'

'You could have told Auntie.'

I shook my head. Women do not understand these things. *Noblesse oblige* means nothing to the gentler sex.

'One does not impart confidential confidences even to Auntie, not if one is a confidant of the right sort.'

'Well, anyway, I know the facts, and I hold Spode, alias Sidcup, in the hollow of my hand. Bless my soul,' she went on, a far-off ecstatic look on her face, 'how well I remember that day at Totleigh Towers. There he was, advancing on you with glittering eyes and foam-flecked lips, and you drew yourself up as cool as some cucumbers, as Anatole would say, and said "One minute, Spode, just one minute. It may interest you to learn that I know all about Eulalie." Gosh, how I admired you!'

'I don't wonder.'

'You were like one of those lion tamers in circuses who defy murderous man-eating monarchs of the jungle.'

'There was a resemblance, no doubt.'

'And how he wilted! I've never seen anything like it. Before my eyes he wilted like a wet sock. And he's going to do it again when he gets here this evening.'

'You propose to draw him aside and tell him you know his guilty secret?'

'Exactly. Strongly recommending him, when Tom shows him the necklace, to say it's a lovely bit of work and worth every penny he paid for it. It can't fail. Fancy him owning Eulalie Sœurs! He must make a packet out of it. I was in there last month, buying some cami-knickers, and the place was doing a roaring trade. Money pouring in like a tidal wave. By the way, laddie, talking of cami-knickers, Florence was showing me hers just now. Not the ones she had on, I don't mean; her reserve supply. She wanted my opinion of them. And I'm sorry to tell you, my poor lamb,' she said, eyeing me with auntly pity, 'that things look pretty serious in that quarter.'

'They do?'

'Extremely serious. She's all set to start those wedding bells ringing out. Somewhere around next November, she seems to think, at St. George's, Hanover Square. Already she is speaking freely of brides-maids and caterers.' She paused, and looked at me in a surprised sort of way. 'You don't seem very upset,' she said. 'Are you one of these men of chilled steel one reads about?'

I spread the hands again, this time without disaster to the breakfast tray.

'Well, I'll tell you, old ancestor. When a fellow has been engaged as often as I have and each time saved from the scaffold at the eleventh hour, he comes to have faith in his star. He feels that all is not lost till they have actually got him at the altar rails with the organ playing "Oh, perfect love" and the clergyman saying "Wilt thou?" At the moment, admittedly, I am in the soup, but it may well be that in God's good time it will be granted to me to emerge unscathed from the tureen.'

'You don't despair?'

'Not at all. I have high hopes that, after they have thought things over, these two proud spirits who have parted brass rags will come together and be reconciled, thus letting me out. The rift was due –'

'I know. She told me.'

'– to the fact that Stilton learned that I had taken Florence to The Mottled Oyster one night about a week ago, and he refused to believe that I had done so merely in order to enable her to accumulate atmosphere for her new book. When he has cooled off and reason has returned to its throne, he may realize how mistaken he was and beg her to forgive him for his low suspicions. I think so, I hope so.'

She agreed that there was something in this and commended me for my spirit, which in her opinion was the right one. My intrepidity reminded her, she said, of the Spartans at Thermopylae, wherever that may be.

'But he's a long way from being in that frame of mind at the moment, according to Florence. She says he is convinced that you two were on an unbridled toot together. And, of course, his finding you in the cupboard in her bedroom at one in the morning was unfortunate.'

'Most. One would gladly have avoided the occurrence.'

'Must have given the man quite a start. What beats me is why he didn't hammer the stuffing out of you. I should have thought that would have been his first move.'

I smiled quietly.

'He has drawn me in the Drones Club Darts sweep.'

'What's that got to do with it?'

'My dear soul, does a fellow hammer the stuffing out of a chap on whose virtuosity at the Darts board he stands to win fifty-six pounds, ten shillings?'

'Oh, I see.'

'So did Stilton. I made the position thoroughly clear to him, and he has ceased to be a menace. However much his thoughts may drift in the direction of stuffing-hammering, he will have to continue to maintain the non-belligerent status of a mild cat in an adage. I have bottled him up good and proper. There was nothing further you wished to discuss?'

'Not that I know of.'

'Then if you will withdraw, I will be getting up and dressing.' I rose from the hay as the door closed, and having bathed, shaved and clad the outer man, took my cigarette out for a stroll in the grounds and messuages.

The sun was now a good bit higher in the heavens than when last observed, and its genial warmth increased the optimism of my mood. Thinking of Stilton and the dead stymie I had laid him, I found myself feeling that it was not such a bad little old world, after all. I don't know anything that braces you more thoroughly than outgeneralling one of the baser sort who has been chucking his weight about and planning to start something. It was with much the same quiet satisfaction which I had experienced when bending Roderick Spode to my will at Totleigh Towers that I contemplated Stilton in his bottled-up state. As Aunt Dahlia had said, quite the lion tamer.

True, as against this, there was Florence – already, it appeared, speaking freely of bridesmaids, caterers and St. George's, Hanover Square – and a lesser man might have allowed her dark shadow to cloud his feeling of *bien-être*. But it is always the policy of the Woosters to count their blessings one by one, and I concentrated my attention exclusively on the bright side of the picture, telling myself that even if an eleventh-hour reprieve failed to materialize and I was compelled to drain the bitter cup, I wouldn't have to do it with two black eyes and a fractured spine, wedding presents from G. D'Arcy Cheesewright. Come what might, I was that much ahead of the game.

I was, in short, in buoyant mood and practically saying 'Tra la', when I observed Jeeves shimmering up in the manner of one desiring audience.

'Ah, Jeeves,' I said. 'Nice morning.'

'Extremely agreeable, sir.'

'Did you want to see me about something?'

'If you could spare me a moment, sir. I was anxious to ascertain if it would be possible for you to dispense with my services today in order that I may go to London. The Junior Ganymede luncheon, sir.'

'I thought that was next week.'

'The date has been put forward to accommodate Sir Everard Everett's butler, who leaves with his employer tomorrow for the

United States of America. Sir Everard is assuming his duties as Britannic ambassador at Washington.'

'Is that so? Good luck to the old blister.'

'Yes, sir.'

'One likes to see these public servants bustling about and earning their salaries.'

'Yes, sir.'

'If one is a taxpayer, I mean, contributing one's whack to those salaries.'

'Precisely, sir. I should be glad if you could see your way to allowing me to attend the function, sir. As I informed you, I am taking the chair.'

Well, of course, when he put it like that, I had no option but to right-ho.

'Certainly, Jeeves. Push along and revel till your ribs squeak. It may be your last chance,' I added significantly.

'Sir?'

'Well, you've often stressed how fussy the brass hats at the Ganymede are about members not revealing the secrets of the club book, and Aunt Dahlia tells me you've just been spilling the whole inner history of Spode and Eulalie Sœurs to her. Won't they drum you out if this becomes known?'

'The contingency is a remote one, sir, and I gladly took the risk, knowing that Mrs. Travers's happiness was at stake.'

'Pretty white, Jeeves.'

'Thank you, sir. I endeavour to give satisfaction. And now I think perhaps, if you will excuse me, sir, I should be starting for the station. The train for London leaves very shortly.'

'Why not drive up in the two-seater?'

'If you could spare it, sir?'

'Of course.'

'Thank you very much, sir. It will be a great convenience.'

He pushed off in the direction of the house, no doubt to go and get the bowler hat which is his inseparable companion when in the metropolis, and scarcely had he left me when I heard my name called in a bleating voice and turned to perceive Percy Gorringe approaching, his tortoiseshell-rimmed spectacles glistening in the sunshine.

My first emotion on beholding him was one of surprise, a feeling that of all the in-and-out performers I had ever met he was the most unpredictable. I mean, you couldn't tell from one minute to another what aspect he was going to present to the world, for he switched from Stormy to Set Fair and from Set Fair to Stormy like a barometer with something wrong with its works. At dinner on the previous night he had been all gaiety and effervescence, and here he was now, only a few hours later, once more giving that impersonation of a dead codfish which had caused Aunt Dahlia to take so strong a line with him. Fixing me with lack-lustre eyes, if lack-lustre is the word I want, and wasting no time on preliminary pip-pippings and pourparlers, he started straight off cleansing his bosom of the perilous stuff that weighs upon the heart.

'Wooster,' he said, 'Florence has just told me a story that shocked me!'

Well, difficult to know what to say to that, of course. One's impulse was to ask what story, adding that if it was the one about the bishop and the lady snake-charmer, one had heard it. And one could, no doubt, have shoved in a thoughtful word or two deploring the growing laxity of speech of the modern girl. I merely said 'Oh, ah?' and waited for further details.

His eye, as Florence's had done on the previous night, rolled in a fine frenzy and glanced from heaven to earth, from earth to heaven. You could see the thing had upset him.

'Shortly after breakfast,' he continued, retrieving the eye and fixing it on me once more, 'finding her alone in the herbaceous border, cutting flowers, I hastened up and asked if I might be allowed to hold the basket.'

'Very civil.'

'She thanked me and said she would be glad if I would do so, and for awhile we talked of neutral subjects. One topic led to another, and eventually I asked her to be my wife.'

''At-a-boy!'

'I beg your pardon?'

'I only said " 'At-a-boy!" '

'Why did you say " 'At-a-boy!"?'

'Sort of cheering you on, as it were.'

'I see. Cheering me on. The expression is a corruption, one assumes, of the phrase "That is the boy" and signifies friendly encouragement?'

'That's right.'

'Then I am surprised in the circumstances – and may I say more than a little disgusted – to hear it from your lips, Wooster. It would have been in better taste to have refrained from cheap taunts and jeers.'

'Eh?'

'If you have triumphed, that is no reason why you should mock those who have been less fortunate.'

'I'm sorry. If you could give me a few footnotes...'

He tchah-ed impatiently.

'I told you that I asked Florence to be my wife, and I also told you that she said something which shocked me profoundly. It was that she was engaged to you.'

I got it now. I saw what he was driving at.

'Oh, ah, yes, of course. Quite. Yes, we would appear to be betrothed.'

'When did this happen, Wooster?'

'Fairly recently.'

He snorted.

'Very recently, I should imagine, seeing that it was only yesterday that she was engaged to Cheesewright. It's all most confusing,' said Percy peevishly. 'It makes one's head swim. One doesn't know where one is.'

I could see his point.

'Bit of a mix-up,' I agreed.

'It's bewildering. I cannot think what she can possibly see in you.'

'No. Very odd, the whole thing.'

He brooded darkly for a while.

'Her recent infatuation for Cheesewright,' he said, teeing off again, 'one could dimly understand. Whatever his mental defects, he is a vigorous young animal, and it is not uncommon to find girls of intellect attracted by vigorous young animals. Bernard Shaw made this the basis of this early novel, *Cashel Byron's Profession*. But *you*! It's inexplicable. A mere weedy butterfly.'

'Would you call me a weedy butterfly?'

'If you can think of a better description, I shall be happy to hear it. I am unable to discern in you the slightest vestige of charm, the smallest trace of any quality that could reasonably be expected to appeal to a girl like Florence. It amazes one that she should wish to have you permanently about the house.'

I don't know if you would call me a touchy man. As a rule, I should say not. But it is not pleasant to find yourself chalked up on the slate as a weedy butterfly, and I confess that I spoke a little shortly.

'Well, there it is,' I said, and went into the silence. And as he, too, seemed disinclined for chit-chat, we stood for some moments like a couple of Trappist monks who have run into each other by chance at the dog races. And I think I would pretty soon have nodded curtly and removed myself, had he not arrested me with an exclamation similar in tone and volume to the one which Stilton had uttered on finding me festooned with hat-boxes in Florence's cupboard. He was looking at me through the windshields with what appeared to be concern, if not horror. It puzzled me. It couldn't have taken him all this time, I felt, to notice the moustache.

'Wooster! Good gracious! You are not wearing a hat!'

'I don't much in the country.'

'But in this hot sun! You might get sunstroke. You ought not to take such risks.'

I must say I was touched by this solicitude. Much of the pique I had been feeling left me. It isn't many fellows, I mean to say, who get all worked up about the well-being of birds who are virtually strangers. It just showed, I thought, that a man may talk a lot of rot about weedy butterflies and still have a tender heart beneath what I should imagine was pretty generally recognized as a fairly repulsive exterior.

'Don't worry,' I said, soothing his alarm.

'But I do worry,' he responded sharply. 'I feel very strongly that you ought either to get a hat or else stay in the shade. I don't want to appear fussy, but your health is naturally a matter of the greatest concern to me. You see, I have drawn you in the Drones Club Darts sweep.'

This got right past me. I could make nothing of it. It sounded to me like straight delirium.

'You've what? How do you mean you've drawn me in the Drones Club Darts sweep?'

'I put it badly. I was agitated. What I should have said was that I have bought you from Cheesewright. He has sold me the ticket bearing your name. So can you wonder that it makes me nervous when I see you going about in this hot sun without a hat?'

In a career liberally spotted with nasty shocks I have had occasion to do quite a bit of reeling and tottering from time to time, but I have seldom reeled and tottered more heartily than I did on hearing these frightful words. I had addressed Aunt Dahlia on the previous night, if you remember, as a fluttering aspen. The description would have fitted me at this moment like the paper on the wall.

This surge of emotion will, I think, be readily understood. My whole foreign policy, as I have made clear, had been built on the fact that I had bottled Stilton up good and proper, and it now appeared, dash it, that I hadn't bottled him up at all. He was once more in the position of an Assyrian fully licensed to come down like a wolf on the fold with his cohorts all gleaming with purple and gold, and the realization that his thirst for vengeance was so pronounced that, rather than forgo his war aims, he was prepared to sacrifice fifty-six quid and a bender was one that froze the marrow.

'There must be a lot of hidden good in Cheesewright,' proceeded Percy. 'I confess frankly that I misjudged him, and, if I had not already returned the galley proofs, I would withdraw that "Caliban at Sunset" thing of mine from *Parnassus*. He tells me that you are a certain winner of this Darts contest, and yet he voluntarily offered to sell me for quite a trivial sum the ticket bearing your name, because, he said, he had taken a great fancy to me and would like to do me a good turn. A big, generous, warm-hearted gesture, and one that restores one's faith in human nature. By the way, Cheesewright is looking for you. He wants to see you about something.'

He repeated his advice with ref. to the hat and moved off, and for quite a while I stood where I was, rigid to the last limb, my numbed bean trying to grapple with this hideous problem which had arisen. It was plain that some diabolically clever counter-move would have to be made and made slippily, but what diabolically clever counter-move? There was what is called the rub.

You see, it wasn't as if I could just leg it from the danger zone, which was what I would have liked to do. It was imperative that I be among those present at Brinkley Court when Spode arrived this evening. Airily though Aunt Dahlia had spoken of making the man play ball, it was quite conceivable that the programme might blow a fuse, in which event the presence on the spot of a quick-thinking nephew would be of the essence. The Woosters do not desert aunts in the time of need.

Eliminating, therefore, the wings of the dove, for which I would gladly have been in the market, what other course presented itself? I freely own that for five minutes or so the thing had me snookered.

But it has often been said of Bertram Wooster that in moments of intense peril he has an uncanny knack of getting inspiration, and this happened now. Suddenly a thought came like a full-blown rose, flushing the brow, and I picked up the feet and lit out for the stables, where my two-seater was housed. It might be that Jeeves had not yet started on the long trail that led to the Junior Ganymede Club, and, if he hadn't, I saw the way out.

16

If you are one of the better element who are never happier than when curled up with the works of B. Wooster, you possibly came across a previous slab of these reminiscences of mine in which I dealt with a visit Jeeves and I paid to Deverill Hall, the rural seat of Esmond Haddock, J.P., and will recall that while under the Haddock roof Jeeves found my Aunt Agatha's son Thos in possession of what is known as a cosh and very prudently impounded it, feeling – as who wouldn't? – that it was the last thing that ought to be at the disposal of that homicidal young thug. The thought which had flushed my brow in the manner described was: Had Jeeves still got it? Everything turned on that.

I found him, richly apparelled and wearing the bowler hat, at the wheel of the car, on the point of putting foot to self-starter. Another moment, and I should have been too late. Racing up, I inaugurated the quiz without delay.

'Jeeves,' I said, 'throw your mind back to that time we stayed at Deverill Hall. Are you throwing?'

'Yes, sir.'

'Then continue to follow me closely. My Aunt Agatha's son, young Thos, was there.'

'Precisely, sir.'

'With the idea of employing it on a schoolmate of his called Stinker, who had incurred his displeasure for some reason, he had purchased before leaving London a cosh.'

'Or blackjack, to use the American term.'

'Never mind American terms, Jeeves. You took the weapon from him.'

'I deemed it wisest, sir.'

'It was wisest. No argument about that. Let a plugugly like young Thos loose in the community with a cosh, and you are inviting disasters and . . . what's the word? Something about cats.'

'Cataclysms, sir?'

'That's it. Cataclysms. Unquestionably you did the right thing. But all that is beside the point. What I am leading up to is this. That cosh, where is it?'

'Among my effects at the apartment, sir.'

'I'll drive with you to London and pick it up.'

'I could bring it with me on my return, sir.'

I did a brief dance step. On his return, forsooth! When would that be? Late at night, probably, because the gang at a hot spot like the Junior Ganymede don't break up a party at the end of lunch. I know what happens when these wild butlers let themselves go. They sit around till all hours, drinking deep and singing close harmony and generally whooping it up like a bunch of the boys in the Malemute saloon. It would mean that for the whole of the long summer day I should be defenceless, an easy prey for a Stilton who, as I had just been informed, was prowling about, seeking whom he might devour.

'That's no good, Jeeves. I require it immediately. Not tonight, not a week from Wednesday, but at the earliest possible moment. I am being hotly pursued by Cheesewright, Jeeves.'

'Indeed, sir?'

'And if I am to stave off the Cheesewright challenge, I shall have need of a weapon. His strength is as the strength of ten, and unarmed I should be corn before his sickle.'

'Extremely well put, sir, if I may say so, and your diagnosis of the situation is perfectly accurate. Mr. Cheesewright's robustness would enable him to crush you like a fly.'

'Exactly.'

'He would obliterate you with a single blow. He would break you in two with his bare hands. He would tear you limb from limb.'

I frowned slightly. I was glad to see that he appreciated the gravity of the situation, but these crude physical details seemed to me uncalled for.

'No need to make a production number of it, Jeeves,' I said with a touch of coldness. 'What I am driving at is that, armed with the cosh, I can face the blighter without a tremor. You agree?'

'Most decidedly, sir.'

'Then shift-ho,' I said, and hurled myself into the vacant seat.

This cosh of which I have been speaking was a small rubber bludgeon which at first sight you might have supposed unequal to the task of coping with an adversary of Stilton Cheesewright's tonnage. In repose, I mean to say, it didn't look like anything so frightfully hot. But I had seen it in action and was hep to what Florence would have called its latent potentialities. At Deverill Hall one night, for the soundest of reasons but too long to go into here, Jeeves had had occasion to bean a policeman with it – Constable Dobbs, a zealous officer – and the smitten slop had dropped as the gentle rain from heaven upon the place beneath.

There is a song, frequently sung by curates at village concerts, which runs:

> I fear no foe in shining armour,
> Though his lance be bright and keen.

Or is it 'swift and keen'? I can't remember. Not that it matters. The point is that those words summed up my attitude to a nicety. They put what I was feeling in a nutshell. With that cosh on my person, I should feel debonair and confident, no matter how many Cheesewrights came bounding at me with slavering jaws.

Everything went according to plan. After an agreeable drive we dropped anchor at the door of Berkeley Mansions and made our way to the flat. There, as foreshadowed, was the cosh. Jeeves handed it over, I thanked him in a few well-chosen words, he went off to his orgy, and I, after a bite of lunch at the Drones, settled myself in the two-seater and turned its nose Worcestershirewards.

The first person I met as I passed through the portals of Brinkley Court some hours later was Aunt Dahlia. She was in the hall, pacing up and down like a distraught tigress. Her exuberance of the morning had vanished completely, leaving her once more the haggard aunt of yesterday, and I was conscious of a quick pang of concern.

'Golly!' I said. 'What's up, old relative? Don't tell me that scheme of yours didn't work?'

She kicked morosely at a handy chair, sending it flying into the unknown.

'It hasn't had a chance to work.'

'Why not? Didn't Spode turn up?'

She gazed about her with sombre eyes, apparently in the hope of finding another chair to kick. There not being one in her immediate sphere of influence, she kicked the sofa.

'He turned up all right, and what happened? Before I could draw him aside and get so much as a word in, Tom swooped on him and took him off to the collection room to look at his foul silver. They've been in there for more than an hour, and how much longer they're going to be, Heaven knows.'

I pursed the lips. One ought, I felt, to have anticipated something of this sort.

'Can't you detach him?'

'No human power can detach a man to whom Tom is talking about his silver collection. He holds him with a glittering eye. All I can hope is that he will be so wrapped up in the silver end of the thing that he'll forget all about the necklace.'

The last thing a nephew of the right sort wants to do is to shove a wallowing aunt still more deeply beneath the surface of the slough of despond than she is already, but I had to shake my head at this.

'I doubt it.'

She gave the sofa another juicy one.

'So do I doubt it. That's why I'm going steadily cuckoo and may at any moment start howling like a banshee. Sooner or later he'll remember to take Spode to the safe, and what I am saying to myself is When? When? I feel like . . . who was the man who sat with a sword dangling over him, suspended by a hair, wondering how long it was going to be before it dropped and gave him a nasty flesh wound?'

She had me there. Nobody I had met. Certainly not one of the fellows at the Drones.

'I couldn't tell you, I'm afraid. Jeeves might know.'

At the mention of that honoured name her eyes lit up.

'Jeeves! Of course! He's the man I want. Where is he?'

'In London. He asked me if he could take the day off. It was the Junior Ganymede monthly luncheon today.'

She uttered a cry which might have been the howl of the banshee to which she had alluded, and gave me the sort of look which in the old tally-ho days she would have given a mentally deficient hound which she had observed suspending its professional activities in order to chase a rabbit.

'You let Jeeves go away at a time like this, when one has never needed him more?'

'I hadn't the heart to refuse. He was taking the chair. He'll be back soon.'

'By which time . . . '

She would have spoken further . . . a good deal further, if I read aright the message in her eyes . . . but before she could get going something whiskered came down the stairs and Percy was with us.

Seeing me, he halted abruptly.

'Wooster!' His agitation was very marked. 'Where have you been all day, Wooster?'

I told him I had driven to London, and he drew his breath in with a hiss.

'In this hot weather? It can't be good for you. You must not overtax yourself, Wooster. You must husband your strength.'

He had chosen the wrong moment for horning in. The old relative turned on him as if he had been someone she had observed heading off the fox, if not shooting it.

'Gorringe, you ghastly sheepfaced fugitive from Hell,' she thundered, forgetting, or so I imagine, that she was a hostess, 'get out of here, blast you! We're in conference.'

I suppose mixing with editors of poetry magazines toughens a fellow, rendering him impervious to verbal assault, for Percy, who might well have been expected to wilt, didn't wilt by a damn sight but drew himself up to his full height, which was about six feet two, and came back at her strongly.

'I am sorry to have intruded at an unseasonable moment, Mrs. Travers,' he said, with a simple dignity that became him well, 'but I have a message for you from Moth-aw, Moth-aw would like to speak to you. She desired me to ask if it would be convenient if she came to your room.'

Aunt Dahlia flung her hands up emotionally. I could understand how she felt. The last thing a woman wants, when distraught, is a chat with someone like Ma Trotter.

'Not now!'

'Later, perhaps?'

'Is it important?'

'I received the impression that it was most important.'

Aunt Dahlia heaved a deep sigh, the sigh of a woman who feels that they are coming over the plate too fast for her.

'Oh, all right. Tell her I'll see her in half an hour. I'm going back to the collection room, Bertie. It's just possible that Tom may have run down by now. But one last word,' she added, as she moved away. 'The next subhuman gargoyle that comes butting in and distracting my thoughts when I am trying to wrestle with vital problems takes his life in his hands. Let him make his will and put in his order for lilies!'

She disappeared at some forty m.p.h., and Percy followed her retreating form with an indulgent eye.

'A quaint character,' he said.

I agreed that the old relative was quaint in spots.

'She reminds me a little of the editress of *Parnassus*. The same tendency to wave her hands and shout, when stirred. But about this drive of yours to London, Wooster. What made you go there?'

'Oh, just one or two things I had to attend to.'

'Well, I am thankful that you got back safely. The toll of the roads is so high these days. I trust you always drive carefully, Wooster? No speeding? No passing on blind corners? Capital, capital. But we were all quite anxious about you. We couldn't think where you could have got to. Cheesewright was particularly concerned. He appeared to think that you had vanished permanently and he said there were all sorts of things he had been hoping to discuss with you. I must let him know you are back. It will relieve his mind.'

He trotted off, and I lit a nonchalant cigarette, calm and collected to the eyebrows. I was perhaps half-way through it and had just blown quite a goodish smoke-ring, when clumping footsteps made themselves heard and Stilton loomed up on the skyline.

I reached a hand into my pocket and got a firm grasp on the old Equalizer.

17

I don't know if you have ever seen a tiger of the jungle drawing a deep breath preparatory to doing a swan dive and landing with both feet on the backbone of one of the minor fauna. Probably not, nor, as a matter of fact, have I. But I should imagine that a t. of the j. at such a moment would look . . . allowing, of course, for the fact that it would not have a pink face and a head like a pumpkin . . . exactly as G. D'Arcy Cheesewright looked as his eyes rested on the Wooster frame. For perhaps a couple of ticks he stood there inflating and deflating his chest. Then he said, as I had rather supposed he would:

'Ho!'

His signature tune, as you might say.

My nonchalance continued undiminished. It would have been idle to pretend that the blister's attitude was not menacing. It was about as menacing as it could jolly well stick. But with my hand on the cosh I faced him without a tremor. Like Caesar's wife, I was ready for anything. I gave him a careless nod.

'Ah, Stilton,' I said. 'How are tricks?'

The question appeared to set the seal on his hotted-up-ness. He gnashed a tooth or two.

'I'll show you how tricks are! I've been looking for you all day.'

'You wished to see me about something?'

'I wished to pull your head off at the roots and make you swallow it.'

I nodded again, carelessly as before.

'Ah, yes. You rather hinted at some such desire last night, did you not? It all comes back to me. Well, I'm sorry, Stilton, but I'm afraid it's off. I have made other plans. Percy Gorringe will no doubt have told you that I ran up to London this morning. I went to get this,' I said, and producing the man of slender physique's best friend, gave it a suggestive waggle.

There is one drawback to not wearing a moustache, and that is that if you don't have one, you've got nothing to twirl when baffled. All you can do is stand with your lower jaw drooping like a tired lily, looking a priceless ass, and that is what Stilton was doing now. His whole demeanour was that of an Assyrian who, having come down like a wolf on the fold, finds in residence not lambs but wild cats, than which, of course, nothing makes an Assyrian feel sillier.

'Amazingly effective little contrivances, these,' I proceeded, rubbing it in. 'You read about them a good deal in mystery thrillers. Coshes they are called, though black-jack is, I believe, the American term.'

He breathed stertorously, his eyes bulging. I suppose he had never come up against anything like this. One gets new experiences.

'You put that thing down!' he said hoarsely.

'I propose to put it down,' I replied, quick as a flash. 'I propose to put it down jolly dashed hard, the moment you make a move, and though I am the merest novice in the use of the cosh, I don't see how I can help hitting a head the size of yours somewhere. And then where will you be, Cheesewright? On the floor, dear old soul, that's where you will be, with me carelessly dusting my hands and putting the instrument back in my pocket. With one of these things in his possession the veriest weakling can lay out the toughest egg colder than a halibut on ice. To put it in a word, Cheesewright, I am armed, and the set-up, as I see it, is this. I take a comfortable stance with the weight balanced on both feet, you make a spring, and I, cool as some cucumbers . . . '

It was a silly thing to say, that about making springs, because it put ideas into his head. He made one on the word 'cucumbers' with such abruptness that I was caught completely unawares. That's the trouble with beefy fellows like Stilton. They are so massive that you don't credit them with the ability to get off the mark like jack rabbits and fly through the air with the greatest of ease. Before I knew what had happened, the cosh, wrenched from my grasp, was sailing across the hall, to come to rest on the floor near Uncle Tom's safe.

I stood there defenceless.

Well, 'stood' is putting it loosely. In crises like this we Woosters do not stand. It was soon made abundantly clear that Stilton was not the only one of our little circle who could get off marks like jack rabbits. I doubt if in the whole of Australia, where this species of animal abounds, you could have found a jack rabbit capable of a tithe of the swift smoothness with which I removed myself from the pulsating centre of things. To do a backward jump of some eleven feet and install myself behind the sofa was with me the work of an instant, and there for awhile the matter rested, because every time he came charging round to my side like a greyhound I went whizzing round to his side like an electric hare, rendering his every effort null and void. Those great Generals, of whom I was speaking earlier, go in for this manœuvre quite a bit. Strategic retreat is the technical term.

How long this round-and-round-the-mulberry-bush sequence would have continued, it is not easy to say, but probably not for any great length of time, for already my partner in the rhythmic doings was beginning to show signs of feeling the pace. Stilton, like so many of these beefy birds, is apt, when not in training for some aquatic contest, to yield to the lure of the flesh pots. This takes its toll. By the end of the first dozen laps, while I remained as fresh as a daisy, prepared to fight it out on this line if it took all summer, he was puffing quite considerably and his brow had become wet with honest sweat.

But, as so often happens on these occasions, the fixture was not played to a finish. Pausing for a moment before starting on lap thirteen, we were interrupted by the entry of Seppings, Aunt Dahlia's butler, who came toddling in, looking rather official.

I was glad to see him myself, for some sort of interruption was just what I had been hoping for, but this turning of the thing into a threesome plainly displeased Stilton, and I could understand why. The man's presence hampered him and prevented him from giving of his best. I have already explained that the Cheesewright code prohibits brawling if there are females around. The same rule holds good when members of the domestic staff appear at the ringside. If butlers butt in while they are in the process of trying to ascertain the colour of some acquaintance's insides, the Cheesewrights cheese it.

But, mark you, they don't like cheesing it, and it is not to be wondered at that, compelled by this major-domo's presence to suspend hostilities, Stilton should have eyed him with ill-concealed animosity. His manner, when he spoke, was brusque.

'What do you want?'

'The door, sir.'

Stilton's ill-concealed animosity became rather worse concealed. So packed indeed, with deleterious animal magnetism was the glance he directed at Seppings that one felt that there was a considerable danger of Aunt Dahlia at no distant date finding herself a butler short.

'What do you mean, you want the door? Which door? What door? What on earth do you want a door for?'

I saw that it was most improbable that he would ever get the thing straight in his mind without a word of explanation, so I supplied it. I always like, if I can, to do the square thing by one and all on these occasions. Scratch Bertram Wooster, I sometimes say, and you find a Boy Scout.

'The front door, Stilton, old dance partner, is what one presumes

Pop Seppings has in mind,' I said. 'I would hazard the guess that the bell rang. Correct, Seppings?'

'Yes, sir,' he replied with quiet dignity. 'The front-door bell rang, and in pursuance of my duties I came to answer it.'

And, his manner suggesting that that in his opinion would hold Stilton for awhile, he carried on as planned.

'What I'll bet has happened, Stilton, old scone,' I said, clarifying the whole situation, 'is that some visitor waits without.'

I was right. Seppings flung wide the gates, there was a flash of blond hair and a whiff of Chanel Number Five and a girl came sailing in, a girl whom I was able to classify at a single glance as a pipterino of the first water.

Those who know Bertram Wooster best are aware that he is not a man who readily slops over when speaking of the opposite sex. He is cool and critical. He weighs his words. So when I describe this girl as a pipterino, you will gather that she was something pretty special. She could have walked into any assembly of international beauty contestants, and the committee of judges would have laid down the red carpet. One could imagine fashionable photographers fighting to the death for her custom.

Like the heroine of *The Mystery of the Pink Crayfish* and, indeed, the heroines of all the thrillers I have ever come across, she had hair the colour of ripe corn and eyes of cornflower blue. Add a tiptilted nose and a figure as full of curves as a scenic railway, and it will not strike you as strange that Stilton, sheathing the sword, should have stood gaping at her dumbly, his aspect that of a man who has been unexpectedly struck by a thunderbolt.

'Is Mrs. Travers around?' inquired this vision, addressing herself to Seppings. 'Will you tell her Miss Morehead has arrived.'

I was astounded. For some reason, possibly because she had three names, the picture I had formed in my mind of Daphne Dolores Morehead was that of an elderly female with a face like a horse and gold-rimmed pince-nez attached to her top button with a black string. Seeing her steadily and seeing her whole, I found myself commending Aunt Dahlia's sagacity in inviting her to Brinkley Court, presumably to help promote the sale of the *Boudoir*. A word from her, advising its purchase, would, I felt, go a long way with L.G. Trotter. He was doubtless a devoted and excellent husband, true as steel to the wife of his b., but even devoted and excellent husbands are apt to react powerfully when girls of the D.D. Morehead type start giving them Treatment A.

Stilton was still goggling at her like a bulldog confronted with a pound of steak, and now, her eyes of cornflower blue becoming accustomed to the dim light of the hall, she took a dekko at him and uttered an exclamation that seemed – oddly, considering what Stilton was like – one of pleasure.

'Mr. Cheesewright!' she said. 'Well, fancy! I thought your face was familiar.' She took another dekko. 'You *are* D'Arcy Cheesewright, who used to row for Oxford?'

Stilton inclined the bean dumbly. He seemed incapable of speech.

'I thought so. Somebody pointed you out to me at the Eights Week ball one year. But I almost didn't recognize you. You had a moustache then. I'm so glad you haven't any longer. You look so much handsomer without it. I do think moustaches are simply awful. I always say that a man who can lower himself to wearing a moustache might just as well grow a beard.'

I could not let this pass.

'There are moustaches and moustaches,' I said, twirling mine. Then, seeing that she was asking herself who this slim, distinguished-looking stranger might be, I tapped myself on the wishbone. 'Wooster, Bertram,' I said. 'I'm Mrs. Travers's nephew, she being my aunt. Should I lead you into her presence? She is probably counting the minutes.'

She pursed the lips dubiously, as if the programme I had suggested deviated in many respects from the ideal.

'Yes, I suppose I ought to be going and saying Hello, but what I would really like would be to explore the grounds. It's such a lovely place.'

Stilton, who was now a pretty vermilion, came partially out of the ether, uttering odd, strangled noises like a man with no roof to his mouth trying to recite 'Gunga Din'. Finally something coherent emerged.

'May I show you round?' he said hoarsely.

'I'd love it.'

'Ho!' said Stilton. He spoke quickly, as if feeling he had been remiss in not saying that earlier, and a moment later they were up and doing. And I, with something of the emotions of Daniel passing out of the stage door of the lions' den, went to my room.

It was cool and restful there. Aunt Dahlia is a woman who believes in doing her guests well in the matter of armchairs and chaises-longues, and the chaise-longue allotted to me yielded gratefully to the form. It was not long before a pleasant drowsiness stole over me. The weary eyelids closed. I slept.

When I woke up half an hour later, my first act was to start with some violence. The brain cleared by slumber, I had remembered the cosh.

I rose to my feet, appalled, and shot from the room. It was imperative that I should recover possession of that beneficent instrument with all possible speed, for though in our recent encounter I had outgeneralled Stilton in round one, foiling him with my superior footwork and ring science, there was no knowing when he might not be feeling ready for round two. A setback may discourage a Cheesewright for the moment, but it does not dispose of him as a logical contender.

The cosh, you will recall, had flashed through the air like a shooting star, to wind up its trip somewhere near Uncle Tom's safe, and I proceeded to the spot on winged feet. And picture my concern on finding on arrival that it wasn't there. The way things disappeared at Brinkley Court ... ladders, coshes and what not ... was enough to make a man throw in his hand and turn his face to the wall.

At this moment I actually did turn my face to the wall, the one the safe was wedged into, and having done so gave another of those violent starts of mine.

And what I saw was enough to make a fellow start with all the violence at his disposal. For two or three ticks I simply couldn't believe it. 'Bertram,' I said to myself, 'the strain has been too much for you. You are cockeyed.' But no. I blinked once or twice to clear the vision, and when I had finished blinking there it was, just as I had seen it the first time.

The safe door was open.

18

It is at moments like this that you catch Bertram Wooster at his superb best, his ice-cold brain working like a machine. Many fellows, I mean to say, seeing that safe door open, would have wasted precious time standing goggling at it, wondering why it was open, who had opened it and why whoever had opened it hadn't shut it again, but not Bertram. Hand him something on a plate with watercress round it, and he does not loiter and linger. He acts. A quick dip inside and a rapid rummaging, and I had the thing all sewed up.

There were half a dozen jewel-cases stowed away on the shelves, and it took a minute or two to open them and examine the contents, but investigation revealed only one pearl necklace, so I was spared anything in the nature of a perplexing choice. Swiftly trouser-pocketing the bijouterie, I shot off to Aunt Dahlia's den like the jack rabbit I had so closely resembled at my recent conference with Stilton. She should, I thought, be there by now, and it was a source of considerable satisfaction to me to feel that I was about to bring the sunshine back into the life of this deserving old geezer. When last seen, she had so plainly been in need of a bit of sunshine.

I found her in *statu quo*, as foreseen, smoking a gasper and spelling her way through her Agatha Christie, but I didn't bring the sunshine into her life, because it was there already. I was amazed at the change in her demeanour since she had gone off droopingly to see if Uncle Tom had finished talking to Spode about old silver. Then, you will recall, her air had been that of one caught in the machinery. Now, she conveyed the impression of having found the blue bird. As she looked up on discovering me in her midst, her face was shining like the seat of a bus-driver's trousers, and it wouldn't have surprised me much if she had started yodelling. Her whole aspect was that of an aunt who on honeydew has fed and drunk the milk of Paradise, and the thought crossed my mind that if she was feeling as yeasty as this before hearing the good news, she might quite easily, when I spilled same, explode with a loud report.

I was not able, however, to reveal the chunk of secret history which

I had up my sleeve, for, as so often happens when I am closeted with this woman, she made it impossible for me to get a syllable in edgeways. Even as I crossed the threshold, words began to flutter from her like bats out of a barn.

'Bertie!' she boomed. 'Just the boy I wanted to see. Bertie, my pet, I have fought the good fight. Do you remember the hymn about "See the troops of Midian prowl and prowl around"? It goes on "Christian, up and smite them", and that is what I have done, in spades. Let me tell you what happened. It will make your eyes pop.'

'I say,' I said, but was able to get no further. She rolled over me like a steam-roller.

'When we parted in the hall not long ago, you will remember, I was bewitched, bothered, and bewildered because I couldn't get hold of Spode to put the bite on him about Eulalie Sœurs, and was going to the collection room on the off-chance of there having been a lull. But when I arrived, I found Tom still gassing away, so I took a seat and sat there hoping that Spode would eventually make a break for the open and give me a chance of having a word with him. But he continued to take it without a murmur, and Tom went rambling on. And then suddenly my bones were turned to water and the collection room swam before my eyes. Without any warning Tom suddenly switched to the subject of the necklace. "You might like to look at it now," he said. "Certainly," said Spode. "It's in the safe in the hall," said Tom. "Let's go," said Spode, and off they went.'

She paused for breath, as even she has to do sometimes.

'I say –' I said.

The lungs refilled, she carried on again.

'I wouldn't have thought my limbs would have been able to support me to the door, much less down a long passage into the hall, but they did. I followed in the wake of the procession, giving at the knees but somehow managing to navigate. What I thought I was doing, joining the party, I don't know, but I suppose I had some vague idea of being present when Tom got the bad news and pleading brokenly for forgiveness. Anyway, I went. Tom opened the safe, and I stood there as if I had been turned into a pillar of salt, like Lot's wife.'

I recalled the incident to which she referred, it having happened to come up in the examination paper that time I won that prize for Scripture Knowledge at my private school, but it's probably new to you, so I will give a brief synopsis. For some reason which has escaped my memory they told this Mrs. Lot, while out walking one day, not to look round or she would be turned into a pillar of salt, so of course she immediately did look round and by what I have always thought an odd coincidence she *was* turned into a pillar of salt. It just shows you, what? I mean to say, you never know where you are these days.

'Time marched on. Tom took out the jewel-case and passed it over to Spode, who said "Ah, this is it, is it?" or some damn silly remark like that, and at that moment, with the hand of doom within a toucher of descending, Seppings appeared, probably sent by my guardian angel, and told Tom he was wanted on the phone. "Eh? What? What?" said Tom, his invariable practice when told he is wanted on the phone, and legged it, followed by Seppings. Woof!' she said, and paused for breath again.

'I say –' I said.

'You can imagine how I felt. That stupendous bit of luck had changed the whole aspect of affairs. For hours I had been wondering how on earth I could get Spode alone, and now I had got him alone. You can bet I didn't waste a second. "Just think, Lord Sidcup," I said winningly, "I haven't had a moment yet to talk to you about all our mutual friends and those happy days at Totleigh Towers. How is dear Sir Watkyn Bassett?" I asked, still winningly. I fairly cooed to the man.'

'I say –' I said.

She squelched me with an imperious gesture.

'Don't interrupt, curse you! I never saw such a chap for wanting to collar the conversation. Gabble, gabble, gabble. Listen, can't you, when I'm telling you the biggest story that has broken around these parts for years. Where was I? Oh, yes. "How is dear Sir Watkyn?" I said, and he said dear Sir Watkyn was pretty oojah-cum-spiff. "And dear Madeline?" I said, and he said dear Madeline was ticking over all right. And then I drew a deep breath and let him have it. "And how is that ladies' underclothing place of yours getting along?" I said. "Eulalie Sœurs, isn't it called? Still coining money, I trust?" And next moment you could have knocked me down with a feather. For with a jolly laugh he replied, "Eulalie Sœurs? Oh, I haven't anything to do with that any longer. I sold out ages ago. It's a company now." And as I stood gaping at him, my whole plan of campaign in ruins, he said, "Well, I may as well have a look at this necklace. Mr. Travers says he is anxious to have my opinion of it." And he pressed his thumb to the catch and the jewel-case flew open. And I was just commending my soul to God and saying to myself that this was the end, when I stubbed my foot against something and looked down and there, lying on the floor . . . you'll scarcely believe this . . . was a cosh.'

She paused again, took on a cargo of breath quickly, and resumed.

'Yessir, a cosh! You wouldn't know what a cosh is, of course, so I'll explain. It's a small rubber instrument, much used by the criminal classes for socking their friends and relations. They wait till their mother-in-law's back is turned and then let her have it on the tortoiseshell comb. It's all the rage in underworld circles, and there it was, as I say, lying at my feet.'

'I say –' I said.

I got the imperious gesture between the eyes once more.

'Well, for a moment, it rang no bell. I picked it up automatically, the good housewife who doesn't like to see things lying around on floors, but it held no message for me. It simply didn't occur to me that my guardian angel had been directing my footsteps and was showing me the way out of my troubles and perplexities. And then suddenly, in a blinding flash, I got it. I realized what that good old guardian angel was driving at. He had at last succeeded in penetrating the bone and getting it into my fat head. There was Spode, with his back turned, starting to take the necklace out of the case . . .'

I gasped gurglingly.

'You didn't cosh him?'

'Certainly I coshed him. What would you have had me do? What would Napoleon have done? I took a nice easy half-swing and let go with lots of follow-through, and he fell to earth he knew not where.'

I could readily believe it. Just so had Constable Dobbs fallen at Deverill Hall.

'He's in bed now, convinced that he had a touch of vertigo and hit his head on the floor. Don't worry about Spode. A good night's rest and a bland diet, and he'll be as right as rain tomorrow. And I've got the necklace, I've got the necklace, I've got the bally necklace, and I feel as if I could pick up a couple of tigers and knock their heads together!'

I gaped at her. The bean was swimming. Through the mist that had risen before the eyes she appeared to be swaying like an aunt caught in a high wind.

'You say you've got the necklace?' I quavered.

'I certainly have.'

'Then what,' I said, in about as hollow a voice as ever proceeded from human lips, 'is this one I've got?'

And I produced my exhibit.

For quite a while it was plain that she had failed to follow the story sequence. She looked at the necklace, then at me, then at the necklace again. It was not until I had explained fully that she got the strength of it.

'Of course, yes,' she said, her brow clearing. 'I see it all now. What with yelling for Tom and telling him Spode had had some sort of seizure and listening to him saying "Oh, my God! Now we'll have to put the frightful fellow up for the night!" and trying to comfort him and helping Seppings tote the remains to bed and all that, I forgot to suggest shutting the safe door. And Tom, of course, never thought of it. He was much too busy tearing his hair and saying this was certainly the last time he would invite a club acquaintance to his house, by golly, it being notorious for the first thing club acquaintances do on finding themselves in somebody's home is to have fits and take advantage of them to stay dug into the woodwork for weeks. And then you came along –'

'– and rummaged in the safe and found a pearl necklace and naturally thought it was yours –'

'– and swiped it. Very decent of you, Bertie, dear, and I appreciate the kind thought. If you had been here this morning, I would have told you that Tom insisted on everybody putting their valuables in the safe, but you had dashed up to London. What took you there, by the way?'

'I went to get the cosh, formerly the property of Aunt Agatha's son, Thos. I have been having trouble of late with Menaces.'

She gazed at me with worshipping eyes, deeply moved.

'Was it you, my heart of gold,' she said brokenly, 'who provided that cosh? I had been putting it down as straight guardian-angel stuff. Oh, Bertie, if ever I called you a brainless poop who ought to be given a scholarship at some good lunatic asylum, I take back the words.'

I thanked her briefly.

'But what happens now?'

'I give three rousing cheers and start strewing roses from my hat.'

I frowned with a touch of impatience.

'I am not talking about you, my dear old ancestor, but about your nephew Bertram, the latter being waist-high in the mulligatawny and liable at any moment to sink without trace. Here I am in possession of somebody's pearl necklace –'

'Ma Trotter's. I recognize it now. She wears it in the evenings.'

'Right. So far, so good. The choker belongs, we find, to Ma Trotter. That point established, what do I do for the best?'

'You put it back.'

'In the safe?'

'That's it. You put it back in the safe.'

It struck me as a most admirable idea, and I wondered why I hadn't thought of it myself.

'You've hit it!' I said. 'Yes, I'll put it back in the safe.'

'I'd run along now, if I were you. No time like the present.'

'I will. Oh, by the way, Daphne Dolores Morehead has arrived. She's out in the grounds with Stilton.'

'What did you think of her?'

'A sight for sore eyes, if I may use the expression. I had no idea they were making female novelists like that these days.'

I would have gone on to amplify the favourable impression the young visitor's outer crust had made on me, but at this moment Mrs. Trotter loomed up in the doorway. She looked at me as if feeling that I was on the whole pretty superfluous.

'Oh, good evening, Mr. Wooster,' she said in a distant sort of way. 'I was hoping to find you alone, Mrs. Travers,' she added with the easy tact which had made her the toast of Liverpool.

'I'm just off,' I assured her. 'Nice evening.'

'Very nice.'

'Well, toodle-oo,' I said, and set a course for the hall, feeling pretty bobbish, for at least a portion of my troubles would soon be over. If, of course, the safe was still open.

It was. And I had reached it and was on the point of whipping out the jewel-case and depositing it, when a voice spoke behind me, and, turning like a startled fawn, I perceived L.G. Trotter.

Since my arrival at Brinkley Court I had not fraternized to any great extent with this weasel-faced old buster. He gave me the impression, as he had done at that dinner of mine, of not being too frightfully keen on the society of his juniors. I was surprised that he should be wanting to chat with me now, and wished that he could have selected some more suitable moment. With that necklace on my person, solitude was what I desired.

'Hey,' he said. 'Where's your aunt?'

'She's in her room,' I replied, 'talking to Mrs. Trotter.'

'Oh? Well, when you see her, tell her I've gone to bed.'

This surprised me.

'To bed? Surely the night is yet young?'

'I've got one of my dyspeptic attacks. You haven't a digestive pill on you?'

'I'm sorry. I came out without any.'

'Hell!' he said, rubbing the abdomen. 'I'm in agony. I feel as if I'd swallowed a couple of wild cats. Hullo,' he proceeded, changing the subject, 'what's that safe door doing open?'

I threw out the suggestion that somebody must have opened it, and he nodded as if thinking well of the theory.

'Damned carelessness,' he said. 'That's the way things get stolen.'

And before my bulging eyes he stepped across and gave the door a shove. It closed with a clang.

'Oof!' he said, massaging the abdomen once more, and with a curt 'Good night', passed up the stairs, leaving me frozen to the spot. Lot's wife couldn't have been stiffer.

Any chance I had of putting things back in the safe had gone with the wind.

19

I don't know that I have a particularly vivid imagination – possibly not, perhaps – but in circs like those which I have just outlined you don't need a very vivid imagination to enable you to spot the shape of things to come. As plainly as if it had been the top line on an oculist's chart, I could see what the future held for Bertram.

As I stood there gaping at the closed door, a vision rose before my eyes, featuring me and an inspector of police, the latter having in his supporting cast an unusually nasty-looking sergeant.

'Are you coming quietly, Wooster?' the inspector was saying.

'Who, me?' I said, quaking in every limb. 'I don't know what you mean.'

'Ha, ha,' laughed the inspector. 'That's good. Eh, Fotheringay?'

'Very rich, sir,' said the sergeant. 'Makes me chuckle, that does.'

'Too late to try anything of that sort, my man,' went on the inspector, becoming grave again. 'The game is up. We have evidence to prove that you went to this safe and from it abstracted a valuable pearl necklace, the property of Mrs. L.G. Trotter. If that doesn't mean five years in the jug for you, I miss my bet.'

'But, honestly, I thought it was Aunt Dahlia's.'

'Ha, ha,' laughed the inspector.

'Ha, ha,' chirped the sergeant.

'A pretty story,' said the inspector. 'Tell that to the jury and see what they think of it. Fotheringay, the handcuffs!'

Such was the v. that rose before my e. as I gaped at that c.d., and I wilted like a salted snail. Outside in the garden birds were singing their evensong, and it seemed to me that each individual bird was saying 'Well, boys, Wooster is for it. We shan't see much of Wooster for the next few years. Too bad, too bad. A nice chap till he took to crime.'

A hollow groan escaped my lips, but before another could follow it I was racing for Aunt Dahlia's room. As I reached it, Ma Trotter came out, gave me an austere look and passed on her way, and I went on into the presence. I found the old relative sitting bolt upright in her chair, staring before her with unseeing eyes, and it was plain that once more something had happened to inject a black frost into her sunny mood. The Agatha Christie had fallen unheeded to the floor, displaced from her lap, no doubt, by a shudder of horror.

Normally, I need scarcely say, my policy on finding this sterling old soul looking licked to a splinter would have been to slap her between the shoulder-blades and urge her to keep her tail up, but my personal troubles left me with little leisure for bracing aunts. Whatever the disaster or cataclysm that had come upon her, I felt, it could scarcely claim to rank in the same class as the one that had come upon me.

'I say,' I said. 'The most frightful thing has happened!'

She nodded sombrely. A martyr at the stake would have been cheerier.

'You bet your heliotrope socks it has,' she responded. 'Ma Trotter has thrown off the mask, curse her. She wants Anatole.'

'Who wouldn't?'

It seemed for a moment as if she were about to haul off and let a loved nephew have it on the side of the head, but with a strong effort she calmed herself. Well, when I say 'calmed herself', she didn't cease to boil briskly, but she confined her activities to the spoken word.

'Don't you understand, ass? She has come out into the open and stated her terms. She says she won't let Trotter buy the *Boudoir* unless I give her Anatole.'

It just shows how deeply my predicament had stirred me that my reaction to this frightful speech was practically nil. Informed at any other time that there was even a remote prospect of that superb disher-up handing in his portfolio and going off to waste his sweetness on the desert air of the Trotter home, I should unquestionably have blenched and gasped and tottered but now, as I say, I heard those words virtually unmoved.

'No, really?' I said. 'I say, listen, old flesh and blood. Just as I got to the safe and was about to restore the Trotter pearls, that chump L. G. Trotter most officiously shut the door, foiling my aims and objects and leaving me in the dickens of a jam. I'm trembling like a leaf.'

'So am I.'

'I don't know what to do.'

'I don't, either.'

'I search in vain for some way out of this what the French call *impasse*.'

'Me, too,' she said, picking up the Agatha Christie and hurling it at a passing vase. When deeply stirred, she is always inclined to kick things and throw things. At Totleigh Towers, during one of our more agitated conferences, she had cleared the mantelpiece in my bedroom of its entire contents, including a terra-cotta elephant and a porcelain statuette of the Infant Samuel in Prayer. 'I don't suppose any woman ever had such a problem to decide. On the one hand, life without Anatole is a thing almost impossible –'

'Here I am, stuck with this valuable pearl necklace, the property of Mrs. L.G. Trotter, and when its loss –'

'– to contemplate. On the other –'

'– is discovered, hues and cries will be raised, inspectors and sergeants sent for –'

'– hand, I must sell the *Boudoir*, or I can't take that necklace of mine out of hock. So –'

'– and I shall be found with what is known as hot ice on my person.'

'Ice!'

'And you know as well as I do what happens to people who are caught in possession of hot ice.'

'Ice!' she repeated and sighed dreamily. 'I think of those prawns in iced aspic of his, and I say to myself that I should be mad to face a lifetime without Anatole's cooking. That *Selle d'Agneau à la Grecque*! That *Mignonette de Poulet Rôti Petit Duc*! Those *Nonats de la Mediterrannée au Fenouil*! And then I feel I must be practical. I've got to get that necklace back, and if the only way of getting it back is to . . . Sweet suffering soupspoons!' she vociferated, if that's the word, anguish written on her every feature. 'I wonder what Tom will say when he hears Anatole is leaving!'

'And I wonder what he'll say when he hears his nephew is doing a stretch in Dartmoor.'

'Eh?'

'Stretch in Dartmoor.'

'Who's going to do a stretch in Dartmoor?'

'I am.'

'You?'

'Me.'

'Why?'

I gave her a look which I suppose, strictly speaking, no nephew should have given an aunt. But I was sorely exasperated.

'Haven't you been listening?' I demanded.

She came back at me with equal heat.

'Of course I haven't been listening. Do you think that when I am faced with the prospect of losing the finest cook in the Midland counties I have time to pay attention to your vapid conversation? What were you babbling about?'

I drew myself up. The word 'babbling' had wounded me.

'I was merely mentioning that, owing to that ass L.G. Trotter having shut the door of the safe before I could deposit the fatal necklace, I am landed with the thing. I described it as hot ice.'

'Oh, that was what you were saying about ice?'

'That was what. I also hazarded the prediction that in about two shakes of a duck's tail inspectors and sergeants would come scooping me up and taking me off to chokey.'

'What nonsense. Why should anyone think you had anything to do with it?'

I laughed. One of those short, bitter ones.

'You don't think it may arouse their suspicions when they find the ruddy thing in my trouser pocket? At any moment I may be caught with the goods on me, and you don't have to read many thrillers to know what happens to unfortunate slobs who are caught with the goods on them. They get it in the neck.'

I could see she was profoundly moved. In my hours of ease this aunt is sometimes uncertain, coy and hard to please and, when I was younger, not infrequently sloshed me on the earhole if my behaviour seemed to her to call for the gesture, but let real peril threaten Bertram and she is in there swinging every time.

'This isn't so good,' she said, picking up a small footstool and throwing it at a china shepherdess on the mantelpiece.

I endorsed this view, expressing the opinion that it was dashed awful.

'You'll have to –'

'Hist!'

'Eh?'

'Hist!'

'What do you mean, Hist?'

What I had meant by the monosyllable was that I had heard footsteps approaching the door. Before I could explain this, the handle turned sharply and Uncle Tom came in.

My ear told me at once that all was not well with this relative by marriage. When Uncle Tom has anything on his mind, he rattles his keys. He was jingling now like a xylophone. His face had the haggard, careworn look which it wears when he hears that week-end guests are expected.

'It's a judgment!' he said, bursting into speech with a whoosh.

Aunt Dahlia masked her agitation with what I imagine she thought to be a genial smile.

'Hullo, Tom, come and join the party. What's a judgment?'

'This is. On me. For weakly allowing you to invite those infernal Trotters here. I knew something awful would happen. I felt it in my bones. You can't fill the house up with people like that without courting disaster. Stands to reason. He's got a face like a weasel, she's twenty pounds overweight, and that son of hers wears whiskers. It was madness ever to let them cross the threshold. Do you know what's happened?'

'No, what?'

'Somebody's pinched her necklace!'

'Good heavens!'

'I thought that would make you sit up,' said Uncle Tom, with gloomy triumph. 'She collared me in the hall just now and said she wanted the thing to wear at dinner tonight, and I took her to the safe and opened it and it wasn't there.'

I told myself that I must keep very cool.

'You mean,' I said, 'that it had gone?'

He gave me rather an unpleasant look.

'You've got a lightning brain!' he said.

Well, I have, of course.

'But how could it have gone?' I asked. 'Was the safe open?'

'No, shut. But I must have left it open. All that fuss of putting that frightful fellow Sidcup to bed distracted my attention.'

I think he was about to say that it just showed what happened when you let people like that into the house, but checked himself on remembering that he was the one who had invited him.

'Well, there it is,' he said. 'Somebody seems to have come along while we were upstairs, seen the safe door open and improved the shining hour. The Trotter woman is raising Cain, and it was only my urgent entreaties that kept her from sending for the police there and then. I told her we could get much better results by making secret inquiries. Didn't want a scandal, I said. But I doubt if I could have persuaded her if it hadn't been that young Gorringe came along and backed me up. Quite an intelligent young fellow, that, though he does wear whiskers.'

I cleared my throat nonchalantly. At least, I tried to do it nonchalantly.

'Then what steps are you taking, Uncle Tom?'

'I'm going to excuse myself during dinner on the plea of a headache – which I've got, I don't mind telling you – and go and search the rooms. Just possible I might dig up something. Meanwhile, I'm off to get a drink. The whole thing has upset me considerably. Will you join me in a quick one, Bertie, me boy?'

'I think I'll stick on here, if you don't mind,' I said. 'Aunt Dahlia and I are talking of this and that.'

He produced a final obligato on the keys.

'Well, suit yourself. But it seems odd to me in my present frame of mind that anyone can refuse a drink. I wouldn't have thought it possible.'

As the door closed behind him, Aunt Dahlia expelled her breath like a death-rattle.

'Golly!' she said.

It seemed to me the *mot juste*.

'What should we do now, do you think?' I queried.

'I know what I'd like to do. I'd like to put the whole thing up to Jeeves, if certain fatheads hadn't let him go off on toots in London just when we need him most.'

'He may be back by now.'

'Ring for Seppings, and ask.'

I pressed the bell.

'Oh, Seppings,' I said, as he entered and You-rang-madam-ed. 'Has Jeeves got back yet?'

'Yes, sir.'

'Then send him here with all speed,' I said.

And a few moments later the man was with us, looking so brainy and intelligent that my heart leaped up as if I had beheld a rainbow in the sky.

'Oh, Jeeves,' I yipped.

'Oh, Jeeves,' yipped Aunt Dahlia, dead-heating with me.

'After you,' I said.

'No, go ahead,' she replied, courteously yielding the floor. 'Your predicament is worse than my predicament. Mine can wait.'

I was touched.

'Very handsome of you, old egg,' I said. 'Much appreciated. Jeeves, your close attention, if you please. Certain problems have arisen.'

'Yes, sir?'

'Two in all.'

'Yes, sir?'

'Shall we call them Problem A and Problem B?'

'Certainly, sir, if you wish.'

'Then here is Problem A, the one affecting me.'

I ran through the scenario, putting the facts clearly and well.

'So there you are, Jeeves. Bend the brain to it. If you wish to pace the corridor, by all means do so.'

'It will not be necessary, sir. One sees what must be done.'

I said I would be glad if he could arrange it so that two could.

'You must restore the necklace to Mrs. Trotter, sir.'

'Give it back to her, you mean?'

'Precisely, sir.'

'But, Jeeves,' I said, my voice shaking a little, 'isn't she going to wonder how I come to have my hooks on the thing? Will she not probe and question, and having probed and questioned rush to the telephone and put in her order for inspectors and sergeants?'

A muscle at the side of his mouth twitched indulgently.

'The restoration would, of course, have to be accomplished with secrecy, sir. I would advocate placing the piece of jewellery in the lady's bedchamber at a moment when it was unoccupied. Possibly while she was at the dinner table.'

'But I should be at the dinner table, too. I can't say "Oh, excuse me" and dash upstairs in the middle of the fish course.'

'I was about to suggest that you allow me to attend to the matter, sir. My movements will be less circumscribed.'

'You mean you'll handle the whole binge?'

'If you will give me the piece of jewellery, sir, I shall be most happy to do so.'

I was overcome. I burned with remorse and shame. I saw how mistaken I had been in supposing that he had been talking through the back of his neck.

'Golly, Jeeves! This is pretty feudal.'

'Not at all, sir.'

'You've solved the whole thing. Rem . . . what's that expression of yours?'

'*Rem acu tetigisti*, sir?'

'That's it. It does mean "You have put your finger on the nub", doesn't it?'

'That would be a rough translation of the Latin, sir. I am happy to have given satisfaction. But did I understand you to say that there was a further matter that was troubling you, sir?'

'Problem B is mine, Jeeves,' said Aunt Dahlia, who during the slice of dialogue had been waiting in the wings, chafing a bit at being withheld from taking the stage. 'It's about Anatole.'

'Yes, madam?'

'Mrs. Trotter wants him.'

'Indeed, madam?'

'And she says she won't let Trotter buy the *Boudoir* unless she gets him. And you know how vital it is that I sell the *Boudoir*. Sweet spirits of nitre!' cried the old relative passionately. 'If only there was some way of inserting a bit of backbone into L.G. Trotter and making him stand up to the woman and defy her!'

'There is, madam.'

Aunt Dahlia leaped about a foot and a quarter. It was as though that calm response had been a dagger of Oriental design thrust into the fleshy part of her leg.

'What did you say, Jeeves? Did you say there was?'

'Yes, madam. I think it will be a reasonably simple matter to induce Mr. Trotter to override the lady's wishes.'

I didn't want to cast a damper over the proceedings, but I had to put in a word here.

'Frightfully sorry to have to dash the cup of joy from your lips, old tortured spirit,' I said, 'but I fear that all this comes under the head of wishful thinking. Pull yourself together, Jeeves. You speak . . . is it airily?'

'Airily or glibly, sir.'

'Thank you, Jeeves. You speak airily or glibly of inducing L.G. Trotter to throw off the yoke and defy his considerably better half, but are you not too . . . dash it, I've forgotten the word.'

'Sanguine, sir?'

'That's it. Sanguine. Brief though my acquaintance with these twain has been, I have got L.G. Trotter's number, all right. His attitude towards Ma Trotter is that of an exceptionally diffident worm towards a sinewy Plymouth Rock or Orpington. A word from her, and he curls up into a ball. So where do you get off with that simple-matter-to-override-wishes stuff?'

I thought I had him there, but no.

'If I might explain. I gather from Mr. Seppings, who has had opportunities of overhearing the lady's conversation, that Mrs. Trotter, being socially ambitious, is extremely anxious to see Mr. Trotter knighted, madam.'

Aunt Dahlia nodded.

'Yes, that's right. She's always talking about it. She thinks it would be one in the eye for Mrs. Alderman Blenkinsop.'

'Precisely, madam.'

I was rather surprised.

'Do they knight birds like him?'

'Oh, yes, sir. A gentleman of Mr. Trotter's prominence in the world of publishing is always in imminent danger of receiving the accolade.'

'Danger? Don't these bozos like being knighted?'

'Not when they are of Mr. Trotter's retiring disposition, sir. He would find it a very testing ordeal. It involves wearing satin knee-breeches and walking backwards with a sword between the legs, not at all the sort of thing a sensitive gentleman of regular habits would enjoy. And he shrinks, no doubt, from the prospect of being addressed for the remainder of his life as Sir Lemuel.'

'His name's not Lemuel?'

'I fear so, sir.'

'Couldn't he use his second name?'

'His second name is Gengulphus.'

'Golly, Jeeves,' I said, thinking of old Uncle Tom Portarlington, 'there's some raw work pulled at the font from time to time, is there not?'

'There is, indeed, sir.'

Aunt Dahlia seemed perplexed, like one who strives in vain to put her finger on the nub.

'Is this all leading up to something, Jeeves?'

'Yes, madam. I was about to hazard the suggestion that were Mr. Trotter to become aware that the alternative to buying *Milady's Boudoir* was the discovery by Mrs. Trotter that he had been offered a knighthood and had declined it, you might find the gentleman more easily moulded than in the past, madam.'

It took Aunt Dahlia right between the eyes like a sock full of wet sand. She tottered, and grabbed for support at the upper part of my right arm, giving it the dickens of a pinch. The anguish caused her next remark to escape me, though as it was no doubt merely 'Gosh!' or 'Lord love a duck!' or something of that sort, I suppose I didn't miss much. When the mists had cleared from my eyes and I was myself again, Jeeves was speaking.

'It appears that Mrs. Trotter some months ago insisted on Mr. Trotter engaging the services of a gentleman's personal gentleman, a young fellow named Worple, and Worple contrived to secure the rough draft of Mr. Trotter's letter of refusal from the wastepaper basket. He had recently become a member of the Junior Ganymede, and in accordance with Rule Eleven he forwarded the document to the secretary for inclusion in the club archives. Through the courtesy of the secretary I was enabled to peruse it after luncheon, and a photostatic copy is to be dispatched to me through the medium of the post. I think that if you were to mention this to Mr. Trotter, madam –'

Aunt Dahlia uttered a whoop similar in timbre to those which she had been accustomed to emit in the old Quorn and Pytchley days when encouraging a bevy of hounds to get on the scent and give it both nostrils.

'We've got him cold!'

'So one is disposed to imagine, madam.'

'I'll tackle him right away.'

'You can't,' I pointed out. 'He's gone to bed. Touch of dyspepsia.'

'Then tomorrow directly after breakfast,' said Aunt Dahlia. 'Oh, Jeeves!'

Emotion overcame her, and she grabbed at my arm again. It was like being bitten by an alligator.

20

At about the hour of nine next morning a singular spectacle might have been observed on the main staircase of Brinkley Court. It was Bertram Wooster coming down to breakfast.

It is a fact well known to my circle that only on very rare occasions do I squash in at the communal morning meal, preferring to chew the kipper or whatever it may be in the seclusion of my bedchamber. But a determined man can nerve himself to almost anything, if necessary, and I was resolved at all cost not to miss the dramatic moment when Aunt Dahlia tore off her whiskers and told a cowering L.G. Trotter that she knew all. It would, I felt, be value for money.

Though slightly on the somnambulistic side, I don't know when I have felt more strongly that the lark was on the wing and the snail on the thorn and God in His Heaven and all right with the world. Thanks to Jeeves's outstanding acumen, Aunt Dahlia's problem was solved, and I was in a position – if I cared to be rude enough – to laugh in the faces of any inspectors and sergeants who might blow in. Furthermore, before retiring to rest on the previous night I had taken the precaution to recover the cosh from the old relative and it was securely on my person once more. Little wonder that, as I entered the dining-room, I was within an ace of bursting into song and piping as the linnets do, as I have heard Jeeves put it.

The first thing I saw on crossing the threshold was Stilton wolfing ham, the next Daphne Dolores Morehead finishing off her repast with toast and marmalade.

'Ah, Bertie, old man,' cried the former, waving a fork in the friendliest manner. 'So there you are, Bertie, old fellow. Come in, Bertie, old chap, come in. Splendid to see you looking so rosy.'

His cordiality would have surprised me more, if I hadn't seen in it a ruse or stratagem designed to put me off my guard and lull me into a false sense of security. Keenly alert, I went to the sideboard and helped myself with my left hand to sausages and bacon, keeping the right hand on the cosh in my side pocket. This jungle warfare teaches a man to take no chances.

'Nice morning,' I said, having taken my seat and dipped the lips into a cup of coffee.

'Lovely,' agreed the Morehead, who was looking more than ever like a dewy flower at daybreak. 'D'Arcy is going to take me for a row on the river.'

'Yes,' said Stilton, giving her a burning glance. 'One feels that Daphne ought to see the river. You might tell your aunt we shall not be back for lunch. Sandwiches and hard-boiled eggs are being provided.'

'By that nice butler.'

'By, as you say, that nice butler, who also thought it might run to a bottle of the best from the oldest bin. We shall be starting almost immediately.'

'I'll be going and getting ready,' said the Morehead.

She rose with a bright smile, and Stilton, full though he was of ham, bounded gallantly to open the door for her. When he returned to the table, he found me rather ostentatiously brandishing the cosh. It seemed to surprise him.

'Hullo!' he said. 'What are you doing with that thing?'

'Oh, nothing,' I replied nonchalantly, resting it by my plate. 'I just thought I would like to have it handy.'

He swallowed a chunk of ham in a puzzled way. Then his face cleared.

'Good Lord! You didn't think I was going to set about you?'

I said that some such idea had crossed my mind, and he uttered an amused laugh.

'Good heavens, no! Why, I look on you as my dearest pal, old man.'

It seemed to me that if yesterday's session was a specimen of the way he comported himself towards his dearest pals, the ones who weren't quite so dear must have a pretty thin time of it. I said as much, and he laughed again as heartily as if he had been standing in the dock at Vinton Street police court with His Worship getting off those nifties of his which convulsed all and sundry.

'Oh, that?' he said, dismissing the incident with an airy wave of the hand. 'Forget all that, dear old chap. Put it right out of your mind, old fellow. Perhaps I was a little cross on the occasion to which you refer, but no longer.'

'No?' I said guardedly.

'Definitely not. I see now that I owe you a deep debt of gratitude. But for you, I might still be engaged to that pill Florence. Thank you, Bertie, old man.'

Well, I said 'Not at all' or 'Don't mention it' or something of that sort, but my head was swimming. What with getting up for breakfast and hearing this Cheesewright allude to Florence as a pill, I felt in a sort of dream.

'I thought you loved her,' I said, digging a bewildered fork into my sausage.

He laughed again. Only a beefy mass of heartiness like G. D'Arcy Cheesewright could have been capable of so much merriment at such an hour.

'Who, me? Good heavens, no! I may have imagined I did once... one of those boyish fancies... but when she said I had a head like a pumpkin, the scales fell from my eyes and I came out of the ether. Pumpkin, forsooth! I don't mind telling you, Bertie, old chap, that there are others – I mention no names – who have described my head as majestic. Yes, I have it from a reliable source that it makes me look a king among men. That will give you a rough idea of what a silly young geezer that blighted Florence Craye is. It is a profound relief to me that you have enabled me to get her out of my hair.'

He thanked me again, and I said 'Don't mention it', or it may have been 'Not at all'. I was feeling dizzier than ever.

'Then you don't think,' I said with a quaver in the v., 'that later on, when the hot blood has cooled, there might be a reconciliation?'

'Not a hope.'

'It happened before.'

'It won't happen again. I know now what love really is, Bertie. I tell you, when somebody – who shall be nameless – gazes into my eyes and says that the first time she saw me – in spite of the fact that I was wearing a moustache fully as foul as that one of yours – something went over her like an electric shock, I feel as if I had just won the Diamond Sculls at Henley. It's all washed up between Florence and me. She's yours, old man. Take her, old chap, take her.'

Well, I said something civil like 'Oh, thanks', but he wasn't listening. A silvery voice had called his name, and pausing but an instant to swallow the last of his ham he shot from the room, his face aglow and his eyes a-sparkle.

He left me with the heart like lead within the bosom and the sausage and bacon turning to ashes in my mouth. This, I could see, was the end. It was plain to the least observant eye that G. D'Arcy Cheesewright had got it properly up his nose. Morehead Preferred were booming, and Craye Ordinaries down in the cellar with no takers.

And I had been so certain that in due season wiser counsels would prevail, causing these two sundered hearts to regret the rift in the lute and decide to have another pop at it, thus saving me from the scaffold once more. But it was not to be. Bertram was for it. He would have to drain the bitter cup, after all.

I was starting on a second instalment of coffee – it tasted like the bitter cup – when L.G. Trotter came in.

The one thing I didn't want in my enfeebled state was to have to swap ideas with Trotters, but when you're alone in a dining-room with a fellow, something in the nature of conversation is inevitable, so, as he poured himself out a cup of tea, I said it was a beautiful morning and recommended the sausages and bacon.

He reacted strongly, shuddering from head to foot.

'Sausages?' he said. 'Bacon?' he said. 'Don't talk to me about sausages and bacon,' he said. 'My dyspepsia's worse than ever.'

Well, if he wanted to thresh out the subject of his aching tum, I was prepared to lend a ready ear, but he skipped on to another topic.

'You married?' he asked.

I winced a trifle and said I wasn't actually married yet.

'And you won't ever be, if you've got a morsel of sense,' he proceeded, and brooded darkly over his tea for a moment. 'You know what happens when you get married? You're bossed. You can't call your soul your own. You become just a cipher in the home.'

I must say I was a bit surprised to find him so confidential to one who was, after all, a fairly mere stranger, but I put it down to the dyspepsia. No doubt the shooting pains had robbed him of his cool judgment.

'Have an egg,' I said, by way of showing him that my heart was in the right place.

He turned green and tied himself into a lovers' knot.

'I won't have an egg! Don't keep telling me to have things. Do you think I could look at eggs, feeling the way I do? It's all this infernal French cooking. No digestion can stand up against it. Marriage!' he said, getting back to the old subject. 'Don't talk to me about marriages. You get married, and first thing you know, you have stepsons rung in on you who grow whiskers and don't do a stroke of honest work. All they do is write poems about sunsets. Pah!'

I'm pretty shrewd, and it flashed upon me at this point that it might quite possibly be his stepson Percy to whom he was guardedly alluding. But before I could verify this suspicion the room had begun to fill up. Round about nine-twenty, which it was now, you generally find the personnel of a country house lining up for the eats. Aunt Dahlia came in and took a fried egg. Mrs. Trotter came in and took a sausage. Percy and Florence came in and took respectively a slice of ham and a portion of haddock. As there were no signs of Uncle Tom, I

presumed that he was breakfasting in bed. He generally does when he
has guests, rarely feeling equal to facing them till he has fortified
himself a bit for the stern ordeal.

Those present had got their heads down and their elbows squared
and were busily employed getting theirs, when Seppings appeared with
the morning papers, and conversation, not that there had ever been
much of it, flagged. It was to a silent gathering that there now entered
a newcomer, a man about seven feet in height with a square, powerful
face, slightly moustached towards the centre. It was some time since
I had set eyes on Roderick Spode, but I had no difficulty in recognizing him. He was one of those distinctive-looking blisters who, once
seen, are never forgotten.

He was looking a little pale, I thought, as if he had recently had an
attack of vertigo and hit his head on the floor. He said 'Good morning'
in what for him was rather a weak voice, and Aunt Dahlia glanced up
from her *Daily Mirror*.

'Why, Lord Sidcup!' she said. 'I never expected that you would be
able to come to breakfast. Are you sure it's wise? Do you feel better
this morning?'

'Considerably better, thank you,' he responded bravely. 'The swelling has to some extent subsided.'

'I'm so glad. That's those cold compresses. I was hoping they would
bring home the bacon. Lord Sidcup,' said Aunt Dahlia, 'had a nasty
fall yesterday evening. We think it must have been a sudden giddiness.
Everything went black, didn't it, Lord Sidcup?'

He nodded, and was plainly sorry next moment that he had done
so, for he winced as I have sometimes winced when rashly oscillating
the bean after some outstanding night of revelry at the Drones.

'Yes,' he said. 'It was all most extraordinary. I was standing there
feeling perfectly well – never better, in fact – when it was as though
something hard had hit me on the head, and I remembered no more
till I came to in my room, with you smoothing my pillow and your
butler mixing me a cooling drink.'

'That's life,' said Aunt Dahlia gravely. 'Yessir, that's life all right.
Here today and gone tomorrow, I often say – Bertie, you hellhound,
take that beastly cigarette of yours outside. It smells like guano.'

I rose, always willing to oblige, and had sauntered about half-way
to the french window, when from the lips of Mrs. L.G. Trotter there
suddenly proceeded what I can only describe as a screech. I don't
know if you have ever inadvertently trodden on an unseen cat. Much
the same sort of thing. Taking a quick look at her, I saw that her face
had become almost as red as Aunt Dahlia's.

'Well!' she ejaculated.

She was staring at *The Times*, which was what she had drawn in the distribution of the morning journals, in much the same manner as a resident of India would have stared at a cobra, had he found it nestling in his bath tub.

'Of all the –' she said, and then words failed her.

L.G. Trotter gave her the sort of look the cobra might have given the resident of India who had barged in on its morning bath. I could understand how he felt. A man with dyspepsia, already out of harmony with his wife, does not like to hear that wife screaming her head off in the middle of breakfast.

'What on earth's the matter?' he said testily.

Her bosom heaved like a stage sea.

'I'll tell you what's the matter. They've gone and knighted Robert Blenkinsop!'

'They have?' said L.G. Trotter. 'Gosh!'

The stricken woman seemed to think 'Gosh!' inadequate.

'Is that all you can say?'

It wasn't. He now said 'Ba goom!' She continued to erupt like one of those volcanoes which spill over from time to time and make the neighbouring householders think a bit.

'Robert Blenkinsop! Robert Berlenkinsop! Of all the iniquitous pieces of idiocy! I don't know what things are coming to nowadays. I never heard of such a . . . May I ask why you are laughing?'

L.G. Trotter curled up beneath her eye like a sheet of carbon paper.

'Not laughing,' he said meekly. 'Just smiling. I was thinking of Bobby Blenkinsop walking backwards with satin knee-breeches on.'

'Oh?' said Ma Trotter, and her voice rang through the room like that of a costermonger indicating to his public that he has brussels sprouts and blood oranges for sale. 'Well, let me tell you that that is never going to happen to you. If ever you are offered a knighthood, Lemuel, you will refuse it. Do you understand? I won't have you cheapening yourself.'

There was a crash. It was Aunt Dahlia dropping her coffee–cup, and I could appreciate her emotion. She was feeling precisely as I had felt on learning from Percy that the Wooster Darts Sweep ticket had changed hands, leaving Stilton free to attack me with tooth and claw. There is nothing that makes a woman sicker than the sudden realization that somebody she thought she was holding in the hollow of her hand isn't in the hollow of her hand by a jugful. So far from being in the hollow of her hand, L.G. Trotter was stepping high, wide and handsome with his hat on the side of his head, and I wasn't surprised that the thing had shaken her to her foundation garments.

In the silence which followed L.G. Trotter's response to this wifely ultimatum – it was, if I remember correctly, 'Okay' – Seppings appeared in the doorway.

He was carrying a silver salver, and on this salver lay a pearl necklace.

21

It is pretty generally recognized in the circles in which he moves that Bertram Wooster is not a man who lightly throws in the towel and admits defeat. Beneath the thingummies of what-d'you-call-it his head, wind and weather permitting, is as a rule bloody but unbowed, and if the slings and arrows of outrageous fortune want to crush his proud spirit, they have to pull their socks up and make a special effort.

Nevertheless, I must confess that when, already weakened by having come down to breakfast, I beheld the spectacle which I have described, I definitely quailed. The heart sank, and, as had happened in the case of Spode, everything went black. Through a murky mist I seemed to be watching a negro butler presenting an inky salver to a Ma Trotter who looked like the end man in a minstrel show.

The floor heaved beneath my feet as if an earthquake had set in with unusual severity. My eye, in a fine frenzy rolling, met Aunt Dahlia's, and I saw hers was rolling, too.

Still, she did her best, as always.

''At-a-boy, Seppings!' she said heartily. 'We were all wondering where that necklace could have got to. It is yours, isn't it, Mrs. Trotter?'

Ma Trotter was scrutinizing the salver through a lorgnette.

'It's mine, all right,' she said. 'But what I'd like to know is how it came into this man's possession.'

Aunt Dahlia continued to do her best.

'You found it on the floor of the hall, I suppose, Seppings, where Lord Sidcup dropped it when he had his seizure?'

A dashed good suggestion, I thought, and it might quite easily have clicked, had not Spode, the silly ass, shoved his oar in.

'I fail to see how that could be so, Mrs. Travers,' he said in that supercilious way of his which has got him so disliked on all sides. 'The necklace I was holding when my senses left me was yours. Mrs. Trotter's was presumably in the safe.'

'Yes,' said Ma Trotter, 'and pearl necklaces don't jump out of safes. I think I'll step to the telephone and have a word with the police.'

Aunt Dahlia raised her eyebrows. It must have taken a bit of doing, but she did it.

'I don't understand you, Mrs. Trotter,' she said, very much the *grande dame*. 'Do you suppose that my butler would break into the safe and steal your necklace?'

Spode horned in again. He was one of those unpleasant men who never know when to keep their big mouths shut.

'Why break?' he said. 'It would not have been necessary to *break* into the safe. The door was already open.'

'Ho!' cried Ma Trotter, reckless of the fact that the copyright of the word was Stilton's. 'So that's how it was. All he had to do was reach in and help himself. The telephone is in the hall, I think?'

Seppings made his first contribution to the feast of reason and flow of soul.

'If I might explain, madam.'

He spoke austerely. The rules of their guild do not permit butlers to give employers' guests dirty looks, but while stopping short of the dirty look he was not affectionate. Her loose talk about police and telephones had caused him to take umbrage, and it was pretty clear that whoever he might select as a companion on his next long walking tour, it would not be Ma Trotter.

'It was not I who found the necklace, madam. Acting upon instructions from Mr. Travers, I instituted a search through the rooms of the staff and discovered the object in the bedchamber of Mr. Wooster's personal attendant, Mr. Jeeves. Upon my drawing this to Mr. Jeeves's attention, he informed me that he had picked it up in the hall.'

'Is that so? Well, tell this man Jeeves to come here at once.'

'Very good, madam.'

Seppings withdrew, and I would have given a good deal to have been able to withdraw myself, for in about another two ticks, I saw, it would be necessary for Bertram Wooster to come clean and reveal all, blazoning forth to the world Aunt Dahlia's recent activities, if blazoning forth to the world is the expression I want, and bathing the unfortunate old egg in shame and confusion. Feudal fidelity would no doubt make Jeeves seal his lips, but you can't let fellows go sealing their lips if it means rendering themselves liable to an exemplary sentence, coupled with some strong remarks from the Bench. Come what might, the dirt would have to be dished. The code of the Woosters is rigid on points like this.

Looking at Aunt Dahlia, I could see that her mind was working along the same lines, and she wasn't liking it by any means. With a face as red as hers she couldn't turn pale, but her lips were tightly set and her hand, as it lathered a slice of toast with marmalade, plainly shook. The look on her dial was the look of a woman who didn't need a fortune-teller and a crystal ball to apprise her of the fact that it would not be long before the balloon went up.

I was gazing at her so intently that it was only when a soft cough broke the silence that I realized that Jeeves had joined the gang. He was standing on the outskirts looking quietly respectful.

'Madam?' he said.

'Hey, you!' said Ma Trotter.

He continued to look quietly respectful. If he resented having the words 'Hey, you!' addressed to him, there was nothing in his manner to show it.

'This necklace,' said Ma Trotter, giving him a double whammy through the lorgnette. 'The butler says he found it in your room.'

'Yes, madam. I was planning after breakfast to make inquiries as to its ownership.'

'You were, were you?'

'I presumed that it was some trinket belonging to one of the housemaids.'

'It was . . . *what*?'

He coughed again, that deferential cough of his which sounds like a well-bred sheep clearing its throat on a distant mountain-top.

'I perceived at once that it was merely an inexpensive imitation made from cultured pearls, madam,' he said.

I don't know if you happen to know the expression 'a stunned silence'. I've come across it in books when one of the characters has unloaded a hot one on the assembled company, and I have always thought it a neat way of describing that sort of stilly hush that pops up on these occasions. The silence that fell on the Brinkley Court breakfast table as Jeeves uttered these words was as stunned as the dickens.

L.G. Trotter was the first to break it.

'What's that? Inexpensive imitation? I paid five thousand pounds for that necklace.'

'Of course you did,' said Ma Trotter with a petulant waggle of the bean. 'The man's intoxicated.'

I felt compelled to intervene in the debate and dispel the miasma of suspicion which had arisen, or whatever it is that miasmas do.

'Intoxicated?' I said. 'At ten in the morning? A laughable theory. But the matter can readily be put to the test. Jeeves, say "Theodore Oswaldtwistle, the thistle sifter, sifting a sack of thistles thrust three thorns through the thick of his thumb".'

He did so with an intonation as clear as a bell, if not clearer.

'You see,' I said, and rested my case.

Aunt Dahlia, who had blossomed like a flower revived with a couple of fluid ounces of the right stuff from a watering-can, chipped in with a helpful word.

'You can bank on Jeeves,' she said. 'If he thinks it's a dud, it is a dud. He knows all about jewellery.'

'Precisely,' I added. 'He has the full facts. He studied under an aunt of his in the profession.'

'Cousin, sir.'

'Of course, yes, cousin. Sorry, Jeeves.'

'Not at all, sir.'

Spode came butting in again.

'Let me see that necklace,' he said authoritatively.

Jeeves drew the salver to his attention.

'You will, I think, support my view, my lord.'

Spode took the contents, glanced at them, sniffed and delivered judgment.

'Perfectly correct. An imitation, and not a very good one.'

'You can't be sure,' said Percy, and got withered by a look.

'Can't be sure?' Spode bristled like a hornet whose feelings have been wounded by a tactless remark. 'Can't be *sure*?'

'Of course he's sure,' I said, not actually slapping him on the back but giving him a back-slapping look designed to show him he had got Bertram Wooster in his corner. 'He knows, as everybody knows, that cultured pearls have a core. You spotted the core in a second, didn't you, Spode, old man, or rather Lord Sidcup, old man?'

I was going on to speak of the practice of introducing a foreign substance into the oyster in order to kid it along and induce it to cover this f.s. with layers of nacre – which I still think is a dirty trick to play on a shellfish which simply wants to be left alone with its thoughts – but Spode had risen. There was dudgeon in his manner.

'All this sort of thing at breakfast!' he said, and I saw what he meant. At home, no doubt, he wrapped himself around the morning egg in cosy seclusion, his daily paper propped up against the coffee-pot and none of this business of naked passions buzzing all over the place. He wiped his mouth, and left via the french window, wincing with a hand to his head as L.G. Trotter spoke in a voice that nearly cracked his tea-cup.

'Emily! Explain this!'

Ma Trotter got the lorgnette working on him, but for all the good it did she might as well have used a monocle. He stared right back at her, and I imagine – couldn't be certain, of course, because his back was to me – that there was in his gaze a steely hardness that turned her bones to water. At any rate, when she spoke, it was like what I have heard Jeeves describe as the earliest pipe of half-awakened birds.

'I can't explain it,' she . . . yes, quavered. I was going to say 'murmured', but quavered hits it off better.

L.G. Trotter barked like a seal.

'I can,' he said. 'You've been giving money on the sly again to that brother of yours.'

This was the first I had heard of any brother of Ma Trotter's, but I wasn't surprised. My experience is that all wives of prosperous business men have shady brothers in the background to whom they slip a bit from time to time.

'I haven't!'

'Don't lie to me!'

'Oh!' cried the shrinking woman, shrinking a bit more, and the spectacle was too much for Percy. All this while he had been sitting tensely where he sat, giving the impression of something stuffed by a good taxidermist, but now, moved by a mother's distress, he rose rather in the manner of one about to reply to the toast of The Ladies. He was looking a little like a cat in a strange alley which is momentarily expecting a half-brick in the short ribs, but his voice, though low, was firm.

'I can explain everything. Moth-aw is innocent. She wanted her necklace cleaned. She entrusted it to me to take to the jeweller's, and I pawned it and had an imitation made. I needed money urgently.'

Aunt Dahlia well-I'll-be-blowed!

'What an extraordinary thing to do!' she said. 'Did you ever hear of anybody doing anything like that, Bertie?'

'New to me, I must confess.'

'Amazing, eh?'

'Bizarre, you might call it.'

'Still, that's how it goes.'

'Yes, that's how it goes.'

'I needed a thousand pounds to put into the play,' said Percy.

L.G. Trotter, who was in good voice this morning, uttered a howl that set the silverware rattling. It was fortunate for Spode that he had removed himself from earshot, for it would certainly have done that head of his no good. Even I, though a strong man, leaped about six inches.

'You put a thousand pounds into a *play*?'

'Into *the* play,' said Percy. 'Florence's and mine. My dramatization of her novel, *Spindrift*. One of our backers had failed us, and rather than disappoint the woman I loved –'

Florence was staring at him, wide-eyed. If you remember, I described her aspect on first glimpsing my moustache as having had in it a touch of the Soul's Awakening. The S.A. was now even more pronounced. It stuck out a mile.

'Percy! You did that for me?'

'And I'd do it again,' said Percy.

L.G. Trotter began to speak. As to whether he opened his remarks with the words 'Ba goom!' I cannot be positive, but there was a 'Ba goom!' implicit in every syllable. The man was what is called beside himself, and one felt a gentle pity for Ma Trotter, little as one liked her. Her reign was over. She had had it. From now on it was plain who was going to be the Führer of the Trotter home. The worm of yesterday – or you might say the worm of ten minutes ago – had become a worm in tiger's clothing.

'This settles it!' he vociferated, I'm pretty sure it's vociferated. 'There won't be any more loafing about London for you, young man. We leave this house this morning –'

'What!' yipped Aunt Dahlia.

'– and the moment we get back to Liverpool you start in at the bottom of the business, as you ought to have done two years ago if I hadn't let myself be persuaded against my better judgment. Five thousand pounds I paid for that necklace, and you . . .'

Emotion overcame him, and he paused.

'But, Mr. Trotter!' There was anguish in Aunt Dahlia's voice. 'You aren't leaving this morning!'

'Yes, I am. Think I'm going to go through another of that French cook's lunches?'

'But I was hoping you would not be going away before we had settled this matter of buying the *Boudoir*. If you could give me a few moments in the library?'

'No time for that. I'm going to drive into Market Snodsbury and see a doctor. Just a chance he may be able to do something to relieve the pain. It's about here that it seems to catch me,' said L.G. Trotter, indicating the fourth button of his waistcoat.

'Tut-tut,' said Aunt Dahlia, and I tut-tutted, too, but nobody else expressed the sympathy the writhing man had a right to expect. Florence was still drinking in Percy with every eye at her disposal, and Percy was bending solicitously over Ma Trotter, who was sitting looking like a survivor of a bomb explosion.

'Come, Moth-aw,' said Percy, hoiking her up from where she roosted. 'I will bathe your temples with eau-de-Cologne.'

With a reproachful look at L.G. Trotter he led her gently from the room. A mother's best friend is her boy.

Aunt Dahlia was still looking aghast, and I knew what was in her mind. Once let this Trotter get away to Liverpool and she would be dished. Delicate negotiations like selling a weekly paper for the gentler sex to a customer full of sales resistance can't be conducted successfully by mail. You have to have men like L.G. Trotter on the spot, kneading their arms and generally giving them the old personality.

'Jeeves!' I cried. I don't know why, because I couldn't see what he could do to help.

He sprang respectfully to life. During the late give-and-take he had been standing in the background with that detached, stuffed-frog look on his face which it always wears when he is present at a free-for-all in which his sense of what is fitting does not allow him to take part. And the spirits rose as I saw from his eye that he was going to rally round.

'If I might make a suggestion, sir.'

'Yes, Jeeves?'

'It occurs to me that one of those morning mixtures of mine would bring relief to Mr. Trotter.'

I gargled. I got his meaning.

'You mean those pick-me-ups you occasionally prepare for me when the state of the old head seems to call for it?'

'Precisely, sir.'

'Would they hit the trot with Mr. Spotter, or rather the other way round?'

'Oh, yes, sir. They act directly on the internal organs.'

It was enough. I saw that, as always, he had *tetigisti*-ed the *rem*. I turned to L.G. Trotter.

'You heard?'

'No, I didn't. How do you expect me to hear things —?'

I checked him with one of my gestures.

'Well, listen now,' I said. 'Be of good cheer, L.G. Trotter, for the United States Marines have arrived. No need for any doctors. Go along with Jeeves, and he will fix you a mixture which will put the old tum in midseason form before you can say "Lemuel Gengulphus".'

He looked at Jeeves with a wild surmise. I heard Aunt Dahlia gasp a gasp.

'Is that right?'

'Yes, sir. I can guarantee the efficacy of the preparation.'

L.G. Trotter emitted a loud 'Woof!'

'Let's go,' he said briefly.

'I'll come with you and hold your hand,' said Aunt Dahlia.

'Just one word,' I said, as the procession started to file out. 'On swallowing the stuff you will have the momentary illusion that you have been struck by lightning. Pay no attention. It's all part of the treatment. But watch the eyeballs, as they are liable, unless checked, to start from the parent sockets and rebound from the opposite wall.'

They passed from the room, and I was alone with Florence.

22

It's an odd thing, but it hadn't occurred to me in the rush and swirl
of recent events that, with people drifting off in twos and threes and –
in the case of Spode – in ones, the time must inevitably come when
this beasel and I would be left face to face in what is called a *solitude
à deux*. And now that this unpleasant state of affairs had come about,
it was difficult to know how to start the conversation. However, I had
a pop at it, the same pop I had had when finding myself closeted with
L.G. Trotter.

'Can I get you a sausage?' I said.

She waved it away. It was plain that the unrest in her soul could
not be lulled with sausages.

'Oh, Bertie,' she said, and paused.

'Or a slice of ham?'

She shook her head. Ham appeared to be just as much a drug in
the market as sausages.

'Oh, Bertie,' she said again.

'Right opposite you,' I said encouragingly.

'Bertie, I don't know what to do.'

She signed off once more, and I stood there waiting for something
to emerge. A half-formed idea of offering her a kipper I dismissed.
Too silly, I mean, keeping on suggesting items on the menu like a
waiter trying to help a customer make up his mind.

'I feel awful!' she said.

'You look fine,' I assured her, but she dismissed the pretty compli-
ment with another wave of the hand.

She was silent again for a moment, and then it came out with a
rush.

'It's about Percy.'

I was nibbling a slice of toast as she spoke, but lowered it courteously.

'Percy?' I said.

'Oh, Bertie,' she proceeded, and from the way her nose wiggled I
could see that she was in quite a state. 'All that that happened just

now . . . when he said that about not disappointing the woman he loved . . . when I realized what he had done . . . just for me . . .'

'I know what you mean,' I said. 'Very white.'

'Something happened to me. It was as though for the first time I was seeing the real Percy. I had always admired his intellect, of course, but now it was different. I seemed to be gazing into his naked soul, and what I saw there . . .'

'Pretty good, was it?' I queried, helping the thing along.

She drew a deep breath.

'I was overcome. I was stunned. I realized that he was just like Rollo Beaminster.'

For a moment I was not abreast. Then I remembered.

'Oh, ah, yes. You didn't get around to telling me much about Rollo, except that he was in a wild mood.'

'Oh, that was quite early in the story, before he and Sylvia came together again.'

'They came together, did they?'

'Yes. She gazed into his naked soul and knew that there could be no other man for her.'

I have already stressed the fact that I was mentally at my brightest this morning, and hearing these words I got the distinct idea that she was feeling pretty pro-Percy as of even date. I might be wrong, of course, but I didn't think so, and it seemed to me that this was a good thing that wanted pushing along. There is, as Jeeves had so neatly put it, a tide in the affairs of men which, taken at the flood, leads on to fortune.

'I say,' I said, 'here's a thought. Why don't you marry Percy?'

She started. I saw that she was trembling. She moved, she stirred, she seemed to feel the rush of life along her keel. In her eyes, as she gazed at me, it wasn't difficult to spot the light of hope.

'But I'm engaged to you,' she faltered, rather giving the impression that she could have kicked herself for being such a chump.

'Oh, that can be readily adjusted,' I said heartily. 'Call it off, is my advice. You don't want a weedy butterfly like me about the home, you want something more in the nature of a soul-mate, a chap with a number nine hat you can sit and hold hands and talk about T.S. Eliot with. And Percy fills the bill.'

She choked a bit. The light of hope was now very pronounced.

'Bertie! You will release me?'

'Certainly, certainly. Frightful wrench, of course, and all that sort of thing, but consider it done.'

'Oh, Bertie!'

She flung herself upon me and kissed me. Unpleasant, of course, but these things have to be faced. As I once heard Anatole remark, one must learn to take a few roughs with a smooth.

We were still linked together in a close embrace, when the silence – we were embracing fairly silently – was broken by what sounded like the heart-cry of one of the local dogs which had bumped its nose against the leg of the table.

It wasn't a dog. It was Percy. He was standing there looking overwrought, and I didn't blame him. Agony, of course, if you love a girl, to come into a room and find her all tangled up with another fellow.

He pulled himself together with a powerful effort.

'Go on,' he said, 'go on. I'm sorry I interrupted you.'

He broke off with a choking gulp, and I could see it was quite a surprise to him when Florence, abruptly detaching herself from me, did a jack-rabbit leap that was almost in the Cheesewright–Wooster class and hurled herself into his arms.

'Eh, what?' he said, plainly missing the gist.

'I love you, Percy!'

'You do?' His face lit up for an instant. Then there was a black-out. 'But you're engaged to Wooster,' he said moodily, eyeing me in a manner that seemed to suggest that in his opinion it was fellows like me who caused half the trouble in the world.

I moved over to the table and took another slice of toast. Cold, of course, but I rather like cold toast, provided there's plenty of butter.

'No, that's off,' I said. 'Carry on, old sport. You have the green light.'

Florence's voice shook.

'Bertie has released me, Percy. I was kissing him because I was so grateful. When I told him I loved you, he released me.'

You could see that Percy was impressed.

'I say! That was very decent of him.'

'He's like that. Bertie is the soul of chivalry.'

'He certainly is. I'm amazed. Nobody would think it, to look at him.'

I was getting about fed up with people saying nobody would think it, to look at me, and it is quite possible that I might at this point have said something a bit biting . . . I don't know what, but something. But before I could assemble the makings Florence suddenly uttered something that was virtually tantamount to a wail of anguish.

'But, Percy, what are we to do? I've only a small dress allowance.'

I didn't follow the trend of her thought. Nor did Percy. Cryptic, I considered it, and I could see he thought so, too.

'What's that got to do with it?' he said.

Florence wrung her hands, a thing I've often heard about but never seen done. It's a sort of circular movement, starting from the wrists.

'I mean, I haven't any money and you haven't any money, except what your stepfather is going to pay you when you join the business. We should have to live in Liverpool. I can't live in Liverpool!'

Well, of course, lots of people do, or so I have been given to understand, but I saw what she meant. Her heart was in London's Bohemia – Bloomsbury, Chelsea, sandwiches and absinthe in the old studio, all that sort of thing, and she hated to give it up. I don't suppose they have studios up Liverpool way.

''Myes,' said Percy.

'You see what I mean?'

'Oh, quite,' said Percy.

He was plainly ill at ease. A strange light had come into his tortoiseshell-rimmed spectacles, and his whiskers quivered gently. For a moment he stood there letting 'I dare not' wait upon 'I would'. Then he spoke.

'Florence, I have a confession to make. I hardly know how to tell you. The truth is that my financial position is reasonably sound. I am not a rich man, but I have a satisfactory income, quite large enough to support the home. I have no intention of going to Liverpool.'

Florence goggled. I have an idea that she was thinking, early though it was, that he had had one over the eight. Her air was that of a girl on the point of asking him to say 'Theodore Oswaldtwistle, the thistle sifter, in sifting a sack of thistles thrust three thorns through the thick of his thumb'. However, all she said was:

'But, Percy darling, you surely can't make much out of your poetry?'

He twiddled his fingers for a moment. You could see he was trying to nerve himself to reveal something he would much have preferred to keep under his hat. I have had the same experience when had up on the carpet by my Aunt Agatha.

'I don't,' he said. 'I only got fifteen shillings for that "Caliban at Sunset" thing of mine in *Parnassus*, and I had to fight like a tiger to get that. The editress wanted to beat me down to twelve-and-six. But I have a . . . an alternative source of revenue.'

'I don't understand.'

He bowed his head.

'You will. My receipts from this – er – alternative source of revenue amounted last year to nearly eight hundred pounds, and this year it should be double that, for my agent has succeeded in establishing me in the American market. Florence, you will shrink from me, but I have to tell you. I write detective stories under the pseudonym of Rex West.'

I wasn't looking at Florence, so I don't know if she shrank from him, but I certainly didn't. I stared at him, agog.

'Rex West? Lord-love-a-duck! Did you write *The Mystery of the Pink Crayfish*?' I gasped.

He bowed his head again.

'I did. And *Murder in Mauve, The Case of the Poisoned Doughnut* and *Inspector Biffen Views the Body*.'

I hadn't happened to get hold of those, but I assured him that I would lose no time in putting them on my library list, and went on to ask a question which had been occupying my mind for quite a while.

'Then who was it who bumped off Sir Eustace Willoughby Bart, with the blunt instrument?'

In a low, toneless voice he said:

'Burwash, the butler.'

I uttered a cry.

'As I suspected! As I suspected from the first!'

I would have probed further into this Art of his, asking him how he thought up these things and did he work regular hours or wait for inspiration, but Florence had taken the floor again. So far from shrinking from him, she was nestling in his arms and covering his face with burning kisses.

'Percy!' She was all over the blighter. 'I think it's wonderful! How frightfully clever of you!'

He tottered.

'You aren't revolted?'

'Of course I'm not. I'm tremendously pleased. Are you working on something now?'

'A novelette. I think of calling it *Blood Will Tell*. It will run to about thirty thousand words. My agent says these American magazines like what they call one-shotters – a colloquial expression, I imagine, for material of a length suitable for publication in a single issue.'

'You must tell me all about it,' said Florence, taking his arm and heading for the french window.

'Hey, just a moment,' I said.

'Yes?' said Percy, turning. 'What is it, Wooster? Talk quickly. I am busy.'

'May I have your autograph?'

He beamed.

'You really want it?'

'I am a great admirer of your work.'

'That is the boy!' said Percy.

He wrote it on the back of an envelope, and they went out hand in hand, these two young folks starting on the long journey together. And I, feeling a bit peckish after this emotional scene, sat down and had another go at the sausages and bacon.

I was still thus engaged when the door opened and Aunt Dahlia came in. A glance was enough to tell me that all was well with the aged relative. On a previous occasion I have described her face as shining like the seat of a bus-driver's trousers. It was doing so now. If she had been going to be Queen of the May, she could not have looked chirpier.

'Has L.G. Trotter signed the papers?' I asked.

'He's going to, the moment he gets his eyeballs back. How right you were about his eyeballs. When last seen, they were ricochetting from wall to wall, with him in hot pursuit. Bertie,' said the old ancestor, speaking in an awed voice, 'what does Jeeves put into those mixtures of his?'

I shook my head.

'Only he and his God know that,' I said gravely.

'They seem powerful stuff. I remember reading somewhere once about a dog that swallowed a bottle of chilli sauce. It was described as putting up quite a performance. Trotter reacted in a somewhat similar manner. I should imagine dynamite was one of the ingredients.'

'Very possibly,' I said. 'But let us not talk of dogs and chilli sauce. Let us rather discuss these happy endings of ours.'

'Endings? In the plural? I've had a happy ending, all right, but you –'

'Me, too. Florence –'

'You don't mean it's off?'

'She's going to marry Percy.'

'Bertie, my beamish boy!'

'Didn't I tell you I had faith in my star? The moral of the whole thing, as I see it, is that you can't keep a good man down, or' – I bowed slightly in her direction – 'a good woman. What a lesson this should be to us, old flesh and blood, never to give up, never to despair. However dark the outlook . . .'

I was about to add 'and however black the clouds' and go on to speak of the sun sooner or later smiling through, but at this moment Jeeves shimmered in.

'Excuse me, madam. Would it be convenient for you to join Mr. Trotter in the library, madam? He is waiting for you there.'

Aunt Dahlia really needs a horse to help her get up speed, but though afoot she made excellent time to the door.

'How is he?' she asked, turning on the threshold.

'Completely restored to health, madam, I am happy to say. He speaks of venturing on a sandwich and a glass of milk at the conclusion of your conference.'

She gave him a long, reverent look.

'Jeeves,' she said, 'you stand alone. I knew you would save the day.'

'Thank you very much, madam.'

'Have you ever tried those mixtures of yours on a corpse?'

'Not yet, madam.'

'You should,' said the old relative, and curvetted out like one of those mettlesome steeds which, though I have never heard one do it myself, say 'Ha!' among the trumpets.

A silence followed her departure, for I was plunged in thought. I was debating within myself whether to take a step of major importance or whether, on the other hand, not to, and at such times one does not talk, one weighs the pros and cons. I was, in short, standing at a man's cross-roads.

That moustache of mine . . .

Pro: I loved the little thing. I fancied myself in it. I had hoped to nurse it through the years with top dressing till it became the talk of the town.

Con: But was it, I asked myself, *safe*? Recalling the effect of its impact on Florence Craye, I saw clearly that it had made me too fascinating. There peril lurked. When you become too fascinating, all sorts of things are liable to occur which you don't want to occur, if you follow me.

A strange calm descended on me, I had made my decision.

'Jeeves,' I said, and if I felt a passing pang, why not? One is but human. 'Jeeves,' I said, 'I'm going to shave my moustache.'

His left eyebrow flickered, showing how deeply the words had moved him.

'Indeed, sir?'

'Yes, you have earned this sacrifice. When I have eaten my fill . . . Good sausages, these.'

'Yes, sir.'

'Made, no doubt, from contented pigs. Did you have some for your breakfast?'

'Yes, sir.'

'Well, as I was saying, when I have eaten my fill, I shall proceed upstairs to my room, I shall lather the upper lip, I shall take razor in hand . . . and *voilà*!'

'Thank you very much, sir,' he said.

JEEVES IN THE OFFING

1

Jeeves placed the sizzling eggs and b. on the breakfast table, and Reginald ('Kipper') Herring and I, licking the lips, squared our elbows and got down to it. A lifelong buddy of mine, this Herring, linked to me by what are called imperishable memories. Years ago, when striplings, he and I had done a stretch together at Malvern House, Bramley-on-Sea, the preparatory school conducted by that prince of stinkers, Aubrey Upjohn M.A., and had frequently stood side by side in the Upjohn study awaiting the receipt of six of the juiciest from a cane of the type that biteth like a serpent and stingeth like an adder, as the fellow said. So we were, you might say, rather like a couple of old sweats who had fought shoulder to shoulder on Crispin's Day, if I've got the name right.

The *plat du jour* having gone down the hatch, accompanied by some fluid ounces of strengthening coffee, I was about to reach for the marmalade, when I heard the telephone tootling out in the hall and rose to attend to it.

'Bertram Wooster's residence,' I said, having connected with the instrument. 'Wooster in person at this end. Oh hullo,' I added, for the voice that boomed over the wire was that of Mrs. Thomas Portarlington Travers of Brinkley Court, Market Snodsbury, near Droitwich – or, putting it another way, my good and deserving Aunt Dahlia. 'A very hearty pip-pip to you, old ancestor,' I said, well pleased, for she is a woman with whom it is always a privilege to chew the fat.

'And a rousing toodle-oo to you, you young blot on the landscape,' she replied cordially. 'I'm surprised to find you up as early as this. Or have you just got in from a night on the tiles?'

I hastened to rebut this slur.

'Certainly not. Nothing of that description whatsoever. I've been upping with the lark this last week, to keep Kipper Herring company. He's staying with me till he can get into his new flat. You remember old Kipper? I brought him down to Brinkley one summer. Chap with a cauliflower ear.'

'I know who you mean. Looks like Jack Dempsey.'

'That's right. Far more, indeed, than Jack Dempsey does. He's on the staff of the *Thursday Review*, a periodical of which you may or may not be a reader, and has to clock in at the office at daybreak. No doubt, when I apprise him of your call, he will send you his love, for I know he holds you in high esteem. The perfect hostess, he often describes you as. Well, it's nice to hear your voice again, old flesh and blood. How's everything down Market Snodsbury way?'

'Oh, we're jogging along. But I'm not speaking from Brinkley. I'm in London.'

'Till when?'

'Driving back this afternoon.'

'I'll give you lunch.'

'Sorry, can't manage it. I'm putting on the nosebag with Sir Roderick Glossop.'

This surprised me. The eminent brain specialist to whom she alluded was a man I would not have cared to lunch with myself, our relations having been on the stiff side since the night at Lady Wickham's place in Hertfordshire when, acting on the advice of my hostess's daughter Roberta, I had punctured his hot-water bottle with a darning needle in the small hours of the morning. Quite unintentional, of course. I had planned to puncture the h-w-b of his nephew Tuppy Glossop, with whom I had a feud on, and unknown to me they had changed rooms. Just one of those unfortunate misunderstandings.

'What on earth are you doing that for?'

'Why shouldn't I? He's paying.'

I saw her point – a penny saved is a penny earned and all that sort of thing – but I continued surprised. It amazed me that Aunt Dahlia, presumably a free agent, should have selected this very formidable loony-doctor to chew the mid-day chop with. However, one of the first lessons life teaches us is that aunts will be aunts, so I merely shrugged a couple of shoulders.

'Well, it's up to you, of course, but it seems a rash act. Did you come to London just to revel with Glossop?'

'No, I'm here to collect my new butler and take him home with me.'

'New butler? What's become of Seppings?'

'He's gone.'

I clicked the tongue. I was very fond of the major-domo in question, having enjoyed many a port in his pantry, and this news saddened me.

'No, really?' I said. 'Too bad. I thought he looked a little frail when I last saw him. Well, that's how it goes. All flesh is grass, I often say.'

'To Bognor Regis, for his holiday.'

I unclicked the tongue.

'Oh, I see. That puts a different complexion on the matter. Odd how all these pillars of the home seem to be dashing away on toots these days. It's like what Jeeves was telling me about the great race movements of the Middle Ages. Jeeves starts his holiday this morning. He's off to Herne Bay for the shrimping, and I'm feeling like that bird in the poem who lost his pet gazelle or whatever the animal was. I don't know what I'm going to do without him.'

'I'll tell you what you're going to do. Have you a clean shirt?'

'Several.'

'And a toothbrush?'

'Two, both of the finest quality.'

'Then pack them. You're coming to Brinkley tomorrow.'

The gloom which always envelops Bertram Wooster like a fog when Jeeves is about to take his annual vacation lightened perceptibly. There are few things I find more agreeable than a sojourn at Aunt Dahlia's rural lair. Picturesque scenery, gravel soil, main drainage, company's own water and, above all, the superb French cheffing of her French chef Anatole, God's gift to the gastric juices. A full hand, as you might put it.

'What an admirable suggestion,' I said. 'You solve all my problems and bring the blue bird out of a hat. Rely on me. You will observe me bowling up in the Wooster sports model tomorrow afternoon with my hair in a braid and a song on my lips. My presence will, I feel sure, stimulate Anatole to new heights of endeavour. Got anybody else staying at the old snake pit?'

'Five inmates in all.'

'Five?' I resumed my tongue-clicking. 'Golly! Uncle Tom must be frothing at the mouth a bit,' I said, for I knew the old buster's distaste for guests in the home. Even a single weekender is sometimes enough to make him drain the bitter cup.

'Tom's not there. He's gone to Harrogate with Cream.'

'You mean lumbago.'

'I don't mean lumbago. I mean Cream. Homer Cream. Big American tycoon, who is visiting these shores. He suffers from ulcers, and his medicine man has ordered him to take the waters at Harrogate. Tom has gone with him to hold his hand and listen to him of an evening while he tells him how filthy the stuff tastes.'

'Antagonistic.'

'What?'

'I mean altruistic. You are probably not familiar with the word, but it's one I've heard Jeeves use. It's what you say of a fellow who gives selfless service, not counting the cost.'

'Selfless service, my foot! Tom's in the middle of a very important business deal with Cream. If it goes through, he'll make a packet free of income tax. So he's sucking up to him like a Hollywood Yes-man.'

I gave an intelligent nod, though this of course was wasted on her because she couldn't see me. I could readily understand my uncle-by-marriage's mental processes. T. Portarlington Travers is a man who has accumulated the pieces of eight in sackfuls, but he is always more than willing to shove a bit extra away behind the brick in the fireplace, feeling – and rightly – that every little bit added to what you've got makes just a little bit more. And if there's one thing that's right up his street, it is not paying income tax. He grudges every penny the Government nicks him for.

'That is why, when kissing me goodbye, he urged me with tears in his eyes to lush Mrs Cream and her son Willie up and treat them like royalty. So they're at Brinkley, dug into the woodwork.'

'Willie, did you say?'

'Short for Wilbert.'

I mused. Willie Cream. The name seemed familiar somehow. I seemed to have heard it or seen it in the papers somewhere. But it eluded me.

'Adela Cream writes mystery stories. Are you a fan of hers? No? Well, start boning up on them, directly you arrive, because every little helps. I've bought a complete set. They're very good.'

'I shall be delighted to run an eye over her material,' I said, for I am what they call an a–something of novels of suspense. Aficionado, would that be it? 'I can always do with another corpse or two. We have established, then, that among the inmates are this Mrs Cream and her son Wilbert. Who are the other three?'

'Well, there's Lady Wickham's daughter Roberta.'

I started violently, as if some unseen hand had goosed me.

'What! Bobbie Wickham? Oh, my gosh!'

'Why the agitation? Do you know her?'

'You bet I know her.'

'I begin to see. Is she one of the gaggle of girls you've been engaged to?'

'Not actually, no. We were never engaged. But that was merely because she wouldn't meet me half way.'

'Turned you down, did she?'

'Yes, thank goodness.'

'Why thank goodness? She's a one-girl beauty chorus.'

'She doesn't try the eyes, I agree.'

'A pippin, if ever there was one.'

'Very true, but is being a pippin everything? What price the soul?'

'Isn't her soul like mother makes?'

'Far from it. Much below par. What I could tell you . . . But no, let it go. Painful subj.'

I had been about to mention fifty-seven or so of the reasons why the prudent operator, if he valued his peace of mind, deemed it best to stay well away from the red-headed menace under advisement, but realized that at a moment when I was wanting to get back to the marmalade it would occupy too much time. It will be enough to say that I had long since come out of the ether and was fully cognisant of the fact that in declining to fall in with my suggestion that we should start rounding up clergymen and bridesmaids, the beasel had rendered me a signal service, and I'll tell you why.

Aunt Dahlia, describing this young blister as a one-girl beauty chorus, had called her shots perfectly correctly. Her outer crust was indeed of a nature to cause those beholding it to rock back on their heels with a startled whistle. But while equipped with eyes like twin stars, hair ruddier than the cherry, oomph, *espièglerie* and all the fixings, B. Wickham had also the disposition and general outlook on life of a ticking bomb. In her society you always had the uneasy feeling that something was likely to go off at any moment with a pop. You never knew what she was going to do next or into what murky depths of soup she would carelessly plunge you.

'Miss Wickham, sir,' Jeeves had once said to me warningly at the time when the fever was at its height, 'lacks seriousness. She is volatile and frivolous. I would always hesitate to recommend as a life partner a young lady with quite such a vivid shade of red hair.'

His judgment was sound. I have already mentioned how with her subtle wiles this girl had induced me to sneak into Sir Roderick Glossop's sleeping apartment and apply the darning needle to his hot-water bottle, and that was comparatively mild going for her. In a word, Roberta, daughter of the late Sir Cuthbert and Lady Wickham of Skeldings Hall, Herts, was pure dynamite and better kept at a distance by all those who aimed at leading the peaceful life. The prospect of being immured with her in the same house, with all the facilities a country house affords an enterprising girl for landing her nearest and dearest in the mulligatawny, made me singularly dubious about the shape of things to come.

And I was tottering under this blow when the old relative administered another, and it was a haymaker.

'And there's Aubrey Upjohn and his stepdaughter Phyllis Mills,' she said. 'That's the lot. What's the matter with you? Got asthma?'

I took her to be alluding to the sharp gasp which had escaped my lips, and I must confess that it had come out not unlike the last words of a dying duck. But I felt perfectly justified in gasping. A weaker man would have howled like a banshee. There floated into my mind something Kipper Herring had once said to me. 'You know, Bertie,' he had said, in philosophical mood, 'we have much to be thankful for in this life of ours, you and I. However rough the going, there is one sustaining thought to which we can hold. The storm clouds may lower and the horizon grow dark, we may get a nail in our shoe and be caught in the rain without an umbrella, we may come down to breakfast and find that someone else has taken the brown egg, but at least we have the consolation of knowing that we shall never see Aubrey Gawd-help-us Upjohn again. Always remember this in times of despondency,' he said, and I always had. And now here the bounder was, bobbing up right in my midst. Enough to make the stoutest-hearted go into his dying-duck routine.

'Aubrey Upjohn?' I quavered. 'You mean *my* Aubrey Upjohn?'

'That's the one. Soon after you made your escape from his chain gang he married Jane Mills, a friend of mine with a colossal amount of money. She died, leaving a daughter. I'm the daughter's godmother. Upjohn's retired now and going in for politics. The hot tip is that the boys in the back room are going to run him as the Conservative candidate in the Market Snodsbury division at the next by-election. What a thrill it'll be for you, meeting him again. Or does the prospect scare you?'

'Certainly not. We Woosters are intrepid. But what on earth did you invite him to Brinkley for?'

'I didn't. I only wanted Phyllis, but he came along, too.'

'You should have bunged him out.'

'I hadn't the heart to.'

'Weak, very weak.'

'Besides, I needed him in my business. He's going to present the prizes at Market Snodsbury Grammar School. We've been caught short as usual, and somebody has got to make a speech on ideals and the great world outside to those blasted boys, so he fits in nicely. I believe he's a very fine speaker. His only trouble is that he's stymied unless he has his speech with him and can read it. Calls it referring to his notes. Phyllis told me that. She types the stuff for him.'

'A thoroughly low trick,' I said severely. 'Even I, who have never soared above the Yeoman's Wedding Song at a village concert, wouldn't have the crust to face my public unless I'd taken the trouble to memorize the words, though actually with the Yeoman's Wedding Song it is possible to get by quite comfortably by keeping singing "Ding dong, ding dong, ding dong, I hurry along". In short . . .'

I would have spoken further, but at this point, after urging me to put a sock in it, and giving me a kindly word of warning not to step on any banana skins, she rang off.

2

I came away from the telephone on what practically amounted to leaden feet. Here, I was feeling, was a nice bit of box fruit. Bobbie Wickham, with her tendency to stir things up and with each new day to discover some new way of staggering civilization, would by herself have been bad enough. Add Aubrey Upjohn, and the mixture became too rich. I don't know if Kipper, when I rejoined him, noticed that my brow was sicklied o'er with the pale cast of thought, as I have heard Jeeves put it. Probably not, for he was tucking into toast and marmalade at the moment, but it was. As had happened so often in the past, I was conscious of an impending doom. Exactly what form this would take I was of course unable to say – it might be one thing or it might be another – but a voice seemed to whisper to me that somehow at some not distant date Bertram was slated to get it in the gizzard.

'That was Aunt Dahlia, Kipper,' I said.

'Bless her jolly old heart,' he responded. 'One of the very best, and you can quote me as saying so. I shall never forget those happy days at Brinkley, and shall be glad at any time that suits her to cadge another invitation. Is she up in London?'

'Till this afternoon.'

'We fill her to the brim with rich foods, of course?'

'No, she's got a lunch date. She's browsing with Sir Roderick Glossop, the loony-doctor. You don't know him, do you?'

'Only from hearing you speak of him. A tough egg, I gather.'

'One of the toughest.'

'He was the chap, wasn't he, who found the twenty-four cats in your bedroom?'

'Twenty-three,' I corrected. I like to get things right. 'They were not my cats. They had been deposited there by my cousins Claude and Eustace. But I found them difficult to explain. He's a rather bad listener. I hope I shan't find him at Brinkley, too.'

'Are you going to Brinkley?'

'Tomorrow afternoon.'

'You'll enjoy that.'

'Well, shall I? The point is a very moot one.'

'You're crazy. Think of Anatole. Those dinners of his! Is the name of the Peri who stood disconsolate at the gate of Eden familiar to you?'

'I've heard Jeeves mention her.'

'Well, that's how I feel when I remember Anatole's dinners. When I reflect that every night he's dishing them up and I'm not there, I come within a very little of breaking down. What gives you the idea that you won't enjoy yourself? Brinkley Court's an earthly Paradise.'

'In many respects, yes, but life there at the moment has its drawbacks. There's far too much of that where-every-prospect-pleases-and-only-man-is-vile stuff buzzing around for my taste. Who do you think is staying at the old dosshouse? Aubrey Upjohn.'

It was plain that I had shaken him. His eyes widened, and an astonished piece of toast fell from his grasp.

'Old Upjohn? You're kidding.'

'No, he's there. Himself, not a picture. And it seems only yesterday that you were buoying me up by telling me I'd never have to see him again. The storm clouds may lower, you said, if you recollect . . .'

'But how does he come to be at Brinkley?'

'Precisely what I asked the aged relative, and she had an explanation that seems to cover the facts. Apparently after we took our eye off him he married a friend of hers, one Jane Mills, and acquired a stepdaughter, Phyllis Mills, whose godmother Aunt Dahlia is. The ancestor invited the Mills girl to Brinkley, and Upjohn came along for the ride.'

'I see. I don't wonder you're trembling like a leaf.'

'Not like a leaf, exactly, but . . . yes, I think you might describe me as trembling. One remembers that fishy eye of his.'

'And the wide, bare upper lip. It won't be pleasant having to gaze at those across the dinner table. Still, you'll like Phyllis.'

'Do you know her?'

'We met out in Switzerland last Christmas. Slap her on the back, will you, and give her my regards. Nice girl, though goofy. She never told me she was related to Upjohn.'

'She would naturally keep a thing like that dark.'

'Yes, one sees that. Just as one would have tried to keep it dark if one had been mixed up in any way with Palmer the poisoner. What ghastly garbage that was he used to fling at us when we were serving our sentence at Malvern House. Remember the sausages on Sunday? And the boiled mutton with caper sauce?'

'And the margarine. Recalling this last, it's going to be a strain having to sit and watch him getting outside pounds of best country butter. Oh, Jeeves,' I said, as he shimmered in to clear the table, 'you never went to a preparatory school on the south coast of England, did you?'

'No, sir, I was privately educated.'

'Ah, then you wouldn't understand. Mr. Herring and I were discussing our former prep-school beak, Aubrey Upjohn, M.A. By the way, Kipper, Aunt Dahlia was telling me something about him which I never knew before and which ought to expose him to the odium of all thinking men. You remember those powerful end-of-term addresses he used to make to us? Well, he couldn't have made them if he hadn't had the stuff all typed out in his grasp, so that he could read it. Without his notes, as he calls them, he's a spent force. Revolting, that, Jeeves, don't you think?'

'Many orators are, I believe, similarly handicapped, sir.'

'Too tolerant, Jeeves, far too tolerant. You must guard against this lax outlook. However, the reason I mention Upjohn to you is that he has come back into my life, or will be so coming in about two ticks. He's staying at Brinkley, and I shall be going there tomorrow. That was Aunt Dahlia on the phone just now, and she demands my presence. Will you pack a few necessaries in a suitcase or so?'

'Very good, sir.'

'When are you leaving on your Herne Bay jaunt?'

'I was thinking of taking a train this morning, sir, but if you would prefer that I remained till tomorrow –'

'No, no, perfectly all right. Start as soon as you like. What's the joke?' I asked, as the door closed behind him, for I observed that Kipper was chuckling softly. Not an easy thing to do, of course, when your mouth's full of toast and marmalade, but he was doing it.

'I was thinking of Upjohn,' he said.

I was amazed. It seemed incredible to me that anyone who had done time at Malvern House, Bramley-on-Sea, could chuckle, softly or otherwise, when letting the mind dwell on that outstanding menace. It was like laughing lightly while contemplating one of those horrors from outer space which are so much with us at the moment on the motion-picture screen.

'I envy you, Bertie,' he went on, continuing to chuckle. 'You have a wonderful treat in store. You are going to be present at the breakfast table when Upjohn opens his copy of this week's *Thursday Review* and starts to skim through the pages devoted to comments on current literature. I should explain that among the books that recently arrived at the office was a slim volume from his pen dealing with the Preparatory School and giving it an enthusiastic build-up. The formative years which we spent there, he said, were the happiest of our life.'

'Gadzooks!'

'He little knew that his brain child would be given to one of the old lags of Malvern House to review. I'll tell you something, Bertie, that every young man ought to know. Never be a stinker, because if you are, though you may flourish for a time like a green bay tree, sooner or later retribution will overtake you. I need scarcely tell you that I ripped the stuffing out of the beastly little brochure. The thought of those sausages on Sunday filled me with the righteous fury of a Juvenal.'

'Of a who?'

'Nobody you know. Before your time. I seemed inspired. Normally, I suppose, a book like that would get me a line and a half in the Other Recent Publications column, but I gave it six hundred words of impassioned prose. How extraordinarily fortunate you are to be in a position to watch his face as he reads them.'

'How do you know he'll read them?'

'He's a subscriber. There was a letter from him on the correspondence page a week or two ago, in which he specifically stated that he had been one for years.'

'Did you sign the thing?'

'No. Ye Ed is not keen on underlings advertising their names.'

'And it was really hot stuff?'

'Red hot. So eye him closely at the breakfast table. Mark his reaction. I confidently expect the blush of shame and remorse to mantle his cheek.'

'The only catch is that I don't come down to breakfast when I'm at Brinkley. Still, I suppose I could make a special effort.'

'Do so. You will find it well worth while,' said Kipper and shortly afterwards popped off to resume the earning of the weekly envelope.

He had been gone about twenty minutes when Jeeves came in, bowler hat in hand, to say goodbye. A solemn moment, taxing our self-control to the utmost. However, we both kept the upper lip stiff, and after we had kidded back and forth for awhile he started to withdraw. He had reached the door when it suddenly occurred to me that he might have inside information about this Wilbert Cream of whom Aunt Dahlia had spoken. I have generally found that he knows everything about everyone.

'Oh, Jeeves,' I said. 'Half a jiffy.'

'Sir?'

'Something I want to ask you. It seems that among my fellow-guests at Brinkley will be a Mrs Homer Cream, wife of an American big butter and egg man, and her son Wilbert, commonly known as Willie, and the name Willie Cream seemed somehow to touch a chord. Rightly or wrongly I associate it with trips we have taken to New York, but in what connection I haven't the vaguest. Does it ring a bell with you?'

'Why yes, sir. References to the gentleman are frequent in the tabloid newspapers of New York, notably in the column conducted by Mr Walter Winchell. He is generally alluded to under the sobriquet of Broadway Willie.'

'Of course! It all comes back to me. He's what they call a playboy.'

'Precisely, sir. Notorious for his escapades.'

'Yes, I've got him placed now. He's the fellow who likes to let off stink bombs in night clubs, which rather falls under the head of carrying coals to Newcastle, and seldom cashes a cheque at his bank without producing a gat and saying, "This is a stick-up." '

'And . . . No, sir, I regret that it has for the moment escaped my memory.'

'What has?'

'Some other little something, sir, that I was told regarding Mr Cream. Should I recall it, I will communicate with you.'

'Yes, do. One wants the complete picture. Oh, gosh!'

'Sir?'

'Nothing, Jeeves. Just a thought has floated into my mind. All right, push off, or you'll miss your train. Good luck to your shrimping net.'

I'll tell you what the thought was that had floated. I have already indicated my qualms at the prospect of being cooped up in the same house with Bobbie Wickham and Aubrey Upjohn, for who could tell what the harvest might be? If in addition to these two heavies I was also to be cheek by jowl with a New York playboy apparently afflicted with bats in the belfry, it began to look as if this visit would prove too much for Bertram's frail strength, and for an instant I toyed with the idea of sending a telegram of regret and oiling out.

Then I remembered Anatole's cooking and was strong again. Nobody who has once tasted them would wantonly deprive himself of that wizard's smoked offerings. Whatever spiritual agonies I might be about to undergo at Brinkley Court, Market Snodsbury, near Droitwich, residence there would at least put me several *Suprêmes de fois gras au champagne* and *Mignonettes de Poulet Petit Duc* ahead of the game. Nevertheless, it would be paltering with the truth to say that I was at my ease as I thought of what lay before me in darkest Worcester-shire, and the hand that lit the after-breakfast gasper shook quite a bit.

At this moment of nervous tension the telephone suddenly gave tongue again, causing me to skip like the high hills, as if the Last Trump had sounded. I went to the instrument all of a twitter.

Some species of butler appeared to be at the other end.

'Mr. Wooster?'

'On the spot.'

'Good morning, sir. Her ladyship wishes to speak to you. Lady Wickham, sir. Here is Mr Wooster, m'lady.'

And Bobbie's mother came on the air.

I should have mentioned, by the way, that during the above exchange of ideas with the butler I had been aware of a distant sound of sobbing, like background music, and it now became apparent that it was from the larynx of the relict of the late Sir Cuthbert that it was proceeding. There was a short intermission before she got the vocal cords working, and while I was waiting for her to start the dialogue I found myself wrestling with two problems that presented themselves – the first, What on earth is this woman ringing me up for?, the second, Having got the number, why does she sob?

It was Problem A that puzzled me particularly, for ever since that hot-water-bottle episode my relations with this parent of Bobbie's had been on the strained side. It was, indeed, an open secret that my standing with her was practically that of a rat of the underworld. I had had this from Bobbie, whose impersonation of her mother dis-cussing me with sympathetic cronies had been exceptionally vivid, and I must confess that I wasn't altogether surprised. No hostess, I mean to say, extending her hospitality to a friend of her daughter's, likes to have the young visitor going about the place puncturing people's water-bottles and leaving at three in the morning without stopping to say good-bye. Yes, I could see her side of the thing all right, and I found it extraordinary that she should be seeking me out on the telephone in this fashion. Feeling as she did so allergic to Bertram, I wouldn't have thought she'd have phoned me with a ten-foot pole.

However, there beyond a question she was.

'Mr Wooster?'

'Oh, hullo, Lady Wickham.'

'Are you there?'

I put her straight on this point, and she took time out to sob again. She then spoke in a hoarse, throaty voice, like Tallulah Bankhead after swallowing a fish bone the wrong way.

'Is this awful news true?'

'Eh?'

'Oh dear, oh dear, oh dear!'

'I don't quite follow.'

'In this morning's *Times*.'

I'm pretty shrewd, and it seemed to me, reading between the lines, that there must have been something in the issue of *The Times* published that morning that for some reason had upset her, though why she should have chosen me to tell her troubles to was a mystery not easy to fathom. I was about to institute inquiries in the hope of spearing a solution, when in addition to sobbing she started laughing in a hyaena-esque manner, making it clear to my trained ear that she was having hysterics. And before I could speak there was a dull thud suggestive of some solid body falling to earth, I knew not where, and when the dialogue was resumed, I found that the butler had put himself on as an understudy.

'Mr Wooster?'

'Still here.'

'I regret to say that her ladyship has fainted.'

'It was she I heard going bump?'

'Precisely, sir. Thank you very much, sir. Good-bye.'

He replaced the receiver and went about his domestic duties, these no doubt including the loosening of the stricken woman's corsets and burning feathers under her nose, leaving me to chew on the situation without further bulletins from the front.

It seemed to me that the thing to do here was to get hold of *The Times* and see what it had to offer in the way of enlightenment. It's a paper I don't often look at, preferring for breakfast reading the *Mirror* and the *Mail*, but Jeeves takes it in and I have occasionally borrowed his copy with a view to having a shot at the crossword puzzle. It struck me as a possibility that he might have left today's issue in the kitchen, and so it proved. I came back with it, lowered myself into a chair, lit another cigarette and proceeded to cast an eye on its contents.

At a cursory glance what might be called swoon material appeared to be totally absent from its columns. The Duchess of something had been opening a bazaar at Wimbledon in aid of a deserving charity, there was an article on salmon fishing on the Wye, and a Cabinet Minister had made a speech about conditions in the cotton industry, but I could see nothing in these items to induce a loss of consciousness. Nor did it seem probable that a woman would have passed out cold on reading that Herbert Robinson (26) of Grove Road, Ponder's End, had been jugged for stealing a pair of green and yellow checked trousers. I turned to the cricket news. Had some friend of hers failed to score in one of yesterday's county matches owing to a doubtful l.b.w. decision?

It was just after I had run the eye down the Births and Marriages that I happened to look at the Engagements, and a moment later I was shooting out of my chair as if a spike had come through its cushioned seat and penetrated the fleshy parts.

'Jeeves!' I yelled, and then remembered that he had long since gone with the wind. A bitter thought, for if ever there was an occasion when his advice and counsel were of the essence, this occ. was that occ. The best I could do, tackling it solo, was to utter a hollow g. and bury the face in the hands. And though I seem to hear my public tut-tutting in disapproval of such neurotic behaviour, I think the verdict of history will be that the paragraph on which my gaze had rested was more than enough to excuse a spot of face-burying.

It ran as follows:

FORTHCOMING MARRIAGES

The engagement is announced between Bertram Wilberforce Wooster of Berkeley Mansions, W.1, and Roberta, daughter of the late Sir Cuthbert Wickham and Lady Wickham of Skeldings Hall, Herts.

3

Well, as I was saying, I had several times when under the influence of her oomph taken up with Roberta Wickham the idea of such a merger, but – and here is the point I would stress – I could have sworn that on each occasion she had declined to co-operate, and that in a manner which left no room for doubt regarding her views. I mean to say, when a girl, offered a good man's heart, laughs like a bursting paper bag and tells him not to be a silly ass, the good man is entitled, I think, to assume that the whole thing is off. In the light of this announcement in *The Times* I could only suppose that on one of these occasions, unnoticed by me possibly because my attention had wandered, she must have drooped her eyes and come through with a murmured 'Right ho.' Though when this could have happened, I hadn't the foggiest.

It was, accordingly, as you will readily imagine, a Bertram Wooster with dark circles under his eyes and a brain threatening to come apart at the seams who braked the sports model on the following afternoon at the front door of Brinkley Court – a Bertram, in a word, who was asking himself what the dickens all this was about. Non-plussed more or less sums it up. It seemed to me that my first move must be to get hold of my fiancée and see if she had anything to contribute in the way of clarifying the situation.

As is generally the case at country houses on a fine day, there seemed to be nobody around. In due season the gang would assemble for tea on the lawn, but at the moment I could spot no friendly native to tell me where I might find Bobbie. I proceeded, therefore, to roam hither and thither about the grounds and messuages in the hope of locating her, wishing that I had a couple of bloodhounds to aid me in my task, for the Travers demesne is a spacious one and there was a considerable amount of sunshine above, though none, I need scarcely mention, in my heart.

And I was tooling along a mossy path with the brow a bit wet with honest sweat, when there came to my ears the unmistakable sound of somebody reading poetry to someone, and the next moment I found myself confronting a mixed twosome who had dropped anchor beneath a shady tree in what is known as a leafy glade.

They had scarcely swum into my ken when the welkin started ringing like billy-o. This was due to the barking of a small dachshund, who now advanced on me with the apparent intention of seeing the colour of my insides. Milder counsels, however, prevailed, and on arriving at journey's end he merely rose like a rocket and licked me on the chin, seeming to convey the impression that in Bertram Wooster he had found just what the doctor ordered. I have noticed before in dogs this tendency to form a beautiful friendship immediately on getting within sniffing distance of me. Something to do, no doubt, with the characteristic Wooster smell, which for some reason seems to speak to their deeps. I tickled him behind the right ear and scratched the base of his spine for a moment or two: then, these civilities concluded, switched my attention to the poetry group.

It was the male half of the sketch who had been doing the reading, a willowy bird of about the tonnage and general aspect of David Niven with ginger hair and a small moustache. As he was unquestionably not Aubrey Upjohn, I assumed that this must be Willie Cream, and it surprised me a bit to find him dishing out verse. One would have expected a New York playboy, widely publicized as one of the lads, to confine himself to prose, and dirty prose, at that. But no doubt these playboys have their softer moments.

His companion was a well-stacked young featherweight, who could be none other than the Phyllis Mills of whom Kipper had spoken. Nice but goofy, Kipper had said, and a glance told me that he was right. One learns, as one goes through life, to spot goofiness in the other sex with an unerring eye, and this exhibit had a sort of mild, Soul's Awakening kind of expression which made it abundantly clear that, while not a super-goof like some of the female goofs I'd met, she was quite goofy enough to be going on with. Her whole aspect was that of a girl who at the drop of a hat would start talking baby talk.

This she now proceeded to do, asking me if I didn't think that Poppet, the dachshund, was a sweet little doggie. I assented rather austerely, for I prefer the shorter form more generally used, and she said she supposed I was Mrs Travers's nephew Bertie Wooster, which, as we knew, was substantially the case.

'I heard you were expected today. I'm Phyllis Mills,' she said, and I said I had divined as much and that Kipper had told me to slap her on the back and give her his best, and she said, 'Oh, Reggie Herring? He's a sweetie-pie, isn't he?' and I agreed that Kipper was one of the sweetie-pies and not the worst of them, and she said, 'Yes, he's a lambkin.'

This duologue had, of course, left Wilbert Cream a bit out of it, just painted on the backdrop as you might say, and for some moments, knitting his brow, plucking at his moustache, shuffling the feet and allowing the limbs to twitch, he had been giving abundant evidence that in his opinion three was a crowd and that what the leafy glade needed to make it all that a leafy glade should be was a complete absence of Woosters. Taking advantage of a lull in the conversation, he said:

'Are you looking for someone?'

I replied that I was looking for Bobbie Wickham.

'I'd go on looking, if I were you. Bound to find her somewhere.'

'Bobbie?' said Phyllis Mills. 'She's down at the lake, fishing.'

'Then what you do,' said Wilbert Cream, brightening, 'is follow this path, bend right, sharp left, bend right again and there you are. You can't miss. Start at once, is my advice.'

I must say I felt that, related as I was by ties of blood, in a manner of speaking, to this leafy glade, it was a bit thick being practically bounced from it by a mere visitor, but Aunt Dahlia had made it clear that the Cream family must not be thwarted or put upon in any way, so I did as he suggested, picking up the feet without anything in the nature of back chat. As I receded, I could hear in my rear the poetry breaking out again.

The lake at Brinkley calls itself a lake, but when all the returns are in it's really more a sort of young pond. Big enough to mess about on in a punt, though, and for the use of those wishing to punt a boathouse has been provided with a small pier or landing stage attached to it. On this, rod in hand, Bobbie was seated, and it was with me the work of an instant to race up and breathe down the back of her neck.

'Hey!' I said.

'Hey to you with knobs on,' she replied. 'Oh, hullo, Bertie. You here?'

'You never spoke a truer word. If you can spare me a moment of your valuable time, young Roberta –'

'Half a second, I think I've got a bite. No, false alarm. What were you saying?'

'I was saying –'

'Oh, by the way, I heard from Mother this morning.'

'I heard from her yesterday morning.'

'I was kind of expecting you would. You saw that thing in *The Times*?'

'With the naked eye.'

'Puzzled you for a moment, perhaps?'

'For several moments.'

'Well, I'll tell you all about that. The idea came to me in a flash.'

'You mean it was you who shoved that communiqué in the journal?'

'Of course.'

'Why?' I said, getting right down to it in my direct way.

I thought I had her there, but no.

'I was paving the way for Reggie.'

I passed a hand over my fevered brow.

'Something seems to have gone wrong with my usually keen hearing,' I said. 'It sounds just as if you were saying "I was paving the way for Reggie." '

'I was. I was making his path straight. Softening up Mother on his behalf.'

I passed another hand over my f.b.

'Now you seem to be saying "Softening up Mother on his behalf." '

'That's what I am saying. It's perfectly simple. I'll put it in words of one syllable for you. I love Reggie. Reggie loves me.'

'Reggie,' of course, is two syllables, but I let it go.

'Reggie who?'

'Reggie Herring.'

I was amazed.

'You mean old Kipper?'

'I wish you wouldn't call him Kipper.'

'I always have. Dash it,' I said with some warmth, 'if a fellow shows up at a private school on the south coast of England with a name like Herring, what else do you expect his playmates to call him? But how do you mean you love him and he loves you? You've never met him.'

'Of course I've met him. We were in the same hotel in Switzerland last Christmas. I taught him to ski,' she said, a dreamy look coming into her twin starlikes. 'I shall never forget the day I helped him unscramble himself after he had taken a toss on the beginners' slope. He had both legs wrapped round his neck. I think that is when love dawned. My heart melted as I sorted him out.'

'You didn't laugh?'

'Of course I didn't laugh. I was all sympathy and understanding.'

For the first time the thing began to seem plausible to me. Bobbie is a fun-loving girl, and the memory of her reaction when in the garden at Skeldings I had once stepped on the teeth of a rake and had the handle jump up and hit me on the tip of the nose was still laid away among my souvenirs. She had been convulsed with mirth.

If, then, she had refrained from guffawing when confronted with the spectacle of Reginald Herring with both legs wrapped round his neck, her emotions must have been very deeply involved.

'Well, all right,' I said. 'I accept your statement that you and Kipper are that way. But why, that being so, did you blazon it forth to the world, if blazoning forth is the expression I want, that you were engaged to me?'

'I told you. It was to soften Mother up.'

'Which sounded to me like delirium straight from the sick bed.'

'You don't get the subtle strategy?'

'Not by several parasangs.'

'Well, you know how you stand with Mother.'

'Our relations are a bit distant.'

'She shudders at the mention of your name. So I thought if she thought I was going to marry you and then found I wasn't, she'd be so thankful for the merciful escape I'd had that she'd be ready to accept anyone as a son-in-law, even someone like Reggie, who, though a wonder man, hasn't got his name in Debrett and isn't any too hot financially. Mother's idea of a mate for me has always been a well-to-do millionaire or a Duke with a large private income. Now do you follow?'

'Oh yes, I follow all right. You've been doing what Jeeves does, studying the psychology of the individual. But do you think it'll work?'

'Bound to. Let's take a parallel case. Suppose your Aunt Dahlia read in the paper one morning that you were going to be shot at sunrise.'

'I couldn't be. I'm never up so early.'

'But suppose she did? She'd be pretty worked up about it, wouldn't she?'

'Extremely, one imagines, for she loves me dearly. I'm not saying her manner toward me doesn't verge at times on the brusque. In childhood days she would occasionally clump me on the side of the head, and since I have grown to riper years she has more than once begged me to tie a brick around my neck and go and drown myself in the pond in the kitchen garden. Nevertheless, she loves her Bertram, and if she heard I was to be shot at sunrise, she would, as you say, be as sore as a gumboil. But why? What's that got to do with it?'

'Well, suppose she then found out it was all a mistake and it wasn't you but somebody else who was to face the firing squad. That would make her happy, wouldn't it?'

'One can picture her dancing all over the place on the tips of her toes.'

'Exactly. She'd be so all over you that nothing you did would be wrong in her eyes. Whatever you wanted to do would be all right with her. Go to it, she would say. And that's how Mother will feel when she learns that I'm not marrying you after all. She'll be so relieved.'

I agreed that the relief would, of course, be stupendous.

'But you'll be giving her the inside facts in a day or two?' I said, for I was anxious to have assurance on this point. A man with an Engagement notice in *The Times* hanging over him cannot but feel uneasy.

'Well, call it a week or two. No sense in rushing things.'

'You want me to sink in?'

'That's the idea.'

'And meanwhile what's the drill? Do I kiss you a good deal from time to time?'

'No, you don't.'

'Right ho. I just want to know where I stand.'

'An occasional passionate glance will be ample.'

'It shall be attended to. Well, I'm delighted about you and Kipper or, as you would prefer to say, Reggie. There's nobody I'd rather see you centre-aisle-ing with.'

'It's very sporting of you to take it like this.'

'Don't give it a thought.'

'I'm awfully fond of you, Bertie.'

'Me, too, of you.'

'But I can't marry everybody, can I?'

'I wouldn't even try. Well, now that we've got all that straight, I suppose I'd better be going and saying "Come aboard" to Aunt Dahlia.'

'What's the time?'

'Close on five.'

'I must run like a hare. I'm supposed to be presiding at the tea table.'

'You? Why you?'

'Your aunt's not here. She found a telegram when she got back yesterday saying that her son Bonzo was sick of a fever at his school, and dashed off to be with him. She asked me to deputy-hostess for her till her return, but I shan't be able to for the next few days. I've got to dash back to Mother. Ever since she saw that thing in *The Times*, she's been wiring me every hour on the hour to come home for a round table conference. What's a guffin?'

'I don't know. Why?'

'That's what she calls you in her latest 'gram. Quote. "Cannot understand how you can be contemplating marrying that guffin." Close quote. I suppose it's more or less the same as a gaby, which was how you figured in one of her earlier communications.'

'That sounds promising.'

'Yes, I think the thing's in the bag. After you, Reggie will come to her like rare and refreshing fruit. She'll lay down the red carpet for him.'

And with a brief 'Whoopee!' she shot off in the direction of the house at forty or so m.p.h. I followed more slowly, for she had given me much food for thought, and I was musing.

Strange, I was feeling, this strong pro-Kipper sentiment in the Wickham bosom. I mean, consider the facts. What with that *espièglerie* of hers, which was tops, she had been pretty extensively wooed in one quarter and another for years, and no business had resulted, so that it was generally assumed that only something extra special in the way of suitors would meet her specifications and that whoever eventually got his nose under the wire would be a king among men and pretty warm stuff. And she had gone and signed up with Kipper Herring.

Mind you, I'm not saying a word against old Kipper. The salt of the earth. But nobody could have called him a knock-out in the way of looks. Having gone in a lot for boxing from his earliest years, he had the cauliflower ear of which I had spoken to Aunt Dahlia and in addition to this a nose which some hidden hand had knocked slightly out of the straight. He would, in short, have been an unsafe entrant to have backed in a beauty contest, even if the only other competitors had been Boris Karloff, King Kong and Oofy Prosser of the Drones.

But then, of course, one had to remind oneself that looks aren't everything. A cauliflower ear can hide a heart of gold, as in Kipper's case it did, his being about as gold as they come. His brain, too, might have helped to do the trick. You can't hold down an editorial post on an important London weekly paper without being fairly well fixed with the little grey cells, and girls admire that sort of thing. And one had to remember that most of the bimbos to whom Roberta Wickham had been giving the bird through the years had been of the huntin', shootin' and fishin' type, fellows who had more or less shot their bolt after saying 'Eh, what?' and slapping their leg with a hunting crop. Kipper must have come as a nice change.

Still, the whole thing provided, as I say, food for thought, and I was in what is called a reverie as I made my way to the house, a reverie so profound that no turf accountant would have given any but the shortest odds against my sooner or later bumping into something. And this, to cut a long story s., I did. It might have been a tree, a bush or a rustic seat. In actual fact it turned out to be Aubrey Upjohn. I came on him round a corner and rammed him squarely before I could put the brakes on. I clutched him round the neck and he clutched me about the middle, and for some moments we tottered to and fro, linked in a close embrace. Then, the mists clearing from my eyes, I saw who it was that I had been treading the measure with.

Seeing him steadily and seeing him whole, as I have heard Jeeves put it, I was immediately struck by the change that had taken place in his appearance since those get-togethers in his study at Malvern House, Bramley-on-Sea, when with a sinking heart I had watched him reach for the whangee and start limbering up the shoulder muscles with a few trial swings. At that period of our acquaintance he had been an upstanding old gentleman about eight feet six in height with burning eyes, foam-flecked lips and flame coming out of both nostrils. He had now shrunk to a modest five foot seven or there-abouts, and I could have felled him with a single blow.

Not that I did, of course. But I regarded him without a trace of the old trepidation. It seemed incredible that I could ever have considered this human shrimp a danger to pedestrians and traffic.

I think this was partly due to the fact that at some point in the fifteen years since our last meeting he had grown a moustache. In the Malvern House epoch what had always struck a chill into the plastic mind had been his wide, bare upper lip, a most unpleasant spectacle to behold, especially when twitching. I wouldn't say the moustache softened his face, but being of the walrus or soup-strainer type it hid some of it, which was all to the good. The up-shot was that instead of quailing, as I had expected to do when we met, I was suave and debonair, possibly a little too much so.

'Oh, hullo, Upjohn!' I said. 'Yoo-hoo!'

'Who you?' he responded, making it sound like a reverse echo.

'Wooster is the name.'

'Oh, Wooster?' he said, as if he had been hoping it would be something else, and one could understand his feelings, of course. No doubt he, like me, had been buoying himself up for years with the thought that we should never meet again and that, whatever brickbats life might have in store for him, he had at least got Bertram out of his system. A nasty jar it must have been for the poor bloke having me suddenly pop up from a trap like this.

'Long time since we met,' I said.

'Yes,' he agreed in a hollow voice, and it was so plain that he was wishing it had been longer that conversation flagged, and there wasn't much in the way of feasts of reason and flows of the soul as we covered the hundred yards to the lawn where the tea table awaited us. I think I may have said 'Nice day, what?' and he may have grunted, but nothing more.

Only Bobbie was present when we arrived at the trough. Wilbert and Phyllis were presumably still in the leafy glade, and Mrs Cream, Bobbie said, worked in her room every afternoon on her new spine-freezer and seldom knocked off for a cuppa. We seated ourselves and had just started sipping, when the butler came out of the house bearing a bowl of fruit and hove to beside the table with it.

Well, when I say 'butler', I use the term loosely. He was dressed like a butler and he behaved like a butler, but in the deepest and truest sense of the word he was not a butler.

Reading from left to right, he was Sir Roderick Glossop.

4

At the Drones Club and other places I am accustomed to frequent you will often hear comment on Bertram Wooster's self-control or sang froid, as it's sometimes called, and it is generally agreed that this is considerable. In the eyes of many people, I suppose, I seem one of those men of chilled steel you read about, and I'm not saying I'm not. But it is possible to find a chink in my armour, and this can be done by suddenly springing eminent loony-doctors on me in the guise of butlers.

It was out of the q. that I could have been mistaken in supposing that it was Sir Roderick Glossop who, having delivered the fruit, was now ambling back to the house. There could not be two men with that vast bald head and those bushy eyebrows, and it would be deceiving the customers to say that I remained unshaken. The effect the apparition had on me was to make me start violently, and we all know what happens when you start violently while holding a full cup of tea. The contents of mine flew through the air and came to rest on the trousers of Aubrey Upjohn, M.A., moistening them to no little extent. Indeed, it would scarcely be distorting the facts to say that he was now not so much wearing trousers as wearing tea.

I could see the unfortunate man felt his position deeply, and I was surprised that he contented himself with a mere 'Ouch!' But I suppose these solid citizens have to learn to curb the tongue. Creates a bad impression, I mean, if they start blinding and stiffing as those more happily placed would be.

But words are not always needed. In the look he now shot at me I seemed to read a hundred unspoken expletives. It was the sort of look the bucko mate of a tramp steamer would have given an able-bodied seaman who for one reason or another had incurred his displeasure.

'I see you have not changed since you were with me at Malvern House,' he said in an extremely nasty voice, dabbing at the trousers with a handkerchief. 'Bungling Wooster we used to call him,' he went on, addressing his remarks to Bobbie and evidently trying to enlist her sympathy. 'He could not perform the simplest action such as holding a cup without spreading ruin and disaster on all sides. It was an axiom at Malvern House that if there was a chair in any room in which he happened to be, Wooster would trip over it. The child,' said Aubrey Upjohn, 'is the father of the man.'

'Frightfully sorry,' I said.

'Too late to be sorry now. A new pair of trousers ruined. It is doubtful if anything can remove the stain of tea from white flannel. Still, one must hope for the best.'

Whether I was right or wrong at this point in patting him on the shoulder and saying 'That's the spirit!' I find it difficult to decide. Wrong, probably, for it did not seem to soothe. He gave me another of those looks and strode off, smelling strongly of tea.

'Shall I tell you something, Bertie?' said Bobbie, following him with a thoughtful eye. 'That walking tour Upjohn was going to invite you to take with him is off. You will get no Christmas present from him this year, and don't expect him to come and tuck you up in bed tonight.'

I upset the milk jug with an imperious wave of the hand.

'Never mind about Upjohn and Christmas presents and walking tours. What is Pop Glossop doing here as the butler?'

'Ah! I thought you might be going to ask that. I was meaning to tell you some time.'

'Tell me now.'

'Well, it was his idea.'

I eyed her sternly. Bertram Wooster has no objection to listening to drivel, but it must not be pure babble from the padded cell, as this appeared to be.

'His idea?'

'Yes.'

'Are you asking me to believe that Sir Roderick Glossop got up one morning, gazed at himself in the mirror, thought he was looking a little pale and said to himself, "I need a change. I think I'll try being a butler for awhile"?'

'No, not that, but . . . I don't know where to begin.'

'Begin at the beginning. Come on now, young B. Wickham, smack into it,' I said, and took a piece of cake in a marked manner.

The austerity of my tone seemed to touch a nerve and kindle the fire that always slept in this vermilion-headed menace to the common weal, for she frowned a displeased frown and told me for heaven's sake to stop goggling like a dead halibut.

'I have every right to goggle like a dead halibut,' I said coldly, 'and I shall continue to do so as long as I see fit. I am under a considerable nervous s. As always seems to happen when you are mixed up in the doings, life has become one damn thing after another, and I think I am justified in demanding an explanation. I await your statement.'

'Well, let me marshal my thoughts.'

She did so, and after a brief intermission, during which I finished my piece of cake, proceeded.

'I'd better begin by telling you about Upjohn, because it all started through him. You see, he's egging Phyllis on to marry Wilbert Cream.'

'When you say egging –'

'I mean egging. And when a man like that eggs, something has to give, especially when the girl's a pill like Phyllis, who always does what Daddy tells her.'

'No will of her own?'

'Not a smidgeon. To give you an instance, a couple of days ago he took her to Birmingham to see the repertory company's performance of Chekhov's *Seagull*, because he thought it would be educational. I'd like to catch anyone trying to make me see Chekhov's *Seagull*, but Phyllis just bowed her head and said, "Yes, Daddy." Didn't even attempt to put up a fight. That'll show you how much of a will of her own she's got.'

It did indeed. Her story impressed me profoundly. I knew Chekhov's *Seagull*. My Aunt Agatha had once made me take her son Thos to a performance of it at the Old Vic, and what with the strain of trying to follow the cock-eyed goings-on of characters called Zarietchnaya and Medvienko and having to be constantly on the alert to prevent Thos making a sneak for the great open spaces, my suffering had been intense. I needed no further evidence to tell me that Phyllis Mills was a girl whose motto would always be 'Daddy knows best.' Wilbert had only got to propose and she would sign on the dotted line because Upjohn wished it.

'Your aunt's worried sick about it.'

'She doesn't approve?'

'Of course she doesn't approve. You must have heard of Willie Cream, going over to New York so much.'

'Why yes, news of his escapades has reached me. He's a playboy.'

'Your aunt thinks he's a screwball.'

'Many playboys are, I believe. Well, that being so, one can understand why she doesn't want those wedding bells to ring out. But,' I said, putting my finger on the *res* in my unerring way, 'that doesn't explain where Pop Glossop comes in.'

'Yes, it does. She got him here to observe Wilbert.'

I found myself fogged.

'Cock an eye at him, you mean? Drink him in, as it were? What good's that going to do?'

She snorted impatiently.

'Observe in the technical sense. You know how these brain specialists work. They watch the subject closely. They engage him in conversation. They apply subtle tests. And sooner or later –'

'I begin to see. Sooner or later he lets fall an incautious word to the effect that he thinks he's a poached egg, and then they've got him where they want him.'

'Well, he does something which tips them off. Your aunt was moaning to me about the situation, and I suddenly had this inspiration of bringing Glossop here. You know how I get sudden inspirations.'

'I do. That hot-water-bottle episode.'

'Yes, that was one of them.'

'Ha!'

'What did you say?'

'Just "Ha!" '

'Why "Ha!"?'

'Because when I think of that night of terror, I feel like saying "Ha!" '

She seemed to see the justice of this. Pausing merely to eat a cucumber sandwich, she proceeded.

'So I said to your aunt, "I'll tell you what to do," I said. "Get Glossop here," I said, "and have him observe Wilbert Cream. Then you'll be in a position to go to Upjohn and pull the rug from under him." '

Again I was not abreast. There had been, as far as I could recollect, no mention of any rug.

'How do you mean?'

'Well, isn't it obvious? "Rope in old Glossop," I said, "and let him observe. Then you'll be in a position," I said, "to go to Upjohn and tell him that Sir Roderick Glossop, the greatest alienist in England, is convinced that Wilbert Cream is round the bend and to ask him if he proposes to marry his stepdaughter to a man who at any moment may be marched off and added to the membership list of Colney Hatch." Even Upjohn would shrink from doing a thing like that. Or don't you think so?'

I weighed this.

'Yes,' I said, 'I should imagine you were right. Quite possibly Upjohn has human feelings, though I never noticed them when I was *in statu pupillari*, as I believe the expression is. One sees now why Glossop is at Brinkley Court. What one doesn't see is why one finds him buttling.'

'I told you that was his idea. He thought he was such a celebrated figure that it would arouse Mrs Cream's suspicions if he came here under his own name.'

'I see what you mean. She would catch him observing Wilbert and wonder why –'

'– and eventually put two and two together –'

'– and start Hey-what's-the-big-idea-ing.'

'Exactly. No mother likes to find that her hostess has got a brain specialist down to observe the son who is the apple of her eye. It hurts her feelings.'

'Whereas, if she catches the butler observing him, she merely says to herself, "Ah, an observant butler." Very sensible. With this deal Uncle Tom's got on with Homer Cream, it would be fatal to risk giving her the pip in any way. She would kick to Homer, and Homer would draw himself up and say "After what has occurred, Travers, I would prefer to break off the negotiations," and Uncle Tom would lose a packet. What is this deal they've got on, by the way? Did Aunt Dahlia tell you?'

'Yes, but it didn't penetrate. It's something to do with some land your uncle owns somewhere, and Mr Cream is thinking of buying it and putting up hotels and things. It doesn't matter, anyway. The fundamental thing, the thing to glue the eye on, is that the Cream contingent have to be kept sweetened at any cost. So not a word to a soul.'

'Quite. Bertram Wooster is not a babbler. No spiller of the beans he. But why are you so certain that Wilbert Cream is loopy? He doesn't look loopy to me.'

'Have you met him?'

'Just for a moment. He was in a leafy glade, reading poetry to the Mills girl.'

She took this big.

'Reading *poetry*? To *Phyllis*?'

'That's right. I thought it odd that a chap like him should be doing such a thing. Limericks, yes. If he had been reciting limericks to her, I could have understood it. But this was stuff from one of those books they bind in limp purple leather and sell at Christmas. I wouldn't care to swear to it, but it sounded to me extremely like Omar Khayyam.'

She continued to take it big.

'Break it up, Bertie, break it up! There's not a moment to be lost. You must go and break it up immediately.'

'Who, me? Why me?'

'That's what you're here for. Didn't your aunt tell you? She wants you to follow Wilbert Cream and Phyllis about everywhere and see that he doesn't get a chance of proposing.'

'You mean that I'm to be a sort of private eye or shamus, tailing them up? I don't like it,' I said dubiously.

'You don't have to like it,' said Bobbie. 'You just do it.'

5

Wax in the hands of the other sex, as the expression is, I went and broke it up as directed, but not blithely. It is never pleasant for a man of sensibility to find himself regarded as a buttinski and a trailing arbutus, and it was thus, I could see at a g., that Wilbert Cream was pencilling me in. At the moment of my arrival he had suspended the poetry reading and had taken Phyllis's hand in his, evidently saying or about to say something of an intimate and tender nature. Hearing my 'What ho', he turned, hurriedly released the fin and directed at me a look very similar to the one I had recently received from Aubrey Upjohn. He muttered something under his breath about someone, whose name I did not catch, apparently having been paid to haunt the place.

'Oh, it's you again,' he said.

Well, it was, of course. No argument about that.

'Kind of at a loose end?' he said. 'Why don't you settle down somewhere with a good book?'

I explained that I had just popped in to tell them that tea was now being served on the main lawn, and Phyllis squeaked a bit, as if agitated.

'Oh, dear!' she said. 'I must run. Daddy doesn't like me to be late for tea. He says it's not respectful to my elders.'

I could see trembling on Wilbert Cream's lips a suggestion as to where Daddy could stick himself and his views on respect to elders, but with a powerful effort he held it back.

'I shall take Poppet for a walk,' he said, chirruping to the dachshund, who was sniffing at my legs, filling his lungs with the delicious Wooster bouquet.

'No tea?' I said.

'No.'

'There are muffins.'

'Tchah!' he ejaculated, if that's the word, and strode off, followed by the low-slung dog, and it was borne in upon me that here was another source from which I could expect no present at Yuletide. His whole demeanour made it plain that I had not added to my little circle of friends. Though going like a breeze with dachshunds, I had failed signally to click with Wilbert Cream.

When Phyllis and I reached the lawn, only Bobbie was at the tea table, and this surprised us both.

'Where's Daddy?' Phyllis asked.

'He suddenly decided to go to London,' said Bobbie.

'To London?'

'That's what he said.'

'Why?'

'He didn't tell me.'

'I must go and see him,' said Phyllis, and buzzed off.

Bobbie seemed to be musing.

'Do you know what I think, Bertie?'

'What?'

'Well, when Upjohn came out just now, he was all of a doodah, and he had this week's *Thursday Review* in his hand. Came by the afternoon post, I suppose. I think he had been reading Reggie's comment on his book.'

This seemed plausible. I number several authors among my aquaintance – the name of Boko Fittleworth is one that springs to the mind – and they invariably become all of a doodah when they read a stinker in the press about their latest effort.

'Oh, you know about that thing Kipper wrote?'

'Yes, he showed it to me one day when we were having lunch together.'

'Very mordant, I gathered from what he told me. But I don't see why that should make Upjohn bound up to London.'

'I suppose he wants to ask the editor who wrote the thing, so that he can horsewhip him on the steps of his club. But of course they won't tell him, and it wasn't signed so . . . Oh, hullo, Mrs Cream.'

The woman she was addressing was tall and thin with a hawk-like face that reminded me of Sherlock Holmes. She had an ink spot on her nose, the result of working on her novel of suspense. It is virtually impossible to write a novel of suspense without getting a certain amount of ink on the beezer. Ask Agatha Christie or anyone.

'I finished my chapter a moment ago, so I thought I would stop for a cup of tea,' said this literateuse. 'No good overdoing it.'

'No. Quit when you're ahead of the game, that's the idea. This is Mrs Travers's nephew Bertie Wooster,' said Bobbie with what I considered a far too apologetic note in her voice. If Roberta Wickham has one fault more pronounced than another, it is that she is inclined

to introduce me to people as if I were something she would much
have preferred to hush up. 'Bertie loves your books,' she added, quite
unnecessarily, and the Cream started like a Boy Scout at the sound
of a bugle.

'Oh, do you?'

'Never happier than when curled up with one of them,' I said,
trusting that she wouldn't ask me which one of them I liked best.

'When I told him you were here, he was overcome.'

'Well, that certainly is great. Always glad to meet the fans. Which
of my books do you like best?'

And I had got as far as 'Er' and was wondering, though not with
much hope, if 'All of them' would meet the case, when Pop Glossop
joined us with a telegram for Bobbie on a salver. From her mother,
I presumed, calling me some name which she had forgotten to insert
in previous communications. Or, of course, possibly expressing once
more her conviction that I was a guffin, which, I thought, having had
time to ponder over it, would be something in the nature of a
bohunkus or a hammerhead.

'Oh, thank you, Swordfish,' said Bobbie, taking the 'gram.

It was fortunate that I was not holding a tea cup as she spoke, for
hearing Sir Roderick thus addressed I gave another of my sudden
starts and, had I had such a cup in my hand, must have strewn its
contents hither and thither like a sower going forth sowing. As it was,
I merely sent a cucumber sandwich flying through the air.

'Oh, sorry,' I said, for it had missed the Cream by a hair's breadth.

I could have relied on Bobbie to shove her oar in. The girl had no
notion of passing a thing off.

'Excuse it, please,' she said. 'I ought to have warned you. Bertie is
training for the Jerk The Cucumber Sandwich event at the next
Olympic Games. He has to be practising all the time.'

On Ma Cream's brow there was a thoughtful wrinkle, as though she
felt unable to accept this explanation of what had occurred. But her
next words showed that it was not on my activities that her mind was
dwelling but on the recent Swordfish. Having followed him with a
keen glance as he faded from view, she said:

'This butler of Mrs Travers'. Do you know where she got him,
Miss Wickham?'

'At the usual pet shop, I think.'

'Had he references?'

'Oh, yes. He was with Sir Roderick Glossop, the brain specialist,
for years. I remember Mrs Travers saying Sir Roderick gave him a
supercolossal reference. She was greatly impressed.'

Ma Cream sniffed.

'References can be forged.'

'Good gracious! Why do you say that?'

'Because I am not at all easy in my mind about this man. He has a criminal face.'

'Well, you might say that about Bertie.'

'I feel that Mrs Travers should be warned. In my *Blackness at Night* the butler turned out to be one of a gang of crooks, planted in the house to make it easy for them to break in. The inside stand, it's called. I strongly suspect that this is why this Swordfish is here, though of course it is quite possible that he is working on his own. One thing I am sure of, and that is that he is not a genuine butler.'

'What makes you think that?' I asked, handkerchiefing my upper slopes, which had become considerably bedewed. I didn't like this line of talk at all. Let the Cream get firmly in her nut the idea that Sir Roderick Glossop was not the butler, the whole butler and nothing but the butler, and disaster, as I saw it, loomed. She would probe and investigate, and before you could say 'What ho' would be in full possession of the facts. In which event, bim would go Uncle Tom's chance of scooping in a bit of easy money. And ever since I've known him failure to get his hooks on any stray cash that's floating around has always put him out of touch with the blue bird. It isn't that he's mercenary. It's just that he loves the stuff.

Her manner suggested that she was glad I had asked her that.

'I'll tell you what makes me think it. He betrays his amateurishness in a hundred ways. This very morning I found him having a long conversation with Wilbert. A real butler would never do that. He would feel it was a liberty.'

I contested this statement.

'Now there,' I said, 'I take issue with you, if taking issue means what I think it means. Many of my happiest hours have been passed chatting with butlers, and it has nearly always happened that it was they who made the first advances. They seek me out and tell me about their rheumatism. Swordfish looks all right to me.'

'You are not a student of criminology, as I am. I have the trained eye, and my judgment is never wrong. That man is here for no good.'

I could see that all this was making Bobbie chafe, but her better self prevailed and she checked the heated retort. She is very fond of T. Portarlington Travers, who, she tells me, is the living image of a wire-haired terrier now residing with the morning stars but at one time very dear to her, and she remembered that for his sake the Cream had to be deferred to and handled with gloves. When she spoke, it was with the mildness of a cushat dove addressing another cushat dove from whom it was hoping to borrow money.

'But don't you think, Mrs. Cream, that it may be just your imagination? You have such a wonderful imagination. Bertie was saying only the other day that he didn't know how you did it. Write all those frightfully imaginative books, I mean. Weren't you, Bertie?'

'My very words.'

'And if you have an imagination, you can't help imagining. Can you, Bertie?'

'Dashed difficult.'

Her honeyed words were wasted. The Cream continued to dig her toes in like Balaam's ass, of whom you have doubtless heard.

'I'm not imagining that that butler is up to something fishy,' she said tartly. 'And I should have thought it was pretty obvious what that something was. You seem to have forgotten that Mr. Travers has one of the finest collections of old silver in England.'

This was correct. Owing possibly to some flaw in his mental make-up, Uncle Tom has been collecting old silver since I was so high, and I suppose the contents of the room on the ground floor where he parks the stuff are worth a princely sum. I knew all about that collection of his, not only because I had had to listen to him for hours on the subject of sconces, foliation, ribbon wreaths in high relief and gadroon borders, but because I had what you might call a personal interest in it, once having stolen an eighteenth-century cow-creamer for him. (Long story. No time to go into it now. You will find it elsewhere in the archives.)

'Mrs Travers was showing it to Willie the other day, and he was thrilled. Willie collects old silver himself.'

With each hour that passed I was finding it more and more difficult to get a toe-hold on the character of W. Cream. An in-and-out performer, if ever there was one. First all that poetry, I mean, and now this. I had always supposed that playboys didn't give a hoot for anything except blondes and cold bottles. It just showed once again that half the world doesn't know how the other three-quarters lives.

'He says there are any number of things in Mr Travers's collection that he would give his back teeth for. There was an eighteenth-century cow-creamer he particularly coveted. So keep your eye on that butler. I'm certainly going to keep mine. Well,' said the Cream, rising, 'I must be getting back to my work. I always like to rough out a new chapter before finishing for the day.'

She legged it, and for a moment silence reigned. Then Bobbie said, 'Phew!' and I agreed that 'Phew!' was the *mot juste*.

'We'd better get Glossop out of here quick,' I said.

'How can we? It's up to your aunt to do that, and she's away.'

'Then I'm jolly well going to get out myself. There's too much impending doom buzzing around these parts for my taste. Brinkley Court, once a peaceful country house, has become like something sinister out of Edgar Allan Poe, and it makes my feet cold. I'm leaving.'

'You can't till your aunt gets back. There has to be some sort of host or hostess here, and I simply must go home tomorrow and see Mother. You'll have to clench your teeth and stick it.'

'And the severe mental strain to which I am being subjected doesn't matter, I suppose?'

'Not a bit. Does you good. Keeps your pores open.'

I should probably have said something pretty cutting in reply to this, if I could have thought of anything, but as I couldn't I didn't.

'What's Aunt Dahlia's address?' I said.

'Royal Hotel, Eastbourne. Why?'

'Because,' I said, taking another cucumber sandwich, 'I'm going to wire her to ring me up tomorrow without fail, so that I can apprise her of what's going on in this joint.'

6

I forget how the subject arose, but I remember Jeeves once saying that sleep knits up the ravelled sleave of care. Balm of hurt minds, he described it as. The idea being, I took it, that if things are getting sticky, they tend to seem less glutinous after you've had your eight hours.

Apple sauce, in my opinion. It seldom pans out that way with me, and it didn't now. I had retired to rest taking a dim view of the current situation at Brinkley Court and opening my eyes to a new day, as the expression is, I found myself taking an even dimmer. Who knew, I asked myself as I practically pushed the breakfast egg away untasted, what Ma Cream might not at any moment uncover? And who could say how soon, if I continued to be always at his side, Wilbert Cream would get it up his nose and start attacking me with tooth and claw? Already his manner was that of a man whom the society of Bertram Wooster had fed to the tonsils, and one more sight of the latter at his elbow might quite easily make him decide to take prompt steps through the proper channels.

Musing along these lines, I had little appetite for lunch, though Anatole had extended himself to the utmost. I winced every time the Cream shot a sharp, suspicious look at Pop Glossop as he messed about at the sideboard, and the long, loving looks her son Wilbert kept directing at Phyllis Mills chilled me to the marrow. At the conclusion of the meal he would, I presumed, invite the girl to accompany him again to that leafy glade, and it was idle to suppose that there would not be pique on his part, or even chagrin, when I came along, too.

Fortunately, as we rose from the table, Phyllis said she was going to her room to finish typing Daddy's speech, and my mind was eased for the nonce. Even a New York playboy, accustomed from his earliest years to pursue blondes like a bloodhound, would hardly follow her there and press his suit.

Seeming himself to recognize that there was nothing constructive to be done in that direction for the moment, he said in a brooding voice that he would take Poppet for a walk. This, apparently, was his invariable method of healing the stings of disappointment, and an excellent thing of course from the point of view of a dog who liked getting around and seeing the sights. They headed for the horizon and passed out of view; the hound gambolling, he not gambolling but swishing his stick a good deal in an overwrought sort of manner, and I, feeling that this was a thing that ought to be done, selected one of Ma Cream's books from Aunt Dahlia's shelves and took it out to read in a deck chair on the lawn. And I should no doubt have enjoyed it enormously, for the Cream unquestionably wielded a gifted pen, had not the warmth of the day caused me to drop off into a gentle sleep in the middle of Chapter Two.

Waking from this some little time later and running an eye over myself to see if the ravelled sleave of care had been knitted up – which it hadn't – I was told that I was wanted on the telephone. I hastened to the instrument, and Aunt Dahlia's voice came thundering over the wire.

'Bertie?'

'Bertram it is.'

'Why the devil have you been such a time? I've been hanging on to this damned receiver a long hour by Shrewsbury clock.'

'Sorry. I came on winged feet, but I was out on the lawn when you broke loose.'

'Sleeping off your lunch, I suppose?'

'My eyes may have closed for a moment.'

'Always eating, that's you.'

'It is customary, I believe, to take a little nourishment at about this hour,' I said rather stiffly. 'How's Bonzo?'

'Getting along.'

'What was it?'

'German measles, but he's out of danger. Well, what's all the excitement about? Why did you want me to phone you? Just so that you could hear Auntie's voice?'

'I am always glad to hear Auntie's voice, but I had a deeper and graver reason. I thought you ought to know about all these lurking perils in the home.'

'What lurking perils?'

'Ma Cream for one. She's hotting up. She entertains suspicions.'

'What of?'

'Pop Glossop. She doesn't like his face.'

'Well, hers is nothing to write home about.'

'She thinks he isn't a real butler.'

From the fact that my ear-drum nearly split in half I deduced that she had laughed a jovial laugh.

'Let her think.'

'You aren't perturbed?'

'Not a bit. She can't do anything about it. Anyway, Glossop ought to be leaving in about a week. He told me he didn't think it would take longer than that to make up his mind about Wilbert. Adela Cream doesn't worry me.'

'Well, if you say so, but I should have thought she was a menace.'

'She doesn't seem so to me. Anything else on your mind?'

'Yes, this Wilbert-Cream-Phyllis-Mills thing.'

'Ah, now you're talking. That's important. Did young Bobbie Wickham tell you that you'd got to stick to Wilbert closer than –'

'A brother?'

'I was going to say porous plaster, but have it your own way. She explained the position of affairs?'

'She did, and it's precisely that that I want to thresh out with you.'

'Do what out?'

'Thresh.'

'All right, start threshing.'

Having given the situation the best of the Wooster brain for some considerable time, I had the *res* all clear in my mind. I proceeded to decant it.

'As we go through this life, my dear old ancestor,' I said, 'we should always strive to see the other fellow's side of a thing, the other fellow in the case under advisement being Wilbert Cream. Has it occurred to you to put yourself in Wilbert Cream's place and ask yourself how he's going to feel, being followed around all the time? It isn't as if he was Mary.'

'What did you say?'

'I said it wasn't as if he was Mary. Mary, as I remember, enjoyed the experience of being tailed up.'

'Bertie, you're tight.'

'Nothing of the kind.'

'Say "British constitution." '

I did so.

'And now "She sells sea shells by the sea shore." '

I reeled it off in a bell-like voice.

'Well, you seem all right,' she said grudgingly. 'How do you mean he isn't Mary? Mary who?'

'I don't think she had a surname, had she? I was alluding to the child who had a little lamb with fleece as white as snow, and everywhere that Mary went the lamb was sure to go. Now I'm not saying that I have fleece as white as snow, but I *am* going everywhere that Wilbert Cream goes, and one speculates with some interest as to what the upshot will be. He resents my constant presence.'

'Has he said so?'

'Not yet. But he gives me nasty looks.'

'That's all right. He can't intimidate me.'

I saw that she was missing the gist.

'Yes, but don't you see the peril that looms?'

'I thought you said it lurked.'

'*And* looms. What I'm driving at is that if I persist in this porous plastering, a time must inevitably come when, feeling that actions speak louder than words, he will haul off and bop me one. In which event, I shall have no alternative but to haul off and bop *him* one. The Woosters have their pride. And when I bop them, they stay bopped till nightfall.'

She bayed like a foghorn, showing that she was deeply stirred.

'You'll do nothing of the sort, unless you want to have an aunt's curse delivered on your doorstep by special messenger. Don't you dare to start mixing it with that man, or I'll tattoo my initials on your chest with a meat axe. Turn the other cheek, you poor fish. If my nephew socked her son, Adela Cream would never forgive me. She would go running to her husband –'

'– and Uncle Tom's deal would be dished. That's the very point I'm trying to make. If Wilbert Cream is bust by anyone, it must be by somebody having no connection with the Travers family. You must at once engage a substitute for Bertram.'

'Are you suggesting that I hire a private detective?'

' "Eye" is the more usual term. No, not that, but you must invite Kipper Herring down here. Kipper is the man you want. He will spring to the task of dogging Wilbert's footsteps, and if Wilbert bops him and he bops Wilbert, it won't matter, he being outside talent. Not that I anticipate that Wilbert will dream of doing so, for Kipper's mere appearance commands respect. The muscles of his brawny arms are strong as iron bands, and he has a cauliflower ear.'

There was a silence of some moments, and it was not difficult to divine that she was passing my words under review, this way and that dividing the swift mind, as I have heard Jeeves put it. When she spoke, it was in quite an awed voice.

'Do you know, Bertie, there are times – rare, yes, but they do happen – when your intelligence is almost human. You've hit it. I never thought of young Herring. Do you think he could come?'

'He was saying to me only the day before yesterday that his dearest wish was to cadge an invitation. Anatole's cooking is green in his memory.'

'Then send him a wire. You can telephone it to the post office. Sign it with my name.'

'Right ho.'

'Tell him to drop everything and come running.'

She rang off, and I was about to draft the communication, when, as so often happens to one on relaxing from a great strain, I became conscious of an imperious desire for a little something quick. Oh, for a beaker full of the warm south, as Jeeves would have said. I pressed the bell, accordingly, and sank into a chair, and presently the door opened and a circular object with a bald head and bushy eyebrows manifested itself, giving me quite a start. I had forgotten that ringing bells at Brinkley Court under prevailing conditions must inevitably produce Sir Roderick Glossop.

It's always a bit difficult to open the conversation with a blend of brain specialist and butler, especially if your relations with him in the past have not been too chummy, and I found myself rather at a loss to know how to set the ball rolling. I yearned for that drink as the hart desireth the water-brook, but if you ask a butler to bring you a whisky-and-soda and he happens to be a brain specialist, too, he's quite apt to draw himself up and wither you with a glance. All depends on which side of him is uppermost at the moment. It was a relief when I saw that he was smiling a kindly smile and evidently welcoming this opportunity of having a quiet chat with Bertram. So long as we kept off the subject of hot-water bottles, it looked as if all would be well.

'Good afternoon, Mr. Wooster. I had been hoping for a word with you in private. But perhaps Miss Wickham has already explained the circumstances? She has? Then that clears the air, and there is no danger of you incautiously revealing my identity. She impressed it upon you that Mrs Cream must have no inkling of why I am here?'

'Oh, rather. Secrecy and silence, what? If she knew you were observing her son with a view to finding out if he was foggy between the ears, there would be umbrage on her part, or even dudgeon.'

'Exactly.'

'And how's it coming along?'

'I beg your pardon?'

'The observing. Have you spotted any dippiness in the subject?'

'If by that expression you mean have I formed any definite views on Wilbert Cream's sanity, the answer is no. It is most unusual for me not to be able to make up my mind after even a single talk with the person I am observing, but in young Cream's case I remain uncertain. On the one hand, we have his record.'

'The stink bombs?'

'Exactly.'

'And the cheque-cashing with levelled gat?'

'Precisely. And a number of other things which one would say pointed to a mental unbalance. Unquestionably Wilbert Cream is eccentric.'

'But you feel the time has not yet come to measure him for the strait waistcoat?'

'I would certainly wish to observe further.'

'Jeeves told me there was something about Wilbert Cream that someone had told him when we were in New York. That might be significant.'

'Quite possibly. What was it?'

'He couldn't remember.'

'Too bad. Well, to return to what I was saying, the young man's record appears to indicate some deep-seated neurosis, if not actual schizophrenia, but against this must be set the fact that he gives no sign of this in his conversation. I was having quite a long talk with him yesterday morning, and found him most intelligent. He is interested in old silver, and spoke with a great deal of enthusiasm of an eighteenth-century cow-creamer in your uncle's collection.'

'He didn't say he *was* an eighteenth-century cow-creamer?'

'Certainly not.'

'Probably just wearing the mask.'

'I beg your pardon?'

'I mean crouching for the spring, as it were. Lulling you into security. Bound to break out sooner or later in some direction or other. Very cunning, these fellows with deep-seated neuroses.'

He shook his head reprovingly.

'We must not judge hastily, Mr. Wooster. We must keep an open mind. Nothing is ever gained by not pausing to weigh the evidence. You may remember that at one time I reached a hasty judgment regarding your sanity. Those twenty-three cats in your bedroom.'

I flushed hotly. The incident had taken place several years previously, and it would have been in better taste, I considered, to have let the dead past bury its dead.

'That was explained fully.'

'Exactly. I was shown to be in error. And that is why I say I must not form an opinion prematurely in the case of Wilbert Cream. I must wait for further evidence.'

'And weigh it?'

'And, as you say, weigh it. But you rang, Mr. Wooster. Is there anything I can do for you?'

'Well, as a matter of fact, I wanted a whisky-and-soda, but I hate to trouble you.'

'My dear Mr. Wooster, you forget that I am, if only temporarily, a butler and, I hope, a conscientious one. I will bring it immediately.'

I was wondering, as he melted away, if I ought to tell him that Mrs. Cream, too, was doing a bit of evidence-weighing, and about him, but decided on the whole better not. No sense in disturbing his peace of mind. It seemed to me that having to answer to the name of Swordfish was enough for him to have to cope with for the time being. Given too much to think about, he would fret and get pale.

When he returned, he brought with him not only the beaker full of the warm south, on which I flung myself gratefully, but a letter which he said had just come for me by the afternoon post. Having slaked the thirst, I glanced at the envelope and saw that it was from Jeeves. I opened it without much of a thrill, expecting that he would merely be informing me that he had reached his destination safely and expressing a hope that this would find me in the pink as it left him at present. In short, the usual guff.

It wasn't the usual guff by a mile and a quarter. One glance at its contents and I was Gosh-ing sharply, causing Pop Glossop to regard me with a concerned eye.

'No bad news, I trust, Mr. Wooster?'

'It depends what you call bad news. It's front page stuff, all right. This is from Jeeves, my man, now shrimping at Herne Bay, and it casts a blinding light on the private life of Wilbert Cream.'

'Indeed? This is most interesting.'

'I must begin by saying that when Jeeves was leaving for his annual vacation, the subject of W. Cream came up in the home, Aunt Dahlia having told me he was one of the inmates here, and we discussed him at some length. I said this, if you see what I mean, and Jeeves said that, if you follow me. Well, just before Jeeves pushed off, he let fall that significant remark I mentioned just now, the one about having heard something about Wilbert and having forgotten it. If it came back to him, he said, he would communicate with me. And he has, by Jove! Do you know what he says in this missive? Give you three guesses.'

'Surely this is hardly the time for guessing games?'

'Perhaps you're right, though they're great fun, don't you think? Well, he says that Wilbert Cream is a . . . what's the word?' I referred to the letter. 'A kleptomaniac,' I said. 'Which means, if the term is not familiar to you, a chap who flits hither and thither pinching everything he can lay his hands on.'

'Good gracious!'

'You might even go so far as "Lor' lumme!" '

'I never suspected this.'

'I told you he was wearing a mask. I suppose they took him abroad to get him away from it all.'

'No doubt.'

'Overlooking the fact that there are just as many things to pinch in England as in America. Does any thought occur to you?'

'It most certainly does. I am thinking of your uncle's collection of old silver.'

'Me, too.'

'It presents a grave temptation to the unhappy young man.'

'I don't know that I'd call him unhappy. He probably thoroughly enjoys lifting the stuff.'

'We must go to the collection room immediately. There may be something missing.'

'Everything except the floor and ceiling, I expect. He would have had difficulty in getting away with those.'

To reach the collection room was not the work of an instant with us, for Pop Glossop was built for stability rather than speed, but we fetched up there in due course and my first emotion on giving it the once-over was one of relief, all the junk appearing to be *in statu quo*. It was only after Pop Glossop had said 'Woof!' and was starting to dry off the brow, for the going had been fast, that I spotted the hiatus.

The cow-creamer was not among those present.

7

This cow-creamer, in case you're interested, was a silver jug or pitcher or whatever you call it shaped, of all silly things, like a cow with an arching tail and a juvenile-delinquent expression on its face, a cow that looked as if it were planning, next time it was milked, to haul off and let the milkmaid have it in the lower ribs. Its back opened on a hinge and the tip of the tail touched the spine, thus giving the householder something to catch hold of when pouring. Why anyone should want such a revolting object had always been a mystery to me, it ranking high up on the list of things I would have been reluctant to be found dead in a ditch with, but apparently they liked that sort of jug in the eighteenth century and, coming down to more modern times, Uncle Tom was all for it and so, according to the evidence of the witness Glossop, was Wilbert. No accounting for tastes is the way one has to look at these things, one man's caviar being another man's major-general, as the old saw says.

However, be that as it may and whether you liked the bally thing or didn't, the point was that it had vanished, leaving not a wrack behind, and I was about to apprise Pop Glossop of this and canvass his views, when we were joined by Bobbie Wickham. She had doffed the shirt and Bermuda-shorts which she had been wearing and was now dressed for her journey home.

'Hullo, souls,' she said. 'How goes it? You look a bit hot and bothered, Bertie. What's up?'

I made no attempt to break the n. gently.

'I'll tell you what's up. You know that cow-creamer of Uncle Tom's?'

'No, I don't. What is it?'

'Sort of cream jug kind of thing, ghastly but very valuable. One would not be far out in describing it as Uncle Tom's ewe lamb. He loves it dearly.'

'Bless his heart.'

'It's all right blessing his heart, but the damn thing's gone.'

The still summer air was disturbed by a sound like beer coming out of a bottle. It was Pop Glossop gurgling. His eyes were round, his nose wiggled, and one could readily discern that this news item had come to him not as rare and refreshing fruit but more like a buffet on the base of the skull with a sock full of wet sand.

'Gone?'

'Gone.'

'Are you sure?'

I said that sure was just what I wasn't anything but.

'It is not possible that you may have overlooked it?'

'You can't overlook a thing like that.'

He re-gurgled.

'But this is terrible.'

'Might be considerably better, I agree.'

'Your uncle will be most upset.'

'He'll have kittens.'

'Kittens?'

'That's right.'

'Why kittens?'

'Why not?'

From the look on Bobbie's face, as she stood listening to our cross-talk act, I could see that the inner gist was passing over her head. Cryptic, she seemed to be registering it as.

'I don't get this,' she said. 'How do you mean it's gone?'

'It's been pinched.'

'Things don't get pinched in country houses.'

'They do if there's a Wilbert Cream on the premises. He's a klep-whatever-it-is,' I said, and thrust Jeeves's letter on her. She perused it with an interested eye and having mastered its contents said, 'Cor chase my Aunt Fanny up a gum tree,' adding that you never knew what was going to happen next these days. There was, however, she said, a bright side.

'You'll be able now to give it as your considered opinion that the man is as loony as a coot, Sir Roderick.'

A pause ensued during which Pop Glossop appeared to be weighing this, possibly thinking back to coots he had met in the course of his professional career and trying to estimate their dippiness as compared with that of W. Cream.

'Unquestionably his metabolism is unduly susceptible to stresses resulting from the interaction of external excitations,' he said, and Bobbie patted him on the shoulder in a maternal sort of way, a thing I wouldn't have cared to do myself though our relations were, as I have indicated, more cordial than they had been at one time, and told him he had said a mouthful.

'That's how I like to hear you talk. You must tell Mrs Travers that when she gets back. It'll put her in a strong position to cope with Upjohn in this matter of Wilbert and Phyllis. With this under her belt, she'll be able to forbid the banns in no uncertain manner. "What price his metabolism?" she'll say, and Upjohn won't know which way to look. So everything's fine.'

'Everything,' I pointed out, 'except that Uncle Tom is short one ewe lamb.'

She chewed the lower lip.

'Yes, that's true. You have a point there. What steps do we take about that?'

She looked at me, and I said I didn't know, and then she looked at Pop Glossop, and he said he didn't know.

'The situation is an extremely delicate one. You concur, Mr. Wooster?'

'Like billy-o.'

'Placed as he is, your uncle can hardly go to the young man and demand restitution. Mrs. Travers impressed it upon me with all the emphasis at her disposal that the greatest care must be exercised to prevent Mr and Mrs Cream taking –'

'Umbrage?'

'I was about to say offence.'

'Just as good, probably. Not much in it either way.'

'And they would certainly take offence, were their son to be accused of theft.'

'It would stir them up like an egg whisk. I mean, however well they know that Wilbert is a pincher, they don't want to have it rubbed in.'

'Exactly.'

'It's one of the things the man of tact does not mention in their presence.'

'Precisely. So really I cannot see what is to be done. I am baffled.'

'So am I.'

'I'm not,' said Bobbie.

I quivered like a startled what-d'you-call-it. She had spoken with a cheery ring in her voice that told an experienced ear like mine that she was about to start something. In a matter of seconds by Shrewsbury clock, as Aunt Dahlia would have said, I could see that she was going to come out with one of those schemes or plans of hers that not only stagger humanity and turn the moon to blood but lead to some unfortunate male – who on the present occasion would, I strongly suspected, be me – getting immersed in what Shakespeare calls a sea of troubles, if it was Shakespeare. I had heard that ring in her voice

before, to name but one time, at the moment when she was pressing
the darning-needle into my hand and telling me where I would find
Sir Roderick Glossop's hot-water bottle. Many people are of the
opinion that Roberta, daughter of the late Sir Cuthbert and Lady
Wickham of Skeldings Hall, Herts., ought not to be allowed at large.
I string along with that school of thought.

Pop Glossop, having only a sketchy acquaintance with this female
of the species and so not knowing that from childhood up her motto
had been 'Anything goes', was all animation and tell-me-more.

'You have thought of some course of action that it will be feasible
for us to pursue, Miss Wickham?'

'Certainly. It sticks out like a sore thumb. Do you know which
Wilbert's room is?'

He said he did.

'And do you agree that if you snitch things when you're staying at
a country house, the only place you can park them in is your room?'

He said that this was no doubt so.

'Very well, then.'

He looked at her with what I have heard Jeeves call a wild surmise.

'Can you be . . . Is it possible that you are suggesting . . . ?'

'That somebody nips into Wilbert's room and hunts around? That's
right. And it's obvious who the people's choice is. You're elected,
Bertie.'

Well, I wasn't surprised. As I say, I had seen it coming. I don't
know why it is, but whenever there's dirty work to be undertaken at
the crossroads, the cry that goes round my little circle is always 'Let
Wooster do it.' It never fails. But though I hadn't much hope that
any words of mine would accomplish anything in the way of averting
the doom, I put in a rebuttal.

'Why me?'

'It's young man's work.'

Though with a growing feeling that I was fighting in the last ditch,
I continued rebutting.

'I don't see that,' I said. 'I should have thought a mature, experienced man of the world would have been far more likely to bring
home the bacon than a novice like myself, who as a child was never
any good at hunt-the-slipper. Stands to reason.'

'Now don't be difficult, Bertie. You'll enjoy it,' said Bobbie, though
where she got that idea I was at a loss to understand. 'Try to imagine
you're someone in the Secret Service on the track of the naval treaty
which was stolen by a mysterious veiled woman diffusing a strange
exotic scent. You'll have the time of your life. What did you say?'

'I said "Ha!" Suppose someone pops in?'

'Don't be silly. Mrs. Cream is working on her book. Phyllis is in her room, typing Upjohn's speech. Wilbert's gone for a walk. Upjohn isn't here. The only character who could pop in would be the Brinkley Court ghost. If it does, give it a cold look and walk through it. That'll teach it not to come butting in where it isn't wanted, ha ha.'

'Ha ha,' trilled Pop Glossop.

I thought their mirth ill-timed and in dubious taste, and I let them see it by my manner as I strode off. For of course I did stride off. These clashings of will with the opposite sex always end with Bertram Wooster bowing to the inev. But I was not in jocund mood, and when Bobbie, speeding me on my way, called me her brave little man and said she had known all along I had it in me, I ignored the remark with a coldness which must have made itself felt.

It was a lovely afternoon, replete with blue sky, beaming sun, buzzing insects and what not, an afternoon that seemed to call to one to be out in the open with God's air playing on one's face and something cool in a glass at one's side, and here was I, just to oblige Bobbie Wickham, tooling along a corridor indoors on my way to search a comparative stranger's bedroom, this involving crawling on floors and routing under beds and probably getting covered with dust and fluff. The thought was a bitter one, and I don't suppose I have ever come closer to saying 'Faugh!' It amazed me that I could have allowed myself to be let in for a binge of this description simply because a woman wished it. Too bally chivalrous for our own good, we Woosters, and always have been.

As I reached Wilbert's door and paused outside doing a bit of screwing the courage to the sticking point, as I have heard Jeeves call it, I found the proceedings reminding me of something, and I suddenly remembered what. I was feeling just as I had felt in the old Malvern House epoch when I used to sneak down to Aubrey Upjohn's study at dead of night in quest of the biscuits he kept there in a tin on his desk, and there came back to me the memory of the occasion when, not letting a twig snap beneath my feet, I had entered his sanctum in pyjamas and a dressing-gown, to find him seated in his chair, tucking into the biscuits himself. A moment fraught with embarrassment. The What-does-this-mean-Wooster-ing that ensued and the aftermath next morning – six of the best on the old spot – had always remained on the tablets of my mind, if that's the expression I want.

Except for the tapping of a typewriter in a room along the corridor, showing that Ma Cream was hard at her self-appointed task of curdling the blood of the reading public, all was still. I stood outside the door for a space, letting 'I dare not' wait upon 'I would', as Jeeves tells me cats do in adages, then turned the handle softly, pushed – also softly – and, carrying on into the interior, found myself confronted by a girl in housemaid's costume who put a hand to her throat like somebody in a play and leaped several inches in the direction of the ceiling.

'Coo!' she said, having returned to terra firma and taken aboard a spot of breath. 'You gave me a start, sir!'

'Frightfully sorry, my dear old housemaid,' I responded cordially. 'As a matter of fact, you gave *me* a start, making two starts in all. I'm looking for Mr. Cream.'

'I'm looking for a mouse.'

This opened up an interesting line of thought.

'You feel there are mice in these parts?'

'I saw one this morning, when I was doing the room. So I brought Augustus,' she said, and indicated a large black cat who until then had escaped my notice. I recognized him as an old crony with whom I had often breakfasted, I wading into the scrambled eggs, he into the saucer of milk.

'Augustus will teach him,' she said.

Now, right from the start, as may readily be imagined, I had been wondering how this housemaid was to be removed, for of course her continued presence would render my enterprise null and void. You can't search rooms with the domestic staff standing on the sidelines, but on the other hand it was impossible for anyone with any claim to be a *preux chevalier* to take her by the slack of her garment and heave her out. For a while the thing had seemed an impasse, but this statement of hers that Augustus would teach the mouse gave me an idea.

'I doubt it,' I said. 'You're new here, aren't you?'

She conceded this, saying that she had taken office only in the previous month.

'I thought as much, or you would be aware that Augustus is a broken reed to lean on in the matter of catching mice. My own acquaintance with him is a longstanding one, and I have come to know his psychology from soup to nuts. He hasn't caught a mouse since he was a slip of a kitten. Except when eating, he does nothing but sleep. Lethargic is the word that springs to the lips. If you cast an eye on him, you will see that he's asleep now.'

'Coo! So he is.'

'It's a sort of disease. There's a scientific name for it. Trau-something. Traumatic symplegia, that's it. This cat has traumatic symplegia. In other words, putting it in simple language adapted to the lay mind, where other cats are content to get their eight hours, Augustus wants his twenty-four. If you will be ruled by me, you will abandon the whole project and take him back to the kitchen. You're simply wasting your time here.'

My eloquence was not without its effect. She said 'Coo!' again, picked up the cat, who muttered something drowsily which I couldn't follow, and went out, leaving me to carry on.

8

The first thing I noticed when at leisure to survey my surroundings was that the woman up top, carrying out her policy of leaving no stone unturned in the way of sucking up to the Cream family, had done Wilbert well where sleeping accommodation was concerned. What he had drawn when clocking in at Brinkley Court was the room known as the Blue Room, a signal honour to be accorded to a bachelor guest, amounting to being given star billing, for at Brinkley, as at most country houses, any old nook or cranny is considered good enough for the celibate contingent. My own apartment, to take a case in point, was a sort of hermit's cell in which one would have been hard put to it to swing a cat, even a smaller one than Augustus, not of course that one often wants to do much cat-swinging. What I'm driving at is that when I blow in on Aunt Dahlia, you don't catch her saying 'Welcome to Meadowsweet Hall, my dear boy. I've put you in the Blue Room, where I am sure you will be comfortable.' I once suggested to her that I be put there, and all she said was '*You?*' and the conversation turned to other topics.

The furnishing of this Blue Room w₃ solid and Victorian, it having been the G.H.Q. of my Uncle Tom's late father, who liked things substantial. There was a four-poster bed, a chunky dressing table, a massive writing table, divers chairs, pictures on the walls of fellows in cocked hats bending over females in muslin and ringlets and over at the far side a cupboard or *armoire* in which you could have hidden a dozen corpses. In short, there was so much space and so many things to shove things behind that most people, called on to find a silver cow-creamer there, would have said 'Oh, what's the use?' and thrown in the towel.

But where I had the bulge on the ordinary searcher was that I am a man of wide reading. Starting in early boyhood, long before they were called novels of suspense, I've read more mystery stories than you could shake a stick at, and they have taught me something – viz. that anybody with anything to hide invariably puts it on top of the cupboard or, if you prefer it, the *armoire*. This is what happened in

Murder at Mistleigh Manor, Three Dead on Tuesday, Excuse my Gat, Guess Who and a dozen more standard works, and I saw no reason to suppose that Wilbert Cream would have deviated from routine. My first move, accordingly, was to take a chair and prop it against the *armoire*, and I had climbed on this and was preparing to subject the top to a close scrutiny, when Bobbie Wickham, entering on noiseless feet and speaking from about eighteen inches behind me, said:

'How are you getting on?'

Really, one sometimes despairs of the modern girl. You'd have thought that this Wickham would have learned at her mother's knee that the last thing a fellow in a highly nervous condition wants, when he's searching someone's room, is a disembodied voice in his immediate ear asking him how he's getting on. The upshot, I need scarcely say, was that I came down like a sack of coals. The pulse was rapid, the blood pressure high, and for awhile the Blue Room pirouetted about me like an adagio dancer.

When Reason returned to its throne, I found that Bobbie, no doubt feeling after that resounding crash that she was better elsewhere, had left me and that I was closely entangled in the chair, my position being in some respects similar to that of Kipper Herring when he got both legs wrapped round his neck in Switzerland. It seemed improbable that I would ever get loose without the aid of powerful machinery.

However, by pulling this way and pushing that, I made progress, and I'd just contrived to de-chair myself and was about to rise, when another voice spoke.

'For Pete's sake!' it said, and, looking up, I found that it was not, as I had for a moment supposed, from the lips of the Brinkley Court ghost that the words had proceeded, but from those of Mrs. Homer Cream. She was looking at me, as Sir Roderick Glossop had recently looked at Bobbie, with a wild surmise, her whole air that of a woman who is not abreast. This time, I noticed, she had an ink spot on her chin.

'Mr. Wooster!' she yipped.

Well, there's nothing much you can say in reply to 'Mr. Wooster!' except 'Oh, hullo,' so I said it.

'You are doubtless surprised,' I was continuing, when she hogged the conversation again, asking me (a) what I was doing in her son's room and (b) what in the name of goodness I thought I was up to.

'For the love of Mike,' she added, driving her point home.

It is frequently said of Bertram Wooster that he is a man who can think on his feet, and if the necessity arises he can also use his loaf when on all fours. On the present occasion I was fortunate in having had that get-together with the housemaid and the cat Augustus, for it gave me what they call in France a *point d'appui*. Removing a portion of chair which had got entangled in my back hair, I said with a candour that became me well:

'I was looking for a mouse.'

If she had replied, 'Ah, yes, indeed. I understand now. A mouse, to be sure. Quite,' everything would have been nice and smooth, but she didn't.

'A mouse?' she said. 'What do you mean?'

Well, of course, if she didn't know what a mouse was, there was evidently a good deal of tedious spadework before us, and one would scarcely have known where to start. It was a relief when her next words showed that that 'What do you mean?' had not been a query but more in the nature of a sort of heart-cry.

'What makes you think there is a mouse in this room?'

'The evidence points that way.'

'Have you seen it?'

'Actually, no. It's been lying what the French call *perdu*.'

'What made you come and look for it?'

'Oh, I thought I would.'

'And why were you standing on a chair?'

'Sort of just trying to get a bird's-eye view, as it were.'

'Do you often go looking for mice in other people's rooms?'

'I wouldn't say often. Just when the spirit moves me, don't you know?'

'I see. Well . . .'

When people say 'Well' to you like that, it usually means that they think you are outstaying your welcome and that the time has come to call it a day. She felt, I could see, that Woosters were not required in her son's sleeping apartment, and realizing that there might be something in this, I rose, dusted the knees of the trousers, and after a courteous word to the effect that I hoped the spine-freezer on which she was engaged was coming out well, left the presence. Happening to glance back as I reached the door, I saw her looking after me, that wild surmise still functioning on all twelve cylinders. It was plain that she considered my behaviour odd, and I'm not saying it wasn't. The behaviour of those who allow their actions to be guided by Roberta Wickham is nearly always odd.

The thing I wanted most at this juncture was to have a heart-to-heart talk with that young *femme fatale*, and after roaming hither and thither for awhile I found her in my chair on the lawn, reading the

Ma Cream book in which I had been engrossed when these doings had started. She greeted me with a bright smile, and said:

'Back already? Did you find it?'

With a strong effort I mastered my emotion and replied curtly but civilly that the answer was in the negative.

'No,' I said, 'I did not find it.'

'You can't have looked properly.'

Again I was compelled to pause and remind myself that an English gentleman does not slosh a sitting redhead, no matter what the provocation.

'I hadn't time to look properly. I was impeded in my movements by half-witted females sneaking up behind me and asking how I was getting on.'

'Well, I wanted to know.' A giggle escaped her. 'You did come down a wallop, didn't you? How art thou fallen from heaven, oh Lucifer, son of the morning, I said to myself. You're so terribly neurotic, Bertie. You must try to be less jumpy. What you need is a good nerve tonic. I'm sure Sir Roderick would shake you up one, if you asked him. And meanwhile?'

'How do you mean, "And meanwhile"?'

'What are your plans now?'

'I propose to hoik you out of that chair and seat myself in it and take that book, the early chapters of which I found most gripping, and start catching up with my reading and try to forget.'

'You mean you aren't going to have another bash?'

'I am not. Bertram is through. You may give this to the press, if you wish.'

'But the cow-creamer. How about your Uncle Tom's grief and agony when he learns of his bereavement?'

'Let Uncle Tom eat cake.'

'Bertie! Your manner is strange.'

'Your manner would be strange if you'd been sitting on the floor of Wilbert Cream's sleeping apartment with a chair round your neck, and Ma Cream had come in.'

'Golly! Did she?'

'In person.'

'What did you say?'

'I said I was looking for a mouse.'

'Couldn't you think of anything better than that?'

'No.'

'And how did it all come out in the end?'

'I melted away, leaving her plainly convinced that I was off my rocker. And so, young Bobbie, when you speak of having another bash, I merely laugh bitterly,' I said, doing so. 'Catch me going into that sinister room again! Not for a million pounds sterling, cash down in small notes.'

She made what I believe, though I wouldn't swear to it, is called a *moue*. Putting the lips together and shoving them out, if you know what I mean. The impression I got was that she was disappointed in Bertram, having expected better things, and this was borne out by her next words.

'Is this the daredevil spirit of the Woosters?'

'As of even date, yes.'

'Are you man or mouse?'

'Kindly do not mention that word "mouse" in my presence.'

'I do think you might try again. Don't spoil the ship for a ha'porth of tar. I'll help you this time.'

'Ha!'

'Haven't I heard that word before somewhere?'

'You may confidently expect to hear it again.'

'No, but listen, Bertie. Nothing can possibly go wrong if we work together. Mrs. Cream won't show up this time. Lightning never strikes twice in the same place.'

'Who made that rule?'

'And if she does . . . Here's what I thought we'd do. You go in and start searching, and I'll stand outside the door.'

'You feel that will be a lot of help?'

'Of course it will. If I see her coming, I'll sing.'

'Always glad to hear you singing, of course, but in what way will that ease the strain?'

'Oh, Bertie, you really are an abysmal chump. Don't you get it? When you hear me burst into song, you'll know there's peril afoot and you'll have plenty of time to nip out of the window.'

'And break my bally neck?'

'How can you break your neck? There's a balcony outside the Blue Room. I've seen Wilbert Cream standing on it, doing his Daily Dozen. He breathes deeply and ties himself into a lovers' knot and –'

'Never mind Wilbert Cream's excesses.'

'I only put that in to make it more interesting. The point is that there is a balcony and once on it you're home. There's a water pipe at the end of it. You just slide down that and go on your way, singing a gypsy song. You aren't going to tell me that you have any objection to sliding down water pipes. Jeeves says you're always doing it.'

I mused. It was true that I had slid down quite a number of water pipes in my time. Circumstances had often so moulded themselves as to make such an action imperative. It was by that route that I had left Skeldings Hall at three in the morning after the hot-water-bottle incident. So while it would be too much, perhaps, to say that I am never happier than when sliding down water pipes, the prospect of doing so caused me little or no concern. I began to see that there was something in this plan she was mooting, if mooting is the word I want.

What tipped the scale was the thought of Uncle Tom. His love for the cow-creamer might be misguided, but you couldn't get away from the fact that he was deeply attached to the beastly thing, and one didn't like the idea of him coming back from Harrogate and saying to himself 'And now for a refreshing look at the old cow-creamer' and finding it was not in residence. It would blot the sunshine from his life, and affectionate nephews hate like the dickens to blot the sunshine from the lives of uncles. It was true that I had said 'Let Uncle Tom eat cake,' but I hadn't really meant it. I could not forget that when I was at Malvern House, Bramley-on-Sea, this relative by marriage had often sent me postal orders sometimes for as much as ten bob. He, in short, had done the square thing by me, and it was up to me to do the s.t. by him.

And so it came about that some five minutes later I stood once more outside the Blue Room with Bobbie beside me, not actually at the moment singing in the wilderness but prepared so to sing if Ma Cream, modelling her strategy on that of the Asyrian, came down like a wolf on the fold. The nervous system was a bit below par, of course, but not nearly so much so as it might have been. Knowing that Bobbie would be on sentry-go made all the difference. Any gangster will tell you that the strain and anxiety of busting a safe are greatly diminished if you've a look-out man ready at any moment to say 'Cheese it, the cops!'

Just to make sure that Wilbert hadn't returned from his hike, I knocked on the door. Nothing stirred. The coast seemed c. I mentioned this to Bobbie, and she agreed that it was as c. as a whistle.

'Now a quick run-through, to see that you have got it straight. If I sing, what do you do?'

'Nip out of the window.'

'And –?'

'Slide down the water pipe.'

'And –?'

'Leg it over the horizon.'

'Right. In you go and get cracking,' she said, and I went in.

The dear old room was just as I'd left it, nothing changed, and my first move, of course, was to procure another chair and give the top of the *armoire* the once-over. It was a set-back to find that the cow-creamer wasn't there. I suppose these kleptomaniacs know a thing or two and don't hide the loot in the obvious place. There was nothing to be done but start the exhaustive search elsewhere, and I proceeded to do so, keeping an ear cocked for any snatch of song. None coming, it was with something of the old debonair Wooster spirit that I looked under this and peered behind that, and I had just crawled beneath the dressing-table in pursuance of my researches, when one of those disembodied voices which were so frequent in the Blue Room spoke, causing me to give my head a nasty bump.

'For goodness' sake!' it said, and I came out like a pickled onion on the end of a fork, to find that Ma Cream was once more a pleasant visitor. She was standing there, looking down at me with a what-the-hell expression on her finely-chiselled face, and I didn't blame her. Gives a woman a start, naturally, to come into her son's bedroom and observe an alien trouser-seat sticking out from under the dressing-table.

We went into our routine.

'Mr. Wooster!'

'Oh, hullo.'

'It's you *again*?'

'Why, yes,' I said, for this of course was perfectly correct, and an odd sound proceeded from her, not exactly a hiccup and yet not quite not a hiccup.

'Are you still looking for that mouse?'

'That's right. I thought I saw it run under there, and I was about to deal with it regardless of its age or sex.'

'What makes you think there is a mouse here?'

'Oh, one gets these ideas.'

'Do you often hunt for mice?'

'Fairly frequently.'

An idea seemed to strike her.

'You don't think you're a cat?'

'No, I'm pretty straight on that.'

'But you pursue mice?'

'Yes.'

'Well, this is very interesting. I must consult my psychiatrist when I get back to New York. I'm sure he will tell me that this mouse-fixation is a symbol of something. Your head feels funny, doesn't it?'

'It does rather,' I said, the bump I had given it had been a juicy one, and the temples were throbbing.

'I thought as much. A sort of burning sensation, I imagine. Now you do just as I tell you. Go to your room and lie down. Relax. Try to get a little sleep. Perhaps a cup of strong tea would help. And . . . I'm trying to think of the name of that alienist I've heard people over here speak so highly of. Miss Wickham mentioned him yesterday. Bossom? Blossom? Glossop, that's it, Sir Roderick Glossop. I think you ought to consult him. A friend of mine is at his clinic now, and she says he's wonderful. Cures the most stubborn cases. Meanwhile, rest is the thing. Go and have a good rest.'

At an early point in these exchanges I had started to sidle to the door, and I now sidled through it, rather like a diffident crab on some sandy beach trying to avoid the attentions of a child with a spade. But I didn't go to my room and relax, I went in search of Bobbie, breathing fire. I wanted to take up with her the matter of that absence of the burst of melody. I mean, considering that a mere couple of bars of some popular song hit would have saved me from an experience that had turned the bones to water and whitened the hair from the neck up, I felt entitled to demand an explanation of why those bars had not emerged.

I found her outside the front door at the wheel of her car.

'Oh, hullo, Bertie,' she said, and a fish on ice couldn't have spoken more calmly. 'Have you got it?'

I ground a tooth or two and waved the arms in a passionate gesture.

'No,' I said, ignoring her query as to why I had chosen this moment to do my Swedish exercises. 'I haven't. But Ma Cream got me.'

Her eyes widened. She squeaked a bit.

'Don't tell me she caught you bending again?'

'Bending is right. I was half-way under the dressing table. You and your singing,' I said, and I'm not sure I didn't add the word 'Forsooth!'

Her eyes widened a bit further, and she squeaked another squeak.

'Oh, Bertie, I'm sorry about that.'

'Me, too.'

'You see, I was called away to the telephone. Mother rang up. She wanted to tell me you were a nincompoop.'

'One wonders where she picks up such expressions.'

'From her literary friends, I suppose. She knows a lot of literary people.'

'Great help to the vocabulary.'

'Yes. She was delighted when I told her I was coming home. She wants to have a long talk.'

'About me, no doubt?'

'Yes, I expect your name will crop up. But I mustn't stay here chatting with you, Bertie. If I don't get started, I shan't hit the old nest till daybreak. It's a pity you made such a mess of things. Poor Mr. Travers, he'll be broken-hearted. Still, into each life some rain must fall,' she said, and drove off, spraying gravel in all directions.

If Jeeves had been there, I would have turned to him and said 'Women, Jeeves!', and he would have said 'Yes, sir' or possibly 'Precisely, sir', and this would have healed the bruised spirit to a certain extent, but as he wasn't I merely laughed a bitter laugh and made for the lawn. A go at Ma Cream's goose-flesher might, I thought, do something to soothe the vibrating ganglions.

And it did. I hadn't been reading long when drowsiness stole over me, the tired eyelids closed, and in another couple of ticks I was off to dreamland, slumbering as soundly as if I had been the cat Augustus. I awoke to find that some two hours had passed, and it was while stretching the limbs that I remembered I hadn't sent that wire to Kipper Herring, inviting him to come and join the gang. I went to Aunt Dahlia's boudoir and repaired this omission, telephoning the communication to someone at the post office who would have been well advised to consult a good aurist. This done, I headed for the open spaces again, and was approaching the lawn with a view to getting on with my reading when, hearing engine noises in the background and turning to cast an eye in their direction, blow me tight if I didn't behold Kipper alighting from his car at the front door.

9

The distance from London to Brinkley Court being a hundred miles or so and not much more than two minutes having elapsed since I had sent off that telegram, the fact that he was now outside the Brinkley front door struck me as quick service. It lowered the record of the chap in the motoring sketch which Catsmeat Potter-Pirbright sometimes does at the Drones Club smoking concert where the fellow tells the other fellow he's going to drive to Glasgow and the other fellow says 'How far is that?' and the fellow says 'Three hundred miles' and the other fellow says 'How long will it take you to get there?' and the fellow says 'Oh, about half an hour, about half an hour.' The What-ho with which I greeted the back of his head as I approached was tinged, accordingly, with a certain bewilderment.

At the sound of the old familiar voice he spun around with something of the agility of a cat on hot bricks, and I saw that his dial, usually cheerful, was contorted with anguish, as if he had swallowed a bad oyster. Guessing now what was biting him, I smiled one of my subtle smiles. I would soon, I told myself, be bringing the roses back to his cheeks.

He gulped a bit, then spoke in a hollow voice, like a spirit at a séance.

'Hullo, Bertie.'

'Hullo.'

'So there you are.'

'Yes, here I am.'

'I was hoping I might run into you.'

'And now the dream's come true.'

'You see, you told me you were staying here.'

'Yes.'

'How's everything?'

'Pretty fruity.'

'Your aunt well?'

'Fine.'

'You all right?'

'More or less.'

'Capital. Long time since I was at Brinkley.'

'Yes.'

'Nothing much changed, I mean.'

'No.'

'Well, that's how it goes.'

He paused and did another splash of gulping, and I could see that we were about to come to the nub, all that had gone before having been merely what they call pour-parlers. I mean the sort of banana oil that passes between statesmen at conferences conducted in an atmosphere of the utmost cordiality before they tear their whiskers off and get down to cases.

I was right. His face working as if the first bad oyster had been followed by a second with even more spin on the ball, he said:

'I saw that thing in *The Times*, Bertie.'

I dissembled. I ought, I suppose, to have started bringing those roses back right away, but I felt it would be amusing to kid the poor fish along for awhile, so I wore the mask.

'Ah, yes. In *The Times*. That thing. Quite. You saw it, did you?'

'At the club, after lunch. I couldn't believe my eyes.'

Well, I hadn't been able to believe mine, either, but I didn't mention this. I was thinking how like Bobbie it was, when planning this scheme of hers, not to have let him in on the ground floor. Slipped her mind, I suppose, or she may have kept it under her hat for some strange reason of her own. She had always been a girl who moved in a mysterious way her wonders to perform.

'And I'll tell you why I couldn't. You'll scarcely credit this, but only a couple of days ago she was engaged to *me*.'

'You don't say?'

'Yes, I jolly well do.'

'Engaged to you, eh?'

'Up to the hilt. And all the while she must have been contemplating this ghastly bit of treachery.'

'A bit thick.'

'If you can tell me anything that's thicker, I shall be glad to hear it. It just shows you what women are like. A frightful sex, Bertie. There ought to be a law. I hope to live to see the day when women are no longer allowed.'

'That would rather put a stopper on keeping the human race going, wouldn't it?'

'Well, who wants to keep the human race going?'

'I see what you mean. Yes, something in that, of course.'

He kicked petulantly at a passing beetle, frowned awhile and resumed.

'It's the cold, callous heartlessness of the thing that shocks me. Not a hint that she was proposing to return me to store. As short a while ago as last week, when we had a bite of lunch together, she was sketching out plans for the honeymoon with the greatest animation. And now this! Without a word of warning. You'd have thought that a girl who was smashing a fellow's life into hash would have dropped him a line, if only a postcard. Apparently that never occurred to her. She just let me get the news from the morning paper. I was stunned.'

'I bet you were. Did everything go black?'

'Pretty black. I took the rest of the day thinking it over, and this morning wangled leave from the office and got the car out and came down here to tell you . . .'

He paused, seeming overcome with emotion.

'Yes?'

'To tell you that, whatever we do, we mustn't let this thing break our old friendship.'

'Of course not. Damn silly idea.'

'It's such a very old friendship.'

'I don't know when I've met an older.'

'We were boys together.'

'In Eton jackets and pimples.'

'Exactly. And more like brothers than anything. I would share my last bar of almond rock with you, and you would cut me in fifty-fifty on your last bag of acid drops. When you had mumps, I caught them from you, and when I had measles, you caught them from me. Each helping each. So we must carry on regardless, just as if this had not happened.'

'Quite.'

'The same old lunches.'

'Oh, rather.'

'And golf on Saturdays and the occasional game of squash. And when you are married and settled down, I shall frequently look in on you for a cocktail.'

'Yes, do.'

'I will. Though I shall have to exercise an iron self-restraint to keep me from beaning that pie-faced little hornswoggler Mrs. Bertram Wooster, *née* Wickham, with the shaker.'

'Ought you to call her a pie-faced little hornswoggler?'

'Why, can you think of something worse?' he said, with the air of one always open to suggestions. 'Do you know Thomas Otway?'

'I don't believe so. Pal of yours?'

'Seventeenth-century dramatist. Wrote *The Orphan*. In which play these words occur. "What mighty ills have not been done by Woman? Who was't betrayed the Capitol? A woman. Who lost Marc Antony the world? A woman. Who was the cause of a long ten years' war and laid at last old Troy in ashes? Woman. Deceitful, damnable, destructive Woman." Otway knew what he was talking about. He had the right slant. He couldn't have put it better if he had known Roberta Wickham personally.'

I smiled another subtle smile. I was finding all this extremely diverting.

'I don't know if it's my imagination, Kipper,' I said, 'but something gives me the impression that at moment of going to press you aren't too sold on Bobbie.'

He shrugged a shoulder.

'Oh, I wouldn't say that. Apart from wishing I could throttle the young twister with my bare hands and jump on the remains with hobnailed boots, I don't feel much about her one way or the other. She prefers you to me, and there's nothing more to be said. The great thing is that everything is all right between you and me.'

'You came all the way here just to make sure of that?' I said, moved.

'Well, there may possibly also have been an idea at the back of my mind that I might get invited to dig in at one of those dinners of Anatole's before going on to book a room at the "Bull and Bush" in Market Snodsbury. How is Anatole's cooking these days?'

'Superber than ever.'

'Continues to melt in the mouth, does it? It's two years since I bit into his products, but the taste still lingers. What an artist!'

'Ah!' I said, and would have bared my head, only I hadn't a hat on.

'Would it run to a dinner invitation, do you think?'

'My dear chap, of course. The needy are never turned from our door.'

'Splendid. And after the meal I shall propose to Phyllis Mills.'

'What!'

'Yes, I know what you're thinking. She is closely related to Aubrey Upjohn, you are saying to yourself. But surely, Bertie, she can't help that.'

'More to be pitied than censured, you think?'

'Exactly. We mustn't be narrow-minded. She is a sweet, gentle girl, unlike certain scarlet-headed Delilahs who shall be nameless, and I am very fond of her.'

'I thought you scarcely knew her.'

'Oh yes, we saw quite a bit of one another in Switzerland. We're great buddies.'

It seemed to me that the moment had come to bring the good news from Aix to Ghent, as the expression is.

'I don't know that I would propose to Phyllis Mills, Kipper. Bobbie might not like it.'

'But that's the whole idea, to show her she isn't the only onion in the stew and that if she doesn't want me, there are others who feel differently. What are you grinning about?'

As a matter of fact, I was smiling subtly, but I let it go.

'Kipper,' I said, 'I have an amazing story to relate.'

I don't know if you happen to take Old Doctor Gordon's Bile Magnesia, which when the liver is disordered gives instant relief, acting like magic and imparting an inward glow? I don't myself, my personal liver being always more or less in mid-season form, but I've seen the advertisements. They show the sufferer before and after taking, in the first case with drawn face and hollow eyes and the general look of one shortly about to hand in his dinner pail, in the second all beans and buck and what the French call *bien être*. Well, what I'm driving at is that my amazing story had exactly the same effect on Kipper as the daily dose for adults . . . He moved, he stirred, he seemed to feel the rush of life along his keel, and while I don't suppose he actually put on several pounds in weight as the tale proceeded, one got the distinct illusion that he was swelling like one of those rubber ducks which you fill with air before inserting them in the bath tub.

'Well, I'll be blowed!' he said, when I had placed the facts before him. 'Well, I'll be a son of a what-not!'

'I thought you would be.'

'Bless her ingenious little heart! Not many girls would have got the grey matter working like that.'

'Very few.'

'What a helpmeet! Talk about service and co-operation. Have you any idea how the thing is working out?'

'Rather smoothly, I think. On reading the announcement in *The Times*, Wickham senior had hysterics and swooned in her tracks.'

'She doesn't like you?'

'That was the impression I got. It has been confirmed by subsequent telegrams to Bobbie in which she refers to me as a guffin and a gaby. She also considers me a nincompoop.'

'Well, that's fine. It looks as though, after you, I shall come to her like . . . it's on the tip of my tongue.'

'Rare and refreshing fruit?'

'Exactly. If you care to have a bet on it, five bob will get you ten that this scenario will end with a fade-out of Lady Wickham folding me in her arms and kissing me on the brow and saying she knows I will make her little girl happy. Gosh, Bertie, when I think that she – Bobbie, I mean, not Lady Wickham – will soon be mine and that shortly after yonder sun has set I shall be tucking into one of Anatole's dinners, I could dance a saraband. By the way, talking of dinner, do you suppose it would also run to a bed? The "Bull and Bush" is well spoken of in the *Automobile Guide*, but I'm always a bit wary of these country pubs. I'd much rather be at Brinkley Court, of which I have such happy memories. Could you swing it with your aunt?'

'She isn't here. She left to minister to her son Bonzo, who is down with German measles at his school. But she rang up this afternoon and instructed me to wire you to come and make a prolonged stay.'

'You're pulling my leg.'

'No, this is official.'

'But what made her think of me?'

'There's something she wants you to do for her.'

'She can have anything she asks, even unto half my kingdom. What does she . . .' He paused, and a look of alarm came into his face. 'Don't tell me she wants me to present the prizes at Market Snodsbury Grammer School, like Gussie?'

He was alluding to a mutual friend of ours of the name of Gussie Fink-Nottle, who, hounded by the aged relative into undertaking this task in the previous summer, had got pickled to the gills and made an outstanding exhibition of himself, setting up a mark at which all future orators would shoot in vain.

'No, no, nothing like that. The prizes this year will be distributed by Aubrey Upjohn.'

'That's a relief. How is he, by the way? You've met him, of course?'

'Oh, yes, we got together. I spilled some tea on him.'

'You couldn't have done better.'

'He's grown a moustache.'

'That eases my mind. I wasn't looking forward to seeing that bare upper lip of his. Remember how it used to make us quail when he twitched it at us? I wonder how he'll react when confronted with not only one former pupil but two, and those two the very brace that have probably haunted him in his dreams for the last fifteen years. Might as well unleash me on him now.'

'He isn't here.'

'You said he was.'

'Yes, he was and he will be, but he isn't. He's gone up to London.'

'Isn't anybody here?'

'Certainly. There's Phyllis Mills –'

'Nice girl.'

'– and Mrs. Homer Cream of New York City, N.Y., and her son Wilbert. And that brings me to the something Aunt Dahlia wants you to do for her.'

I was pleased, as I put him hep on the Wilbert-Phyllis situation and revealed the part he was expected to play in it, to note that he showed no signs of being about to issue the presidential veto. He followed the set-up intelligently and when I had finished said that of course he would be only too willing to oblige. It wasn't much, he said, to ask of a fellow who esteemed Aunt Dahlia as highly as he did and who ever since she had lushed him up so lavishly two summers ago had been wishing there was something he could do in the way of buying back.

'Rely on me, Bertie,' he said. 'We can't have Phyllis tying herself up with a man who on the evidence would appear to be as nutty as a fruit cake. I will be about this Cream's bed and about his board, spying out all his ways. Every time he lures the poor girl into a leafy glade, I will be there, nestling behind some wild flower all ready to pop out and gum the game at the least indication that he is planning to get mushy. And now if you would show me to my room, I will have a bath and brush-up so as to be all sweet and fresh for the evening meal. Does Anatole still do those *Timbales de ris de veau Toulousiane?*'

'And the *Sylphids à la crême d'écrevisses.*'

'There is none like him, none,' said Kipper, moistening the lips with the tip of the tongue and looking like a wolf that has just spotted its Russian peasant. 'He stands alone.'

10

As I hadn't the remotest which rooms were available and which weren't, getting Kipper dug in necessitated ringing for Pop Glossop. I pressed the button and he appeared, giving me, as he entered, the sort of conspiratorial glance the acting secretary of a secret society would have given a friend on the membership roll.

'Oh, Swordfish,' I said, having given him a conspiratorial glance in return, for one always likes to do the civil thing, 'this is Mr. Herring, who has come to join our little group.'

He bowed from the waist, not that he had much waist.

'Good evening, sir.'

'He will be staying some time. Where do we park him?'

'The Red Room suggests itself, sir.'

'You get the Red Room, Kipper.'

'Right ho.'

'I had it last year. 'Tis not as deep as a well nor as wide as a church door, but 'tis enough, 'twill serve,' I said, recalling a gag of Jeeves's. 'Will you escort Mr. Herring thither, Swordfish?'

'Very good, sir.'

'And when you have got him installed, perhaps I could have a word with you in your pantry,' I said, giving him a conspiratorial glance.

'Certainly, sir,' he responded, giving me a conspiratorial glances.

It was one of those big evenings for conspiratorial glances.

I hadn't been waiting in the pantry long when he navigated over the threshold, and my first act was to congratulate him on the excellence of his technique. I had been much impressed by all that 'Very good, sir,' 'Certainly, sir,' bowing-from-the-waist stuff. I said that Jeeves himself couldn't have read his lines better, and he simpered modestly and said that one picked up these little tricks of the trade from one's own butler.

'Oh, by the way,' I said, 'where did you get the Swordfish?'

He smiled indulgently.

'That was Miss Wickham's suggestion.'

'I thought as much.'

'She informed me that she had always dreamed of one day meeting a butler called Swordfish. A charming young lady. Full of fun.'

'It may be fun for her,' I said with one of my bitter laughs, 'but it isn't so diverting for the unfortunate toads beneath the harrow whom she plunges so ruthlessly in the soup. Let me tell you what occurred after I left you this afternoon.'

'Yes, I am all eagerness to hear.'

'Then pin your ears back and drink it in.'

If I do say so, I told my story well, omitting no detail however slight. It had him Bless-my-soul-ing throughout, and when I had finished he t'ck-t'ck-t'ck-ed and said it must have been most unpleasant for me, and I said that 'unpleasant' covered the facts like the skin on a sausage.

'But I think that in your place I should have thought of an explanation of your presence calculated to carry more immediate conviction than that you were searching for a mouse.'

'Such as?'

'It is hard to say on the spur of the moment.'

'Well, it was on the spur of the m. that I had to say it,' I rejoined with some heat. 'You don't get time to polish your dialogue and iron out the bugs in the plot when a woman who looks like Sherlock Holmes catches you in her son's room with your rear elevation sticking out from under the dressing-table.'

'True. Quite true. But I wonder . . .'

'Wonder what?'

'I do not wish to hurt your feelings.'

'Go ahead. My feelings have been hurt so much already that a little bit extra won't make any difference.'

'I may speak frankly?'

'Do.'

'Well, then, I am wondering if it was altogether wise to entrust this very delicate operation to a young fellow like yourself. I am coming round to the view you put forward when we were discussing the matter with Miss Wickham. You said, if you recall, that the enterprise should have been placed in the hands of a mature, experienced man of the world and not in those of one of less ripe years who as a child had never been expert at hunt-the-slipper. I am, you will agree, mature, and in my earlier days I won no little praise for my skill at hunt-the-slipper. I remember one of the hostesses whose Christmas parties I attended comparing me to a juvenile bloodhound. An extravagant encomium, of course, but that is what she said.'

I looked at him with a wild surmise. It seemed to me that there was but one meaning to be attached to his words.

'You aren't thinking of having a pop at it yourself?'

'That is precisely my intention, Mr. Wooster.'

'Lord love a duck!'

'The expression is new to me, but I gather from it that you consider my conduct eccentric.'

'Oh, I wouldn't say that, but do you realize what you are letting yourself in for? You won't enjoy meeting Ma Cream. She has an eye like . . . what are those things that have eyes? Basilisks, that's the name I was groping for. She has an eye like a basilisk. Have you considered the possibility of having that eye go through you like a dose of salts?'

'Yes, I can envisage the peril. But the fact is, Mr. Wooster, I regard what has happened as a challenge. My blood is up.'

'Mine froze.'

'And you may possibly not believe me, but I find the prospect of searching Mr. Cream's room quite enjoyable.'

'Enjoyable?'

'Yes. In a curious way it restores my youth. It brings back to me my preparatory school days, when I would often steal down at night to the headmaster's study to eat his biscuits.'

I started. I looked at him with a kindling eye. Deep had called to deep, and the cockles of the heart were warmed.

'Biscuits?'

'He kept them in a tin on his desk.'

'You really used to do that at your prep school?'

'Many years ago.'

'So did I,' I said, coming within an ace of saying, 'My brother!'

He raised his bushy eyebrows, and you could see that his heart's cockles were warmed, too.

'Indeed? Fancy that! I had supposed the idea original with myself, but no doubt all over England today the rising generation is doing the same thing. So you too have lived in Arcady? What kind of biscuits were yours? Mine were mixed.'

'The ones with pink and white sugar on?'

'In many instances, though some were plain.'

'Mine were ginger nuts.'

'Those are very good, too, of course, but I prefer the mixed.'

'So do I. But you had to take what you could get in those days. Were you ever copped?'

'I am glad to say never.'

'I was once. I can feel the place in frosty weather still.'

'Too bad. But these things will happen. Embarking on the present venture, I have the sustaining thought that if the worst occurs and I am apprehended, I can scarcely be given six of the best bending over a chair, as we used to call it. Yes, you may leave this little matter entirely to me, Mr. Wooster.'

'I wish you'd call me Bertie.'

'Certainly, certainly.'

'And might I call you Roderick?'

'I shall be delighted.'

'Or Roddy? Roderick's rather a mouthful.'

'Whichever you prefer.'

'And you are really going to hunt the slipper?'

'I am resolved to do so. I have the greatest respect and affection for your uncle and appreciate how deeply wounded he would be, were this prized object to be permanently missing from his collection. I would never forgive myself if in the endeavour to recover his property, I were to leave any –'

'Stone unturned?'

'I was about to say avenue unexplored. I shall strain every –'

'Sinew?'

'I was thinking of the word nerve.'

'Just as *juste*. You'll have to bide your time, of course.'

'Quite.'

'And await your opportunity.'

'Exactly.'

'Opportunity knocks but once.'

'So I understand.'

'I'll give you one tip. The thing isn't on top of the cupboard or *armoire*.'

'Ah, that is helpful.'

'Unless of course he's put it there since. Well, anyway, best of luck, Roddy.'

'Thank you, Bertie.'

If I had been taking Old Doctor Gordon's Bile Magnesia regularly, I couldn't have felt more of an inward glow as I left him and headed for the lawn to get the Ma Cream book and return it to its place on the shelves of Aunt Dahlia's boudoir. I was lost in admiration of Roddy's manly spirit. He was well stricken in years, fifty if a day, and it thrilled me to think that there was so much life in the old dog still. It just showed . . . well, I don't know what, but something. I found myself musing on the boy Glossop, wondering what he had been like in his biscuit-snitching days. But except that I knew he wouldn't have been bald then, I couldn't picture him. It's often this way when one contemplates one's seniors. I remember how amazed I was to learn that my Uncle Percy, a tough old egg with apparently not a spark of humanity in him, had once held the metropolitan record for being chucked out of Covent Garden Balls.

I got the book, and ascertaining after reaching Aunt Dahlia's lair that there remained some twenty minutes before it would be necessary to start getting ready for the evening meal I took a seat and resumed my reading. I had had to leave off at a point where Ma Cream had just begun to spit on her hands and start filling the customers with pity and terror. But I hadn't put more than a couple of clues and a mere sprinkling of human gore under my belt, when the door flew open and Kipper appeared. And as the eye rested on him, he too filled me with pity and terror, for his map was flushed and his manner distraught. He looked like Jack Dempsey at the conclusion of his first conference with Gene Tunney, the occasion, if you remember, when he forgot to duck.

He lost no time in bursting into speech.

'Bertie! I've been hunting for you all over the place!'

'I was having a chat with Swordfish in his pantry. Something wrong?'

'Something wrong!'

'Don't you like the Red Room?'

'The Red Room!'

I gathered from his manner that he had not come to beef about his sleeping accommodation.

'Then what is your little trouble?'

'My little trouble!'

I felt that this sort of thing must be stopped at its source. It was only ten minutes to dressing-for-dinner time, and we could go on along these lines for hours.

'Listen, old crumpet,' I said patiently. 'Make up your mind whether you are my old friend Reginald Herring or an echo in the Swiss mountains. If you're simply going to repeat every word I say –'

At this moment Pop Glossop entered with the cocktails, and we cheesed the give-and-take. Kipper drained his glass to the lees and seemed to become calmer. When the door closed behind Roddy and he was at liberty to speak, he did so quite coherently. Taking another beaker, he said:

'Bertie, the most frightful thing has happened.'

I don't mind saying that the heart did a bit of sinking. In an earlier conversation with Bobbie Wickham it will be recalled that I had compared Brinkley Court to one of those joints the late Edgar Allan Poe used to write about. If you are acquainted with his works, you will remember that in them it was always tough going for those who stayed in country houses, the visitor being likely at any moment to encounter a walking corpse in a winding sheet with blood all over it. Prevailing conditions at Brinkley were not perhaps quite as testing as that, but the atmosphere had undeniably become sinister, and here was Kipper more than hinting that he had a story to relate which would deepen the general feeling that things were hotting up.

'What's the matter?' I said.

'I'll tell you what's the matter,' he said.

'Yes, do,' I said, and he did.

'Bertie,' he said, taking a third one. 'I think you will understand that when I read that announcement in *The Times* I was utterly bowled over?'

'Oh quite. Perfectly natural.'

'My head swam, and –'

'Yes, you told me. Everything went black.'

'I wish it had stayed black,' he said bitterly, 'but it didn't. After awhile the mists cleared, and I sat there seething with fury. And after I had seethed for a bit I rose from my chair, took pen in hand and wrote Bobbie a stinker.'

'Oh, gosh!'

'I put my whole soul into it.'

'Oh, golly!'

'I accused her in set terms of giving me the heave-ho in order that she could mercenarily marry a richer man. I called her a carrot-topped Jezebel whom I was thankful to have got out of my hair. I . . . Oh, I can't remember what else I said but, as I say, it was a stinker.'

'But you never mentioned a word about this when I met you.'

'In the ecstasy of learning that that *Times* thing was just a ruse and that she loved me still it passed completely from my mind. When it suddenly came back to me just now, it was like getting hit in the eye with a wet fish. I reeled.'

'Squealed?'

'Reeled. I felt absolutely boneless. But I had enough strength to stagger to the telephone. I rang up Skeldings Hall and was informed that she had just arrived.'

'She must have driven like an inebriated racing motorist.'

'No doubt she did. Girls will be girls. Anyway, she was there. She told me with a merry lilt in her voice that she had found a letter from me on the hall table and could hardly wait to open it. In a shaking voice I told her not to.'

'So you were in time.'

'In time, my foot! Bertie, you're a man of the world. You've known a good many members of the other sex in your day. What does a girl do when she is told not to open a letter?'

I got his drift.

'Opens it?'

'Exactly. I heard the envelope rip, and the next moment . . . No, I'd rather not think of it.'

'She took umbrage?'

'Yes, and she also took my head off. I don't know if you have ever been in a typhoon on the Indian Ocean.'

'No, I've never visited those parts.'

'Nor have I, but from what people tell me what ensued must have been very like being in one. She spoke for perhaps five minutes –'

'By Shrewsbury clock.'

'What?'

'Nothing. What did she say?'

'I can't repeat it all, and wouldn't if I could.'

'And what did you say?'

'I couldn't get a word in edgeways.'

'One can't sometimes.'

'Women talk so damn quick.'

'How well I know it! And what was the final score?'

'She said she was thankful that I was glad to have got her out of my hair, because she was immensely relieved to have got me out of hers, and that I had made her very happy because now she was free to marry you, which had always been her dearest wish.'

In this hair-raiser of Ma Cream's which I had been perusing there was a chap of the name of Scarface McColl, a gangster of sorts, who, climbing into the old car one morning and twiddling the starting key, went up in fragments owing to a business competitor having inserted a bomb in his engine, and I had speculated for a moment, while reading, as to how he must have felt. I knew now. Just as he had done, I rose. I sprang to the door, and Kipper raised an eyebrow.

'Am I boring you?' he said rather stiffly.

'No, no. But I must go and get my car.'

'You going for a ride?'

'Yes.'

'But it's nearly dinner time.'

'I don't want any dinner.'

'Where are you going?'

'Herne Bay.'

'Why Herne Bay?'

'Because Jeeves is there, and this thing must be placed in his hands without a moment's delay.'

'What can Jeeves do?'

'That,' I said, 'I cannot say, but he will do something. If he has been eating plenty of fish, as no doubt he would at a seashore resort, his brain will be at the top of its form, and when Jeeves's brain is at the top of its form, all you have to do is press a button and stand out of the way while he takes charge.'

11

It's considerably more than a step from Brinkley Court to Herne Bay, the one being in the middle of Worcestershire and the other on the coast of Kent, and even under the best of conditions you don't expect to do the trip in a flash. On the present occasion, held up by the Arab steed getting taken with a fit of the vapours and having to be towed to a garage for medical treatment, I didn't fetch up at journey's end till well past midnight. And when I rolled round to Jeeves's address on the morrow, I was informed that he had gone out early and they didn't know when he would be back. Leaving word for him to ring me at the Drones, I returned to the metropolis and was having the pre-dinner keg of nails in the smoking-room when his call came through.

'Mr. Wooster? Good evening, sir. This is Jeeves.'

'And not a moment too soon,' I said, speaking with the emotion of a lost lamb which after long separation from the parent sheep finally manages to spot it across the meadow. 'Where have you been all this time?'

'I had an appointment to lunch with a friend at Folkestone, sir, and while there was persuaded to extend my visit in order to judge a seaside bathing belles contest.'

'No, really? You do live, don't you?'

'Yes, sir.'

'How did it go off?'

'Quite satisfactorily, sir, thank you.'

'Who won?'

'A Miss Marlene Higgins of Brixton, sir, with Miss Lana Brown of Tulse Hill and Miss Marilyn Bunting of Penge honourably mentioned. All most attractive young ladies.'

'Shapely?'

'Extremely so.'

'Well, let me tell you, Jeeves, and you can paste this in your hat, shapeliness isn't everything in this world. In fact, it sometimes seems to me that the more curved and lissome the members of the opposite

sex, the more likely they are to set Hell's foundations quivering. I'm
sorely beset, Jeeves. Do you recall telling me once about someone who
told somebody he could tell him something which would make him
think a bit? Knitted socks and porcupines entered into it, I remember.'

'I think you may be referring to the ghost of the father of Hamlet,
Prince of Denmark, sir. Addressing his son, he said "I could a tale
unfold whose lightest word would harrow up thy soul, freeze thy young
blood, make thy two eyes, like stars, start from their spheres, thy
knotted and combined locks to part and each particular hair to stand
on end like quills upon the fretful porpentine." '

'That's right. Locks, of course, not socks. Odd that he should have
said porpentine when he meant porcupine. Slip of the tongue, no
doubt, as so often happens with ghosts. Well, he had nothing on me,
Jeeves. It's a tale of that precise nature that I am about to unfold.
Are you listening?'

'Yes, sir.'

'Then hold on to your hat and don't miss a word.'

When I had finished unfolding, he said, 'I can readily appreciate
your concern, sir. The situation, as you say, is one fraught with
anxiety,' which is pitching it strong for Jeeves, he as a rule coming
through with a mere 'Most disturbing, sir.'

'I will come to Brinkley Court immediately, sir.'

'Will you really? I hate to interrupt your holiday.'

'Not at all, sir.'

'You can resume it later.'

'Certainly, sir, if that is convenient to you.'

'But now –'

'Precisely sir. Now, if I may borrow a familiar phrase –'

'– is the time for all good men to come to the aid of the party?'

'The very words I was about to employ, sir. I will call at the
apartment at as early an hour tomorrow as is possible.'

'And we'll drive down together. Right,' I said, and went off to my
simple but wholesome dinner.

It was with . . . well, not quite an uplifted heart . . . call it a heart
lifted about half way . . . that I started out for Brinkley on the following
afternoon. The thought that Jeeves was at my side, his fish-fed brain
at my disposal, caused a spot of silver lining to gleam through the
storm clouds, but only a spot, for I was asking myself if even Jeeves
might not fail to find a solution of the problem that had raised its
ugly head. Admittedly expert though he was at joining sundered
hearts, he had rarely been up against a rift within the lute so complete
as that within the lute of Roberta Wickham and Reginald Herring,

and as I remember hearing him say once, 'tis not in mortals to command success. And at the thought of what would ensue, were he to fall down on the assignment, I quivered like something in aspic. I could not forget that Bobbie, while handing Kipper his hat, had expressed in set terms her intention of lugging me to the altar rails and signalling to the clergyman to do his stuff. So as I drove along the heart, as I have indicated, was uplifted only to a medium extent.

When we were out of the London traffic and it was possible to converse without bumping into buses and pedestrians, I threw the meeting open for debate.

'You have not forgotten our telephone conversation of yestreen, Jeeves?'

'No, sir.'

'You have the salient points docketed in your mind?'

'Yes, sir.'

'Have you been brooding on them?'

'Yes, sir.'

'Got a bite of any sort?'

'Not yet, sir.'

'No, I hardly expected you would. These things always take time.'

'Yes, sir.'

'The core of the matter is,' I said, twiddling the wheel to avoid a passing hen, 'that in Roberta Wickham we are dealing with a girl of high and haughty spirit.'

'Yes, sir.'

'And girls of high and haughty spirit need kidding along. This cannot be done by calling them carrot-topped Jezebels.'

'No, sir.'

'I know if anyone called me a carrot-topped Jezebel, umbrage is the first thing I'd take. Who was Jezebel, by the way? The name seems familiar, but I can't place her.'

'A character in the Old Testament, sir. A queen of Israel.'

'Of course, yes. Be forgetting my own name next. Eaten by dogs, wasn't she?'

'Yes, sir.'

'Can't have been pleasant for her.'

'No, sir.'

'Still, that's the way the ball rolls. Talking of being eaten by dogs, there's a dachshund at Brinkley who when you first meet him will give you the impression that he plans to convert you into a light snack between his regular meals. Pay no attention. It's all eyewash. His belligerent attitude is simply –'

'Sound and fury signifying nothing, sir?'

'That's it. Pure swank. A few civil words, and he will be grappling you . . . what's that expression I've heard you use?'

'Grappling me to his soul with hoops of steel, sir?'

'In the first two minutes. He wouldn't hurt a fly, but he has to put up a front because his name's Poppet. One can readily appreciate that when a dog hears himself addressed day in and day out as Poppet, he feels he must throw his weight about. His self-respect demands it.'

'Precisely, sir.'

'You'll like Poppet. Nice dog. Wears his ears inside out. Why do dachshunds wear their ears inside out?'

'I could not say, sir.'

'Nor me. I've often wondered. But this won't do, Jeeves. Here we are, yakking about Jezebels and dachshunds, when we ought to be concentrating our minds on . . .'

I broke off abruptly. My eye had been caught by a wayside inn. Well, not actually so much by the wayside inn as by what was standing outside it – to wit, a scarlet roadster which I recognized instantly as the property of Bobbie Wickham. One saw what had happened. Driving back to Brinkley after a couple of nights with Mother, she had found the going a bit warm and had stopped off at this hostelry for a quick one. And a very sensible thing to do, too. Nothing picks one up more than a spot of sluicing on a hot summer afternoon.

I applied the brakes.

'Mind waiting here a minute, Jeeves?'

'Certainly, sir. You wish to speak to Miss Wickham?'

'Ah, you spotted her car?'

'Yes, sir. It is distinctly individual.'

'Like its owner. I have a feeling that I may be able to accomplish something in the breach-healing way with a honeyed word or two. Worth trying, don't you think?'

'Unquestionably, sir.'

'At a time like this one doesn't want to leave any avenue unturned.'

The interior of the wayside inn – the 'Fox and Goose', not that it matters – was like the interiors of all wayside inns, dark and cool and smelling of beer, cheese, coffee, pickles and the sturdy English peasantry. Entering, you found yourself in a cosy nook with tankards on the walls and chairs and tables dotted hither and thither. On one of the chairs at one of the tables Bobbie was seated with a glass and a bottle of ginger ale before her.

'Good Lord, Bertie!' she said as I stepped up and what-ho-ed. 'Where did you spring from?'

I explained that I was on my way back to Brinkley from London in my car.

'Be careful someone doesn't pinch it. I'll bet you haven't taken out the keys.'

'No, but Jeeves is there, keeping watch and ward, as you might say.'

'Oh, you've brought Jeeves with you? I thought he was on his holiday.'

'He very decently cancelled it.'

'Pretty feudal.'

'Very. When I told him I needed him at my side, he didn't hesitate.'

'What do you need him at your side for?'

The moment had come for the honeyed word. I lowered my voice to a confidential murmur, but on her inquiring if I had laryngitis raised it again.

'I had an idea that he might be able to do something.'

'What about?'

'About you and Kipper,' I said, and started to feel my way cautiously towards the core and centre. It would be necessary, I knew, to pick my words with c., for with girls of high and haughty spirit you have to watch your step, especially if they have red hair, like Bobbie. If they think you're talking out of turn, dudgeon ensues, and dudgeon might easily lead her to reach for the ginger ale bottle and bean me with it. I don't say she would, but it was a possibility that had to be taken into account. So I sort of eased into the agenda.

'I must begin by saying that Kipper has given me a full eyewitness's – well, earwitness's I suppose you'd say – report of that chat you and he had over the telephone, and no doubt you are saying to yourself that it would have been in better taste for him to have kept it under his hat. But you must remember that we were boys together, and a fellow naturally confides in a chap he was boys together with. Anyway, be that as it may, he poured out his soul to me, and he hadn't been pouring long before I was able to see that he was cut to the quick. His blood pressure was high, his eye rolled in what they call a fine frenzy, and he was death-where-is-thy-sting-ing like nobody's business.'

I saw her quiver and kept a wary eye on the ginger ale bottle. But even if she had raised it and brought it down on the Wooster bean, I couldn't have been more stunned than I was by the words that left her lips.

'The poor lamb!'

I had ordered a gin and tonic. I now spilled a portion of this.

'Did you say poor lamb?'

'You bet I said poor lamb, though "Poor sap" would perhaps be a better description. Just imagine him taking all that stuff I said seriously. He ought to have known I didn't mean it.'

I groped for the gist.

'You were just making conversation?'

'Well, blowing off steam. For heaven's sake, isn't a girl allowed to blow off some steam occasionally? I never dreamed it would really upset him. Reggie always takes everything so literally.'

'Then is the position that the laughing love god is once more working at the old stand?'

'Like a beaver.'

'In fact, to coin a phrase, you're sweethearts still?'

'Of course. I may have meant what I said at the time, but only for about five minutes.'

I drew a deep breath, and a moment later wished I hadn't, because I drew it while drinking the remains of my gin and tonic.

'Does Kipper know of this?' I said, when I had finished coughing.

'Not yet. I'm on my way to tell him.'

I raised a point on which I particularly desired assurance.

'Then what it boils down to is – No wedding bells for me?'

'I'm afraid not.'

'Quite all right. Anything that suits you.'

'I don't want to get jugged for bigamy.'

'No, one sees that. And your selection for the day is Kipper. I don't blame you. The ideal mate.'

'Just the way I look at it. He's terrific, isn't he?'

'Colossal.'

'I wouldn't marry anyone else if they came to me bringing apes, ivory and peacocks. Tell me what he was like as a boy.'

'Oh, much the same as the rest of us.'

'Nonsense!'

'Except, of course, for rescuing people from burning buildings and saving blue-eyed children from getting squashed by runaway horses.'

'He did that a lot?'

'Almost daily.'

'Was he the Pride of the School?'

'Oh, rather.'

'Not that it was much of a school to be the pride of, from what he tells me. A sort of Dotheboys Hall, wasn't it?'

'Conditions under Aubrey Upjohn were fairly tough. One's mind reverts particularly to the sausages on Sunday.'

'Reggie was very funny about those. He said they were made not from contented pigs but from pigs which had expired, regretted by all, of glanders, the botts and tuberculosis.'

'Yes, that would be quite a fair description of them, I suppose. You going?' I said, for she had risen.

'I can't wait for another minute. I want to fling myself into Reggie's arms. If I don't see him soon, I shall pass out.'

'I know how you feel. The chap in the Yeoman's Wedding Song thought along those same lines, only the way he put it was "Ding dong, ding dong, ding dong, I hurry along." At one time I often used to render the number at village concerts, and there was a nasty Becher's Brook to get over when you got to "For it is my wedding morning," because you had to stretch out the "mor" for about ten minutes, which tested the lung power severely. I remember the vicar once telling me –'

Here I was interrupted, as I'm so often interrupted when giving my views on the Yeoman's Wedding Song, by her saying that she was dying to hear all about it but would rather wait till she could get it in my autobiography. We went out together, and I saw her off and returned to where Jeeves kept his vigil in the car, all smiles. I was all smiles, I mean, not Jeeves. The best he ever does is to let his mouth twitch slightly on one side, generally the left. I was in rare fettle, and the heart had touched a new high. I don't know anything that braces one up like finding you haven't got to get married after all.

'Sorry to keep you waiting, Jeeves,' I said. 'Hope you weren't bored?'

'Oh no, sir, thank you. I was quite happy with my Spinoza.'

'Eh?'

'The copy of Spinoza's *Ethics* which you kindly gave me some time ago.'

'Oh, ah, yes, I remember. Good stuff?'

'Extremely, sir.'

'I suppose it turns out in the end that the butler did it. Well, Jeeves, you'll be glad to hear that everything's under control.'

'Indeed, sir?'

'Yes, rift in lute mended and wedding bells liable to ring out at any moment. She's changed her mind.'

'*Varium et mutabile semper femina*, sir.'

'I shouldn't wonder. And now,' I said, climbing in and taking the wheel, 'I'll unfold the tale of Wilbert and the cow-creamer, and if that doesn't make your knotted locks do a bit of starting from their spheres, I for one shall be greatly surprised.'

12

Arriving at Brinkley in the quiet evenfall and putting the old machine away in the garage, I noticed that Aunt Dahlia's car was there and gathered from this that the aged relative was around and about once more. Nor was I in error. I found her in her boudoir getting outside a dish of tea and a crumpet. She greeted me with one of those piercing view-halloos which she had picked up on the hunting field in the days when she had been an energetic chivvier of the British fox. It sounded like a gas explosion and went through me from stem to stern. I've never hunted myself, but I understand that half the battle is being able to make noises like some jungle animal with dyspepsia, and I believe that Aunt Dahlia in her prime could lift fellow-members of the Quorn and Pytchley out of their saddles with a single yip, though separated from them by two ploughed fields and a spinney.

'Hullo, ugly,' she said. 'Turned up again, have you?'

'Just this moment breasted the tape.'

'Been to Herne Bay, young Herring tells me.'

'Yes, to fetch Jeeves. How's Bonzo?'

'Spotty but cheerful. What did you want Jeeves for?'

'Well, as it turns out, his presence isn't needed, but I only discovered that when I was half-way here. I was bringing him along to meditate . . . no, it isn't meditate . . . to mediate, that's the word, between Bobbie Wickham and Kipper. You knew they were betrothed?'

'Yes, she told me.'

'Did she tell you about shoving that thing in *The Times* saying she was engaged to me?'

'I was the first in whom she confided. I got a good laugh out of that.'

'More than Kipper did, because it hadn't occurred to the cloth-headed young nitwit to confide in him. When he read the announcement, he reeled and everything went black. It knocked his faith in woman for a loop, and after seething for a while he sat down and wrote her a letter in the Thomas Otway vein.'

'In the who's vein?'

'You are not familiar with Thomas Otway? Seventeenth-century dramatist, celebrated for making bitter cracks about the other sex. Wrote a play called *The Orphan*, which is full of them.'

'So you do read something beside the comics?'

'Well, actually I haven't steeped myself to any great extent in Thos's output, but Kipper told me about him. He held the view that women are a mess, and Kipper passed this information on to Bobbie in this letter of which I speak. It was a snorter.'

'And you never thought of explaining to him, I suppose?'

'Of course I did. But by that time she'd got the letter.'

'Why didn't the idiot tell her not to open it?'

'It was his first move. "I've found a letter from you here, precious," she said. "On no account open it, angel," he said. So of course she opened it.'

She pursed the lips, nodded the loaf, and ate a moody piece of crumpet.

'So that's why he's been going about looking like a dead fish. I suppose Roberta broke the engagement?'

'In a speech lasting five minutes without a pause for breath.'

'And you brought Jeeves along to mediate?'

'That was the idea.'

'But if things have gone as far as that . . .'

'You doubt whether even Jeeves can heal the rift?' I patted her on the top knot. 'Dry the starting tear, old ancestor, it's healed. I met her at a pub on the way here, and she told me that almost immediately after she had flipped her lid in the manner described she had a change of heart. She loves him still with a passion that's more like boiling oil than anything, and when we parted she was tooling off to tell him so. By this time they must be like ham and eggs again. It's a great burden off my mind, because, having parted brass rags with Kipper, she announced her intention of marrying me.'

'A bit of luck for you, I should have thought.'

'Far from it.'

'Why? You were crazy about the girl once.'

'But no longer. The fever has passed, the scales have fallen from my eyes, and we're just good friends. The snag in this business of falling in love, aged relative, is that the parties of the first part so often get mixed up with the wrong parties of the second part, robbed of their cooler judgment by the parties of the second part's glamour. Put it like this. The male sex is divided into rabbits and non-rabbits and the female sex into dashers and dormice, and the trouble is that the male rabbit has a way of getting attracted by the female dasher (who would be fine for the male non-rabbit) and realizing too late that he ought to have been concentrating on some mild, gentle dormouse with whom he could settle down peacefully and nibble lettuce.'

'The whole thing, in short, a bit of a mix-up?'

'Exactly. Take me and Bobbie. I yield to no one in my appreciation of her *espièglerie*, but I'm one of the rabbits and always have been while she is about as pronounced a dasher as ever dashed. What I like is the quiet life, and Roberta Wickham wouldn't recognize the quiet life if you brought it to her on a plate with watercress round it. She's all for not letting the sun go down without having started something calculated to stagger humanity. In a word, she needs the guiding hand, which is a thing I couldn't supply her with. Whereas from Kipper she will get it in abundance, he being one of those tough non-rabbits for whom it is child's play to make the little woman draw the line somewhere. That is why the union of these twain has my support and approval and why, when she told me all that in the pub, I felt like doing a buck-and-wing dance. Where is Kipper? I should like to shake him by the hand and pat his back.'

'He went on a picnic with Wilbert and Phyllis.'

The significance of this did not escape me.

'Tailing up stuff, eh? Right on the job, is he?'

'Wilbert is constantly under his eye.'

'And if ever a man needed to be constantly under an eye, it's the above kleptomaniac.'

'The what?'

'Haven't you been told? Wilbert's a pincher.'

'How do you mean, a pincher?'

'He pinches things. Everything that isn't nailed down is grist to his mill.'

'Don't be an ass.'

'I'm not being an ass. He's got Uncle Tom's cow-creamer.'

'I know.'

'You know?'

'Of course I know.'

Her . . . what's the word? . . . phlegm, is it? . . . something beginning with a p . . . astounded me. I had expected to freeze her young – or, rather, middle-aged – blood and have her perm stand on end like quills upon the fretful porpentine, and she hadn't moved a muscle.

'Beshrew me,' I said, 'you take it pretty calmly.'

'Well, what's there to get excited about? Tom sold him the thing.'

'What?'

'Wilbert got in touch with him at Harrogate and put in his bid, and Tom phoned me to give it to him. Just shows how important that deal must be to Tom. I'd have thought he would rather have parted with his eyeteeth.'

I drew a deep breath, this time fortunately unmixed with gin and tonic. I was profoundly stirred.

'You mean,' I said, my voice quavering like that of a coloratura soprano, 'that I went through that soul-shattering experience all for nothing?'

'Who's been shattering your soul, if any?'

'Ma Cream. By popping in while I was searching Wilbert's room for the loathsome object. Naturally I thought he'd swiped it and hidden it there.'

'And she caught you?'

'Not once, but twice.'

'What did she say?'

'She recommended me to take treatment from Roddy Glossop, of whose skill in ministering to the mentally afflicted she had heard such good reports. One sees what gave her the idea. I was half-way under the dressing-table at the moment, and no doubt she thought it odd.'

'Bertie! How absolutely priceless!'

The adjective 'priceless' seemed to me an ill-chosen one, and I said so. But my words were lost in the gale of mirth into which she now exploded. I had never heard anyone laugh so heartily, not even Bobbie on the occasion when the rake jumped up and hit me on the tip of the nose.

'I'd have given fifty quid to have been there,' she said, when she was able to get the vocal cords working. 'Half-way under the dressing-table, were you?'

'The second time. When we first forgathered, I was sitting on the floor with a chair round my neck.'

'Like an Elizabethan ruff, as worn by Thomas Botway.'

'Otway,' I said stiffly. As I have mentioned, I like to get things right. And I was about to tell her that what I had hoped for from a blood relation was sympathy and condolence rather than this crackling of thorns under a pot, as it is sometimes called, when the door opened and Bobbie came in.

The moment I cast an eye on her, it seemed to me that there was something strange about her aspect. Normally, this beasel presents to the world the appearance of one who is feeling that if it isn't the best of all possible worlds, it's quite good enough to be going on with till a better one comes along. Verve, I mean, and animation and all that sort of thing. But now there was a listlessness about her, not the listlessness of the cat Augustus but more that of the female in the picture in the Louvre, of whom Jeeves, on the occasion when he lugged me there to take a dekko at her, said that here was the head upon which all the ends of the world are come. He drew my attention, I remember, to the weariness of the eyelids. I got just the same impression of weariness from Bobbie's eyelids.

Unparting her lips which were set in a thin line as if she had just been taking a suck at a lemon, she said:

'I came to get that book of Mrs Cream's that I was reading, Mrs. Travers.'

'Help yourself, child,' said the ancestor. 'The more people in this joint reading her stuff, the better. It all goes to help the composition.'

'So you got here all right, Bobbie,' I said. 'Have you seen Kipper?'

I wouldn't say she snorted, but she certainly sniffed.

'Bertie,' she said in a voice straight from the Frigidaire, 'will you do me a favour?'

'Of course. What?'

'Don't mention that rat's name in my presence,' she said, and pushed off, the eyelids still weary.

She left me fogged and groping for the inner meaning, and I could see from Aunt Dahlia's goggling eyes that the basic idea hadn't got across with her either.

'Well!' she said. 'What's all this? I thought you told me she loved young Herring with a passion like boiling oil.'

'That was her story.'

'The oil seems to have gone off the boil. Yes, sir, if that was the language of love, I'll eat my hat,' said the blood relation, alluding, I took it, to the beastly straw contraption in which she does her gardening, concerning which I can only say that it is almost as foul as Uncle Tom's Sherlock Holmes deerstalker, which has frightened more crows than any other lid in Worcestershire. 'They must have had a fight.'

'It does look like it,' I agreed, 'and I don't understand how it can have happened considering that she left me with the love light in her eyes and can't have been back here more than about half an hour. What, one asks oneself, in so short a time can have changed a girl full of love and ginger ale into a girl who speaks of the adored object as "that rat" and doesn't want to hear his name mentioned? These are deep waters. Should I send for Jeeves?'

'What on earth can Jeeves do?'

'Well, now you put it that way, I'm bound to admit that I don't know. It's just that one drops into the habit of sending for Jeeves whenever things have gone agley, if that's the word I'm thinking of. Scotch, isn't it? Agley, I mean. It sounds Scotch to me. However, passing lightly over that, the thing to do when you want the low-down is to go to the fountainhead and get it straight from the horse's mouth. Kipper can solve this mystery. I'll pop along and find him.'

I was, however, spared the trouble of popping, for at this moment he entered left centre.

'Oh, there you are, Bertie,' he said. 'I heard you were back. I was looking for you.'

He had spoken in a low, husky sort of way, like a voice from the tomb, and I now saw that he was exhibiting all the earmarks of a man who has recently had a bomb explode in his vicinity. His shoulders sagged and his eyes were glassy. He looked, in short, like the fellow who hadn't started to take Old Doctor Gordon's Bile Magnesia, and I snapped into it without preamble. This was no time for being tactful and pretending not to notice.

'What's all this strained-relations stuff between you and Bobbie, Kipper?' I said, and when he said, 'Oh, nothing,' rapped the table sharply and told him to cut out the coy stuff and come clean.

'Yes,' said Aunt Dahlia. 'What's happened, young Herring?'

I think for a moment he was about to draw himself up with hauteur and say he would prefer, if we didn't mind, not to discuss his private affairs, but when he was half-way up he caught Aunt Dahlia's eye and returned to position one. Aunt Dahlia's eye, while not in the same class as that of my Aunt Agatha, who is known to devour her young and conduct human sacrifices at the time of the full moon, has lots of authority. He subsided into a chair and sat there looking filleted.

'Well, if you must know,' he said, 'she's broken the engagement.'

This didn't get us any farther. We had assumed as much. You don't go calling people rats if love still lingers.

'But it's only an hour or so,' I said, 'since I left her outside a hostelry called the "Fox and Goose", and she had just been giving you a rave notice. What came unstuck? What did you do to the girl?'

'Oh, nothing.'

'Come, come!'

'Well, it was this way.'

There was a pause here while he said that he would give a hundred quid for a stiff whisky-and-soda, but as this would have involved all the delay of ringing for Pop Glossop and having it fetched from the lowest bin, Aunt Dahlia would have none of it. In lieu of the desired

refreshment she offered him a cold crumpet, which he declined, and
told him to get on with it.

'Where I went wrong,' he said, still speaking in that low, husky
voice as if he had been a ghost suffering from catarrh, 'was in getting
engaged to Phyllis Mills.'

'What?' I cried.

'What?' cried Aunt Dahlia.

'Egad!' I said.

'What on earth did you do that for?' said Aunt Dahlia.

He shifted uneasily in his chair, like a man troubled with ants in
the pants.

'It seemed a good idea at the time,' he said. 'Bobbie had told me
on the telephone that she never wanted to speak to me again in this
world or the next, and Phyllis had been telling me that, while she
shrank from Wilbert Cream because of his murky past, she found him
so magnetic that she knew she wouldn't be able to refuse him if he
proposed, and I had been commissioned to stop him proposing, so I
thought the simplest thing to do was to get engaged to her myself.
So we talked it over, and having reached a thorough understanding
that it was simply a ruse and nothing binding on either side, we
announced it to Cream.'

'Very shrewd,' said Aunt Dahlia. 'How did he take it?'

'He reeled.'

'Lot of reeling there's been in this business,' I said. 'You reeled, if
you recollect, when you remembered you'd written that letter to
Bobbie.'

'And I reeled again when she suddenly appeared from nowhere just
as I was kissing Phyllis.'

I pursed the lips. Getting a bit French, this sequence, it seemed to
me.

'There was no need for you to do that.'

'No need, perhaps, but I wanted to make it look natural to Cream.'

'Oh, I see. Driving it home, as it were?'

'That was the idea. Of course I wouldn't have done it if I'd known
that Bobbie had changed her mind and wanted things to be as they
were before that telephone conversation. But I didn't know. It's just
one of life's little ironies. You get the same sort of thing in Thomas
Hardy.'

I knew nothing of this T. Hardy of whom he spoke, but I saw what
he meant. It was like what's always happening in the novels of
suspense, where the girl goes around saying, 'Had I but known.'

'Didn't you explain?'

He gave me a pitying look.

'Have you ever tried explaining something to a red-haired girl who's madder than a wet hen?'

I took his point.

'What happened then?'

'Oh, she was very lady-like. Talked amiably of this and that till Phyllis had left us. Then she started in. She said she had raced here with a heart overflowing with love, longing to be in my arms, and a jolly surprise it was to find those arms squeezing the stuffing out of another and . . . Oh, well, a lot more along those lines. The trouble is, she's always been a bit squiggle-eyed about Phyllis, because in Switzerland she held the view that we were a shade too matey. Nothing in it, of course.'

'Just good friends?'

'Exactly.'

'Well, if you want to know what I think,' said Aunt Dahlia.

But we never did get around to knowing what she thought, for at this moment Phyllis came in.

13

Giving the wench the once-over as she entered, I found myself well able to understand why Bobbie on observing her entangled with Kipper had exploded with so loud a report. I'm not myself, of course, an idealistic girl in love with a member of the staff of the *Thursday Review* and never have been, but if I were I know I'd get the megrims somewhat severely if I caught him in a clinch with anyone as personable as this stepdaughter of Aubrey Upjohn, for though shaky on the I.Q., physically she was a pipterino of the first water. Her eyes were considerably bluer than the skies above, she was wearing a simple summer dress which accentuated rather than hid the graceful outlines of her figure, if you know what I mean, and it was not surprising that Wilbert Cream, seeing her, should have lost no time in reaching for the book of poetry and making a bee line with her to the nearest leafy glade.

'Oh, Mrs. Travers,' she said, spotting Aunt Dahlia, 'I've just been talking to Daddy on the telephone.'

This took the old ancestor's mind right off the tangled affairs of the Kipper-Bobbie axis, to which a moment before she had been according her best attention, and I didn't wonder. With the prize-giving at Market Snodsbury Grammar School, a function at which all that was bravest and fairest in the neighbourhood would be present, only two days away, she must have been getting pretty uneasy about the continued absence of the big shot slated to address the young scholars on ideals and life in the world outside. If you are on the board of governors of a school and have contracted to supply an orator for the great day of the year, you can be forgiven for feeling a trifle jumpy when you learn that the silver-tongued one has gadded off to the metropolis, leaving no word as to when he will be returning, if ever. For all she knew, Upjohn might have got the holiday spirit and be planning to remain burning up the boulevards indefinitely, and of course nothing gives a big beano a black eye more surely than the failure to show up of the principal speaker. So now she quite naturally blossomed like a rose in June and asked if the old son of a bachelor had mentioned anything about when he was coming back.

'He's coming back tonight. He says he hopes you haven't been worrying.'

A snort of about the calibre of an explosion in an ammunition dump escaped my late father's sister.

'Oh, does he? Well, I've a piece of news for him. I *have* been worrying. What's kept him in London so long?'

'He's been seeing his lawyer about this libel action he's bringing against the *Thursday Review*.'

I have often asked myself how many inches it was that Kipper leaped from his chair at these words. Sometimes I think it was ten, sometimes only six, but whichever it was he unquestionably came up from the padded seat like an athlete competing in the Sitting High Jump event. Scarface McColl couldn't have risen more nippily.

'Against the *Thursday Review*?' said Aunt Dahlia. 'That's your rag, isn't it, young Herring? What have they done to stir him up?'

'It's this book Daddy wrote about preparatory schools. He wrote a book about preparatory schools. Did you know he had written a book about preparatory schools?'

'Hadn't an inkling. Nobody tells me anything.'

'Well, he wrote this book about preparatory schools. It was about preparatory schools.'

'About preparatory schools, was it?'

'Yes, about preparatory schools.'

'Thank God we've got that straightened out at last. I had a feeling we should get somewhere if we dug long enough. And –?'

'And the *Thursday Review* said something libellous about it, and Daddy's lawyer says the jury ought to give Daddy at least five thousand pounds. Because they libelled him. So he's been in London all this time seeing his lawyer. But he's coming back tonight. He'll be here for the prize-giving, and I've got his speech all typed out and ready for him. Oh, there's my precious Poppet,' said Phyllis, as a distant barking reached the ears. 'He's asking for his dinner, the sweet little angel. All right, darling, Mother's coming,' she fluted, and buzzed off on the errand of mercy.

A brief silence followed her departure.

'I don't care what you say,' said Aunt Dahlia at length in a defiant sort of way. 'Brains aren't everything. She's a dear, sweet girl. I love her like a daughter, and to hell with anyone who calls her a half-wit. Why, hullo,' she proceeded, seeing that Kipper was slumped back in his chair trying without much success to hitch up a drooping lower jaw. 'What's eating you, young Herring?'

I could see that Kipper was in no shape for conversation, so took it upon myself to explain.

'A certain stickiness has arisen, aged relative. You heard what P. Mills said before going to minister to Poppet. Those words tell the story.'

'What do you mean?'

'The facts are readily stated. Upjohn wrote this slim volume, which, if you recall, was about preparatory schools, and in it, so Kipper tells me, said that the time spent in these establishments was the happiest of our lives. Ye Ed passed it on to Kipper for comment, and he, remembering the dark days at Malvern House, Bramley-on-Sea, when he and I were plucking the gowans fine there, slated it with no uncertain hand. Correct, Kipper?'

He found speech, if you could call making a noise like a buffalo taking its foot out of a swamp finding speech.

'But, dash it,' he said, finding a bit more, 'it was perfectly legitimate criticism. I didn't mince my words, of course –'

'It would be interesting to find out what these unminced words were,' said Aunt Dahlia, 'for among them there appear to have been one or two which seem likely to set your proprietor back five thousand of the best and brightest. Bertie, get your car out and go to Market Snodsbury station and see if the bookstall has a copy of this week's . . . No, wait, hold the line. Cancel that order. I shan't be a minute,' she said, and went out, leaving me totally fogged as to what she was up to. What aunts are up to is never an easy thing to divine.

I turned to Kipper.

'Bad show,' I said.

From the way he writhed I gathered that he was feeling it could scarcely be worse.

'What happens when an editorial assistant on a weekly paper lets the bosses in for substantial libel damages?'

He was able to answer that one.

'He gets the push and, what's more, finds it pretty damned difficult to land another job. He's on the black list.'

I saw what he meant. These birds who run weekly papers believe in watching the pennies. They like to get all that's coming to them and when the stuff, instead of pouring in, starts pouring out as the result of an injudicious move on the part of a unit of the staff, what they do to that unit is plenty. I think Kipper's outfit was financed by some sort of board or syndicate, but boards and syndicates are just as sensitive about having to cough up as individual owners. As Kipper had indicated, they not only give the erring unit the heave-ho but pass the word round to the other boards and syndicates.

'Herring?' the latter say when Kipper comes seeking employment. 'Isn't he the bimbo who took the bread out of the mouths of the *Thursday Review* people? Chuck the blighter out of the window and we want to see him bounce.' If this action of Upjohn's went through, his chances of any sort of salaried post were meagre, if not slim. It might be years before all was forgiven and forgotten.

'Selling pencils in the gutter is about the best I'll be able to look forward to,' said Kipper, and he had just buried his face in his hands, as fellows are apt to do when contemplating a future that's a bit on the bleak side, when the door opened, to reveal not, as I had expected, Aunt Dahlia, but Bobbie.

'I got the wrong book,' she said. 'The one I wanted was –'

Then her eye fell on Kipper and she stiffened in every limb, rather like Lot's wife, who, as you probably know, did the wrong thing that time there was all that unpleasantness with the cities of the plain and got turned into a pillar of salt, though what was the thought behind this I've never been able to understand. Salt, I mean. Seems so bizarre somehow and not at all what you would expect.

'Oh!' she said haughtily, as if offended by this glimpse into the underworld, and even as she spoke a hollow groan burst from Kipper's interior and he raised an ashen face. And at the sight of that ashen f. the haughtiness went out of Roberta Wickham with a whoosh, to be replaced by all the old love, sympathy, womanly tenderness and what not, and she bounded at him like a leopardess getting together with a lost cub.

'Reggie! Oh, Reggie! Reggie, darling, what is it?' she cried, her whole demeanour undergoing a marked change for the better. She was, in short, melted by his distress, as so often happens with the female sex. Poets have frequently commented on this. You are probably familiar with the one who said 'Oh, woman in our hours of ease tum tumty tiddly something please, when something something something some-thing brow, a something something something thou.'

She turned on me with an animal snarl.

'What have you been doing to the poor lamb?' she demanded, giving me one of the nastiest looks seen that summer in the midland counties, and I had just finished explaining that it was not I but Fate or Destiny that had removed the sunshine from the poor lamb's life, when Aunt Dahlia returned. She had a slip of paper in her hand.

'I was right,' she said. 'I knew Upjohn's first move on getting a book published would be to subscribe to a press-cutting agency. I found this on the hall table. It's your review of his slim volume, young Herring, and having run an eye over it I'm not surprised that he's a little upset. I'll read it to you.'

As might have been expected, this having been foreshadowed a good deal in one way and another, what Kipper had written was on the severe side, and as far as I was concerned it fell into the rare and refreshing fruit class. I enjoyed every minute of it. It concluded as follows:

'Aubrey Upjohn might have taken a different view of preparatory schools if he had done a stretch at the Dotheboys Hall conducted by him at Malvern House, Bramley-on-Sea, as we had the misfortune to do. We have not forgotten the sausages on Sunday, which were made not from contented pigs but from pigs which had expired, regretted by all, of glanders, the botts and tuberculosis.'

Until this passage left the aged relative's lips Kipper had been sitting with the tips of his fingers together, nodding from time to time as much as to say 'Caustic, yes, but perfectly legitimate criticism,' but on hearing this excerpt he did another of his sitting high jumps, lowering all previous records by several inches. It occurred to me as a passing thought that if all other sources of income failed, he had a promising future as an acrobat.

'But I never wrote that,' he gasped.

'Well, it's here in cold print.'

'Why, that's libellous!'

'So Upjohn and his legal eagle seem to feel. And I must say it reads like a pretty good five thousand pounds' worth to me.'

'Let me look at that,' yipped Kipper. 'I don't understand this. No, half a second, darling. Not now. Later. I want to concentrate,' he said, for Bobbie had flung herself on him and was clinging to him like the ivy on the old garden wall.

'Reggie!' she wailed – yes, wail's the word. 'It was me!'

'Eh?'

'That thing Mrs Travers just read. You remember you showed me the proof at lunch that day and told me to drop it off at the office, as you had to rush along to keep a golf date. I read it again after you'd gone, and saw you had left out that bit about the sausages – accidentally, I thought – and it seemed to me so frightfully funny and clever that . . . Well, I put it in at the end. I felt it just rounded the thing off.'

14

There was silence for some moments, broken only by the sound of an aunt saying 'Lord love a duck!' Kipper stood blinking, as I had sometimes seen him do at the boxing tourneys in which he indulged when in receipt of a shrewd buffet on some tender spot like the tip of the nose. Whether or not the idea of taking Bobbie's neck in both hands and twisting it into a spiral floated through his mind, I cannot say, but if so it was merely the ideal dream of a couple of seconds or so, for almost immediately love prevailed. She had described him as a lamb, and it was with all the mildness for which lambs are noted that he now spoke.

'Oh, I see. So that's how it was.'

'I'm so sorry.'

'Don't mention it.'

'Can you ever forgive me?'

'Oh, rather.'

'I meant so well.'

'Of course you did.'

'Will you really get into trouble about this?'

'There may be some slight unpleasantness.'

'Oh, Reggie!'

'Quite all right.'

'I've ruined your life.'

'Nonsense. The *Thursday Review* isn't the only paper in London. If they fire me, I'll accept employment elsewhere.'

This scarcely squared with what he had told me about being blacklisted, but I forbore to mention this, for I saw that his words had cheered Bobbie up considerably, and I didn't want to bung a spanner into her mood of *bien être*. Never does to dash the cup of happiness from a girl's lips when after plumbing the depths she has started to take a swig at it.

'Of course!' she said. 'Any paper would be glad to have a valuable man like you.'

'They'll fight like tigers for his services,' I said, helping things along. 'You don't find a chap like Kipper out of circulation for more than a day or so.'

'You're so clever.'

'Oh, thanks.'

'I don't mean you, ass, I mean Reggie.'

'Ah, yes. Kipper has what it takes, all right.'

'All the same,' said Aunt Dahlia, 'I think, when Upjohn arrives, you had better do all you can to ingratiate yourself with him.'

I got her meaning. She was recommending that grappling-to-the-soul-with-hoops-of-steel stuff.

'Yes,' I said. 'Exert the charm, Kipper, and there's a chance he might call the thing off.'

'Bound to,' said Bobbie. 'Nobody can resist you, darling.'

'Do you think so, darling?'

'Of course I do, darling.'

'Well, let's hope you're right, darling. In the meantime,' said Kipper, 'if I don't get that whisky-and-soda soon, I shall disintegrate. Would you mind if I went in search of it, Mrs. Travers?'

'It's the very thing I was about to suggest myself. Dash along and drink your fill, my unhappy young stag at eve.'

'I'm feeling rather like a restorative, too,' said Bobbie.

'Me also,' I said, swept along on the tide of the popular movement. 'Though I would advise,' I said, when we were outside, 'making it port. More authority. We'll look in on Swordfish. He will provide.'

We found Pop Glossop in his pantry polishing silver, and put in our order. He seemed a little surprised at the inrush of such a multitude, but on learning that our tongues were hanging out obliged with a bottle of the best, and after we had done a bit of tissue-restoring, Kipper, who had preserved a brooding silence since entering, rose and left us, saying that if we didn't mind he would like to muse apart for awhile. I saw Pop Glossop give him a sharp look as he went out and knew that Kipper's demeanour had roused his professional interest, causing him to scent in the young visitor a potential customer. These brain specialists are always on the job and never miss a trick. Tactfully waiting till the door had closed, he said:

'Is Mr Herring an old friend of yours, Mr. Wooster?'

'Bertie.'

'I beg your pardon. Bertie. You have known him for some time?'

'Practically from the egg.'

'And is Miss Wickham a friend of his?'

'Reggie Herring and I are engaged, Sir Roderick,' said Bobbie. Her words seemed to seal the Glossop lips. He said 'Oh' and began to talk about the weather and continued to do so until Bobbie, who since Kipper's departure had been exhibiting signs of restlessness, said she thought she would go and see how he was making out. Finding himself de-Wickham-ed, he unsealed his lips without delay.

'I did not like to mention it before Miss Wickham, as she and Mr. Herring are engaged, for one is always loath to occasion anxiety, but that young man has a neurosis.'

'He isn't always as dippy as he looked just now.'

'Nevertheless –'

'And let me tell you something, Roddy. If you were as up against it as he is, you'd have a neurosis, too.'

And feeling that it would do no harm to get his views on the Kipper situation, I unfolded the tale.

'So you see the posish,' I concluded. 'The only way he can avoid the fate that is worse than death – viz. letting his employers get nicked for a sum beyond the dreams of avarice – is by ingratiating himself with Upjohn, which would seem to any thinking man a shot that's not on the board. I mean, he had four years with him at Malvern House and didn't ingratiate himself once, so it's difficult to see how he's going to start doing it now. It seems to me the thing's an impasse. French expression,' I explained, 'meaning that we're stymied good and proper with no hope of finding a formula.'

To my surprise, instead of clicking the tongue and waggling the head gravely to indicate that he saw the stickiness of the dilemma, he chuckled fatly, as if having spotted an amusing side to the thing which had escaped me. Having done this, he blessed his soul, which was his way of saying 'Gorblimey'.

'It really is quite extraordinary, my dear Bertie,' he said, 'how associating with you restores my youth. Your lightest word seems to bring back old memories. I find myself recollecting episodes in the distant past which I have not thought of for years and years. It is as though you waved a magic wand of some kind. This matter of the problem confronting your friend Mr. Herring is a case in point. While you were telling me of his troubles, the mists shredded away, the hands of the clock turned back, and I was once again a young fellow in my early twenties, deeply involved in the strange affair of Bertha Simmons, George Lanchester and Bertha's father, old Mr. Simmons, who at that time resided in Putney. He was in the imported lard and butter business.'

'The what was that strange affair again?'

He repeated the cast of characters, asked me if I would care for another drop of port, a suggestion with which I readily fell in, and proceeded.

'George, a young man of volcanic passions, met Bertha Simmons at a dance at Putney Town Hall in aid of the widows of deceased railway porters and became instantly enamoured. And his love was returned. When he encountered Bertha next day in Putney High Street and, taking her off to a confectioner's for an ice cream, offered her with it his hand and heart, she accepted them enthusiastically. She said that when they were dancing together on the previous night something had seemed to go all over her, and he said he had had exactly the same experience.'

'Twin souls, what?'

'A most accurate description.'

'In fact, so far, so good.'

'Precisely. But there was an obstacle, and a very serious one. George was a swimming instructor at the local baths, and Mr. Simmons had higher views for his daughter. He forbade the marriage. I am speaking, of course, of the days when fathers did forbid marriage. It was only when George saved him from drowning that he relented and gave the young couple his consent and blessing.'

'How did that happen?'

'Perfectly simple. I took Mr. Simmons for a stroll on the river bank and pushed him in, and George, who was waiting in readiness, dived into the water and pulled him out. Naturally I had to undergo a certain amount of criticism of my clumsiness, and it was many weeks before I received another invitation to Sunday supper at Chatsworth, the Simmons residence, quite a privation in those days when I was a penniless medical student and perpetually hungry, but I was glad to sacrifice myself to help a friend and the results, as far as George was concerned, were of the happiest. And what crossed my mind, as you were telling me of Mr. Herring's desire to ingratiate himself with Mr. Upjohn, was that a similar — is "set-up" the term you young fellows use? — would answer in his case. All the facilities are here at Brinkley Court. In my rambles about the grounds I have noticed a small but quite adequate lake, and . . . well, there you have it, my dear Bertie. I throw it out, of course, merely as a suggestion.'

His words left me all of a glow. When I thought how I had misjudged him in the days when our relations had been distant, I burned with shame and remorse. It seemed incredible that I could ever have looked on this admirable loony-doctor as the menace in the treatment. What a lesson, I felt, this should teach all of us that a man may have a bald head and bushy eyebrows and still remain at heart a jovial sportsman and one of the boys. There was about an inch of the ruby juice nestling in my glass, and as he finished speaking I raised the beaker in a reverent toast. I told him he had hit the bull's eye and was entitled to a cigar or coconut according to choice.

'I'll go and take the matter up with my principals immediately.'

'Can Mr. Herring swim?'

'Like several fishes.'

'Then I see no obstacle in the path.'

We parted with mutual expressions of good will, and it was only after I had emerged into the summer air that I remembered I hadn't told him that Wilbert had purchased, not pinched, the cow-creamer, and for a moment I thought of going back to apprise him. But I thought again, and didn't. First things first, I said to myself, and the item at the top of the agenda paper was the bringing of a new sparkle to Kipper's eyes. Later on, I told myself, would do, and carried on to where he and Bobbie were pacing the lawn with bowed heads. It would not be long, I anticipated, before I would be bringing those heads up with a jerk.

Nor was I in error. Their enthusiasm was unstinted. Both agreed unreservedly that if Upjohn had the merest spark of human feeling in him, which of course had still to be proved, the thing was in the bag.

'But you never thought this up yourself, Bertie,' said Bobbie, always inclined to underestimate the Wooster shrewdness. 'You've been talking to Jeeves.'

'No, as a matter of fact, it was Swordfish who had the idea.'

Kipper seemed surprised.

'You mean you told him about it?'

'I thought it the strategic move. Four heads are better than three.'

'And he advised shoving Upjohn into the lake?'

'That's right.'

'Rather a peculiar butler.'

I turned this over in my mind.

'Peculiar? Oh, I don't know. Fairly run-of-the-mill I should call him. Yes, more or less the usual type,' I said.

15

With self all eagerness and enthusiasm for the work in hand, straining at the leash, as you might say, and full of the will to win, it came as a bit of a damper when I found on the following afternoon that Jeeves didn't think highly of Operation Upjohn. I told him about it just before starting out for the tryst, feeling that it would be helpful to have his moral support, and was stunned to see that his manner was austere and even puff-faced. He was giving me a description at the time of how it felt to act as judge at a seaside bathing belles contest, and it was with regret that I was compelled to break into this, for he had been holding me spellbound.

'I'm sorry, Jeeves,' I said, consulting my watch, 'but I shall have to be dashing off. Urgent appointment. You must tell me the rest later.'

'At any time that suits you, sir.'

'Are you doing anything for the next half hour or so?'

'No, sir.'

'Not planning to curl up in some shady nook with a cigarette and Spinoza?'

'No, sir.'

'Then I strongly advise you to come down to the lake and witness a human drama.'

And in a few brief words I outlined the programme and the events which had led up to it. He listened attentively and raised his left eyebrow a fraction of an inch.

'Was this Miss Wickham's idea, sir?'

'No. I agree that it sounds like one of hers, but actually it was Sir Roderick Glossop who suggested it. By the way, you were probably surprised to find him buttling here.'

'It did occasion me a momentary astonishment, but Sir Roderick explained the circumstances.'

'Fearing that if he didn't let you in on it, you might unmask him in front of Mrs. Cream?'

'No doubt, sir. He would naturally wish to take all precautions. I gathered from his remarks that he has not yet reached a definite conclusion regarding the mental condition of Mr. Cream.'

'No, he's still observing. Well, as I say, it was from his fertile bean that the idea sprang. What do you think of it?'

'Ill-advised, sir, in my opinion.'

I was amazed. I could hardly b. my e.

'Ill-advised?'

'Yes, sir.'

'But it worked without a hitch in the case of Bertha Simmons, George Lanchester and old Mr. Simmons.'

'Very possibly, sir.'

'Then why this defeatist attitude?'

'It is merely a feeling, sir, due probably to my preference for finesse. I mistrust these elaborate schemes. One cannot depend on them. As the poet Burns says, the best laid plans of mice and men gang aft agley.'

'Scotch, isn't it, that word?'

'Yes, sir.'

'I thought as much. The "gang" told the story. Why do Scotsmen say gang?'

'I have no information, sir. They have not confided in me.'

I was getting a bit peeved by now, not at all liking the sniffiness of his manner. I had expected him to speed me on my way with words of encouragement and uplift, not to go trying to blunt the keen edge of my zest like this. I was rather in the position of a child who runs to his mother hoping for approval and endorsement of something he's done, and is awarded instead a brusque kick in the pants. It was with a good deal of warmth that I came back at him.

'So you think the poet Burns would look askance at this enterprise of ours, do you? Well, you can tell him from me he's an ass. We've thought the thing out to the last detail. Miss Wickham asks Mr. Upjohn to come for a stroll with her. She leads him to the lake. I am standing on the brink, ostensibly taking a look at the fishes playing amongst the reeds. Kipper, ready to the last button, is behind a neighbouring tree. On the cue "Oh, look!" from Miss Wickham, accompanied by business of pointing with girlish excitement at something in the water, Upjohn bends over to peer. I push, Kipper dives in, and there we are. Nothing can possibly go wrong.'

'Just as you say, sir. But I still have that feeling.'

The blood of the Woosters is hot, and I was about to tell him in set terms what I thought of his bally feeling, when I suddenly spotted what it was that was making him crab the act. The green-eyed monster had bitten him. He was miffed because he wasn't the brains behind this binge, the blue prints for it having been laid down by a rival. Even great men have their weaknesses. So I held back the acid crack I might have made, and went off with a mere 'Oh, yeah?' No sense in twisting the knife in the wound, I mean.

All the same, I remained a bit hot under the collar, because when you're all strung up and tense and all that, the last thing you want is people upsetting you by bringing in the poet Burns. I hadn't told him, but our plans had already nearly been wrecked at the outset by the unfortunate circumstance of Upjohn, while in the metropolis, having shaved his moustache, this causing Kipper to come within a toucher of losing his nerve and calling the whole thing off. The sight of that bare expanse or steppe of flesh beneath the nose, he said, did something to him, bringing back the days when he had so often found his blood turning to ice on beholding it. It had required quite a series of pep talks to revive his manly spirits.

However, there was good stuff in the lad, and though for a while the temperature of his feet had dropped sharply, threatening to reduce him to the status of a non-cooperative cat in an adage, at 3.30 Greenwich Mean Time he was at his post behind the selected tree, resolved to do his bit. He poked his head round the tree as I arrived, and when I waved a cheery hand at him, waved a fairly cheery hand at me. Though I only caught a glimpse of him, I could see that his upper lip was stiff.

There being no signs as yet of the female star and her companion, I deduced that I was a bit on the early side. I lit a cigarette and stood awaiting their entrance, and was pleased to note that conditions could scarcely have been better for the coming water fête. Too often on an English summer day you find the sun going behind the clouds and a nippy wind springing up from the north east, but this afternoon was one of those still, sultry afternoons when the slightest movement brings the persp. in beads to the brow, an afternoon, in short, when it would be a positive pleasure to be shoved into a lake. 'Most refreshing,' Upjohn would say to himself as the cool water played about his limbs.

I was standing there running over the stage directions in my mind to see that I had got them all clear, when I beheld Wilbert Cream approaching, the dog Poppet curvetting about his ankles. On seeing me, the hound rushed forward with uncouth cries as was his wont, but on heaving alongside and getting a whiff of Wooster Number Five calmed down, and I was at liberty to attend to Wilbert, who I could see desired speech with me.

He was looking, I noticed, fairly green about the gills, and he conveyed the same suggestion of having just swallowed a bad oyster which I had observed in Kipper on his arrival at Brinkley. It was plain that the loss of Phyllis Mills, goofy though she unquestionably was, had hit him a shrewd wallop, and I presumed that he was coming to me for sympathy and heart balm, which I would have been only too pleased to dish out. I hoped, of course, that he would make it crisp and remove himself at an early date, for when the moment came for the balloon to go up I didn't want to be hampered by an audience. When you're pushing someone into a lake, nothing embarrasses you more than having the front seats filled up with goggling spectators.

It was not, however, on the subject of Phyllis that he proceeded to touch.

'Oh, Wooster,' he said, 'I was talking to my mother a night or two ago.'

'Oh, yes?' I said, with a slight wave of the hand intended to indicate that if he liked to talk to his mother anywhere, all over the house, he had my approval.

'She tells me you are interested in mice.'

I didn't like the trend the conversation was taking, but I preserved my aplomb.

'Why, yes, fairly interested.'

'She says she found you trying to catch one in my bedroom!'

'Yes, that's right.'

'Good of you to bother.'

'Not at all. Always a pleasure.'

'She says you seemed to be making a very thorough search of my room.'

'Oh, well, you know, when one sets one's hand to the plough.'

'You didn't find a mouse?'

'No, no mouse. Sorry.'

'I wonder if by any chance you happened to find an eighteenth-century cow-creamer?'

'Eh?'

'A silver jug shaped like a cow.'

'No. Why, was it on the floor somewhere?'

'It was in a drawer of the bureau.'

'Ah, then I would have missed it.'

'You'd certainly miss it now. It's gone.'

'Gone?'

'Gone.'

'You mean disappeared, as it were?'

'I do.'

'Strange.'

'Very strange.'

'Yes, does seem extremely strange, doesn't it?'

I had spoken with all the old Wooster coolness, and I doubt if a casual observer would have detected that Bertram was not at his ease, but I can assure my public that he wasn't by a wide margin. My heart had leaped in the manner popularized by Kipper Herring and Scarface McColl, crashing against my front teeth with a thud which must have been audible in Market Snodsbury. A far less astute man would have been able to divine what had happened. Not knowing the score owing to having missed the latest stop-press news and looking on the cow-creamer purely in the light of a bit of the swag collected by Wilbert in the course of his larcenous career, Pop Glossop, all zeal, had embarked on the search he had planned to make, and intuition, developed by years of hunt-the-slipper, had led him to the right spot. Too late I regretted sorely that, concentrating so tensely on Operation Upjohn, I had failed to place the facts before him. Had he but known, about summed it up.

'I was going to ask you,' said Wilbert, 'if you think I should inform Mrs. Travers.'

The cigarette I was smoking was fortunately one of the kind that make you nonchalant, so it was nonchalantly – or fairly nonchalantly – that I was able to reply.

'Oh, I wouldn't do that.'

'Why not?'

'Might upset her.'

'You consider her a sensitive plant?'

'Oh, very. Rugged exterior, of course, but you can't go by that. No, I'd just wait awhile, if I were you. I expect it'll turn out that the thing's somewhere you put it but didn't think you'd put it. I mean, you often put a thing somewhere and think you've put it somewhere else and then find you didn't put it somewhere else but somewhere. I don't know if you follow me?'

'I don't.'

'What I mean is, just stick around and you'll probably find the thing.'

'You think it will return?'

'I do.'

'Like a homing pigeon?'

'That's the idea.'

'Oh?' said Wilbert, and turned away to greet Bobbie and Upjohn, who had just arrived on the boathouse landing stage. I had found his manner a little peculiar, particularly that last 'Oh?' but I was glad that there was no lurking suspicion in his mind that I had taken the bally thing. He might so easily have got the idea that Uncle Tom, regretting having parted with his ewe lamb, had employed me to recover it privily, this being the sort of thing, I believe, that collectors frequently do. Nevertheless, I was still much shaken, and I made a mental note to tell Roddy Glossop to slip it back among his effects at the earliest possible moment.

I shifted over to where Bobbie and Upjohn were standing, and though up and doing with a heart for any fate couldn't help getting that feeling you get at times like this of having swallowed a double portion of butterflies. My emotions were somewhat similar to those I had experienced when I first sang the Yeoman's Wedding Song. In public, I mean, for of course I had long been singing it in my bath.

'Hullo, Bobbie,' I said.

'Hullo, Bertie,' she said.

'Hullo, Upjohn,' I said.

The correct response to this would have been 'Hullo, Wooster', but he blew up in his lines and merely made a noise like a wolf with its big toe caught in a trap. Seemed a bit restive, I thought, as if wishing he were elsewhere.

Bobbie was all girlish animation.

'I've been telling Mr. Upjohn about that big fish we saw in the lake yesterday, Bertie.'

'Ah yes, the big fish.'

'It was a whopper, wasn't it?'

'Very well-developed.'

'I brought him down here to show it to him.'

'Quite right. You'll enjoy the big fish, Upjohn.'

I had been perfectly correct in supposing him to be restive. He did his wolf impersonation once more.

'I shall do nothing of the sort,' he said, and you couldn't find a better word than 'testily' to describe the way he spoke. 'It is most inconvenient for me to be away from the house at this time. I am expecting a telephone call from my lawyer.'

'Oh, I wouldn't bother about telephone calls from lawyers,' I said heartily. 'These legal birds never say anything worth listening to. Just gab gab gab. You'll never forgive yourself if you miss the big fish. You were saying, Upjohn?' I broke off courteously, for he had spoken.

'I am saying, Mr. Wooster, that both you and Miss Wickham are labouring under a singular delusion in supposing that I am interested

in fish, whether large or small. I ought never to have left the house.
I shall return there at once.'

'Oh, don't go yet,' I said.

'Wait for the big fish,' said Bobbie.

'Bound to be along shortly,' I said.

'At any moment now,' said Bobbie.

Her eyes met mine, and I read in them the message she was trying
to convey – viz. that the time had come to act. There is a tide in the
affairs of men which taken at the flood leads on to fortune. Not my
own. Jeeves's. She bent over and pointed with an eager finger.

'Oh, look!' she cried.

This, as I had explained to Jeeves, should have been the cue for
Upjohn to bend over, too, thus making it a simple task for me to do
my stuff, but he didn't bend over an inch. And why? Because at this
moment the goof Phyllis, suddenly appearing in our midst, said:

'Daddy, dear, you're wanted on the telephone.'

Upon which, standing not on the order of his going, Upjohn was
off as if propelled from a gun. He couldn't have moved quicker if he
had been the dachshund Poppet, who at this juncture was running
round in circles, trying, if I read his thoughts aright, to work off the
rather heavy lunch he had had earlier in the afternoon.

One began to see what the poet Burns had meant. I don't know
anything that more promptly gums up a dramatic sequence than the
sudden and unexpected exit of an important member of the cast at a
critical point in the proceedings. I was reminded of the time when we
did *Charley's Aunt* at the Market Snodsbury Town Hall in aid of the
local church organ fund and half-way through the second act, just
when we were all giving of our best, Catsmeat Potter-Pirbright, who
was playing Lord Fancourt Babberley, left the stage abruptly to attend
to an unforeseen nose bleed.

As far as Bobbie and I were concerned, silence reigned, this novel
twist in the scenario having wiped speech from our lips, as the
expression is, but Phyllis continued vocal.

'I found this darling pussycat in the garden,' she said, and for the
first time I observed that she was bearing Augustus in her arms. He
was looking a bit disgruntled, and one could readily see why. He
wanted to catch up with his sleep and was being kept awake by the
endearments she was murmuring in his ear.

She lowered him to the ground.

'I brought him here to talk to Poppet. Poppet loves cats, don't
you angel? Come and say how-d'you-do to the sweet pussykins,
darling.'

I shot a quick look at Wilbert Cream, to see how he was reacting to this. It was the sort of observation which might well have quenched the spark of love in his bosom, for nothing tends to cool the human heart more swiftly than babytalk. But so far from being revolted he was gazing yearningly at her as if her words were music to his ears. Very odd, I felt, and I was just saying to myself that you never could tell, when I became aware of a certain liveliness in my immediate vicinity.

At the moment when Augustus touched ground and curling himself into a ball fell into a light doze, Poppet had completed his tenth lap and was preparing to start on his eleventh. Seeing Augustus, he halted in mid-stride, smiled broadly, turned his ears inside out, stuck his tail straight up at right angles to the parent body and bounded forward, barking merrily.

I could have told the silly ass his attitude was all wrong. Roused abruptly from slumber, the most easy-going cat is apt to wake up cross. Already Augustus had had much to endure from Phyllis, who had doubtless jerked him out of dreamland when scooping him up in the garden, and all this noise and heartiness breaking out just as he dropped off again put the lid on his sullen mood. He spat peevishly, there was a sharp yelp, and something long and brown came shooting between my legs, precipitating itself and me into the depths. The waters closed about me, and for an instant I knew no more.

When I rose to the surface, I found that Poppet and I were not the only bathers. We had been joined by Wilbert Cream, who had dived in, seized the hound by the scruff of the neck, and was towing him at a brisk pace to the shore. And by one of those odd coincidences I was at this moment seized by the scruff of the neck myself.

'It's all right, Mr. Upjohn, keep quite cool, keep quite . . . What the hell are you doing here, Bertie?' said Kipper, for it was he. I may have been wrong, but it seemed to me that he spoke petulantly.

I expelled a pint or so of H_2O.

'You may well ask,' I said, moodily detaching a water beetle from my hair. 'I don't know if you know the meaning of the word "agley", Kipper, but that, to put it in a nutshell, is the way things have ganged.'

16

Reaching the mainland some moments later and squelching back to the house, accompanied by Bobbie, like a couple of Napoleons squelching back from Moscow, we encountered Aunt Dahlia, who, wearing that hat of hers that looks like one of those baskets you carry fish in, was messing about in the herbaceous border by the tennis lawn. She gaped at us dumbly for perhaps five seconds, then uttered an ejaculation, far from suitable to mixed company, which she had no doubt picked up from fellow-Nimrods in her hunting days. Having got this off the chest, she said:

'What's been going on in this joint? Wilbert Cream came by here just now, soaked to the eyebrows, and now you two appear, leaking at every seam. Have you all been playing water polo with your clothes on?'

'Not so much water polo, more that seaside bathing belles stuff,' I said. 'But it's a long story, and one feels that the cagey thing for Kipper and me to do now is to nip along and get into some dry things, not to linger conferring with you, much,' I added courteously, 'as we always enjoy your conversation.'

'The extraordinary thing is that I saw Upjohn not long ago, and he was as dry as a bone. How was that? Couldn't you get him to play with you?'

'He had to go and talk to his lawyer on the phone,' I said, and leaving Bobbie to place the facts before her, we resumed our squelching. And I was in my room, having shed the moistened outer crust and substituted something a bit more *sec* in pale flannel, when there was a knock on the door. I flung wide the gates and found Bobbie and Kipper on the threshold.

The first thing I noticed about their demeanour was the strange absence of gloom, despondency and what not. I mean, considering that it was little more than a quarter of an hour since all our hopes and dreams had taken the knock, one would have expected their hearts to be bowed down with weight of woe, but their whole aspect was one of buck and optimism. It occurred to me as a possible solution that

with that bulldog spirit of never admitting defeat which has made
Englishmen – and, of course, Englishwomen – what they are they had
decided to have another go along the same lines at some future date,
and I asked if this was the case.

The answer was in the negative. Kipper said No, there was no
likelihood of getting Upjohn down to the lake again, and Bobbie said
that even if they did, it wouldn't be any good, because I would be
sure to mess things up once more.

This stung me, I confess.

'How do you mean, mess things up?'

'You'd be bound to trip over your flat feet and fall in, as you did
today.'

'Pardon me,' I said, preserving with an effort the polished suavity
demanded from an English gentleman when chewing the rag with one
of the other sex, 'you're talking through the back of your fatheaded
little neck. I did not trip over my flat feet. I was hurled into the
depths by an Act of God, to wit, a totally unexpected dachshund
getting between my legs. If you're going to blame anyone blame the
goof Phyllis for bringing Augustus there and calling him in his hearing
a sweet pussykins. Naturally it made him sore and disinclined to stand
any lip from barking dogs.'

'Yes,' said Kipper, always the staunch pal. 'It wasn't Bertie's fault,
angel. Say what you will of dachshunds, their peculiar shape makes
them the easiest breed of dog to trip over in existence. I feel that
Bertie emerges without a stain on his character.'

'I don't,' said Bobbie. 'Still, it doesn't matter.'

'No, it doesn't really matter,' said Kipper, 'because your aunt has
suggested a scheme that's just as good as the Lanchester-Simmons
thing, if not better. She was telling Bobbie about the time when Boko
Fittleworth was trying to ingratiate himself with your Uncle Percy,
and you very sportingly offered to go and call your Uncle Percy a lot
of offensive names, so that Boko, hovering outside the door, could
come in and stick up for him, thus putting himself in solid with him.
You probably remember the incident?'

I quivered. I remembered the incident all right.

'She thinks the same treatment would work with Upjohn, and I'm
sure she's right. You know how you feel when you suddenly discover
you've a real friend, a fellow who thinks you're terrific and won't hear
a word said against you. It touches you. If you had anything in the
nature of a prejudice against the chap, you change your opinion of
him. You feel you can't do anything to injure such a sterling bloke.
And that's how Upjohn is going to feel about me, Bertie, when I come

in and lend him my sympathy and support as you stand there calling him all the names you can think of. You must have picked up dozens from your aunt. She used to hunt, and if you hunt, you have to know all the names there are because people are always riding over hounds and all that. Ask her to jot down a few of the best on a half sheet of notepaper.'

'He won't need that,' said Bobbie. 'He's probably got them all tucked away in his mind.'

'Of course. Learned them at her knee as a child. Well, that's the set-up, Bertie. You wait your opportunity and corner Upjohn somewhere and tower over him –'

'As he crouches in his chair.'

'– and shake your finger in his face and abuse him roundly. And when he's quailing beneath your scorn and wishing some friend in need would intervene and save him from this terrible ordeal, I come in, having heard all. Bobbie suggests that I knock you down, but I don't think I could do that. The recollection of our ancient friendship would make me pull my punch. I shall simply rebuke you. "Wooster," I shall say, "I am shocked. Shocked and astounded. I cannot understand how you can talk like that to a man I have always respected and looked up to, a man in whose preparatory school I spent the happiest years of my life. You strangely forget yourself, Wooster." Upon which, you slink out, bathed in shame and confusion, and Upjohn thanks me brokenly and says if there is anything he can do for me, I have only to name it.'

'I still think you ought to knock him down.'

'Having endeared myself to him thus –'

'Much more box-office.'

'Having endeared myself to him thus, I lead the conversation round to the libel suit.'

'One good punch in the eye would do it.'

'I say that I have seen the current issue of the *Thursday Review*, and I can quite understand him wanting to mulct the journal in substantial damages, but "Don't forget, Mr. Upjohn," I say, "that when a weekly paper loses a chunk of money, it has to retrench, and the way it retrenches is by getting rid of the more junior members of its staff. You wouldn't want me to lose my job, would you, Mr. Upjohn?" He starts. "Are you on the staff of the *Thursday Review*?" he says. "For the time being, yes," I say. "But if you bring that suit, I shall be selling pencils in the street." This is the crucial moment. Looking into his eyes, I can see that he is thinking of that five thousand quid, and for an instant quite naturally he hesitates. Then his better self prevails. His eyes soften. They fill with tears. He clasps my hand. He tells me he could use five thousand quid as well as the next man, but no money in the world would make him dream of doing an injury to the fellow who championed him so stoutly against the louse Wooster, and the scene ends with our going off together to Swordfish's pantry for a drop of port, probably with our arms round each other's waists, and that night he writes a letter to his lawyer telling him to call the suit off. Any questions?'

'Not from me. It isn't as if he could find out that it was you who wrote that review. It wasn't signed.'

'No, thank heaven for the editorial austerity that prevented that.'

'I can't see a flaw in the scenario. He'll have to withdraw the suit.'

'In common decency, one would think. The only thing that remains is to choose a time and place for Bertie to operate.'

'No time like the present.'

'But how do we locate Upjohn?'

'He's in Mr. Travers's study. I saw him through the french window.'

'Excellent. Then, Bertie, if you're ready . . .'

It will probably have been noticed that during these exchanges I had taken no part in the conversation. This was because I was fully occupied with envisaging the horror that lay before me. I knew that it did lie before me, of course, for where the ordinary man would have met the suggestion they had made with a firm *nolle prosequi*, I was barred from doing this by the code of the Woosters, which, as is pretty generally known, renders it impossible for me to let a pal down. If the only way of saving a boyhood friend from having to sell pencils in the street – though I should have thought that blood oranges would have been a far more lucrative line – was by wagging my finger in the face of Aubrey Upjohn and calling him names, that finger would have to be wagged and those names called. The ordeal would whiten my hair from the roots up and leave me a mere shell of my former self, but it was one that I must go through. Mine not to reason why, as the fellow said.

So I uttered a rather husky 'Right ho' and tried not to think of how the Upjohn face looked without its moustache. For what chilled the feet most was the mental picture of that bare upper lip which he had so often twitched at me in what are called days of yore. Dimly, as we started off for the arena, I could hear Bobbie saying 'My hero!' and Kipper asking anxiously if I was in good voice, but it would have taken a fat lot more than my-hero-ing and solicitude about my vocal cords to restore tone to Bertram's nervous system. I was, in short, feeling like an inexperienced novice going up against the heavyweight champion when in due course I drew up at the study door, opened it and tottered in. I could not forget that an Aubrey Upjohn who for years had been looking strong parents in the eye and making them wilt, and whose toughness was a byword in Bramley-on-Sea, was not a man lightly to wag a finger in the face of.

Uncle Tom's study was a place I seldom entered during my visits to Brinkley Court, because when I did go there he always grabbed me and started to talk about old silver, whereas if he caught me in the open he often touched on other topics, and the way I looked at it was that there was no sense in sticking one's neck out. It was more than a year since I had been inside this sanctum, and I had forgotten how extraordinarily like its interior was to that of Aubrey Upjohn's lair at Malvern House. Discovering this now and seeing Aubrey Upjohn seated at the desk as I had so often seen him sit on the occasions when he had sent for me to discuss some recent departure of mine from the straight and narrow path, I found what little was left of my sang froid expiring with a pop. And at the same time I spotted the flaw in this scheme I had undertaken to sit in on – viz. that you can't just charge into a room and start calling someone names – out of a blue sky, as it were – you have to lead up to the thing. Pourparlers, in short, are of the essence.

So I said 'Oh, hullo,' which seemed to me about as good a pourparler as you could have by way of an opener. I should imagine that those statesmen of whom I was speaking always edge into their conferences conducted in an atmosphere of the utmost cordiality in some such manner.

'Reading?' I said.

He lowered his book – one of Ma Cream's, I noticed – and flashed an upper lip at me.

'Your powers of observation have not led you astray, Wooster. I *am* reading.'

'Interesting book?'

'Very. I am counting the minutes until I can resume its perusal undisturbed.'

I'm pretty quick, and I at once spotted that the atmosphere was not of the utmost cordiality. He hadn't spoken matily, and he wasn't eyeing me matily. His whole manner seemed to suggest that he felt that I was taking up space in the room which could have been better employed for other purposes.

However, I persevered.

'I see you've shaved off your moustache.'

'I have. You do not feel, I hope, that I pursued a mistaken course?'

'Oh no, rather not. I grew a moustache myself last year, but had to get rid of it.'

'Indeed?'

'Public sentiment was against it.'

'I see. Well, I should be delighted to hear more of your reminiscences, Wooster, but at the moment I am expecting a telephone call from my lawyer.'

'I thought you'd had one.'

'I beg your pardon?'

'When you were down by the lake, didn't you go off to talk to him?'

'I did. But when I reached the telephone, he had grown tired of waiting and had rung off. I should never have allowed Miss Wickham to take me away from the house.'

'She wanted you to see the big fish.'

'So I understood her to say.'

'Talking of fish, you must have been surprised to find Kipper here.'

'Kipper?'

'Herring.'

'Oh, Herring,' he said, and one spotted the almost total lack of animation in his voice. And conversation had started to flag, when the door flew open and the goof Phyllis bounded in, full of girlish excitement.

'Oh, Daddy,' she burbled, 'are you busy?'

'No, my dear.'

'Can I speak to you about something?'

'Certainly. Goodbye, Wooster.'

I saw what this meant. He didn't want me around. There was nothing for it but to ooze out through the french window, so I oozed, and had hardly got outside when Bobbie sprang at me like a leopardess.

'What on earth are you fooling about for like this, Bertie?' she stage-whispered. 'All that rot about moustaches. I thought you'd be well into it by this time.'

I pointed out that as yet Aubrey Upjohn had not given me a cue.

'You and your cues!'

'All right, me and my cues. But I've got to sort of lead the conversation in the right direction, haven't I?'

'I see what Bertie means, darling,' said Kipper. 'He wants –'

'A *point d'appui*.'

'A what?' said Bobbie.

'Sort of jumping-off place.'

The beasel snorted.

'If you ask me, he's lost his nerve. I knew this would happen. The worm has got cold feet.'

I could have crushed her by drawing her attention to the fact that worms don't have feet, cold or piping hot, but I had no wish to bandy words.

'I must ask you, Kipper,' I said with frigid dignity, 'to request your girl friend to preserve the decencies of debate. My feet are not cold. I am as intrepid as a lion and only too anxious to get down to brass tacks, but just as I was working round to the *res*, Phyllis came in. She said she had something she wanted to speak to him about.'

Bobbie snorted again, this time in a despairing sort of way.

'She'll be there for hours. It's no good waiting.'

'No,' said Kipper. 'May as well call it off for the moment. We'll let you know time and place of next fixture, Bertie.'

'Oh, thanks,' I said, and they drifted away.

And about a couple of minutes later, as I stood there brooding on Kipper's sad case, Aunt Dahlia came along. I was glad to see her. I thought she might possibly come across with aid and comfort, for though, like the female in the poem I was mentioning, she sometimes inclined to be a toughish egg in hours of ease, she could generally be relied on to be there with the soothing solace when one had anything wrong with one's brow.

As she approached, I got the impression that her own brow had for some reason taken it on the chin. Quite a good deal of that upon-which-all-the-ends-of-the-earth-are-come stuff, it seemed to me.

Nor was I mistaken.

'Bertie,' she said, heaving-to beside me and waving a trowel in an overwrought manner, 'do you know what?'

'No, what?'

'I'll tell you what,' said the aged relative, rapping out a sharp monosyllable such as she might have uttered in her Quorn and Pytchley days on observing a unit of the pack of hounds chasing a rabbit. 'That ass Phyllis has gone and got engaged to Wilbert Cream!'

17

Her words gave me quite a wallop. I don't say I reeled, and everything didn't actually go black, but I was shaken, as what nephew would not have been. When a loved aunt has sweated herself to the bone trying to save her god-child from the clutches of a New York playboy and learns that all her well-meant efforts have gone blue on her, it's only natural for her late brother's son to shudder in sympathy.

'You don't mean that?' I said. 'Who told you?'

'She did.'

'In person?'

'In the flesh. She came skipping to me just now, clapping her little hands and bleating about how very, very happy she was, dear Mrs. Travers. The silly young geezer. I nearly conked her one with my trowel. I'd always thought her half-baked, but now I think they didn't even put her in the oven.'

'But how did it happen?'

'Apparently that dog of hers joined you in the water.'

'Yes, that's right, he took his dip with the rest of us. But what's that got to do with it?'

'Wilbert Cream dived in and saved him.'

'He could have got ashore perfectly well under his own steam. In fact, he was already on his way, doing what looked like an Australian crawl.'

'That wouldn't occur to a pinhead like Phyllis. To her Wilbert Cream is the man who rescued her dachshund from a watery grave. So she's going to marry him.'

'But you don't marry fellows because they rescue dachshunds.'

'You do, if you've a mentality like hers.'

'Seems odd.'

'And is. But that's how it goes. Girls like Phyllis Mills are an open book to me. For four years I was, if you remember, the proprietor and editress of a weekly paper for women.' She was alluding to the periodical entitled *Milady's Boudoir*, to the Husbands and Brothers page of which I once contributed an article or 'piece' on What The

Well-Dressed Man is Wearing. It had recently been sold to a mug up Liverpool way, and I have never seen Uncle Tom look chirpier than when the deal went through, he for those four years having had to foot the bills.

'I don't suppose,' she continued, 'that you were a regular reader, so for your information there appeared in each issue a short story, and in seventy per cent of those short stories the hero won the heroine's heart by saving her dog or her cat or her canary or whatever foul animal she happened to possess. Well, Phyllis didn't write all those stories, but she easily might have done, for that's the way her mind works. When I say mind,' said the blood relation, 'I refer to the quarter-teaspoonful of brain which you might possibly find in her head if you sank an artesian well. Poor Jane!'

'Poor who?'

'Her mother. Jane Mills.'

'Oh, ah, yes. She was a pal of yours, you told me.'

'The best I ever had, and she was always saying to me "Dahlia, old girl, if I pop off before you, for heaven's sake look after Phyllis and see that she doesn't marry some ghastly outsider. She's sure to want to. Girls always do, goodness knows why," she said, and I knew she was thinking of her first husband, who was a heel to end all heels and a constant pain in the neck to her till one night he most fortunately walked into the River Thames while under the influence of the sauce and didn't come up for days. "Do stop her," she said, and I said "Jane, you can rely on me." And now this happens.'

I endeavoured to soothe.

'You can't blame yourself.'

'Yes, I can.'

'It isn't your fault.'

'I invited Wilbert Cream here.'

'Merely from a wifely desire to do Uncle Tom a bit of good.'

'And I let Upjohn stick around, always at her elbow egging her on.'

'Yes, Upjohn's the bird I blame.'

'Me, too.'

'But for his – undue influence, do they call it? – Phyllis would have remained a bachelor or spinster or whatever it is. "Thou art the man, Upjohn!" seems to me the way to sum it up. He ought to be ashamed of himself.'

'And am I going to tell him so! I'd give a tenner to have Aubrey Upjohn here at this moment.'

'You can get him for nothing. He's in Uncle Tom's study.'

Her face lit up.

'He is?' She threw her head back and inflated the lungs. 'UPJOHN!' she boomed, rather like someone calling the cattle home across the sands of Dee, and I issued a kindly word of warning.

'Watch that blood pressure, old ancestor.'

'Never you mind my blood pressure. You let it alone, and it'll leave you alone. UPJOHN!'

He appeared in the french window, looking cold and severe, as I had so often seen him look when hobnobbing with him in his study at Malvern House, self not there as a willing guest but because I'd been sent for. ('I should like to see Wooster in my study immediately after morning prayers' was the formula.)

'Who is making that abominable noise? Oh, it's you, Dahlia.'

'Yes, it's me.'

'You wished to see me?'

'Yes, but not the way you're looking now. I'd have preferred you to have fractured your spine or at least to have broken a couple of ankles and got a touch of leprosy.'

'My dear Dahlia!'

'I'm not your dear Dahlia. I'm a seething volcano. Have you seen Phyllis?'

'She has just left me.'

'Did she tell you?'

'That she was engaged to Wilbert Cream? Certainly.'

'And I suppose you're delighted?'

'Of course I am.'

'Yes, of course you are! I can well imagine that it's your dearest wish to see that unfortunate muttonheaded girl become the wife of a man who lets off stink bombs in night clubs and pinches the spoons and has had three divorces already and who, if the authorities play their cards right, will end up cracking rocks in Sing-Sing. That is unless the loony-bin gets its bid in first. Just a Prince Charming, you might say.'

'I don't understand you.'

'Then you're an ass.'

'Well, really!' said Aubrey Upjohn, and there was a dangerous note in his voice. I could see that the relative's manner, which was not affectionate, and her words, which lacked cordiality, were peeving him. It looked like an odds-on shot that in about another two ticks he would be giving her the Collect for the Day to write out ten times or even instructing her to bend over while he fetched his whangee. You can push these preparatory schoolmasters just so far.

'A fine way for Jane's daughter to end up. Mrs Broadway Willie!'

'Broadway Willie?'

'That's what he's called in the circles in which he moves, into which he will now introduce Phyllis. "Meet the moll," he'll say, and then he'll teach her in twelve easy lessons how to make stink bombs, and the children, if and when, will be trained to pick people's pockets as they dandle them on their knee. And you'll be responsible, Aubrey Upjohn!'

I didn't like the way things were trending. Admittedly the aged relative was putting up a great show and it was a pleasure to listen to her, but I had seen Upjohn's lip twitch and that look of smug satisfaction come into his face which I had so often seen when he had been counsel for the prosecution in some case in which I was involved and had spotted a damaging flaw in my testimony. The occasion when I was on trial for having broken the drawing-room window with a cricket ball springs to the mind. It was plain to an eye as discerning as mine that he was about to put it across the old flesh and blood properly, making her wish she hadn't spoken. I couldn't see how, but the symptoms were all there.

I was right. That twitching lip had not misled me.

'If I might be allowed to make a remark, my dear Dahlia,' he said, 'I think we are talking at cross purposes. You appear to be under the impression that Phyllis is marrying Wilbert's younger brother Wilfred, the notorious playboy whose escapades have caused the family so much distress and who, as you are correct in saying, is known to his disreputable friends as Broadway Willie. Wilfred, I agree, would make – and on three successive occasions has made – a most undesirable husband, but no one to my knowledge has ever spoken a derogatory word of Wilbert. I know few young men who are more generally respected. He is a member of the faculty of one of the greatest American universities, over in this country on his sabbatical. He teaches romance languages.'

Stop me if I've told you this before, I rather fancy I have, but once when I was up at Oxford and chatting on the river bank with a girl called something that's slipped my mind there was a sound of barking and a great hefty dog of the Hound of the Baskervilles type came galloping at me, obviously intent on mayhem, its whole aspect that of a dog that has no use for Woosters. And I was just commending my soul to God and thinking that this was where my new flannel trousers got about thirty bobs' worth of value bitten out of them, when the girl, waiting till she saw the whites of its eyes, with extraordinary presence of mind opened a coloured Japanese umbrella in the animal's face. Upon which, with a startled exclamation it did three back somersaults and retired into private life.

And the reason I bring this up now is that, barring the somersaults, Aunt Dahlia's reaction to this communiqué was precisely that of the above hound to the Japanese umbrella. The same visible taken-abackness. She has since told me that her emotions were identical with those she had experienced when she was out with the Pytchley and riding over a ploughed field in rainy weather, and the horse of a sports-lover in front of her suddenly kicked three pounds of wet mud into her face.

She gulped like a bulldog trying to swallow a sirloin steak many sizes too large for its thoracic cavity.

'You mean there are two of them?'

'Exactly.'

'And Wilbert isn't the one I thought he was?'

'You have grasped the position of affairs to a nicety. You will appreciate now, my dear Dahlia,' said Upjohn, speaking with the same unction, if that's the word, with which he had spoken when unmasking his batteries and presenting unshakable proof that yours was the hand, Wooster, which propelled this cricket ball, 'that your concern, though doing you the greatest credit, has been needless. I could wish Phyllis no better husband. Wilbert has looks, brains, character . . . and excellent prospects,' he added, rolling the words round his tongue like vintage port. 'His father, I should imagine, would be worth at least twenty million dollars, and Wilbert is the elder son. Yes, most satisfactory, most . . .'

As he spoke, the telephone rang, and with a quick 'Ha!' he shot back into the study like a homing rabbit.

18

For perhaps a quarter of a minute after he had passed from the scene the aged relative stood struggling for utterance. At the end of this period she found speech.

'Of all the damn silly fatheaded things!' she vociferated, if that's the word. 'With a million ruddy names to choose from, these ruddy Creams call one ruddy son Wilbert and the other ruddy son Wilfred, and both these ruddy sons are known as Willie. Just going out of their way to mislead the innocent bystander. You'd think people would have more consideration.'

Again I begged her to keep an eye on her blood pressure and not get so worked up, and once more she brushed me off, this time with a curt request that I would go and boil my head.

'You'd be worked up if you had just been scored off by Aubrey Upjohn, with that loathsome self-satisfied look on his face as if he'd been rebuking a pimply pupil at his beastly school for shuffling his feet in church.'

'Odd, that,' I said, struck by the coincidence. 'He once rebuked me for that very reason. And I had pimples.'

'Pompous ass!'

'Shows what a small world it is.'

'What's he doing here anyway? I didn't invite him.'

'Bung him out. I took this point up with you before, if you remember. Cast him into the outer darkness, where there is wailing and gnashing of teeth.'

'I will, if he gives me any more of his lip.'

'I can see you're in a dangerous mood.'

'You bet I'm in a dangerous . . . My God! He's with us again!'

And A. Upjohn was indeed filtering through the french window. But he had lost the look of which the ancestor had complained, the one he was wearing now seeming to suggest that since last heard from something had occurred to wake the fiend that slept in him.

'Dahlia!' he . . . yes better make it vociferated once more, I'm pretty sure it's the word I want.

The fiend that slept in Aunt Dahlia was also up on its toes. She gave him a look which, if directed at an erring member of the personnel of the Quorn or Pytchley hound ensemble, would have had that member sticking his tail between his legs and resolving for the future to lead a better life.

'Now what?'

Just as Aunt Dahlia had done, Aubrey Upjohn struggled for utterance. Quite a bit of utterance-struggling there had been around these parts this summer afternoon.

'I have just been speaking to my lawyer on the telephone,' he said, getting going after a short stage wait. 'I had asked him to make inquiries and ascertain the name of the author of that libellous attack on me in the columns of the *Thursday Review*. He did so, and has now informed me that it was the work of my former pupil, Reginald Herring.'

He paused at this point, to let us chew it over, and the heart sank. Mine, I mean. Aunt Dahlia's seemed to be carrying on much as usual. She scratched her chin with her trowel, and said:

'Oh, yes?'

Upjohn blinked, as if he had been expecting something better than this in the way of sympathy and concern.

'Is that all you can say?'

'That's the lot.'

'Oh? Well, I am suing the paper for heavy damages, and furthermore, I refuse to remain in the same house with Reginald Herring. Either he goes, or I go.'

There was the sort of silence which I believe cyclones drop into for a second or two before getting down to it and starting to give the populace the works. Throbbing? Yes, throbbing wouldn't be a bad word to describe it. Nor would electric, for the matter of that, and if you care to call it ominous, it will be all right with me. It was a silence of the type that makes the toes curl and sends a shiver down the spinal cord as you stand waiting for the bang. I could see Aunt Dahlia swelling slowly like a chunk of bubble gum, and a less prudent man than Bertram Wooster would have warned her again about her blood pressure.

'I beg your pardon?' she said.

He repeated the key words.

'Oh?' said the relative, and went off with a pop. I could have told Upjohn he was asking for it. Normally as genial a soul as ever broke biscuit, this aunt, when stirred, can become the haughtiest of *grandes dames* before whose wrath the stoutest quail, and she doesn't, like some, have to use a lorgnette to reduce the citizenry to pulp, she does it all with the naked eye. 'Oh?' she said. 'So you have decided to revise my guest list for me? You have the nerve, the – the –'

I saw she needed helping out.

'Audacity,' I said, throwing her the line.

'The audacity to dictate to me who I shall have in my house.'

It should have been 'whom', but I let it go.

'You have the –'

'Crust.'

'– the immortal rind,' she amended, and I had to admit it was stronger, 'to tell me whom' – she got it right that time – 'I may entertain at Brinkley Court and who' – wrong again – 'I may not. Very well, if you feel unable to breathe the same air as my friends, you must please yourself. I believe the "Bull and Bush" in Market Snodsbury is quite comfortable.'

'Well spoken of in the *Automobile Guide*,' I said.

'I shall go there,' said Upjohn. 'I shall go there as soon as my things are packed. Perhaps you will be good enough to tell your butler to pack them.'

He strode off, and she went into Uncle Tom's study, me following, she still snorting. She rang the bell.

Jeeves appeared.

'Jeeves?' said the relative, surprised. 'I was ringing for –'

'It is Sir Roderick's afternoon off, madam.'

'Oh? Well, would you mind packing Mr. Upjohn's things, Jeeves? He is leaving us.'

'Very good, madam.'

'And you can drive him to Market Snodsbury, Bertie.'

'Right ho,' I said, not much liking the assignment, but liking less the idea of endeavouring to thwart this incandescent aunt in her current frame of mind.

Safety first, is the Wooster slogan.

19

It isn't much of a run from Brinkley Court to Market Snodsbury, and I deposited Upjohn at the 'Bull and Bush' and started m-p-h-ing homeward in what you might call a trice. We parted, of course, on rather distant terms, but the great thing when you've got an Upjohn on your books is to part and not be fussy about how it's done, and had it not been for all this worry about Kipper, for whom I was now mourning in spirit more than ever, I should have been feeling fine.

I could see no happy issue for him from the soup in which he was immersed. No words had been exchanged between Upjohn and self on the journey out, but the glimpses I had caught of his face from the corner of the eyes had told me that he was grim and resolute, his supply of the milk of human kindness plainly short by several gallons. No hope, it seemed to me, of turning him from his fell purpose.

I garaged the car and went to Aunt Dahlia's sanctum to ascertain whether she had cooled off at all since I had left her, for I was still anxious about that blood pressure of hers. One doesn't want aunts going up in a sheet of flame all over the place.

She wasn't there, having, I learned later, withdrawn to her room to bathe her temples with eau de Cologne and do Yogi deep-breathing, but Bobbie was, and not only Bobbie but Jeeves. He was handing her something in an envelope, and she was saying 'Oh, Jeeves, you've saved a human life,' and he was saying 'Not at all, miss.' The gist, of course, escaped me, but I had no leisure to probe into gists.

'Where's Kipper?' I asked, and was surprised to note that Bobbie was dancing round the room on the tips of her toes uttering animal cries, apparently ecstatic in their nature.

'Reggie?' she said, suspending the farmyard imitations for a moment. 'He went for a walk.'

'Does he know that Upjohn's found out he wrote that thing?'

'Yes, your aunt told him.'

'Then we ought to be in conference.'

'About Upjohn's libel action? It's all right about that. Jeeves has pinched his speech.'

I could make nothing of this. It seemed to me that the beasel spoke in riddles.

'Have you an impediment in your speech, Jeeves?'

'No, sir.'

'Then what, if anything, does the young prune mean?'

'Miss Wickham's allusion is to the typescript of the speech which Mr Upjohn is to deliver tomorrow to the scholars of Market Snodsbury Grammar School, sir.'

'She said you'd pinched it.'

'Precisely, sir.'

I started.

'You don't mean –'

'Yes, he does,' said Bobbie, resuming the Ballet Russe movements. 'Your aunt told him to pack Upjohn's bags, and the first thing he saw when he smacked into it was the speech. He trousered it and brought it along to me.'

I raised an eyebrow.

'Well, really, Jeeves!'

'I deemed it best, sir.'

'And did you deem right!' said Bobbie, executing a Nijinsky whatever-it's-called. 'Either Upjohn agrees to drop that libel suit or he doesn't get these notes, as he calls them, and without them he won't be able to utter a word. He'll have to come across with the price of the papers. Won't he, Jeeves?'

'He would appear to have no alternative, miss.'

'Unless he wants to get up on that platform and stand there opening and shutting his mouth like a goldfish. We've got him cold.'

'Yes, but half a second,' I said.

I spoke reluctantly. I didn't want to damp the young ball of worsted in her hour of joy, but a thought had occurred to me.

'I see the idea, of course. I remember Aunt Dahlia telling me about this strange inability of Upjohn's to be silver-tongued unless he has the material in his grasp, but suppose he says he's ill and can't appear.'

'He won't.'

'I would.'

'But you aren't trying to get the Conservative Association of the Market Snodsbury division to choose you as their candidate at the coming by-election. Upjohn is, and it's vitally important for him to address the multitude tomorrow and make a good impression, because half the selection committee have sons at the school and will be there, waiting to judge for themselves how good he is as a speaker. Their last nominee stuttered, and they didn't discover it till the time came for him to dish it out to the constituents. They don't want to make a mistake this time.'

'Yes, I get you now,' I said. I remembered that Aunt Dahlia had spoken to me of Upjohn's political ambitions.

'So that fixes that,' said Bobbie. 'His future hangs on this speech, and we've got it and he hasn't. We take it from there.'

'And what exactly is the procedure?'

'That's all arranged. He'll be ringing up any moment now, making inquiries. When he does, you step to the telephone and outline the position of affairs to him.'

'Me?'

'That's right.'

'Why me?'

'Jeeves deems it best.'

'Well, really, Jeeves! Why not Kipper?'

'Mr Herring and Mr Upjohn are not on speaking terms, sir.'

'So you can see what would happen if he heard Reggie's voice. He would hang up haughtily, and all the weary work to do again. Whereas he'll drink in your every word.'

'But, dash it –'

'And, anyway, Reggie's gone for a walk and isn't available. I do wish you wouldn't always be so difficult, Bertie. Your aunt tells me it was just the same when you were a child. She'd want you to eat your cereal, and you would stick your ears back and be stubborn and non-cooperative, like Jonah's ass in the Bible.'

I could not let this go uncorrected. It's pretty generally known that when at school I won a prize for Scripture Knowledge.

'Balaam's ass. Jonah was the chap who had the whale. Jeeves!'

'Sir?'

'To settle a bet, wasn't it Balaam's ass that entered the *nolle prosequi*?'

'Yes, sir.'

'I told you so,' I said to Bobbie, and would have continued grinding her into the dust, had not the telephone at this moment tinkled, diverting my mind from the point at issue. The sound sent a sudden chill through the Wooster limbs, for I knew what it portended.

Bobbie, too, was not unmoved.

'Hullo!' she said. 'This if I mistake not, is our client now. In you go, Bertie. Over the top and best of luck.'

I have mentioned before that Bertram Wooster, chilled steel when dealing with the sterner sex, is always wax in a woman's hands, and the present case was no exception to the r. Short of going over Niagara

Falls in a barrel, I could think of nothing I wanted to do less than chat with Aubrey Upjohn at this juncture, especially along the lines indicated, but having been requested by one of the delicately nurtured to take on the grim task, I had no option. I mean, either a chap's *preux* or he isn't, as the Chevalier Bayard used to say.

But as I approached the instrument and unhooked the thing you unhook, I was far from being at my most nonchalant, and when I heard Upjohn are-you-there-ing at the other end my manly spirit definitely blew a fuse. For I could tell by his voice that he was in the testiest of moods. Not even when conferring with me at Malvern House, Bramley-on-Sea, on the occasion when I put sherbet in the ink, had I sensed in him a more marked stirred-up-ness.

'Hullo? Hullo? Hullo? Are you there? Will you kindly answer me? This is Mr. Upjohn speaking.'

They always say that when the nervous system isn't all it should be the thing to do is to take a couple of deep breaths. I took six, which of course occupied a certain amount of time, and the delay noticeably increased his umbrage. Even at this distance one could spot what I believe is called the deleterious animal magnetism.

'Is that Brinkley Court?'

I could put him straight there. None other, I told him.

'Who are you?'

I had to think for a moment. Then I remembered.

'This is Wooster, Mr. Upjohn.'

'Well, listen to me carefully, Wooster.'

'Yes, Mr. Upjohn. How do you like the "Bull and Bush"? Everything pretty snug?'

'What did you say?'

'I was asking if you like the "Bull and Bush".'

'Never mind the "Bull and Bush".'

'No, Mr. Upjohn.'

'This is of vital importance. I wish to speak to the man who packed my things.'

'Jeeves.'

'What?'

'Jeeves.'

'What do you mean by Jeeves?'

'Jeeves.'

'You keep saying "Jeeves" and it makes no sense. Who packed my belongings?'

'Jeeves.'

'Oh, Jeeves is the man's name?'

'Yes, Mr. Upjohn.'

'Well, he carelessly omitted to pack the notes for my speech at Market Snodsbury Grammar School tomorrow.'

'No, really! I don't wonder you're sore.'

'Saw whom?'

'Sore with an r.'

'What?'

'No, sorry. I mean with an o-r-e.'

'Wooster!'

'Yes, Mr. Upjohn.'

'Are you intoxicated?'

'No, Mr. Upjohn.'

'Then you are drivelling. Stop drivelling, Wooster.'

'Yes, Mr. Upjohn.'

'Send for this man Jeeves immediately and ask him what he did with the notes for my speech.'

'Yes, Mr. Upjohn.'

'At once! Don't stand there saying "Yes, Mr. Upjohn".'

'No, Mr. Upjohn.'

'It is imperative that I have them in my possession immediately.'

'Yes, Mr. Upjohn.'

Well, I suppose, looking at it squarely, I hadn't made much real progress and a not too close observer might quite possibly have got the impression that I had lost my nerve and was shirking the issue, but that didn't in my opinion justify Bobbie at this point in snatching the receiver from my grasp and bellowing the word 'Worm!' at me.

'What did you call me?' said Upjohn.

'I didn't call you anything,' I said. 'Somebody called me something.'

'I wish to speak to this man Jeeves.'

'You do, do you?' said Bobbie. 'Well, you're going to speak to me. This is Roberta Wickham, Upjohn. If I might have your kind attention for a moment.'

I must say that, much as I disapproved in many ways of this carrot-topped Jezebel, as she was sometimes called, there was no getting away from it that she had mastered the art of talking to retired preparatory schoolmasters. The golden words came pouring out like syrup. Of course, she wasn't handicapped, as I had been, by having sojourned for some years beneath the roof of Malvern House, Bramley-on-Sea, and having at a malleable age associated with this old Frankenstein's monster when he was going good, but even so her performance deserved credit.

Beginning with a curt 'Listen, Buster,' she proceeded to sketch out with admirable clearness the salient points in the situation as she envisaged it, and judging from the loud buzzing noises that came over the wire, clearly audible to me though now standing in the background, it was evident that the nub was not escaping him. They were the buzzing noises of a man slowly coming to the realization that a woman's hand had got him by the short hairs.

Presently they died away, and Bobbie spoke.

'That's fine,' she said. 'I was sure you'd come round to our view. Then I will be with you shortly. Mind there's plenty of ink in your fountain pen.'

She hung up and legged it from the room, once more giving vent to those animal cries, and I turned to Jeeves as I had so often turned to him before when musing on the activities of the other sex.

'Women, Jeeves!'

'Yes, sir.'

'Were you following all that?'

'Yes, sir.'

'I gather that Upjohn, vowing . . . How does it go?'

'Vowing he would ne'er consent, consented, sir.'

'He's withdrawing the suit.'

'Yes, sir. And Miss Wickham prudently specified that he do so in writing.'

'Thus avoiding all ranygazoo?'

'Yes, sir.'

'She thinks of everything.'

'Yes, sir.'

'I thought she was splendidly firm.'

'Yes, sir.'

'It's the red hair that does it, I imagine.'

'Yes, sir.'

'If anyone had told me that I should live to hear Aubrey Upjohn addressed as "Buster". . .'

I would have spoken further, but before I could get under way the door opened, revealing Ma Cream, and he shimmered silently from the room. Unless expressly desired to remain, he always shimmers off when what is called the Quality arrive.

20

This was the first time I had seen Ma Cream today, she having gone off around noon to lunch with some friends in Birmingham, and I would willingly not have seen her now, for something in her manner seemed to suggest that she spelled trouble. She was looking more like Sherlock Holmes than ever. Slap a dressing-gown on her and give her a violin, and she could have walked straight into Baker Street and no questions asked. Fixing me with a penetrating eye, she said:

'Oh, there you are, Mr. Wooster. I was looking for you.'

'You wished speech with me?'

'Yes. I wanted to say that now perhaps you'd believe me.'

'I beg your pardon?'

'About that butler.'

'What about him?'

'I'll tell you about him. I'd sit down, if I were you. It's a long story.'

I sat down. Glad to, as a matter of fact, for the legs were feeling weak.

'You remember I told you I mistrusted him from the first?'

'Oh ah, yes. You did, didn't you?'

'I said he had a criminal face.'

'He can't help his face.'

'He can help being a crook and an imposter. Calls himself a butler, does he? The police could shake that story. He's no more a butler than I am.'

I did my best.

'But think of those references of his.'

'I am thinking of them.'

'He couldn't have stuck it out as major-domo to a man like Sir Roderick Glossop, if he'd been dishonest.'

'He didn't.'

'But Bobbie said –'

'I remember very clearly what Miss Wickham said. She told me he had been with Sir Roderick Glossop for years.'

'Well, then.'

'You think that puts him in the clear?'

'Certainly.'

'I don't, and I'll tell you why. Sir Roderick Glossop has a large clinic down in Somersetshire at a place called Chuffnell Regis, and a friend of mine is there. I wrote to her asking her to see Lady Glossop and get all the information she could about a former butler of hers named Swordfish. When I got back from Birmingham just now, I found a letter from her. She says that Lady Glossop told her she had never employed a butler called Swordfish. Try that one on for size.'

I continued to do my best. The Woosters never give up.

'You don't know Lady Glossop, do you?'

'Of course I don't, or I'd have written to her direct.'

'Charming woman, but with a memory like a sieve. The sort who's always losing one glove at the theatre. Naturally she wouldn't remember a butler's name. She probably thought all along it was Fotheringay or Binks or something. Very common, that sort of mental lapse. I was up at Oxford with a man called Robinson, and I was trying to think of his name the other day and the nearest I could get to it was Fosdyke. It only came back to me when I saw in *The Times* a few days ago that Herbert Robinson (26) of Grove Road, Ponder's End, had been had up at Bosher Street police court, charged with having stolen a pair of green and yellow checked trousers. Not the same chap, of course, but you get the idea. I've no doubt that one of these fine mornings Lady Glossop will suddenly smack herself on the forehead and cry "Swordfish! Of *course*! And all this time I've been thinking of the honest fellow as Catbird!" '

She sniffed. And if I were to say that I liked the way she sniffed, I would be wilfully deceiving my public. It was the sort of sniff Sherlock Holmes would have sniffed when about to clap the darbies on the chap who had swiped the Maharajah's ruby.

'Honest fellow, did you say? Then how do you account for this? I saw Willie just now, and he tells me that a valuable eighteenth-century cow-creamer which he bought from Mr. Travers is missing. And where is it, you ask? At this moment it is tucked away in Swordfish's bedroom in a drawer under his clean shirts.'

In stating that the Woosters never give up, I was in error. These words caught me amidships and took all the fighting spirit out of me, leaving me a spent force.

'Oh, is it?' I said. Not good, but the best I could do.

'Yes, sir, that's where it is. Directly Willie told me the thing had gone, I knew where it had gone to. I went to this man Swordfish's room and searched it, and there it was. I've sent for the police.'

Again I had that feeling of having been spiritually knocked base over apex. I gaped at the woman.

'You've sent for the police?'

'I have, and they're sending a sergeant. He ought to be here at any moment. And shall I tell you something? I'm going now to stand outside Swordfish's door, to see that nobody tampers with the evidence. I'm not going to take any chances. I wouldn't want to say anything to suggest that I don't trust you implicitly, Mr. Wooster, but I don't like the way you've been sticking up for this fellow. You've been far too sympathetic with him for my taste.'

'It's just that I think he may have yielded to sudden temptation and all that.'

'Nonsense. He's probably been acting this way all his life.. I'll bet he was swiping things as a small boy.'

'Only biscuits.'

'I beg your pardon?'

'Or crackers you would call them, wouldn't you? He was telling me he occasionally pinched a cracker or two in his salad days.'

'Well, there you are. You start with crackers and you end up with silver jugs. That's life,' she said, and buzzed off to keep her vigil, leaving me kicking myself because I'd forgotten to say anything about the quality of mercy not being strained. It isn't, as I dare say you know, and a mention of this might just have done the trick.

I was still brooding on this oversight and wondering what was to be done for the best, when Bobbie and Aunt Dahlia came in, looking like a young female and an elderly female who were sitting on top of the world.

'Roberta tells me she has got Upjohn to withdraw the libel suit,' said Aunt Dahlia. 'I couldn't be more pleased, but I'm blowed if I can imagine how she did it.'

'Oh, I just appealed to his better feelings,' said Bobbie, giving me one of those significant glances. I got the message. The ancestor, she was warning me, must never learn that she had achieved her ends by jeopardizing the delivery of the Upjohn speech to the young scholars of Market Snodsbury Grammar School on the morrow. 'I told him that the quality of mercy . . . What's the matter, Bertie?'

'Nothing. Just starting.'

'What do you want to start for?'

'I believe Brinkley Court is open for starting in at about this hour, is it not? The quality of mercy, you were saying?'

'Yes. It isn't strained.'

'I believe not.'

'And in case you didn't know, it's twice bless'd and becomes the thronèd monarch better than his crown. I drove over to the "Bull and Bush" and put this to Upjohn, and he saw my point. So now everything's fine.'

I uttered a hacking laugh.

'No,' I said, in answer to a query from Aunt Dahlia. 'I have not accidentally swallowed my tonsils, I was merely laughing hackingly. Ironical that the young blister should say that everything is fine, for at this very moment disaster stares us in the eyeball. I have a story to relate which I think you will agree falls into the fretful porpentine class,' I said, and without further pourparlers I unshipped my tale.

I had anticipated that it would shake them to their foundation garments, and it did. Aunt Dahlia reeled like an aunt struck behind the ear with a blunt instrument, and Bobbie tottered like a red-haired girl who hadn't known it was loaded.

'You see the set-up,' I continued, not wanting to rub it in but feeling that they should be fully briefed. 'Glossop will return from his afternoon off to find the awful majesty of the Law waiting for him, complete with handcuffs. We can hardly expect him to accept an exemplary sentence without a murmur, so his first move will be to establish his innocence by revealing all. "True," he will say, "I did pinch this bally cow-creamer, but merely because I thought Wilbert had pinched it and it ought to be returned to store," and he will go on to explain his position in the house – all this, mind you, in front of Ma Cream. So what ensues? The sergeant removes the gloves from his wrists, and Ma Cream asks you if she may use your telephone for a moment, as she wishes to call her husband on long distance. Pop Cream listens attentively to the tale she tells, and when Uncle Tom looks in on him later, he finds him with folded arms and a forbidding scowl. "Travers," he says, "the deal's off." "Off?" quivers Uncle Tom. "Off," says Cream. "O-ruddy-double-f. I don't do business with guys whose wives bring in loony-doctors to observe my son." A short while ago Ma Cream was urging me to try something on for size. I suggest that you do the same for this.'

Aunt Dahlia had sunk into a chair and was starting to turn purple. Strong emotion always has this effect on her.

'The only thing left, it seems to me,' I said, 'is to put our trust in a higher power.'

'You're right,' said the relative, fanning her brow. 'Go and fetch Jeeves, Roberta. And what you do, Bertie, is get out that car of yours and scour the countryside for Glossop. It may be possible to head him off. Come on, come on, let's have some service. What are you waiting for?'

I hadn't exactly been waiting. I'd only been thinking that the enterprise had more than a touch of looking for a needle in a haystack about it. You can't find loony-doctors on their afternoon off just by driving around Worcestershire in a car; you need bloodhounds and handkerchiefs for them to sniff at and all that professional stuff. Still, there it was.

'Right ho,' I said. 'Anything to oblige.'

21

And, of course, as I had anticipated from the start, the thing was a wash-out. I stuck it out for about an hour and then, apprised by a hollow feeling in the midriff that the dinner hour was approaching, laid a course for home.

Arriving there, I found Bobbie in the drawing-room. She had the air of a girl who was waiting for something, and when she told me that the cocktails would be coming along in a moment, I knew what it was.

'Cocktails, eh? I could do with one or possibly more,' I said. 'My fruitless quest has taken it out of me. I couldn't find Glossop anywhere. He must be somewhere, of course, but Worcestershire hid its secret well.'

'Glossop?' she said, seeming surprised. 'Oh, he's been back for ages.'

She wasn't half as surprised as I was. The calm with which she spoke amazed me.

'Good Lord! This is the end.'

'What is?'

'This is. Has he been pinched?'

'Of course not. He told them who he was and explained everything.'

'Oh, gosh!'

'What's the matter? Oh, of course, I was forgetting. You don't know the latest developments. Jeeves solved everything.'

'He did?'

'With a wave of the hand. It was so simple, really. One wondered why one hadn't thought of it oneself. On his advice, Glossop revealed his identity and said your aunt had got him down here to observe *you*.'

I reeled, and might have fallen, had I not clutched at a photograph on a near-by table of Uncle Tom in the uniform of the East Worcestershire Volunteers.

'*No?*' I said.

'And of course it carried immediate conviction with Mrs. Cream. Your aunt explained that she had been uneasy about you for a long time, because you were always doing extraordinary things like sliding down water-pipes and keeping twenty-three cats in your bedroom and all that, and Mrs. Cream recalled the time when she had found you hunting for mice under her son's dressing-table, so she quite agreed that it was high time you were under the observation of an experienced eye like Glossop's. She was greatly relieved when Glossop assured her that he was confident of effecting a cure. She said we must all be very, very kind to you. So everything's nice and smooth. It's extraordinary how things turn out for the best, isn't it?' she said, laughing merrily.

Whether I would or would not at this juncture have taken her in an iron grasp and shaken her till she frothed is a point on which I can make no definite announcement. The chivalrous spirit of the Woosters would probably have restrained me, much as I resented that merry laughter, but as it happened the matter was not put to the test, for at this moment Jeeves entered, bearing a tray on which were glasses and a substantial shaker filled to the brim with the juice of the juniper berry. Bobbie drained her beaker with all possible speed and left us, saying that if she didn't get dressed, she'd be late for dinner, and Jeeves and I were alone, like a couple of bimbos in one of those movies where two strong men stand face to face and might is the only law.

'Well, Jeeves,' I said.

'Sir?'

'Miss Wickham has been telling me all.'

'Ah yes, sir.'

'The words "Ah yes, sir" fall far short of an adequate comment on the situation. A nice ... what is it? Begins with an i ... im-something.'

'Imbroglio, sir?'

'That's it. A nice imbroglio you've landed me in. Thanks to you...'

'Yes, sir.'

'Don't say "Yes, sir." Thanks to you I have been widely publicized as off my rocker.'

'Not widely, sir. Merely to your immediate circle now resident at Brinkley Court.'

'You have held me up at the bar of world opinion as a man who has not got all his marbles.'

'It was not easy to think of an alternative scheme, sir.'

'And let me tell you,' I said, and I meant this to sting, 'it's amazing that you got away with it.'

'Sir?'

'There's a flaw in your story that sticks up like a sore thumb.'

'Sir?'

'It's no good standing there saying "Sir?", Jeeves. It's obvious. The cow-creamer was in Glossop's bedroom. How did he account for that?'

'On my suggestion, sir, he explained that he had removed it from your room, where he had ascertained that you had hidden it after purloining it from Mr. Cream.'

I started.

'You mean,' I . . . yes, thundered would be the word, 'You mean that I am now labelled not only as a loony in a general sort of way but also as a klept-whatever-it-is?'

'Merely to your immediate circle now resident at Brinkley Court, sir.'

'You keep saying that, and you must know it's the purest apple sauce. You don't really think the Creams will maintain a tactful reserve? They'll dine out on it for years. Returning to America, they'll spread the story from the rockbound coasts of Maine to the Everglades of Florida, with the result that when I go over there again, keen looks will be shot at me at every house I go into and spoons counted before I leave. And do you realize that in a few shakes I've got to show up at dinner and have Mrs. Cream being very, very kind to me? It hurts the pride of the Woosters, Jeeves.'

'My advice, sir, would be to fortify yourself for the ordeal.'

'How?'

'There are always cocktails, sir. Should I pour you another?'

'You should.'

'And we must always remember what the poet Longfellow said, sir.'

'What was that?'

'Something attempted, something done, has earned a night's repose. You have the satisfaction of having sacrificed yourself in the interests of Mr. Travers.'

He had found a talking point. He had reminded me of those postal orders, sometimes for as much as ten bob, which Uncle Tom had sent me in the Malvern House days. I softened. Whether or not a tear rose to my eye, I cannot say, but it may be taken as official that I softened.

'How right you are, Jeeves!' I said.

STIFF UPPER LIP, JEEVES

1

I marmaladed a slice of toast with something of a flourish, and I don't suppose I have ever come much closer to saying 'Tra-la-la' as I did the lathering, for I was feeling in mid-season form this morning. God, as I once heard Jeeves put it, was in His Heaven and all was right with the world. (He added, I remember, some guff about larks and snails, but that is a side issue and need not detain us.)

It is no secret in the circles in which he moves that Bertram Wooster, though as glamorous as one could wish when night has fallen and the revels get under way, is seldom a ball of fire at the breakfast table. Confronted with the eggs and b., he tends to pick cautiously at them, as if afraid they may leap from the plate and snap at him. Listless, about sums it up. Not much bounce to the ounce.

But today vastly different conditions had prevailed. All had been verve, if that's the word I want, and animation. Well, when I tell you that after sailing through a couple of sausages like a tiger of the jungles tucking into its luncheon coolie I was now, as indicated, about to tackle the toast and marmalade, I fancy I need say no more.

The reason for this improved outlook on the proteins and carbohydrates is not far to seek. Jeeves was back, earning his weekly envelope once more at the old stand. Her butler having come down with an ailment of some sort, my Aunt Dahlia, my good and deserving aunt, had borrowed him for a house party she was throwing at Brinkley Court, her Worcestershire residence, and he had been away for more than a week. Jeeves, of course, is a gentleman's gentleman, not a butler, but if the call comes, he can buttle with the best of them. It's in the blood. His Uncle Charlie is a butler, and no doubt he has picked up many a hint on technique from him.

He came in a little later to remove the debris, and I asked him if he had had a good time at Brinkley.

'Extremely pleasant, thank you, sir.'

'More than I had in your absence. I felt like a child of tender years deprived of its Nannie. If you don't mind me calling you a Nannie.'

'Not at all, sir.'

Though, as a matter of fact, I was giving myself a slight edge, putting it that way. My Aunt Agatha, the one who eats broken bottles and turns into a werewolf at the time of the full moon, generally refers to Jeeves as my keeper.

'Yes, I missed you sorely, and had no heart for whooping it up with the lads at the Drones. From sport to sport they . . . how does that gag go?'

'Sir?'

'I heard you pull it once with reference to Freddie Widgeon, when one of his girls had given him the bird. Something about hurrying.'

'Ah yes, sir. From sport to sport they hurry me, to stifle my regret –'

'And when they win a smile from me, they think that I forget. That was it. Not your own, by any chance?'

'No, sir. An old English drawing-room ballad.'

'Oh? Well, that's how it was with me. But tell me all about Brinkley. How was Aunt Dahlia?'

'Mrs. Travers appeared to be in her customary robust health, sir.'

'And how did the party go off?'

'Reasonably satisfactorily, sir.'

'Only reasonably?'

'The demeanour of Mr. Travers cast something of a gloom on the proceedings. He was low-spirited.'

'He always is when Aunt Dahlia fills the house with guests. I've known even a single foreign substance in the woodwork to make him drain the bitter cup.'

'Very true, sir, but on this occasion I think his despondency was due principally to the presence of Sir Watkyn Bassett.'

'You don't mean that old crumb was there?' I said, Great-Scott-ing, for I knew that if there is one man for whose insides my Uncle Tom has the most vivid distaste, it is this Bassett. 'You astound me, Jeeves.'

'I, too, must confess to a certain surprise at seeing the gentleman at Brinkley Court, but no doubt Mrs. Travers felt it incumbent upon her to return his hospitality. You will recollect that Sir Watkyn recently entertained Mrs. Travers and yourself at Totleigh Towers.'

I winced. Intending, I presumed, merely to refresh my memory, he had touched an exposed nerve. There was some cold coffee left in the pot, and I took a sip to restore my equanimity.

'The word "entertained" is not well chosen, Jeeves. If locking a fellow in his bedroom, as near as a toucher with gyves upon his wrists, and stationing the local police force on the lawn below to ensure that he doesn't nip out of the window at the end of a knotted sheet is your idea of entertaining, it isn't mine, not by a jugful.'

I don't know how well up you are in the Wooster archives, but if you have dipped into them to any extent, you will probably recall the sinister affair of Sir Watkyn Bassett and my visit to his Gloucestershire home. He and my Uncle Tom are rival collectors of what are known as objets d'art, and on one occasion he pinched a silver cow-creamer, as the revolting things are called, from the relation by marriage, and Aunt Dahlia and self went to Totleigh to pinch it back, an enterprise which, though crowned with success, as the expression is, so nearly landed me in the jug that when reminded of that house of horror I still quiver like an aspen, if aspens are the things I'm thinking of.

'Do you ever have nightmares, Jeeves?' I asked, having got through with my bit of wincing.

'Not frequently, sir.'

'Nor me. But when I do, the set-up is always the same. I am back at Totleigh Towers with Sir W. Bassett, his daughter Madeline, Roderick Spode, Stiffy Byng, Gussie Fink-Nottle and the dog Bartholomew, all doing their stuff, and I wake, if you will pardon the expression so soon after breakfast, sweating at every pore. Those were the times that . . . what, Jeeves?'

'Tried men's souls, sir.'

'They certainly did – in spades. Sir Watkyn Bassett, eh?' I said thoughtfully. 'No wonder Uncle Tom mourned and would not be comforted. In his position I'd have been low-spirited myself. Who else were among those present?'

'Miss Bassett, sir, Miss Byng, Miss Byng's dog and Mr. Fink-Nottle.'

'Gosh! Practically the whole Totleigh Towers gang. Not Spode?'

'No, sir. Apparently no invitation had been extended to his lordship.'

'His what?'

'Mr. Spode, if you recall, recently succeeded to the title of Lord Sidcup.'

'So he did. I'd forgotten. But Sidcup or no Sidcup, to me he will always be Spode. There's a bad guy, Jeeves.'

'Certainly a somewhat forceful personality, sir.'

'I wouldn't want him in my orbit again.'

'I can readily understand it, sir.'

'Nor would I willingly foregather with Sir Watkyn Bassett, Madeline Bassett, Stiffy Byng and Bartholomew. I don't mind Gussie. He looks like a fish and keeps newts in a glass tank in his bedroom, but one condones that sort of thing in an old schoolfellow, just as one condones in an old Oxford friend such as the Rev. H.P. Pinker the habit of tripping over his feet and upsetting things. How was Gussie? Pretty bobbish?'

'No, sir. Mr. Fink-Nottle, too, seemed to me low-spirited.'

'Perhaps one of his newts had got tonsilitis or something.'

'It is conceivable, sir.'

'You've never kept newts, have you?'

'No, sir.'

'Nor have I. Nor, to the best of my knowledge, have Einstein, Jack Dempsey and the Archbishop of Canterbury, to name but three others. Yet Gussie revels in their society and is never happier than when curled up with them. It takes all sorts to make a world, Jeeves.'

'It does, indeed, sir. Will you be lunching in?'

'No, I've a date at the Ritz,' I said, and went off to climb into the outer crust of the English gentleman.

As I dressed, my thoughts returned to the Bassetts, and I was still wondering why on earth Aunt Dahlia had allowed the pure air of Brinkley Court to be polluted by Sir Watkyn and associates, when the telephone rang and I went into the hall to answer it.

'Bertie?'

'Oh, hullo, Aunt Dahlia.'

There had been no mistaking that loved voice. As always when we converse on the telephone, it had nearly fractured my ear-drum. This aunt was at one time a prominent figure in hunting circles, and when in the saddle, so I'm told, could make herself heard not only in the field or meadow where she happened to be, but in several adjoining counties. Retired now from active fox-chivvying, she still tends to address a nephew in the tone of voice previously reserved for rebuking hounds for taking time off to chase rabbits.

'So you're up and about, are you?' she boomed. 'I thought you'd be in bed, snoring your head off.'

'It is a little unusual for me to be in circulation at this hour,' I agreed, 'but I rose today with the lark and, I think, the snail. Jeeves!'

'Sir?'

'Didn't you tell me once that snails were early risers?'

'Yes, sir. The poet Browning in his *Pippa Passes*, having established that the hour is seven a.m., goes on to say, "The lark's on the wing, the snail's on the thorn." '

'Thank you, Jeeves. I was right, Aunt Dahlia. When I slid from between the sheets, the lark was on the wing, the snail on the thorn.'

'What the devil are you babbling about?'

'Don't ask me, ask the poet Browning. I was merely apprising you that I was up betimes. I thought it was the least I could do to celebrate Jeeves's return.'

'He got back all right, did he?'

'Looking bronzed and fit.'

'He was in rare form here. Bassett was terrifically impressed.'

I was glad to have this opportunity of solving the puzzle which had been perplexing me.

'Now there,' I said, 'you have touched on something I'd very much like to have information *re*. What on earth made you invite Pop Bassett to Brinkley?'

'I did it for the wife and kiddies.'

I eh-what-ed. 'You wouldn't care to amplify that?' I said. 'It got past me to some extent.'

'For Tom's sake, I mean,' she replied with a hearty laugh that rocked me to my foundations. 'Tom's been feeling rather low of late because of what he calls iniquitous taxation. You know how he hates to give up.'

I did, indeed. If Uncle Tom had his way, the Revenue authorities wouldn't get so much as a glimpse of his money.

'Well, I thought having to fraternize with Bassett would take his mind off it – show him that there are worse things in this world than income tax. Our doctor here gave me the idea. He was telling me about a thing called Hodgkin's Disease that you cure by giving the patient arsenic. The principle's the same. That Bassett really is the limit. When I see you, I'll tell you the story of the black amber statuette. It's a thing he's just bought for his collection. He was showing it to Tom when he was here, gloating over it. Tom suffered agonies, poor old buzzard.'

'Jeeves told me he was low-spirited.'

'So would you be, if you were a collector and another collector you particularly disliked had got hold of a thing you'd have given your eyeteeth to have in your own collection.'

'I see what you mean,' I said, marvelling, as I had often done before, that Uncle Tom could attach so much value to objects which I personally would have preferred not to be found dead in a ditch with. The cow-creamer I mentioned earlier was one of them, being a milk jug shaped like a cow, of all ghastly ideas. I have always maintained fearlessly that the spiritual home of all these fellows who collect things is a padded cell in a loony bin.

'It gave Tom the worst attack of indigestion he's had since he was last lured into eating lobster. And talking of indigestion, I'm coming up to London for the day the day after tomorrow and shall require you to give me lunch.'

I assured her that that should be attended to, and after the exchange of a few more civilities she rang off.

'That was Aunt Dahlia, Jeeves,' I said, coming away from the machine.

'Yes, sir, I fancied I recognized Mrs. Travers's voice.'

'She wants me to give her lunch the day after tomorrow. I think we'd better have it here. She's not keen on restaurant cooking.'

'Very good, sir.'

'What's this black amber statuette thing she was talking about?'

'It is a somewhat long story, sir.'

'Then don't tell me now. If I don't rush, I shall be late for my date.'

I reached for the umbrella and hat, and was heading for the open spaces, when I heard Jeeves give that soft cough of his and, turning, saw that a shadow was about to fall on what had been a day of joyous reunion. In the eye which he was fixing on me I detected the aunt-like gleam which always means that he disapproves of something, and when he said in a soupy tone of voice 'Pardon me, sir, but are you proposing to enter the Ritz Hotel in that hat?' I knew that the time had come when Bertram must show that iron resolution of his which has been so widely publicized.

In the matter of head-joy Jeeves is not in tune with modern progressive thought, his attitude being best described, perhaps, as hidebound, and right from the start I had been asking myself what his reaction would be to the blue Alpine hat with the pink feather in it which I had purchased in his absence. Now I knew. I could see at a g. that he wanted no piece of it.

I, on the other hand, was all for this Alpine lid. I was prepared to concede that it would have been more suitable for rural wear, but against this had to be set the fact that it unquestionably lent a *diablerie* to my appearance, and mine is an appearance that needs all the *diablerie* it can get. In my voice, therefore, as I replied, there was a touch of steel.

'Yes, Jeeves, that, in a nutshell, is what I am proposing to do. Don't you like this hat?'

'No, sir.'

'Well, I do,' I replied rather cleverly, and went out with it tilted just that merest shade over the left eye which makes all the difference.

2

My date at the Ritz was with Emerald Stoker, younger offspring of that pirate of the Spanish Main, old Pop Stoker, the character who once kidnapped me on board his yacht with a view to making me marry his elder daughter Pauline. Long story, I won't go into it now, merely saying that the old fathead had got entirely the wrong angle on the relations between his ewe lamb and myself, we being just good friends, as the expression is. Fortunately it all ended happily, with the popsy linked in matrimony with Marmaduke, Lord Chuffnell, an ancient buddy of mine, and we're still good friends. I put in an occasional week-end with her and Chuffy, and when she comes to London on a shopping binge or whatever it may be, I see to it that she gets her calories. Quite natural, then, that when her sister Emerald came over from America to study painting at the Slade, she should have asked me to keep an eye on her and give her lunch from time to time. Kindly old Bertram, the family friend.

I was a bit late, as I had foreshadowed, in getting to the tryst, and she was already there when I arrived. It struck me, as it did every time I saw her, how strange it is that members of a family can be so unlike each other – how different in appearance, I mean, Member A. so often is from Member B., and for the matter of that Member B. from Member C., if you follow what I'm driving at. Take the Stoker troupe, for instance. To look at them, you'd never have guessed they were united by ties of blood. Old Stoker resembled one of those fellows who play bit parts in gangster pictures: Pauline was of a beauty so radiant that strong men whistled after her in the street; while Emerald, in sharp contra-distinction, was just ordinary, no different from a million other nice girls except perhaps for a touch of the Pekinese about the nose and eyes and more freckles than you usually see.

I always enjoyed putting on the nosebag with her, for there was a sort of motherliness about her which I found restful. She was one of those soothing, sympathetic girls you can take your troubles to, confident of having your hand held and your head patted. I was still a bit ruffled about Jeeves and the Alpine hat and of course told her all about it, and nothing could have been in better taste than her attitude. She said it sounded as if Jeeves must be something like her father – she had never met him – Jeeves, I mean, not her father, whom of course she had met frequently – and she told me I had been quite right in displaying the velvet hand in the iron glove, or rather the other way around, isn't it, because it never did to let oneself be bossed. Her father, she said, always tried to boss everybody, and in her opinion one of these days some haughty spirit was going to haul off and poke him in the nose – which, she said, and I agreed with her, would do him all the good in the world.

I was so grateful for these kind words that I asked her if she would care to come to the theatre on the following night, I knowing where I could get hold of a couple of tickets for a well-spoken-of musical, but she said she couldn't make it.

'I'm going down to the country this afternoon to stay with some people. I'm taking the four o'clock train at Paddington.'

'Going to be there long?'

'About a month.'

'At the same place all the time?'

'Of course.'

She spoke lightly, but I found myself eyeing her with a certain respect. Myself, I've never found a host and hostess who could stick my presence for more than about a week. Indeed, long before that as a general rule the conversation at the dinner table is apt to turn on the subject of how good the train service to London is, those present obviously hoping wistfully that Bertram will avail himself of it. Not to mention the time-tables left in your room with a large cross against the 2.35 and the legend 'Excellent train. Highly recommended.'

'Their name's Bassett.' I started visibly. 'They live in Gloucestershire.' I started visibly. 'Their house is called –'

'Totleigh Towers?'

She started visibly, making three visible starts in all.

'Oh, do you know them? Well, that's fine. You can tell me about them.'

This surprised me somewhat.

'Why, don't *you* know them?'

'I've only met Miss Bassett. What are the rest of them like?'

It was a subject on which I was a well-informed source, but I hesitated for a moment, asking myself if I ought to reveal to this frail girl what she was letting herself in for. Then I decided that the truth must be told and nothing held back. Cruel to hide the facts from her and allow her to go off to Totleigh Towers unprepared.

'The inmates of the leper colony under advisement,' I said, 'consist of Sir Watkyn Bassett, his daughter Madeline, his niece Stephanie Byng, a chap named Spode who recently took to calling himself Lord Sidcup, and Stiffy Byng's Aberdeen terrier Bartholomew, the last of whom you would do well to watch closely if he gets anywhere near your ankles, for he biteth like a serpent and stingeth like an adder. So you've met Madeline Bassett? What did you think of her?'

She seemed to weigh this. A moment or two passed before she surfaced again. When she spoke, it was with a spot of wariness in her voice.

'Is she a great friend of yours?'

'Far from it.'

'Well, she struck me as a drip.'

'She is a drip.'

'Of course, she's very pretty. You have to hand her that.'

I shook the loaf.

'Looks are not everything. I admit that any redblooded Sultan or Pasha, if offered the opportunity of adding M. Bassett to the personnel of his harem, would jump to it without hesitation, but he would regret his impulsiveness before the end of the first week. She's one of those soppy girls, riddled from head to foot with whimsy. She holds the view that the stars are God's daisy chain, that rabbits are gnomes in attendance on the Fairy Queen, and that every time a fairy blows its wee nose a baby is born, which, as we know, is not the case. She's a drooper.'

'Yes, that's how she seemed to me. Rather like one of the lovesick maidens in *Patience*.'

'Eh?'

'*Patience*. Gilbert and Sullivan. Haven't you ever seen it?'

'Oh yes, now I recollect. My Aunt Agatha made me take her son Thos to it once. Not at all a bad little show, I thought, though a bit highbrow. We now come to Sir Watkyn Bassett, Madeline's father.'

'Yes, she mentioned her father.'

'And well she might.'

'What's he like?'

'One of those horrors from outer space. It may seem a hard thing to say of any man, but I would rank Sir Watkyn Bassett as an even bigger stinker than your father.'

'Would you call Father a stinker?'

'Not to his face, perhaps.'

'He thinks you're crazy.'

'Bless his old heart.'

'And you can't say he's wrong. Anyway, he's not so bad, if you rub him the right way.'

'Very possibly, but if you think a busy man like myself has time to go rubbing your father, either with or against the grain, you are greatly mistaken. The word "stinker", by the way, reminds me that there is one redeeming aspect of life at Totleigh Towers, the presence in the neighbouring village of the Rev. H.P. ("Stinker") Pinker, the local curate. You'll like him. He used to play football for England. But watch out for Spode. He's about eight feet high and has the sort of eye that can open an oyster at sixty paces. Take a line through gorillas you have met, and you will get the idea.'

'You do seem to have some nice friends.'

'No friends of mine. Though I'm fond of young Stiffy and am always prepared to clasp her to my bosom, provided she doesn't start something. But then she always does start something. I think that completes the roster. Oh no, Gussie. I was forgetting Gussie.'

'Who's he?'

'Fellow I've known for years and years. He's engaged to Madeline Bassett. Chap named Gussie Fink-Nottle.'

She uttered a sharp squeak.

'Does he wear horn-rimmed glasses?'

'Yes.'

'And keep newts?'

'In great profusion. Why, do you know him?'

'I've met him. We met at a studio party.'

'I didn't know he ever went to studio parties.'

'He went to this one, and we talked most of the evening. I thought he was a lamb.'

'You mean a fish.'

'I don't mean a fish.'

'He looks like a fish.'

'He does not look like a fish.'

'Well, have it your own way,' I said tolerantly, knowing it was futile to attempt to reason with a girl who had spent an evening vis-à-vis Gussie Fink-Nottle and didn't think he looked like a fish. 'So there you are, that's Totleigh Towers. Wild horses wouldn't drag me there, not that I suppose they would ever try, but you'll probably have a good enough time,' I said, for I didn't wish to depress her unduly. 'It's a beautiful place, and it isn't as if you were going there to pinch a cow-creamer.'

'To what a what?'

'Nothing, nothing. I was just thinking of something,' I said, and turned the conv. to other topics.

She gave me the impression, when we parted, of being a bit pensive, which I could well understand, and I wasn't feeling too unpensive myself. There's a touch of the superstitious in my make-up, and the way the Bassett ménage seemed to be raising its ugly head, if you know what I mean, struck me as sinister. I had a . . . what's the word? . . . begins with a p . . . pre-something . . . presentiment, that's the baby . . . I had a presentiment that I was being tipped off by my guardian angel that Totleigh Towers was trying to come back into my life and that I would be well advised to watch my step and keep an eye skinned.

It was consequently a thoughtful Bertram Wooster who half an hour later sat toying with a stoup of malvoisie in the smoking room of the Drones Club. To the overtures of fellow-members who wanted to hurry me from sport to sport I turned a deaf ear, for I wished to brood. And I was trying to tell myself that all this Totleigh Towers business was purely coincidental and meant nothing, when the smoking-room waiter slid up and informed me that a gentleman stood without, asking to have speech with me. A clerical gentleman named Pinker, he said, and I gave another of my visible starts, the presentiment stronger on the wing than ever.

It wasn't that I had any objection to the sainted Pinker. I loved him like a b. We were up at Oxford together, and our relations have always been on strictly David and Jonathan lines. But while technically not a resident of Totleigh Towers, he helped the Vicar vet the souls of the local yokels in the adjoining village of Totleigh-in-the-Wold, and that was near enough to it to make this sudden popping up of his deepen the apprehension I was feeling. It seemed to me that it only needed Sir Watkyn Bassett, Madeline Bassett, Roderick Spode and the dog Bartholomew to saunter in arm in arm, and I would have a full hand. My respect for my guardian angel's astuteness hit a new high. A gloomy bird, with a marked disposition to take the dark view and make one's flesh creep, but there was no gainsaying that he knew his stuff.

'Bung him in,' I said dully, and in due season the Rev. H.P. Pinker lumbered across the threshold and advancing with outstretched hand tripped over his feet and upset a small table, his almost invariable practice when moving from spot to spot in any room where there's furniture.

3

Which was odd, when you came to think of it, because after representing his University for four years and his country for six on the football field, he still turns out for the Harlequins when he can get a Saturday off from saving souls, and when footballing is as steady on his pins as a hart or roe or whatever the animals are that don't trip over their feet and upset things. I've seen him a couple of times in the arena, and was profoundly impressed by his virtuosity. Rugby football is more or less a sealed book to me, I never having gone in for it, but even I could see that he was good. The lissomness with which he moved hither and thither was most impressive, as was his homicidal ardour when doing what I believe is called tackling. Like the Canadian Mounted Police he always got his man, and when he did so the air was vibrant with the excited cries of morticians in the audience making bids for the body.

He's engaged to be married to Stiffy Byng, and his long years of football should prove an excellent preparation for setting up house with her. The way I look at it is that when a fellow has had pluguglies in cleated boots doing a Shuffle-Off-To-Buffalo on his face Saturday after Saturday since he was a slip of a boy, he must get to fear nothing, not even marriage with a girl like Stiffy, who from early childhood has seldom let the sun go down without starting some loony enterprise calculated to bleach the hair of one and all.

There was plenty and to spare of the Rev. H.P. Pinker. Even as a boy, I imagine, he must have burst seams and broken try-your-weight machines, and grown to man's estate he might have been Roderick Spode's twin brother. Purely in the matter of thews, sinews and tonnage, I mean of course, for whereas Roderick Spode went about seeking whom he might devour and was a consistent menace to pedestrians and traffic, Stinker, though no doubt a fiend in human shape when assisting the Harlequins Rugby football club to dismember some rival troupe of athletes, was in private life a gentle soul with whom a child could have played. In fact, I once saw a child doing so.

Usually when you meet this man of God, you find him beaming. I believe his merry smile is one of the sights of Totleigh-in-the-Wold, as it was of Magdalen College, Oxford, when we were up there together. But now I seemed to note in his aspect a certain gravity, as if he had just discovered a schism in his flock or found a couple of choir boys smoking reefers in the churchyard. He gave me the impression of a two-hundred-pound curate with something on his mind beside his hair. Upsetting another table, he took a seat and said he was glad he had caught me.

'I thought I'd find you at the Drones.'

'You have,' I assured him. 'What brings you to the metrop?'

'I came up for a Harlequins committee meeting.'

'And how were they all?'

'Oh, fine.'

'That's good. I've been worrying myself sick about the Harlequins committee. Well, how have you been keeping, Stinker?'

'I've been all right.'

'Are you free for dinner?'

'Sorry, I've got to get back to Totleigh.'

'Too bad. Jeeves tells me Sir Watkyn and Madeline and Stiffy have been staying with my aunt at Brinkley.'

'Yes.'

'Have they returned?'

'Yes.'

'And how's Stiffy?'

'Oh, fine.'

'And Bartholomew?'

'Oh, fine.'

'And your parishioners? Going strong, I trust?'

'Oh yes, they're fine.'

I wonder if anything strikes you about the slice of give-and-take I've just recorded. No? Oh, surely. I mean, here were we, Stinker Pinker and Bertram Wooster, buddies who had known each other virtually from the egg, and we were talking like a couple of strangers making conversation on a train. At least, he was, and more and more I became convinced that his bosom was full of the perilous stuff that weighs upon the heart, as I remember Jeeves putting it once.

I persevered in my efforts to uncork him.

'Well, Stinker,' I said, 'what's new? Has Pop Bassett given you that vicarage yet?'

This caused him to open up a bit. His manner became more animated.

'No, not yet. He doesn't seem able to make up his mind. One day he says he will, the next day he says he's not so sure, he'll have to think it over.'

I frowned. I disapproved of this shilly-shallying. I could see how it must be throwing a spanner into Stinker's whole foreign policy, putting him in a spot and causing him alarm and despondency. He can't marry Stiffy on a curate's stipend, so they've got to wait till Pop Bassett gives him a vicarage which he has in his gift. And while I personally, though fond of the young gumboil, would run a mile in tight shoes to avoid marrying Stiffy, I knew him to be strongly in favour of signing her up.

'Something always happens to put him off. I think he was about ready to close the deal before he went to stay at Brinkley, but most unfortunately I bumped into a valuable vase of his and broke it. It seemed to rankle rather.'

I heaved a sigh. It's always what Jeeves would call most disturbing to hear that a chap with whom you have plucked the gowans fine, as the expression is, isn't making out as well as could be wished. I was all set to follow this Pinker's career with considerable interest, but the way things were shaping it began to look as if there wasn't going to be a career to follow.

'You move in a mysterious way your wonders to perform, Stinker. I believe you would bump into something if you were crossing the Gobi desert.'

'I've never been in the Gobi desert.'

'Well, don't go. It isn't safe. I suppose Stiffy's sore about this . . . what's the word? . . . Not vaseline . . . Vacillation, that's it. She chafes, I imagine, at this vacillation on Bassett's part and resents him letting "I dare not" wait upon "I would", like the poor cat in the adage. Not my own, that, by the way. Jeeves's. Pretty steamed up, is she?'

'She is rather.'

'I don't blame her. Enough to upset any girl. Pop Bassett has no right to keep gumming up the course of true love like this.'

'No.'

'He needs a kick in the pants.'

'Yes.'

'If I were Stiffy, I'd put a toad in his bed or strychnine in his soup.'

'Yes. And talking of Stiffy, Bertie —'

He broke off, and I eyed him narrowly. There could be no question to my mind that I had been right about that perilous stuff. His bosom was obviously chock full of it.

'There's something the matter, Stinker.'

'No, there isn't. Why do you say that?'

'Your manner is strange. You remind me of a faithful dog looking up into its proprietor's face as if it were trying to tell him something. Are you trying to tell me something?'

He swallowed once or twice, and his colour deepened, which took a bit of doing, for even when his soul is in repose he always looks like a clerical beetroot. It was as though the collar he buttons at the back was choking him. In a hoarse voice he said:

'Bertie.'

'Hullo?'

'Bertie.'

'Still here, old man, and hanging on your lips.'

'Bertie, are you busy just now?'

'Not more than usual.'

'You could get away for a day or two?'

'I suppose one might manage it.'

'Then can you come to Totleigh?'

'To stay with you, do you mean?'

'No, to stay at Totleigh Towers.'

I stared at the man, wide-eyed as the expression is. Had it not been that I knew him to be abstemiousness itself, rarely indulging in anything stronger than a light lager, and not even that during Lent, I should have leaped to the conclusion that there beside me sat a curate who had been having a couple. My eyebrows rose till they nearly disarranged my front hair.

'Stay *where*? Stinker, you're not yourself, or you wouldn't be gibbering like this. You can't have forgotten the ordeal I passed through last time I went to Totleigh Towers.'

'I know. But there's something Stiffy wants you to do for her. She wouldn't tell me what it was, but she said it was most important and that you would have to be on the spot to do it.'

I drew myself up. I was cold and resolute.

'You're crazy, Stinker!'

'I don't see why you say that.'

'Then let me explain where your whole scheme falls to the ground. To begin with, is it likely that after what has passed between us Sir Watkyn B. would issue an invitation to one who has always been to him a pain in the neck to end all pains in the neck? If ever there was a man who was all in favour of me taking the high road while he took the low road, it is this same Bassett. His idea of a happy day is one spent with at least a hundred miles between him and Bertram.'

'Madeline would invite you, if you sent her a wire asking if you could come for a day or two. She never consults Sir Watkyn about guests. It's an understood thing that she has anyone she wants to at the house.'

This I knew to be true, but I ignored the suggestion and proceeded remorselessly.

'In the second place, I know Stiffy. A charming girl whom, as I was telling Emerald Stoker, I am always prepared to clasp to my bosom, at least I would be if she wasn't engaged to you, but one who is a cross between a ticking bomb and a poltergeist. She lacks that balanced judgment which we like to see in girls. She gets ideas, and if you care to call them bizarre ideas, it will be all right with me. I need scarcely remind you that when I last visited Totleigh Towers she egged you on to pinch Constable Eustace Oates's helmet, the one thing a curate should shrink from doing if he wishes to rise to heights in the Church. She is, in short, about as loony a young shrimp as ever wore a wind-swept hair-do. What this commission is that she has in mind for me we cannot say, but going by the form book I see it as something totally unfit for human consumption. Didn't she even hint at its nature?'

'No. I asked, of course, but she said she would rather keep it under her hat till she saw you.'

'She won't see me.'

'You won't come to Totleigh?'

'Not within fifty miles of the sewage dump.'

'She'll be terribly disappointed.'

'You will administer spiritual solace. That's your job. Tell her these things are sent to try us.'

'She'll probably cry.'

'Nothing better for the nervous system. It does something, I forget what, to the glands. Ask any well-known Harley Street physician.'

I suppose he saw that my iron front was not to be shaken, for he made no further attempt to sell the idea to me. With a sigh that seemed to come up from the soles of the feet, he rose, said goodbye, knocked over the glass from which I had been refreshing myself and withdrew.

Knowing how loath Bertram Wooster always is to let a pal down and fail him in his hour of need, you are probably thinking that this distressing scene had left me shaken, but as a matter of fact it had bucked me up like a day at the seaside.

Let's just review the situation. Ever since breakfast my guardian angel had been scaring the pants off me by practically saying in so many words that Totleigh Towers was all set to re-enter my life, and it was now clear that what he had had in mind had been the imminence of this plea to me to go there, he feeling that in a weak moment I might allow myself to be persuaded against my better judgment. The peril was now past. Totleigh Towers had made its spring and missed by a mile, and I no longer had a thing to worry about. It was with a light heart that I joined a group of pleasure-seekers who were playing Darts and cleaned them up with effortless skill. Three o'clock was approaching when I left the club en route for home, and it must have been getting on for half past when I hove alongside the apartment house where I have my abode.

There was a cab standing outside, laden with luggage. From its window Gussie Fink-Nottle's head was poking out, and I remember thinking once again how mistaken Emerald Stoker had been about his appearance. Seeing him steadily, if not whole, I could detect in his aspect no trace of the lamb, but he was looking so like a halibut that if he hadn't been wearing horn-rimmed spectacles, a thing halibuts seldom do, I might have supposed myself to be gazing on something a.w.o.l. from a fishmonger's slab.

I gave him a friendly yodel, and he turned the spectacles in my direction.

'Oh, hullo, Bertie,' he said, 'I've just been calling on you. I left a message with Jeeves. Your aunt told me to tell you she's coming to London the day after tomorrow and she wants you to give her lunch.'

'Yes, she was on the phone to that effect this morning. I suppose she thought you'd forget to notify me. Come in and have some orange juice,' I said, for it is to that muck that he confines himself whilst making whoopee.

He looked at his watch, and his eyes lost the gleam that always comes into them when orange juice is mentioned.

'I wish I could, but I can't,' he sighed. 'I should miss my train. I'm off to Totleigh on the four o'clock at Paddington.'

'Oh, really? Well, look out for a friend of yours, who'll be on it. Emerald Stoker.'

'Stoker? Stoker? Emerald Stoker?'

'Girl with freckles. American. Looks like a Pekinese of the better sort. She tells me she met you at a studio party the other day, and you talked about newts.'

His face cleared.

'Of course, yes. Now I've placed her. I didn't get her name that day. Yes, we had a long talk about newts. She used to keep them herself as a child, only she called them guppies. A most delightful girl. I shall enjoy seeing her again. I don't know when I've met a girl who attracted me more.'

'Except, of course, Madeline.'

His face darkened. He looked like a halibut that's taken offence at a rude remark from another halibut.

'Madeline! Don't talk to me about Madeline! Madeline makes me sick!' he hissed. 'Paddington!' he shouted to the charioteer and was gone with the wind, leaving me gaping after him, all of a twitter.

4

And I'll tell you why I was all of a t. My critique of her when chatting with Emerald Stoker will have shown how allergic I was to this Bassett beazel. She was scarcely less of a pain in the neck to me than I was to her father or Roderick Spode. Nevertheless, there was a grave danger that I might have to take her for better or for worse, as the book of rules puts it.

The facts may be readily related. Gussie, enamoured of the Bassett, would have liked to let her in on the way he felt, but every time he tried to do so his nerve deserted him and he found himself babbling about newts. At a loss to know how to swing the deal, he got the idea of asking me to plead his cause, and when I pleaded it, the Bassett, as pronounced a fathead as ever broke biscuit, thought I was pleading mine. She said she was so sorry to cause me pain, but her heart belonged to Gussie. Which would have been fine, had she not gone on to say that if anything should ever happen to make her revise her conviction that he was a king among men and she was compelled to give him the heave-ho, I was the next in line, and while she could never love me with the same fervour she felt for Gussie, she would do her best to make me happy. I was, in a word, in the position of a Vice-President of the United States of America who, while feeling that he is all right so far, knows that he will be for it at a moment's notice if anything goes wrong with the man up top.

Little wonder, then, that Gussie's statement that Madeline made him sick smote me like a ton of bricks and had me indoors and bellowing for Jeeves before you could say What ho. As had so often happened before, I felt that my only course was to place myself in the hands of a higher power.

'Sir?' he said, manifesting himself.

'A ghastly thing has happened, Jeeves! Disaster looms.'

'Indeed, sir? I am sorry to hear that.'

There's one thing you have to give Jeeves credit for. He lets the dead past bury its d. He and the young master may have had differences about Alpine hats with pink feathers in them, but when he sees the y.m. on the receiving end of the slings and arrows of outrageous fortune, he sinks his dudgeon and comes through with the feudal spirit at its best. So now, instead of being cold and distant and aloof, as a lesser man would have been, he showed the utmost agitation and concern. That is to say, he allowed one eyebrow to rise perhaps an eighth of an inch, which is as far as he ever goes in the way of expressing emotion.

'What would appear to be the trouble, sir?'

I sank into a chair and mopped the frontal bone. Not for many a long day had I been in such a doodah.

'I've just seen Gussie Fink-Nottle.'

'Yes, sir. Mr. Fink-Nottle was here a moment ago.'

'I met him outside. He was in a cab. And do you know what?'

'No, sir.'

'I happened to mention Miss Bassett's name, and he said – follow this closely, Jeeves – he said – I quote – "Don't talk to me about Madeline. Madeline makes me sick." Close quotes.'

'Indeed, sir?'

'Those are not the words of love.'

'No, sir.'

'They are the words of a man who for some reason not disclosed is fed to the front teeth with the adored object. I hadn't time to go into the matter, because a moment later he was off like a scalded cat to Paddington, but it's pretty clear there must have been a rift in the what-d'you-call-it. Begins with an l.'

'Would lute be the word for which you are groping, sir?'

'Possibly. I don't know that I'd care to bet on it.'

'The poet Tennyson speaks of the little rift within the lute, that by and by will make the music mute and ever widening slowly silence all.'

'Then lute it is. And we know what's going to happen if this particular lute goes phut.'

We exchanged significant glances. At least, I gave him a significant glance, and he looked like a stuffed frog, his habit when being discreet. He knows just how I'm situated as regards M. Bassett, but naturally we don't discuss it except by going into the sig-glance-stuffed-frog routine. I mean, you can't talk about a thing like that. I don't know if it would actually come under the head of speaking lightly of a woman's name, but it wouldn't be seemly, and the Woosters are sticklers for seemliness. So, for that matter, are the Jeeveses.

'What ought I to do, do you think?'

'Sir?'

'Don't stand there saying "Sir?" You know as well as I do that a situation has arisen which calls for the immediate coming of all good men to the aid of the party. It is of the essence that Gussie's engagement does not spring a leak. Steps must be taken.'

'It would certainly seem advisable, sir.'

'But what steps? I ought, of course, to hasten to the seat of war and try to start the dove of peace going into its act – have a bash, in other words, at seeing what a calm, kindly man of the world can do to bring the young folks together, if you get what I mean.'

'I apprehend you perfectly, sir. Your role, as I see it, would be that of what the French call the *raisonneur*.'

'You're probably right. But mark this. Apart from the fact that the mere thought of being under the roof of Totleigh Towers again is one that freezes the gizzard, there's another snag. I was talking to Stinker Pinker just now, and he says that Stiffy Byng has something she wants me to do for her. Well, you know the sort of thing Stiffy generally wants people to do. You recall the episode of Constable Oates's helmet?'

'Very vividly, sir.'

'Oates had incurred her displeasure by reporting to her Uncle Watkyn that her dog Bartholomew had spilled him off his bicycle, causing him to fall into a ditch and sustain bruises and contusions, and she persuaded Harold Pinker, a man in holy orders who buttons his collar at the back, to pinch his helmet for her. And that was comparatively mild for Stiffy. There are no limits, literally none, to what she can think of when she gives her mind to it. The imagination boggles at the thought of what she may be cooking up for me.'

'Certainly you may be pardoned for feeling apprehensive, sir.'

'So there you are. I'm on the horns of . . . what are those things you get on the horns of?'

'Dilemmas, sir.'

'That's right. I'm on the horns of a dilemma. Shall I, I ask myself, go and see what I can accomplish in the way of running repairs on the lute, or would it be more prudent to stay put and let nature take its course, trusting to Time, the great healer, to do its stuff?'

'If I might make a suggestion, sir?'

'Press on, Jeeves.'

'Would it not be possible for you to go to Totleigh Towers, but to decline to carry out Miss Byng's wishes?'

I weighed this. It was, I could see, a thought.

'Issue a *nolle prosequi*, you mean? Tell her to go and boil her head?'

'Precisely, sir.'

I eyed him reverently.

'Jeeves,' I said, 'as always, you have found the way. I'll wire Miss Bassett asking if I can come, and I'll wire Aunt Dahlia that I can't give her lunch, as I'm leaving town. And I'll tell Stiffy that whatever she has in mind, she gets no service and co-operation from me. Yes, Jeeves, you've hit it. I'll go to Totleigh, though the flesh creeps at the prospect. Pop Bassett will be there. Spode will be there. Stiffy will be there. The dog Bartholomew will be there. It makes one wonder why so much fuss has been made about those half-a-league half-a-league half-a-league-onward bimbos who rode into the Valley of Death. They weren't going to find Pop Bassett at the other end. Ah well, let us hope for the best.'

'The only course to pursue, sir.'

'Stiff upper lip, Jeeves, what?'

'Indubitably, sir. That, if I may say so, is the spirit.'

5

As Stinker had predicted, Madeline Bassett placed no obstacle in the way of my visiting Totleigh Towers. In response to my invitation-cadging missive she gave me the green light, and an hour or so after her telegram had arrived Aunt Dahlia rang up from Brinkley, full of eagerness to ascertain what the hell, she having just received my wire saying that owing to absence from the metropolis I would be unable to give her the lunch for which she had been budgeting.

Her call came as no surprise. I had anticipated that there might be a certain liveliness on the Brinkley front. The old flesh-and-blood is a genial soul who loves her Bertram dearly, but she is a woman of imperious spirit. She dislikes having her wishes thwarted, and her voice came booming at me like a pack of hounds in full cry.

'Bertie, you foul young blot on the landscape!'

'Speaking.'

'I got your telegram.'

'I thought you would. Very efficient, the gramming service.'

'What do you mean, you're leaving town? You never leave town except to come down here and wallow in Anatole's cooking.'

Her allusion was to her peerless French chef, at the mention of whose name the mouth starts watering automatically. God's gift to the gastric juices I have sometimes called him.

'Where are you going?'

My mouth having stopped watering, I said I was going to Totleigh Towers, and she uttered an impatient snort.

'There's something wrong with this blasted wire. It sounded as if you were saying you were going to Totleigh Towers.'

'I am.'

'To Totleigh *Towers?*'

'I leave this afternoon.'

'What in the world made them invite you?'

'They didn't. I invited myself.'

'You mean you're deliberately seeking the society of Sir Watkyn Bassett? You must be more of an ass than even I have ever thought you. And I speak as a woman who has just had the old bounder in her hair for more than a week.'

I saw her point, and hastened to explain.

'I admit Pop Bassett is a bit above the odds,' I said, 'and unless one is compelled by circumstances it is always wisest not to stir him, but a sharp crisis has been precipitated in my affairs. All is not well between Gussie Fink-Nottle and Madeline Bassett. Their engagement is tottering toward the melting pot, and you know what that engagement means to me. I'm going down there to try to heal the rift.'

'What can you do?'

'My role, as I see it, will be that of what the French call the *raisonneur*.'

'And what does that mean?'

'Ah, there you have me, but that's what Jeeves says I'll be.'

'Are you taking Jeeves with you?'

'Of course. Do I ever stir foot without him?'

'Well, watch out, that's all I say to you, watch out. I happen to know that Bassett is making overtures to him.'

'How do you mean, overtures?'

'He's trying to steal him from you.'

I reeled, and might have fallen, had I not been sitting at the time. 'Incredulous!'

'If you mean incredible, you're wrong. I told you how he had fallen under Jeeves's spell when he was here. He used to follow him with his eyes as he buttled, like a cat watching a duck, as Anatole would say. And one morning I heard him making him a definite proposition. Well? What's the matter with you? Have you fainted?'

I told her that my momentary silence had been due to the fact that her words had stunned me, and she said she didn't see why, knowing Bassett, I should be so surprised.

'You can't have forgotten how he tried to steal Anatole. There isn't anything to which that man won't stoop. He has no conscience whatsoever. When you get to Totleigh, go and see someone called Plank and ask him what he thinks of Sir Watkyn ruddy Bassett. He chiselled this poor devil Plank out of a . . . Oh, hell!' said the aged relative as a voice intoned 'Thur-ree minutes', and she hung up, having made my flesh creep as nimbly as if she had been my guardian angel, on whose talent in that direction I have already touched.

It was still creeping with undiminished gusto as I steered the sports model along the road to Totleigh-in-the-Wold that afternoon. I was convinced, of course, that Jeeves would never dream of severing relations with the old firm, and when urged to do so by this blighted Bassett would stop his ears like the deaf adder, which, as you probably know, made a point of refusing to hear the voice of the charmer, charm he never so wisely. But the catch is that you can be convinced about a thing and nevertheless get pretty jumpy when you muse on it, and it was in no tranquil mood that I eased the Arab steed through the gates of Totleigh Towers and fetched up at the front door.

I don't know if you happen to have come across a hymn, the chorus of which goes:

> Tum tumty tumty tumty
> Tum tiddly om pom isle,
> Where every prospect pleases
> And only man is vile

or words to that effect, but the description would have fitted Totleigh Towers like the paper on the wall. Its façade, its spreading grounds, rolling parkland, smoothly shaven lawns and what not were all just like Mother makes, but what percentage was there in that, when you knew what was waiting for you inside? It's never a damn bit of use a prospect pleasing, if the gang that goes with it lets it down.

This lair of old Bassett's was one of the fairly stately homes of England – not a show place like the joints you read about with three hundred and sixty-five rooms, fifty-two staircases and twelve court-yards, but definitely not a bungalow. He had bought it furnished some time previously from a Lord somebody who needed cash, as so many do these days.

Not Pop Bassett, though. In the evening of his life he had more than a sufficiency. It would not be going too far, indeed, to describe him as stinking rich. For a great part of his adult life he had been a metropolitan police magistrate, and in that capacity once fined me five quid for a mere light-hearted peccadillo on Boat Race Night, when a mild reprimand would more than have met the case. It was shortly after this that a relative died and left him a vast fortune. That, at least, was the story given out. What really happened, of course, was that all through his years as a magistrate he had been trousering the fines, amassing the stuff in sackfuls. Five quid here, five quid there, it soon mounts up.

We had made goodish going on the road, and it wasn't more than about four-forty when I rang the front-door bell. Jeeves took the car to the stables, and the butler – Butterfield was his name, I remembered – led me to the drawing-room.

'Mr. Wooster,' he said, loosing me in.

I was not surprised to find tea in progress, for I had heard the clinking of cups. Madeline Bassett was at the controls, and she extended a drooping hand to me.

'Bertie! How nice to see you.'

I can well imagine that a casual observer, if I had confided to him my qualms at the idea of being married to this girl, would have raised his eyebrows and been at a loss to understand, for she was undeniably an eyeful, being slim, svelte and bountifully equipped with golden hair and all the fixings. But where the casual observer would have been making his bloomer was in overlooking that squashy soupiness of hers, that subtle air she had of being on the point of talking babytalk. She was the sort of girl who puts her hands over a husband's eyes, as he is crawling in to breakfast with a morning head, and says 'Guess who?'

I once stayed at the residence of a newly-married pal of mine, and his bride had had carved in large letters over the fireplace in the drawing-room, where it was impossible to miss it, the legend 'Two Lovers Built This Nest', and I can still recall the look of dumb anguish in the other half of the sketch's eyes every time he came in and saw it. Whether Madeline Bassett, on entering the marital state, would go to such an awful extreme, one could not say, but it seemed most probable, and I resolved that when I started trying to reconcile her and Gussie, I would not scamp my work but would give it everything I had.

'You know Mr. Pinker,' she said, and I perceived that Stinker was present. He was safely wedged in a chair and hadn't, as far as I could see, upset anything yet, but he gave me the impression of a man who was crouching for the spring and would begin to operate shortly. There was a gate-leg table laden with muffins and cucumber sandwiches which I foresaw would attract him like a magnet.

On seeing me, he had started visibly, dropping a plate with half a muffin on it, and his eyes had widened. I knew what he was thinking, of course. He supposed that my presence must be due to a change of heart. Rejoice with me, for I have found the sheep which was lost, he was no doubt murmuring to himself. I mourned in spirit a bit for the poor fish, knowing what a nasty knock he had coming to him when he got on to it that nothing was going to induce me to undertake whatever the foul commission might be that Stiffy had earmarked for me. On that point I was resolved to be firm, no matter what spiritual agonies he and she suffered in the process. I had long since learned that the secret of a happy and successful life was to steer clear of any project masterminded by that young scourge of the species.

The conversation that followed was what you might call . . . I've forgotten the word, but it begins with a d. I mean, with Stinker within earshot Madeline and I couldn't get down to brass tacks, so we just chewed the fat . . . desultory, that's the word I wanted. We just chewed the fat in a desultory way. Stinker said he was there to talk over the forthcoming school treat with Sir Watkyn, and I said 'Oh, is there a school treat coming up?' and Madeline said it was taking place the day after tomorrow and owing to the illness of the vicar Mr. Pinker would be in sole charge, and Stinker winced a bit, as if he didn't like the prospect much.

Madeline asked if I had had a nice drive down, and I said 'Oh, splendid.' Stinker said Stiffy would be so pleased I had come, and I smiled one of my subtle smiles. And then Butterfield came in and said Sir Watkyn could see Mr. Pinker now, and Stinker oozed off. And the moment the door had closed behind curate and butler, Madeline clasped her hands, gave me one of those squashy looks, and said:

'Oh, Bertie, you should not have come here. I had not the heart to deny your pathetic request – I knew how much you yearned to see me again, however briefly, however hopelessly – but was it *wise*? Is it not merely twisting the knife in the wound? Will it not simply cause you needless pain to be near me, knowing we can never be more than just good friends? It is useless, Bertie. You must not hope. I love Augustus.'

Her words, as you may well imagine, were music to my e. She wouldn't, I felt, have come out with anything as definite as this if there had been a really serious spot of trouble between her and Gussie. Obviously that crack of his about her making him sick had been a mere passing what-d'you–call-it, the result of some momentary attack of the pip caused possibly by her saying he smoked too much or something of the sort. Anyway, whatever it was that had rifted the lute was now plainly forgotten and forgiven, and I was saying to myself that, the way things looked, I ought to be able to duck out of here immediately after breakfast tomorrow, when I noticed that a look of pain had spread over her map and that the eyes were dewy.

'It makes me so sad to think of your hopeless love, Bertie,' she said, adding something which I didn't quite catch about moths and stars. 'Life is so tragic, so cruel. But what can I do?'

'Not a thing,' I said heartily. 'Just carry on regardless.'

'But it breaks my heart.'

And with these words she burst into what are sometimes called uncontrollable sobs. She sank into her chair, covering her face with her hands, and it seemed to me that the civil thing to do was to pat her head. This project I now carried out, and I can see, looking back, that it was a mistake. I remember Monty Bodkin of the Drones, who once patted a weeping female on the head, unaware that his betrothed was standing in his immediate rear, drinking the whole thing in, telling me that the catch in this head-patting routine is that, unless you exercise the greatest care, you forget to take your hand off. You just stand there resting it on the subject's bean, and this is apt to cause spectators to purse their lips.

Monty fell into this error and so did I. And the lip-pursing was attended to by Spode, who chanced to enter at this moment. Seeing the popsy bathed in tears, he quivered from stem to stern.

'Madeline!' he yipped. 'What's the matter?'

'It is nothing, Roderick, nothing,' she replied chokingly.

She buzzed off, no doubt to bathe her eyes, and Spode pivoted round and gave me a penetrating look. He had grown a bit, I noticed, since I had last seen him, being now about nine foot seven. In speaking of him to Emerald Stoker I had, if you remember, compared him to a gorilla, and what I had had in mind had been the ordinary run-of-the-mill gorilla, not the large economy size. What he was looking like now was King Kong. His fists were clenched, his eyes glittered, and the dullest observer could have divined that it was in no sunny spirit that he was regarding Bertram.

6

To ease the strain, I asked him if he would have a cucumber sandwich, but with an impassioned gesture he indicated that he was not in the market for cucumber sandwiches, though I could have told him, for I had found them excellent, that he was passing up a good thing.

'A muffin?'

No, not a muffin, either. He seemed to be on a diet.

'Wooster,' he said, his jaw muscles moving freely, 'I can't make up my mind whether to break your neck or not.'

'Not' would have been the way my vote would have been cast, but he didn't give me time to say so.

'I was amazed when I heard from Madeline that you had had the effrontery to invite yourself here. Your motive, of course, was clear. You have come to try to undermine her faith in the man she loves and sow doubts in her mind. Like a creeping snake,' he added, and I was interested to learn that this was what snakes did. 'You had not the elementary decency, when she had made her choice, to accept her decision and efface yourself. You hoped to win her away from Fink-Nottle.'

Feeling that it was about time I said something, I got as far as 'I –', but he shushed me with another of those impassioned gestures. I couldn't remember when I'd met anyone so resolved on hogging the conversation.

'No doubt you will say that your love was so overpowering that you could not resist the urge to tell her of it and plead with her. Utter nonsense. Despicable weakness. Let me tell you, Wooster, that I have loved that girl for years and years, but never by word or look have I so much as hinted it to her. It was a great shock to me when she became engaged to this man Fink-Nottle, but I accepted the situation because I thought that that was where her happiness lay. Though stunned, I kept –'

'A stiff upper lip?'

'– my feelings to myself. I sat –'

'Like Patience on a monument.'

'– tight, and said nothing that would give her a suspicion of how I felt. All that mattered was that she should be happy. If you ask me if I approve of Fink-Nottle as a husband for her, I admit frankly that I do not. To me he seems to possess all the qualities that go to make the perfect pill, and I may add that my opinion is shared by her father. But he is the man she has chosen and I abide by her choice. I do not crawl behind Fink-Nottle's back and try to prejudice her against him.'

'Very creditable.'

'What did you say?'

I said I had said it did him credit. Very white of him, I said I thought it.

'Oh? Well, I suggest to you, Wooster, that you follow my example. And let me tell you that I shall be watching you closely, and I shall expect to see less of this head-stroking you were doing when I came in. If I don't, I'll –'

Just what he proposed to do he did not reveal, though I was able to hazard a guess, for at this moment Madeline returned. Her eyes were pinkish and her general aspect down among the wines and spirits.

'I will show you your room, Bertie,' she said in a pale, saintlike voice, and Spode gave me a warning look.

'Be careful, Wooster, be very careful,' he said as we went out.

Madeline seemed surprised.

'Why did Roderick tell you to be careful?'

'Ah, that we shall never know. Afraid I might slip on the parquet floor, do you think?'

'He sounded as if he was angry with you. Had you been quarrelling?'

'Good heavens, no. Our talk was conducted throughout in an atmosphere of the utmost cordiality.'

'I thought he might be annoyed at your coming here.'

'On the contrary. Nothing could have exceeded the warmth of his "Welcome to Totleigh Towers".'

'I'm so glad. It would pain me so much if you and he were . . . Oh, there's Daddy.'

We had reached the upstairs corridor, and Sir Watkyn Bassett was emerging from his room, humming a light air. It died on his lips as he saw me, and he stood staring at me aghast. He reminded me of one of those fellows who spend the night in haunted houses and are found next morning dead to the last drop with a look of awful horror on their faces.

'Oh, Daddy,' said Madeline. 'I forgot to tell you. I asked Bertie to come here for a few days.'

Pop Bassett swallowed painfully.

'When you say a few days – ?'

'At least a week, I hope.'

'Good God!'

'If not longer.'

'Great heavens!'

'There is tea in the drawing-room, Daddy.'

'I need something stronger than tea,' said Pop Bassett in a low, husky voice, and he tottered off, a broken man. The sight of his head disappearing as he made for the lower regions where the snootful awaited him brought to my mind a poem I used to read as a child. I've forgotten most of it, but it was about a storm at sea and the punch line ran "We are lost," the captain shouted, as he staggered down the stairs.'

'Daddy seems upset about something,' said Madeline.

'He did convey that impression,' I said, speaking austerely, for the old blister's attitude had offended me. I could make allowances for him, because naturally a man of regular habits doesn't like suddenly finding Woosters in his midst, but I did feel that he might have made more of an effort to bear up. Think of the Red Indians, Bassett, I would have said to him, had we been on better terms, pointing out that they were never in livelier spirits than when being cooked on both sides at the stake.

This painful encounter, following so quickly on my conversation, if you could call it a conversation, with Spode, might have been expected to depress me, but this was far from being the case. I was so uplifted by the official news that all was well between M. Bassett and G. Fink-Nottle that I gave it little thought. It's never, of course, the ideal set-up to come to stay at a house where your host shudders to the depths of his being at the mere sight of you and is compelled to rush to where the bottles are and get a restorative, but the Woosters can take the rough with the s., and the bonging of the gong for dinner some little time later found me in excellent fettle. It was to all intents and purposes with a song on my lips that I straightened my tie and made my way to the trough.

Dinner is usually the meal at which you catch Bertram at his best, and certainly it's the meal I always most enjoy. Many of my happiest hours have been passed in the society of the soup, the fish, the pheasant or whatever it may be, the soufflé, the fruits in their season and the spot of port to follow. They bring out the best in me. 'Wooster,' those who know me have sometimes said, 'may be a pretty total loss during the daytime hours, but plunge the world in darkness, switch on the soft lights, uncork the champagne and shove a dinner into him, and you'd be surprised.'

But if I am to sparkle and charm all and sundry, I make one provision – viz. that the company be congenial. And anything less congenial than the Co. on this occasion I have seldom encountered. Sir Watkyn Bassett, who was plainly still much shaken at finding me on the premises, was very far from being the jolly old Squire who makes the party go from the start. Beyond shooting glances at me over his glasses, blinking as if he couldn't bring himself to believe I was real and looking away with a quick shudder, he contributed little or nothing to what I have heard Jeeves call the feast of reason and the flow of soul. Add Spode, strong and silent, Madeline Bassett, mournful and drooping, Gussie, also apparently mournful, and Stiffy, who seemed to be in a kind of daydream, and you had something resembling a wake of the less rollicking type.

Sombre, that's the word I was trying to think of. The atmosphere was sombre. The whole binge might have been a scene from one of those Russian plays my Aunt Agatha sometimes makes me take her son Thos to at the Old Vic in order to improve his mind, which, as is widely known, can do with all the improvement that's coming to it.

It was toward the middle of the meal that, feeling that it was about time somebody said something, I drew Pop Bassett's attention to the table's centrepiece. In any normal house it would have been a bowl of flowers or something of that order, but this being Totleigh Towers it was a small black figure carved of some material I couldn't put a name to. It was so gosh-awful in every respect that I presumed it must be something he had collected recently. My Uncle Tom is always coming back from sales with similar eyesores.

'That's new, isn't it?' I said, and he started violently. I suppose he'd just managed to persuade himself that I was merely a mirage and had been brought up with a round turn on discovering that I was there in the flesh.

'That thing in the middle of the table that looks like the end man in a minstrel show. It's something you got since . . . er . . . since I was here last, isn't it?'

Tactless of me, I suppose, to remind him of that previous visit of mine, and I oughtn't to have brought it up, but these things slip out.

'Yes,' he said, having paused for a moment to shudder. 'It is the latest addition to my collection.'

'Daddy bought it from a man named Plank who lives not far from here at Hockley-cum-Meston,' said Madeline.

'Attractive little bijou,' I said. It hurt me to look at it, but I felt that nothing was to be lost by giving him the old oil. 'Just the sort of thing Uncle Tom would like to have. By Jove,' I said, remembering, 'Aunt Dahlia was speaking to me about it on the phone yesterday, and she told me Uncle Tom would give his eyeteeth to have it in his collection. I'm not surprised. It looks valuable.'

'It's worth a thousand pounds,' said Stiffy, coming out of her coma and speaking for the first time.

'As much as that? Golly!' Amazing, I was thinking, that magistrates could get to be able to afford expenditure on that scale just by persevering through the years fining people and sticking to the money. 'What is it? Soapstone?'

I had said the wrong thing.

'Amber,' Pop Bassett snapped, giving me the sort of look he had given me in heaping measure on the occasion when I had stood in the dock before him at Bosher Street police court. 'Black amber.'

'Of course, yes. That's what Aunt Dahlia said, I recall. She spoke very highly of it, let me tell you, extremely highly.'

'Indeed?'

'Oh, absolutely.'

I had been hoping that this splash of dialogue would have broken the ice, so to speak, and started us off kidding back and forth like the guys and dolls in one of those old-world salons you read about. But no. Silence fell again, and eventually, at long last, the meal came to an end, and two minutes later I was on my way to my room, where I proposed to pass the rest of the evening with an Erle Stanley Gardner I'd brought with me. No sense, as I saw it, in going and mixing with the mob in the drawing-room and having Spode glare at me and Pop Bassett sniff at me and Madeline Bassett as likely as not sing old English folk songs at me till bedtime. I was aware that in executing this quiet sneak I was being guilty of a social *gaffe* which would have drawn raised eyebrows from the author of a book of etiquette, but the great lesson we learn from life is to know when and when not to be in the centre of things.

7

I haven't mentioned it till now, having been all tied up with other matters, but during dinner, as you may well imagine, something had been puzzling me not a little – the mystery, to wit, of what on earth had become of Emerald Stoker.

At that lunch of ours she had told me in no uncertain terms that she was off to Totleigh on the four o'clock train that afternoon, and however leisurely its progress it must have got there by this time, because Gussie had travelled on it and he had fetched up at the joint all right. But I could detect no sign of her on the premises. It seemed to me, sifting the evidence, that only one conclusion could be arrived at, that she had been pulling the Wooster leg.

But why? With what motive? That was what I was asking myself as I sneaked up the stairs to where Erle Stanley Gardner awaited me. If you had cared to describe me as perplexed and bewildered, you would have been perfectly correct.

Jeeves was in my room when I got there, going about his gentleman's gentlemanly duties, and I put my problem up to him.

'Did you ever see a film called *The Vanishing Lady*, Jeeves?'

'No, sir. I rarely attend cinematographic performances.'

'Well, it was about a lady who vanished, if you follow what I mean, and the reason I bring it up is that a female friend of mine has apparently disappeared into thin air, leaving not a wrack behind, as I once heard you put it.'

'Highly mysterious, sir.'

'You said it. I seek in vain for a solution. When I gave her lunch yesterday, she told me she was off on the four o'clock train to go and stay at Totleigh Towers, and the point I want to drive home is that she hasn't arrived. You remember the day I lunched at the Ritz?'

'Yes, sir. You were wearing an Alpine hat.'

'There is no need to dwell on the Alpine hat, Jeeves.'

'No, sir.'

'If you really want to know, several fellows at the Drones asked me where I had got it.'

'No doubt with a view to avoiding your hatter, sir.'

I saw that nothing was to be gained by bandying words. I turned the conversation to a pleasanter and less controversial subject.

'Well, Jeeves, you'll be glad to hear that everything's all right.'

'Sir?'

'About that lute we were speaking of. No rift. Sound as a bell. I have it straight from the horse's mouth that Miss Bassett and Gussie are sweethearts still. The relief is stupendous.'

I hadn't expected him to clap his hands and leap about, because of course he never does, but I wasn't prepared for the way he took this bit of hot news. He failed altogether to string along with my jocund mood.

'I fear, sir, that you are too sanguine. Miss Bassett's attitude may well be such as you have described, but on Mr. Fink-Nottle's side, I am sorry to say there exists no little dissatisfaction and resentment.'

The smile which had been splitting my face faded. It's never easy to translate what Jeeves says into basic English, but I had been able to grab this one off the bat, and what I believe the French call a *frisson* went through me like a dose of salts.

'You mean she's a sweetheart still, but he isn't?'

'Precisely, sir. I encountered Mr. Fink-Nottle in the stable yard as I was putting away the car, and he confided his troubles to me. His story occasioned me grave uneasiness.'

Another *frisson* passed through my frame. I had the unpleasant feeling you get sometimes that centipedes in large numbers are sauntering up and down your spinal column. I feared the worst.

'But what's happened?' I faltered, if faltered's the word.

'I regret to inform you, sir, that Miss Bassett has insisted on Mr. Fink-Nottle adopting a vegetarian diet. His mood is understandably disgruntled and rebellious.'

I tottered. In my darkest hour I had never anticipated anything as bad as this. You wouldn't think it to look at him, because he's small and shrimplike and never puts on weight, but Gussie loves food. Watching him tucking into his rations at the Drones, a tapeworm would raise its hat respectfully, knowing that it was in the presence of a master. Cut him off, therefore, from the roasts and boileds and particularly from cold steak and kidney pie, a dish of which he is inordinately fond, and you turned him into something fit for treasons, stratagems and spoils, as the fellow said – the sort of chap who would break an engagement as soon as look at you. At the moment of my entry I had been about to light a cigarette, and now the lighter fell from my nerveless hand.

'She's made him become a *vegetarian*?'

'So Mr. Fink-Nottle informed me, sir.'

'No chops?'

'No, sir.'

'No steaks?'

'No, sir.'

'Just spinach and similar garbage?'

'So I gather, sir.'

'But why?'

'I understand that Miss Bassett has recently been reading the life of the poet Shelley, sir, and has become converted to his view that the consumption of flesh foods is unspiritual. The poet Shelley held strong opinions on this subject.'

I picked up the lighter in a sort of trance. I was aware that Madeline B. was as potty as they come in the matter of stars and rabbits and what happened when fairies blew their wee noses, but I had never dreamed that her goofiness would carry her to such lengths as this. But as the picture rose before my eyes of Gussie at the dinner table picking with clouded brow at what had unquestionably looked like spinach, I knew that his story must be true. No wonder Gussie in agony of spirit had said that Madeline made him sick. Just so might a python at a Zoo have spoken of its keeper, had the latter suddenly started feeding it cheese straws in lieu of the daily rabbit.

'But this is frightful, Jeeves!'

'Certainly somewhat disturbing, sir.'

'If Gussie is seething with revolt, anything may happen.'

'Yes, sir.'

'Is there nothing we can do?'

'It might be possible for you to reason with Miss Bassett, sir. You would have a talking point. Medical research has established that the ideal diet is one in which animal and vegetable foods are balanced. A strict vegetarian diet is not recommended by the majority of doctors, as it lacks sufficient protein and in particular does not contain the protein which is built up of the amino-acids required by the body. Competent observers have traced some cases of mental disorder to this shortage.'

'You'd tell her that?'

'It might prove helpful, sir.'

'I doubt it,' I said, blowing a despondent smoke ring. 'I don't think it would sway her.'

'Nor on consideration do I, sir. The poet Shelley regarded the matter from the humanitarian standpoint rather than that of bodily health.

He held that we should show reverence for other life forms, and it is his views that Miss Bassett has absorbed.'

A hollow groan escaped me.

'Curse the poet Shelley! I hope he trips over a loose shoelace and breaks his ruddy neck.'

'Too late, sir. He is no longer with us.'

'Blast all vegetables!'

'Yes, sir. Your concern is understandable. I may mention that the cook expressed herself in a somewhat similar vein when I informed her of Mr. Fink-Nottle's predicament. Her heart melted in sympathy with his distress.'

I was in no mood to hear about cooks' hearts, soluble or otherwise, and I was about to say so, when he proceeded.

'She instructed me to apprise Mr. Fink-Nottle that if he were agreeable to visiting the kitchen at some late hour when the household had retired for the night, she would be happy to supply him with cold steak and kidney pie.'

It was as if the sun had come smiling through the clouds or the long shot on which I had placed my wager had nosed its way past the opposition in the last ten yards and won by a short head. For the peril that had threatened to split the Bassett-Fink-Nottle axis had been averted. I knew Gussie from soup to nuts. Cut him off from the proteins and the amino-acids, and you soured his normally amiable nature, turning him into a sullen hater of his species who asked nothing better than to bite his n. and dearest and bite them good. But give him this steak and kidney pie outlet, thus allowing him to fulfil what they call his legitimate aspirations, and chagrin would vanish and he would become his old lovable self once more. The dark scowl would be replaced by the tender simper, the acid crack by the honeyed word, and all would be hotsy-totsy once more with his love life. My bosom swelled with gratitude to the cook whose quick thinking had solved the problem and brought home the bacon.

'Who is she, Jeeves?'

'Sir?'

'This life-saving cook. I shall want to give her a special mention in my evening prayers.'

'She is a woman of the name of Stoker, sir.'

'*Stoker*? Did you say Stoker?'

'Yes, sir.'

'Odd!'

'Sir?'

'Nothing. Just a rather strange coincidence. Have you told Gussie?'

'Yes, sir. I found him most co-operative. He plans to present himself in the kitchen shortly after midnight. Cold steak and kidney pie is, of course, merely a palliative –'

'On the contrary. It's Gussie's favourite dish. I've known him to order it even on curry day at the Drones. He loves the stuff.'

'Indeed, sir? That is very gratifying.'

'Gratifying is the word. What a lesson this teaches us, Jeeves, never to despair, never to throw in the towel and turn our face to the wall, for there is always hope.'

'Yes, sir. Would you be requiring anything further?'

'Not a thing, thanks. My cup runneth over.'

'Then I will be saying good night, sir.'

'Good night, Jeeves.'

After he had gone, I put in about half an hour on my Erle Stanley Gardner, but I found rather a difficulty in following the thread and keeping my attention on the clues. My thoughts kept straying to this epoch-making cook. Strange, I felt, that her name should be Stoker. Some relation, perhaps.

I could picture the woman so exactly. Stout, red-faced, spectacled, a little irritable, perhaps, if interrupted when baking a cake or thinking out a sauce, but soft as butter at heart. No doubt something in Gussie's wan aspect had touched her. 'That boy needs feeding up, poor little fellow', or possibly she was fond of goldfish and had been drawn to him because he reminded her of them. Or she may have been a Girl Guide. At any rate, whatever the driving motive behind her day's good deed, she had deserved well of Bertram, and I told myself that a thumping tip should reward her on my departure. Purses of gold should be scattered, and with a lavish hand.

I was musing thus and feeling more benevolent every minute, when who should blow in but Gussie in person, and I had been right in picturing his aspect as wan. He wore the unmistakable look of a man who has been downing spinach for weeks.

I took it that he had come to ask me what I was doing at Totleigh Towers, a point on which he might naturally be supposed to be curious, but that didn't seem to interest him. He plunged without delay into as forceful a denunciation of the vegetable world as I've ever heard, oddly enough being more bitter about Brussels sprouts and broccoli than about spinach, which I would have expected him to feature. It was some considerable time before I could get a word in, but when I did my voice dripped with sympathy.

'Yes, Jeeves was telling me about that,' I said, 'and my heart bled for you.'

'And so it jolly well ought to have done – in buckets – if you've a spark of humanity in you,' he retorted warmly. 'Words cannot describe the agonies I've suffered, particularly when staying at Brinkley Court.'

I nodded. I knew just what an ordeal it must have been. With Aunt Dahlia's peerless chef wielding the skillet, the last place where you want to be on a vegetarian diet is Brinkley. Many a time when enjoying the old relative's hospitality I've regretted that I had only one stomach to give to the evening's bill of fare.

'Night after night I had to refuse Anatole's unbeatable eatables, and when I tell you that two nights in succession he gave us those *Mignonettes de Poulet Petit Duc* of his and on another occasion his *Timbales de Ris de Veau Toulousiane*, you will appreciate what I went through.'

It being my constant policy to strew a little happiness as I go by, I hastened to point out the silver lining in the c's.

'Your sufferings must have been terrible,' I agreed. 'But courage, Gussie. Think of the cold steak and kidney pie.'

I had struck the right note. His drawn face softened.

'Jeeves told you about that?'

'He said the cook had it all ready and waiting for you, and I remember thinking at the time that she must be a pearl among women.'

'That is not putting it at all too strongly. She's an angel in human shape. I spotted her solid merits the moment I saw her.'

'You've seen her?'

'Of course I've seen her. You can't have forgotten that talk we had when I was in the cab, about to start off for Paddington. Though why you should have got the idea that she looks like a Pekinese is more than I can imagine.'

'Eh? Who?'

'Emerald Stoker. She doesn't look in the least like a Pekinese.'

'What's Emerald Stoker got to do with it?'

He seemed surprised.

'Didn't she tell you?'

'Tell me what?'

'That she was on her way here to take office as the Totleigh Towers cook.'

I goggled. I thought for a moment that the privations through which he was passing must have unhinged this newt-fancier's brain.

'Did you say *cook*?'

'I'm surprised she didn't tell you. I suppose she felt that you weren't to be trusted to keep her secret. She would, of course, have spotted you as a babbler from the outset. Yes, she's the cook all right.'

'But *why* is she the cook?' I said, getting down to the *res* in that direct way of mine.

'She explained that fully to me on the train. It appears that she's dependent on a monthly allowance from her father in New York, and normally she gets by reasonably comfortably on this. But early this month she was unfortunate in her investments on the turf. Sunny Jim in the three o'clock at Kempton Park.'

I recalled the horse to which he referred. Only prudent second thoughts had kept me from having a bit on it myself.

'The animal ran sixth in a field of seven and she lost her little all. She was then faced with the alternative of applying to her father for funds, which would have necessitated a full confession of her rash act, or of seeking some gainful occupation which would tide her over till, as she put it, the United States Marines arrived.'

'She could have touched me or her sister Pauline.'

'My good ass, a girl like that doesn't borrow money. Much too proud. She decided to become a cook. She tells me she didn't hesitate more than about thirty seconds before making her choice.'

I wasn't surprised. To have come clean to the paternal parent would have been to invite hell of the worst description. Old Stoker was not the type of father who laughs indulgently when informed by a daughter that she has lost her chemise and foundation garments at the races. I don't suppose he has ever laughed indulgently in his life. I've never seen him even smile. Apprised of his child's goings-on, he would unquestionably have blown his top and reduced her to the level of a fifth-rate power. I have been present on occasions when the old gawd-help-us was going good, and I can testify that his boiling point is low. Quite rightly had she decided that silence was best.

It was quite a load off my mind to be able to file away the Emerald Stoker mystery in my case book as solved, for I dislike being baffled and the thing had been weighing on me, but there were one or two small points to be cleared up.

'How did she happen to come to Totleigh?'

'I must have been responsible for that. During our talk at that studio party I remember mentioning that Sir Watkyn was in the market for a cook, and I suppose I must have given her his address, for she applied for the post and got it. These American girls have such enterprise.'

'Is she enjoying her job?'

'Thoroughly, according to Jeeves. She's teaching the butler Rummy.'

'I hope she skins him to the bone.'

'No doubt she will when he is sufficiently advanced to play for money. And she tells me she loves to cook. What's her cooking like?'

I could answer that. She had once or twice given me dinner at her flat, and the browsing had been impeccable.

'It melts in the mouth.'

'It hasn't melted in mine,' said Gussie bitterly. 'Ah well,' he added, a softer light coming into his eyes, 'there's always that steak and kidney pie.'

And on this happier note he took his departure.

8

It was pretty late when I finished the perusal of my Erle Stanley
Gardner and later when I woke from the light doze into which I had
fallen on closing the volume. Totleigh Towers had long since called
it a day, and all was still throughout the house except for a curious
rumbling noise proceeding from my interior. After bending an ear to
this for awhile I was able to see what was causing it. I had fed sparsely
at the dinner table, with the result that I had become as hungry as
dammit.

I don't know if you have had the same experience, but a thing I've
always found about myself is that it takes very little to put me off my
feed. Let the atmosphere at lunch or dinner be what you might call
difficult, and my appetite tends to dwindle. I've often had this happen
when breaking bread with my Aunt Agatha, and it had happened again
at tonight's meal. What with the strain of constantly catching Pop
Bassett's eye and looking hastily away and catching Spode's and
looking hastily away and catching Pop's again, I had done far less than
justice to Emerald Stoker's no doubt admirable offerings. You read
stories sometimes where someone merely toys with his food or even
pushes away his plate untasted, and that substantially was what I had
done. So now this strange hollow feeling, as if some hidden hand had
scooped out my insides with a tablespoon.

This imperative demand for sustenance had probably been coming
on during my Erle Stanley Gardnering, but I had been so intent on
trying to keep tabs on the murder gun and the substitute gun and the
gun which Perry Mason had buried in the shrubbery that I hadn't
noticed it. Only now had the pangs of hunger really started to throw
their weight about, and more and more clearly as they did so there
rose before my eyes the vision of that steak and kidney pie which was
lurking in the kitchen, and it was as though I could hear a soft voice
calling to me 'Come and get it.'

It's odd how often you find that out of evil cometh good, as the
expression is. Here was a case in point. I had always thought of my
previous visit to Totleigh Towers as a total loss. I saw now that I had

been wrong. It had been an ordeal testing the nervous system to the utmost, but there was one thing about it to be placed on the credit side of the ledger. I allude to the fact that it had taught me the way to the kitchen. The route lay down the stairs, through the hall, into the dining-room and through the door at the end of the last named. Beyond the door I presumed that there was some sort of passage or corridor and then you were in the steak and kidney pie zone. A simple journey, not to be compared for complexity with some I had taken at night in my time.

With the Woosters to think is to act, and scarcely more than two minutes later I was on my way.

It was dark on the stairs and just as dark, if not darker, in the hall. But I was making quite satisfactory progress and was about half-way through the latter, when an unforeseen hitch occurred. I bumped into a human body, the last thing I had expected to encounter en route, and for an instant . . . well, I won't say that everything went black, because everything was black already, but I was considerably perturbed. My heart did one of those spectacular leaps Nijinsky used to do in the Russian Ballet, and I was conscious of a fervent wish that I could have been elsewhere.

Elsewhere, however, being just where I wasn't, I had no option but to grapple with this midnight marauder, and when I did so I was glad to find that he was apparently one who had stunted his growth by smoking as a boy. There was a shrimp-like quality about him which I found most encouraging. It seemed to me that it would be an easy task to throttle him into submission, and I was getting down to it with a hearty good will when my hand touched what were plainly spectacles and at the same moment a stifled 'Hey, look out for my glasses!' told me my diagnosis had been all wrong. This was no thief in the night, but an old crony with whom in boyhood days I had often shared my last bar of milk chocolate.

'Oh, hullo, Gussie,' I said. 'Is that you? I thought you were a burglar.'

There was a touch of asperity in his voice as he replied:

'Well, I wasn't.'

'No, I see that now. Pardonable mistake, though, you must admit.'

'You nearly gave me heart failure.'

'I, too, was somewhat taken aback. No one more surprised than the undersigned when you suddenly popped up. I thought I had a clear track.'

'Where to?'

'Need you ask? The steak and kidney pie. If you've left any.'

'Yes, there's quite a bit left.'

'Was it good?'

'Delicious.'

'Then I think I'll be getting along. Good night, Gussie. Sorry you were troubled.'

Continuing on my way, I think I must have lost my bearings a little. Shaken, no doubt, by the recent encounter. These get-togethers take their toll. At any rate, to cut a long story s., what happened was that as I felt my way along the wall I collided with what turned out to be a grandfather clock, for the existence of which I had not budgeted, and it toppled over with a sound like the delivery of several tons of coal through the roof of a conservatory. Glass crashed, pulleys and things parted from their moorings, and as I stood trying to separate my heart from the front teeth in which it had become entangled, the lights flashed on and I beheld Sir Watkyn Bassett.

It was a moment fraught with embarrassment. It's bad enough to be caught by your host prowling about his house after hours even when said host is a warm admirer and close personal friend, and I have, I think, made it clear that Pop Bassett was not one of my fans. He could barely stand the sight of me by daylight, and I suppose I looked even worse to him at one o'clock in the morning.

My feeling of having been slapped between the eyes with a custard pie was deepened by the spectacle of his dressing-gown. He was a small man . . . you got the impression, seeing him, that when they were making magistrates there wasn't enough material left over when they came to him . . . and for some reason not easy to explain it nearly always happens that the smaller the ex-magistrate, the louder the dressing-gown. His was a bright purple number with yellow frogs, and I am not deceiving my public when I say that it smote me like a blow, rendering me speechless.

Not that I'd have felt chatty even if he had been upholstered in something quiet in dark blue. I don't believe you can ever be completely at your ease in the company of someone before whom you've stood in the dock saying 'Yes, your worship' and 'No, your worship' and being told by him that you're extremely lucky to get off with a fine and not fourteen days without the option. This is particularly so if you have just smashed a grandfather clock whose welfare is no doubt very near his heart. At any rate, be that as it may, he was the one to open the conversation, not me.

'Good God!' he said, speaking with every evidence of horror. 'You!'

A thing I never know, and probably never will, is what to say when somebody says 'You!' to me. A mild 'Oh, hullo' was the best I could do on this occasion, and I felt at the time it wasn't good. Better, of course, than 'What ho, there, Bassett!' but nevertheless not good.

'Might I ask what you are doing here at this hour, Mr. Wooster?'

Well, I might have laughed a jolly laugh and replied 'Upsetting grandfather clocks', keeping it light, as it were, if you know what I mean, but something told me it wouldn't go so frightfully well. I had what amounted to an inspiration.

'I came down to get a book. I'd finished my Erle Stanley Gardner and I couldn't seem to drop off to sleep, so I came to see if I couldn't pick up something from your shelves. And in the dark I bumped into the clock.'

'Indeed?' he said, putting a wealth of sniffiness into the word. A thing about this undersized little son of a bachelor I ought to have mentioned earlier is that during his career on the bench he was one of those unpleasant sarcastic magistrates who get themselves so disliked by the criminal classes. You know the type. Their remarks are generally printed in the evening papers with the word 'laughter' after them in brackets, and they count the day lost when they don't make some unfortunate pickpocket or some wretched drunk and disorderly feel like a piece of cheese. I know that on the occasion when we stood face to face in Bosher Street police court he convulsed the audience with three solid jokes at my expense in the first two minutes, bathing me in confusion. 'Indeed?' he said. 'Might I inquire why you were conducting your literary researches in the dark? It would surely have been well within the scope of even your limited abilities to press a light switch.'

He had me there, of course. The best I could say was that I hadn't thought of it, and he sniffed a nasty sniff, as much as to suggest that I was just the sort of dead-from-the-neck-up dumb brick who wouldn't have thought of it. He then turned to the subject of the clock, one which I would willingly have left unventilated. He said he had always valued it highly, it being more or less the apple of his eye.

'My father bought it many years ago. He took it everywhere with him.'

Here again I might have lightened things by asking him if his parent wouldn't have found it simpler to have worn a wrist-watch, but I felt once more that he was not in the mood.

'My father was in the Diplomatic service, and was constantly transferred from one post to another. He was never parted from the clock. It accompanied him in perfect safety from Rome to Vienna, from Vienna to Paris, from Paris to Washington, from Washington to Lisbon. One would have said it was indestructible. But it had still to pass the supreme test of encountering Mr. Wooster, and that was too much for it. It did not occur to Mr. Wooster . . . one cannot think of everything . . . that light may be obtained by pressing a light switch, so he –'

Here he broke off, not so much because he had finished what he had to say as because at this point in the conversation I sprang on to the top of a large chest which stood some six or seven feet distant from the spot where we were chewing the fat. I may have touched the ground once while in transit, but not more than once and that once not willingly. A cat on hot bricks could not have moved with greater nippiness.

My motives in doing so were founded on a solid basis. Toward the later stages of his observations on the clock I had gradually become aware of a curious sound, as if someone in the vicinity was gargling mouthwash, and looking about me I found myself gazing into the eyes of the dog Bartholomew, which were fixed on me with the sinister intentness which is characteristic of this breed of animal. Aberdeen terriers, possibly owing to their heavy eyebrows, always seem to look at you as if they were in the pulpit of the church of some particularly strict Scottish sect and you were a parishioner of dubious reputation sitting in the front row of the stalls.

Not that I noticed his eyes very much, my attention being riveted on his teeth. He had an excellent set and was baring them, and all I had ever heard of his tendency to bite first and ask questions afterwards passed through my mind in a flash. Hence the leap for life. The Woosters are courageous, but they do not take chances.

Pop Bassett was plainly nonplussed, and it was only when his gaze, too, fell upon Bartholomew that he abandoned what must have been his original theory, that Bertram had cracked under the strain and would do well to lose no time in seeing a good mental specialist. He eyed Bartholomew coldly and addressed him as if he had been up before him in his police court.

'Go away, sir! Lie down, sir! Go away!' he said, rasping, if that's the word.

Well, I could have told him that you can't talk to an Aberdeen terrier in that tone of voice for, except perhaps for Doberman pinschers, there is no breed of dog quicker to take offence.

'Really, the way my niece allows this infernal animal to roam at large about the –'

'House' I suppose he was about to say, but the word remained unspoken. It was a moment for rapid action, not for speech. The gargling noise had increased in volume, and Bartholomew was flexing his muscles and getting under way. He moved, he stirred, he seemed to feel the rush of life along his keel, as the fellow said, and Pop Bassett with a lissomness of which I would not have suspected him took to himself the wings of the dove and floated down beside me on the chest. Whether he clipped a second or two off my time I cannot say, but I rather think he did.

'This is intolerable!' he said as I moved courteously to make room for him, and I could see the thing from his point of view. All he asked from life, now that he had made his pile, was to be as far away as possible from Bertram Wooster, and here he was cheek by jowl, as you might say, on a rather uncomfortable chest with him. A certain peevishness was inevitable.

'Not too good,' I agreed. 'Unquestionably open to criticism, the animal's behaviour.'

'He must be off his head. He knows me perfectly well. He sees me every day.'

'Ah,' I said, putting my finger on the weak spot in his argument, 'but I don't suppose he's ever seen you in that dressing-gown.'

I had been too outspoken. He let me see at once that he had taken umbrage.

'What's wrong with my dressing-gown?' he demanded hotly.

'A bit on the bright side, don't you think?'

'No, I do not.'

'Well, that's how it would strike a highly-strung dog.'

I paused here to chuckle softly, and he asked what the devil I was giggling about. I put him abreast.

'I was merely thinking that I wish we *could* strike the highly-strung dog. The trouble on these occasions is that one is always weaponless. It was the same some years ago when an angry swan chased self and friend on to the roof of a sort of boathouse building at my Aunt Agatha's place in Hertfordshire. Nothing would have pleased us better than to bung a brick at the bird, or slosh him with a boathook, but we had no brick and were short of boathooks. We had to wait till Jeeves came along, which he eventually did in answer to our cries. It would have thrilled you to have seen Jeeves on that occasion. He advanced dauntlessly and –'

'Mr. Wooster!'

'Speaking.'

'Kindly spare me your reminiscences.'

'I was merely saying –'

'Well, don't.'

Silence fell. On my part, a wounded silence, for all I'd tried to do was take his mind off things with entertaining chit-chat. I moved an inch or two away from him in a marked manner. The Woosters do not force their conversation on the unwilling.

All this time Bartholomew had been trying to join us, making a series of energetic springs. Fortunately Providence in its infinite wisdom had given Scotties short legs, and though full of the will to win he could accomplish nothing constructive. However much an Aberdeen terrier may bear 'mid snow and ice a banner with the strange device Excelsior, he nearly always has to be content with dirty looks and the sharp, passionate bark.

Some minutes later my fellow-rooster came out of the silence. No doubt the haughtiness of my manner had intimidated him, for there was a mildness in his voice which had not been there before.

'Mr. Wooster.'

I turned coldly.

'Were you addressing me, Bassett?'

'There must be something we can do.'

'You might fine the animal five pounds.'

'We cannot stay here all night.'

'Why not? What's to stop us?'

This held him. He relapsed into silence once more. And we were sitting there like a couple of Trappist monks, when a voice said 'Well, for heaven's sake!' and I perceived that Stiffy was with us.

Not surprising, of course, that she should have turned up sooner or later. If Scotties come, I ought to have said to myself, can Stiffy be far behind?

9

Considering that so substantial a part of her waking hours is devoted to thrusting innocent bystanders into the soup, Stiffy is far prettier than she has any right to be. She's on the small side – petite, I believe, is the technical term – and I have always felt that when she and Stinker walk up the aisle together, if they ever do, their disparity in height should be good for a laugh or two from the ringside pews. The thought has occurred to me more than once that the correct response for Stinker to make, when asked by the M.C. if he is prepared to take this Stephanie to be his wedded wife, would be, 'Why, certainly, what there is of her.'

'What on earth do you two think you're doing?' she inquired, not unnaturally surprised to see her uncle and an old friend in our current position. 'And why have you been upsetting the furniture?'

'That was me,' I said. 'I bumped into the grandfather clock. I'm as bad as Stinker, aren't I, bumping into things, ha-ha.'

'Less of the ha-ha,' she riposted warmly. 'And don't mention yourself in the same breath as my Harold. Well, that doesn't explain why you're sitting up there like a couple of buzzards on a tree top.'

Pop Bassett intervened, speaking at his sniffiest. Her comparison of him to a buzzard, though perfectly accurate, seemed to have piqued him.

'We were savagely attacked by your dog.'

'Not so much attacked,' I said, 'as given nasty looks. We didn't vouchsafe him time to attack us, deeming it best to get out of his sphere of influence before he could settle down to work. He's been trying to get at us for the last two hours, at least it seems like two hours.'

She was quick to defend the dumb chum.

'Well, how can you blame the poor angel? Naturally he thought you were international spies in the pay of Moscow. Prowling about the house at this time of night. I can understand Bertie doing it, because he was dropped on the head as a baby, but I'm surprised at you, Uncle Watkyn. Why don't you go to bed?'

'I shall be delighted to go to bed,' said Pop Bassett stiffly, 'if you will kindly remove this animal. He is a public menace.'

'Very highly-strung,' I put in. 'We were remarking on it only just now.'

'He's all right, if you don't go out of your way to stir him up. Get back to your basket, Bartholomew, you bounder,' said Stiffy, and such was the magic of her personality that the hound turned on its heel without a word and passed into the night.

Pop Bassett climbed down from the chest, and directed a fishy magisterial look at me.

'Good night, Mr. Wooster. If there is any more of my furniture you wish to break, pray consider yourself at perfect liberty to indulge your peculiar tastes,' he said, and he, too, passed into the night.

Stiffy looked after him with a thoughtful eye.

'I don't believe Uncle Watkyn likes you, Bertie. I noticed the way he kept staring at you at dinner, as if appalled. Well, I don't wonder your arrival hit him hard. It did me. I've never been so surprised in my life as when you suddenly bobbed up like a corpse rising to the surface of a sheet of water. Harold told me he had pleaded with you to come here, but nothing would induce you. What made you change your mind?'

In my previous sojourn at Totleigh Towers circumstances had compelled me to confide in this young prune my position as regarded her cousin Madeline, so I had no hesitation now in giving her the low-down.

'I learned that there was trouble between Madeline and Gussie, due, I have since been informed, to her forcing him to follow in the footsteps of the poet Shelley and become a vegetarian, and I felt that I might accomplish something as a *raisonneur*.'

'As a whatonneur?'

'I thought that would be a bit above your head. It's a French expression meaning, I believe, though I would have to check with Jeeves, a calm kindly man of the world who intervenes when a rift has occurred between two loving hearts and brings them together again. Very essential in the present crisis.'

'You mean that if Madeline hands Gussie the pink slip, she'll marry you?'

'That, broadly, is about the strength of it. And while I admire and respect Madeline, I'm all against the idea of having her smiling face peeping at me over the coffee pot for the rest of my life. So I came along here to see what I could do.'

'Well, you couldn't have come at a better moment. Now you're here, you can get cracking on that job Harold told you I want you to do for me.'

I saw that the time had come for some prompt in-the-bud-nipping.

'Include me out. I won't touch it. I know you and your jobs.'

'But this is something quite simple. You can do it on your head. And you'll be bringing sunshine and happiness into the life of a poor slob who can do with a bit of both. Were you ever a Boy Scout?'

'Not since early boyhood.'

'Then you've lots of leeway to make up in the way of kind deeds. This'll be a nice start for you. The facts are as follows.'

'I don't want to hear them.'

'You would prefer that I recalled Bartholomew and told him to go on where he left off?'

She had what Jeeves had called a talking point.

'Very well. Tell me all. But briefly.'

'It won't take long, and then you can be off to beddy-bye. You remember that little black statuette thing on the table at dinner.'

'Ah yes, the eyesore.'

'Uncle Watkyn bought it from a man called Plank.'

'So I gathered.'

'Well, do you know what he paid him for it?'

'A thousand quid, didn't you say?'

'No, I didn't. I said it was worth that. But he got it out of this poor blighter Plank for a fiver.'

'You're kidding.'

'No, I'm not. He paid him five pounds. He makes no secret of it. When we were at Brinkley, he was showing the thing to Mr. Travers and telling him all about it . . . how he happened to see it on Plank's mantelpiece and spotted how valuable it was and told Plank it was worth practically nothing but he would give him five pounds for it because he knew how hard up he was. He gloated over how clever he had been, and Mr. Travers writhed like an egg whisk.'

I could well believe it. If there's one thing that makes a collector spit blood, it's hearing about another collector getting a bargain.

'How do you know Plank was hard up?'

'Well, would he have let the thing go for a fiver if he wasn't?'

'Something in that.'

'You can't say Uncle Watkyn isn't a dirty dog.'

'I would never dream of saying he isn't – and always has been – the dirtiest of dogs. It bears out what I have frequently maintained, that there are no depths to which magistrates won't stoop. I don't wonder you look askance. Your Uncle Watkyn stands revealed as a chiseller of the lowest type. But nothing to be done about it, of course.'

'I don't know so much about that.'

'Why, have you tried doing anything?'

'In a sort of way. I arranged that Harold should preach a very strong sermon on Naboth's Vineyard. Not that I suppose you've ever heard of Naboth's Vineyard.'

I bridled. She had offended my *amour propre*.

'I doubt if there's a man in London and the home counties who has the facts relating to Naboth's Vineyard more thoroughly at his fingertips than me. The news may not have reached you, but when at school I once won a prize for Scripture Knowledge.'

'I bet you cheated.'

'Not at all. Sheer merit. Did Stinker co-operate?'

'Yes, he thought it was a splendid idea and went about sucking throat pastilles for a week, so as to be in good voice. The set-up was the same as the play in *Hamlet*. You know. With which to catch the conscience of the king and all that.'

'Yes, I see the strategy all right. How did it all work out?'

'It didn't. Harold lives in the cottage of Mrs. Bootle, the postman's wife, where they only have oil lamps, and the sermon was on a table with a lamp on it, and he bumped into the table and upset the lamp and it burned the sermon and he hadn't time to write it out again, so he had to dig out something on another topic from the old stockpile. He was terribly disappointed.'

I pursed my lips, and was on the point of saying that of all the web-footed muddlers in existence H.P. Pinker took the well-known biscuit, when it occurred to me that it might possibly hurt her feelings, and I desisted. The last thing I wanted was to wound the child, particularly when I remembered that crack of hers about recalling Bartholomew.

'So we've got to handle the thing another way, and that's where you come in.'

I smiled a tolerant smile.

'I can see where you're heading,' I said. 'You want me to go to your Uncle Watkyn and slip a jack under his better self. "Play the game, Bassett," you want me to say, "Let conscience be your guide, Bassett," trying to drive it into his nut how wrong it is to put over a fast one on the widow and the orphan. I am assuming for purposes of argument that Plank is an orphan, though possibly not a widow. But my misguided young shrimp, do you really suppose that Pop Bassett looks on me as a friend and counsellor to whom he is always willing to lend a ready ear? You yourself were stressing only a moment ago how allergic he was to the Wooster charm. It's no good me talking to him.'

'I don't want you to.'

'Then what do you want me to do?'

'I want you to pinch the thing and return it to Plank, who will then sell it to Mr. Travers at a proper price. The idea of Uncle Watkyn only giving him a fiver for it! We can't have him getting away with raw work like that. He needs a sharp lesson.'

I smiled another tolerant smile. The young boll weevil amused me. I was thinking how right I had been in predicting that any job assigned by her to anyone would be unfit for human consumption.

'Well, really, Stiffy!'

The quiet rebuke in my voice ought to have bathed her in shame and remorse, but it didn't. She came back at me strongly.

'I don't know what you're Well-really-ing about. You're always pinching things, aren't you? Policemen's helmets and things like that.'

I inclined the bean. It was true that I had once lived in Arcady.

'There is,' I was obliged to concede, 'a certain substance in what you say. I admit that in my time I may have removed a lid or two from the upper stories of members of the constabulary –'

'Well, then.'

'– but only on Boat Race Night and when the heart was younger than it is as of even date. It was an episode of the sort that first brought me and your Uncle Watkyn together. But you can take it from me that the hot blood has cooled and I'm a reformed character. My answer to your suggestion is No.'

'No?'

'N-ruddy-o,' I said, making it clear to the meanest intelligence. 'Why don't you pinch the thing yourself?'

'It wouldn't be any good. I couldn't take it to Plank. I'm confined to barracks. Bartholomew bit the butler, and the sins of the Scottie are visited upon its owner. I do think you might reconsider, Bertie.'

'Not a hope.'

'You're a blighter!'

'But a blighter who knows his own mind and is not to be shaken by argument or plea, however specious.'

She was silent for a space. Then she gave a little sigh.

'Oh, dear,' she said. 'And I did hope I wouldn't have to tell Madeline about Gussie.'

I gave another of those visible starts of mine. I've seldom heard words I liked the sound of less. Fraught with sinister significance they seemed to me.

'Do you know what happened tonight, Bertie? I was roused from sleep about an hour ago, and what do you think roused me? Stealthy footsteps, no less. I crept out of my room, and I saw Gussie sneaking down the stairs. All was darkness, of course, but he had a little torch and it shone on his spectacles. I followed him. He went to the kitchen. I peered in, and there was the cook shovelling cold steak and kidney pie into him like a stevedore loading a grain ship. And the thought flashed into my mind that if Madeline heard of this, she would give him the bum's rush before he knew what had hit him.'

'But a girl doesn't give a fellow the bum's rush just because she's told him to stick to the sprouts and spinach and she hears that he's been wading into the steak and kidney pie,' I said, trying to reassure myself but not getting within several yards of it.

'I bet Madeline would.'

And so, thinking it over, did I. You can't judge goofs like Madeline Bassett by ordinary standards. What the normal popsy would do and what she would do in any given circumstances were two distinct and separate things. I had not forgotten the time when she had severed relations with Gussie purely because through no fault of his own he got stinko when about to present the prizes at Market Snodsbury Grammar School.

'You know how high her ideals are. Yes, sir, if someone were to drop an incautious word to her about tonight's orgy, those wedding bells would not ring out. Gussie would be at liberty, and she would start looking about her for somebody else to fill the vacant spot. I really think you'll have to reconsider that decision of yours, Bertie, and do just this one more bit of pinching.'

'Oh, my sainted aunt!'

I spoke as harts do when heated in the chase and panting for cooling streams. It would have been plain to a far less astute mind than mine that this blighted Byng had got me by the short hairs and was in a position to dictate tactics and strategy.

Blackmail, of course, but the gentler sex love blackmail. Not once but on several occasions has my Aunt Dahlia bent me to her will by threatening that if I didn't play ball she would bar me from her table, thus dashing Anatole's lunches and dinners from my lips. Show me a delicately nurtured female, and I will show you a ruthless Napoleon of Crime prepared without turning a hair to put the screws on some unfortunate male whose services she happens to be in need of. There ought to be a law.

'It looks as if the die were cast,' I said reluctantly.

'It is,' she assured me.

'You're really adamant?'

'Couldn't be more so. My heart bleeds for Plank, and I'm going to see that justice is done.'

'Right ho, then. I'll have a crack at it.'

'That's my little man. The whole thing's so frightfully easy and simple. All you have to do is lift the thing off the dining-room table and smuggle it over to Plank. Think how his face'll light up when you walk in on him with it. "My hero!" I expect he'll say.'

And with a laugh which, though silvery, grated on my ear like a squeaking slate pencil, she buzzed off.

10

Proceeding to my room and turning in between the sheets, I composed myself for sleep, but I didn't get a lot of it and what I did get was much disturbed by dreams of being chased across difficult country by sharks, some of them looking like Stiffy, some like Sir Watkyn Bassett, others like the dog Bartholomew. When Jeeves came shimmering in next morning with the breakfast tray, I lost no time in supplying him with full information *re* the harrow I found myself the toad under.

'You see the posish, Jeeves,' I concluded. 'When the loss of the thing is discovered and the hue and cry sets in, who will be the immediate suspect? Wooster, Bertram. My name in this house is already mud, and the men up top will never think of looking further for the guilty party. On the other hand, if I refuse to sit in, Stiffy will consider herself scorned, and we all know what happens when you scorn a woman. She'll tell Madeline Bassett that Gussie has been at the steak and kidney pie, and ruin and desolation will ensue. I see no way of beating the game.'

To my surprise, instead of raising an eyebrow the customary eighth of an inch and saying 'Most disturbing, sir,' he came within an ace of smiling. That is to say, the left corner of his mouth quivered almost imperceptibly before returning to position one.

'You cannot accede to Miss Byng's request, sir.'

I took an astonished sip of coffee. I couldn't follow his train of thought. It seemed to me that he couldn't have been listening.

'But if I don't, she'll squeal to the F.B.I.'

'No, sir, for the lady will be forced to admit that it is physically impossible for you to carry out her wishes. The statuette is no longer at large. It has been placed in Sir Watkyn's collection room behind a stout steel door.'

'Good Lord! How do you know?'

'I chanced to pass the dining-room, sir, and inadvertently overheard a conversation between Sir Watkyn and his lordship.'

'Call him Spode.'

'Very good, sir. Mr. Spode was observing to Sir Watkyn that he had not at all liked the interest you displayed in the figurine at dinner last night.'

'I was just giving Pop B. the old salve in the hope of sweetening the atmosphere a bit.'

'Precisely, sir, but your statement that the object was "just the sort of thing Uncle Tom would like to have" made a deep impression on Mr. Spode. Remembering the unfortunate episode of the cow-creamer, which did so much to mar the pleasantness of your previous visit to Totleigh Towers, he informed Sir Watkyn that he had revised his original view that you were here to attempt to lure Miss Bassett from Mr. Fink-Nottle, and that he was now convinced that your motive in coming to the house had to do with the figurine, and that you were planning to purloin it on Mr. Travers's behalf. Sir Watkyn, who appeared much moved, accepted the theory in toto, all the more readily because of an encounter which he said he had had with you in the early hours of this morning.'

I nodded.

'Yes, we got together in the hall at, I suppose, about one a.m. I had gone down to see if I could get a bit of that steak and kidney pie.'

'I quite understand, sir. It was an injudicious thing to do, if I may say so, but the claims of steak and kidney pie are of course paramount. It was immediately after this that Sir Watkyn fell in with Mr. Spode's suggestion that the statuette be placed under lock and key in the collection room. I presume that it is now there, and when it is explained to Miss Byng that only by means of burglar's tools or a flask of trinitrotoluol could you obtain access to it and that neither of these is in your possession, I am sure the lady will see reason and recede from her position.'

Only the circumstance of my being in bed at the moment kept me from dancing a few carefree steps.

'You speak absolute sooth, Jeeves. This lets me out.'

'Completely, sir.'

'Perhaps you wouldn't mind going and explaining the position of affairs to Stiffy now. You can tell the story so much better than I could, and she ought to be given the low-down as soon as possible. I don't know where she is at this time of day, but you'll find her messing about somewhere, I've no doubt.'

'I saw Miss Byng in the garden with Mr. Pinker, sir. I think she was trying to prepare him for his approaching ordeal.'

'Eh?'

'If you recall, sir, owing to the temporary indisposition of the vicar, Mr. Pinker will be in sole charge of the school treat tomorrow, and he views the prospect with not unnatural qualms. There is a somewhat lawless element among the school children of Totleigh-in-the-Wold, and he fears the worst.'

'Well, tell Stiffy to take a couple of minutes off from the pep talk and listen to your communiqué.'

'Very good, sir.'

He was absent quite a time – so long, in fact, that I was dressed when he returned.

'I saw Miss Byng, sir.'

'And – ?'

'She is still insistent that you restore the statuette to Mr. Plank.'

'She's cuckoo. I can't get into the collection room.'

'No, sir, but Miss Byng can. She informs me that not long ago Sir Watkyn chanced to drop his key, and she picked it up and omitted to apprise him. Sir Watkyn had another key made, but the original remains in Miss Byng's possession.'

I clutched the brow.

'You mean she can get into the room any time she feels like it?'

'Precisely, sir. Indeed, she has just done so.'

And so saying he fished the eyesore from an inner pocket and handed it to me.

'Miss Byng suggests that you take the object to Mr. Plank after luncheon. In her droll way she said the meal – I quote her words – would put the necessary stuffing into you and nerve you for the . . . It is somewhat early, sir, but shall I get you a little brandy?'

'Not a little, Jeeves,' I said. 'Fetch the cask.'

I don't know how Emerald Stoker was with brush and palette, never having seen any of her output, but she unquestionably had what it takes where cooking was concerned, and any householder would have been glad to sign her up for the duration. The lunch she provided was excellent, everything most toothsome.

But with this ghastly commission of Stiffy's on the agenda paper, I had little appetite for her offerings. The brow was furrowed, the manner distrait, the stomach full of butterflies.

'Jeeves,' I said as he accompanied me to my car at the conclusion of the meal, speaking rather peevishly, perhaps, for I was not my usual sunny self, 'doesn't it strike you as odd that, with infant mortality so rife, a girl like Stiffy should have been permitted to survive into the early twenties? Some mismanagement there. What's the tree I read about somewhere that does you in if you sit under it?'

'The Upas tree, sir.'

'She's a female Upas tree. It's not safe to come near her. Disaster on every side is what she strews. And another thing. It's all very well for her to say . . . glibly?'

'Or airily, sir. The words are synonymous.'

'It's all very well for her to say glibly or airily "Take this blasted eyesore to Plank," but how do I find him? I can't go rapping on every door in Hockley-cum-Meston, saying "Excuse me, are you Plank?" It'd be like looking for a needle in a haystack.'

'A very colourful image, sir. I appreciate your difficulty. I would suggest that you proceed to the local post office and institute inquiries there. Post office officials invariably have information at their disposal as to the whereabouts of dwellers in the vicinity.'

He had not erred. Braking the car in the Hockley-cum-Meston High Street, I found that the post office was one of those shops you get in villages, where in addition to enjoying the postal facilities you can purchase cigarettes, pipe tobacco, wool, lollipops, string, socks, boots, overalls, picture postcards and bottles containing yellow non-alcoholic drinks, probably fizzy. In answer to my query the old lady behind the counter told me I would find Plank up at the big house with the red shutters about half a mile further back along the road. She seemed a bit disappointed that information was all I was after and that I had no intention of buying a pair of socks or a ball of string, but she bore up philosophically, and I toddled back to the car.

I remembered the house she had spoken of, having passed it on my way. Imposing mansion with a lot of land. This Plank, I took it, would be some sort of labourer on the estate. I pictured him as a sturdy, gnarled old fellow whose sailor son had brought home the eyesore from one of his voyages, and neither of them had had the foggiest that it was valuable. 'I'll put it on the mantelpiece, Dad,' no doubt the son had said. 'It'll look well up there,' to which the old gaffer had replied 'Aye, lad, gormed if 'twon't look gradely on the mantelpiece.' Or words to that effect. I can't do the dialect, of course. So they had shoved it on the mantelpiece, and then along had come Sir Watkyn Bassett with his smooth city ways and made suckers out of parent and offspring. Happening all the time, that sort of thing.

I reached the house and was about to knock on the door, when there came bustling up an elderly gentleman with a square face, much tanned as if he had been sitting out in the sun quite a lot without his parasol.

'Oh, there you are,' he said. 'Hope I haven't kept you waiting. We were having football practice, and I lost track of the time. Come in, my dear fellow, come in.'

I need scarcely say that this exuberant welcome to one who, whatever his merits, was a total stranger warmed my heart quite a good deal.

It was with the feeling that his attitude did credit to Gloucestershire hospitality that I followed him through a hall liberally besprinkled with the heads of lions, leopards, gnus and other fauna into a room with french windows opening on the front garden. Here he left me while he went off to fetch drinks, his first question having been Would I care for one for the tonsils, to which I had replied with considerable enthusiasm that I would. When he returned, he found me examining the photographs on the wall. The one on which my eye was resting at the moment was a school football group, and it was not difficult to spot the identity of the juvenile delinquent holding the ball and sitting in the middle.

'You?' I said.

'That's me,' he replied. 'My last year at school. I skippered the side that season. That's old Scrubby Willoughby sitting next to me. Fast wing threequarter, but never would learn to give the reverse pass.'

'He wouldn't?' I said, shocked. I hadn't the remotest what he was talking about, but he had said enough to show me that this Willoughby must have been a pretty dubious character, and when he went on to tell me that poor old Scrubby had died of cirrhosis of the liver in the Federal Malay States, I wasn't really surprised. I imagine these fellows who won't learn to give the reverse pass generally come to a fairly sticky end.

'Chap on my other side is Smiler Todd, prop forward.'

'Prop forward, eh?'

'And a very good one. Played for Cambridge later on. You fond of Rugger?'

'I don't think I know him.'

'Rugby football.'

'Oh, ah. No, I've never gone in for it.'

'You haven't?'

'No.'

'Good God!'

I could see that I had sunk pretty low in his estimation, but he was a host and managed to fight down the feeling of nausea with which my confession had afflicted him.

'I've always been mad keen on Rugger. Didn't get much of it after leaving school, as they stationed me in West Africa. Tried to teach the natives there the game, but had to give it up. Too many deaths, with the inevitable subsequent blood feuds. Retired now and settled down here. I'm trying to make Hockley-cum-Meston the best football village in these parts, and I will say for the lads that they're coming on nicely. What we need is a good prop forward, and I can't find one. But you don't want to hear all this. You want to know about my

Brazilian expedition.'

'Oh, have you been to Brazil?'

I seemed to have said the wrong thing, as one so often does. He stared.

'Didn't you know I'd been to Brazil?'

'Nobody tells me anything.'

'I should have thought they'd have briefed you at the office. Seems silly to send a reporter all the way down here without telling him what they're sending him for.'

I'm pretty astute, and I saw there had been a mix-up somewhere.

'Were you expecting a reporter?'

'Of course I was. Aren't you from the *Daily Express*?'

'Sorry, no.'

'I thought you must be the chap who was coming to interview me about my Brazilian explorations.'

'Oh, you're an explorer?'

Again I had said the wrong thing. He was plainly piqued.

'What did you think I was? Does the name Plank mean nothing to you?'

'Is your name Plank?'

'Of course it is.'

'Well, what a very odd coincidence,' I said, intrigued. 'I'm looking for a character called Plank. Not you, somebody else. The bimbo I want is a sturdy tiller of the soil, probably gnarled, with a sailor son. As you have the same name as him, you'll probably be interested in the story I'm about to relate. I have here,' I said, producing the black amber thing, 'a what-not.'

He gaped at it.

'Where did you get that? That's the bit of native sculpture I picked up on the Congo and then sold to Sir Watkyn Bassett.'

I was amazed.

'*You* sold it to him?'

'Certainly.'

'Well, shiver my timbers!'

I was conscious of a Boy Scoutful glow. I liked this Plank, and I rejoiced that it was in my power to do him as good a turn as anyone had ever done anybody. God bless Bertram Wooster, I felt he'd be saying in another couple of ticks. For the first time I was glad that Stiffy had sent me on this mission.

'Then I'll tell you what,' I said. 'If you'll just give me five pounds –'

I broke off. He was looking at me with a cold, glassy stare, as no doubt he had looked at the late lions, leopards and gnus whose remains were to be viewed on the walls of the outer hall. Fellows at the Drones who have tried to touch Ooofy Prosser, the club millionaire, for a trifle to see them through till next Wednesday have described him to me as looking just like that.

'Oh, so that's it!' he said, and even Pop Bassett could not have spoken more nastily. 'I've got your number now. I've met your sort all over the world. You won't get any five pounds, my man. You sit where you are and don't move. I'm going to call the police.'

'It will not be necessary, sir,' said a respectful voice, and Jeeves entered through the french window.

11

His advent drew from me a startled goggle and, I rather think, a cry of amazement. Last man I'd expected to see, and how he had got here defeated me. I've sometimes felt that he must dematerialize himself like those fellows in India – fakirs, I think they're called – who fade into thin air in Bombay and turn up five minutes later in Calcutta or points west with all the parts reassembled.

Nor could I see how he had divined that the young master was in sore straits and in urgent need of his assistance, unless it was all done by what I believe is termed telepathy. Still, here he was, with his head bulging at the back and on his face that look of quiet intelligence which comes from eating lots of fish, and I welcomed his presence. I knew from experience what a wizard he was at removing the oppressed from the soup, and the soup was what I was at this point in my affairs deeply immersed in.

'Major Plank?' he said.

Plank, too, was goggling.

'Who on earth are you?'

'Chief Inspector Witherspoon, sir, of Scotland Yard. Has this man been attempting to obtain money from you?'

'Just been doing that very thing.'

'As I suspected. We have had our eye on him for a long time, but till now have never been able to apprehend him in the act.'

'Notorious crook, is he?'

'Precisely, sir. He is a confidence man of considerable eminence in the underworld, who makes a practice of calling at houses and extracting money from their owners with some plausible story.'

'He does more than that. He pinches things from people and tries to sell them. Look at that statuette he's holding. It's a thing I sold to Sir Watkyn Bassett, who lives at Totleigh-in-the-Wold, and he had the cool cheek to come here and try to sell it to me for five pounds.'

'Indeed, sir? With your permission I will impound the object.'

'You'll need it as evidence?'

'Exactly, sir. I shall now take him to Totleigh Towers and confront him with Sir Watkyn.'

'Yes, do. That'll teach him. Nasty hangdog look the fellow's got. I suspected from the first he was wanted by the police. Had him under observation for a long time, have you?'

'For a very long time, sir. He is known to us at the Yard as Alpine Joe, because he always wears an Alpine hat.'

'He's got it with him now.'

'He never moves without it.'

'You'd think he'd have the sense to adopt some rude disguise.'

'You would indeed, sir, but the mental processes of a man like that are hard to follow.'

'Then there's no need for me to phone the local police?'

'None, sir. I will take him into custody.'

'You wouldn't like me to hit him over the head first with a Zulu knobkerrie?'

'Unnecessary, sir.'

'It might be safer.'

'No, sir, I am sure he will come quietly.'

'Well, have it your own way. But don't let him give you the slip.'

'I will be very careful, sir.'

'And shove him into a dungeon with dripping walls and see to it that he is well gnawed by rats.'

'Very good, sir.'

What with all the stuff about reverse passes and prop forwards, plus the strain of seeing gentlemen's personal gentlemen appear from nowhere and of having to listen to that loose talk about Zulu knob-kerries, the Wooster bean was not at its best as we moved off, and there was nothing in the way of conversational give-and-take until we had reached my car, which I had left at the front gate.

'Chief Inspector *who*?' I said, recovering a modicum of speech as we arrived at our objective.

'Witherspoon, sir.'

'Why Witherspoon? On the other hand,' I added, for I like to look on both sides of a thing, 'why not Witherspoon? However, that is not germane to the issue and can be reserved for discussion later. The real point – the nub – the thing that should be threshed out imme-diately – is how on earth do you come to be here?'

'I anticipated that my arrival might occasion you a certain surprise, sir. I hastened after you directly I learned of the revelation Sir Watkyn had made to Miss Byng, for I foresaw that your interview with Major

Plank would be embarrassing, and I hoped to be able to intercept you before you could establish communication with him.'

Practically all of this floated past me.

'How do you mean, the revelation Pop Bassett made to Stiffy?'

'It occurred shortly after luncheon, sir. Miss Byng informs me that she decided to approach Sir Watkyn and make a last appeal to his better feelings. As you are aware, the matter of the statuette has always been one that affected her deeply. She thought that if she reproached Sir Watkyn with sufficient vehemence, something constructive might result. Greatly to her astonishment, she had hardly begun to speak when Sir Watkyn, chuckling heartily, asked her if she could keep a secret. He then revealed that there was no foundation for the story he had told Mr. Travers and that in actual fact he had paid Major Plank a thousand pounds for the object.'

It took me perhaps a quarter of a minute to sort all this out.

'A thousand quid?'

'Yes, sir.'

'Not a fiver?'

'No, sir.'

'You mean he lied to Uncle Tom?'

'Yes, sir.'

'What on earth did he do that for?'

I thought he would say he hadn't a notion, but he didn't.

'I think Sir Watkyn's motive was obvious, sir.'

'Not to me.'

'He acted from a desire to exasperate Mr. Travers. Mr. Travers is a collector, and collectors are never pleased when they learn that a rival collector has acquired at an insignificant price an *objet d'art* of great value.'

It penetrated. I saw what he meant. The discovery that Pop Bassett had got hold of a thousand-quid thingummy for practically nothing would have been gall and w. to Uncle Tom. Stiffy had described him as writhing like an egg whisk, and I could well believe it. It must have been agony for the poor old buster.

'You've hit it, Jeeves. It's just what Pop Bassett would do. Nothing would please him better than to spoil Uncle Tom's day. What a man, Jeeves!'

'Yes, sir.'

'Would you like to have a mind like his?'

'No, sir.'

'Nor me. It just shows how being a magistrate saps the moral fibre. I remember thinking as I stood before him in the dock that he had a shifty eye and that I wouldn't trust him as far as I could throw an elephant. I suppose all magistrates are like that.'

'There may be exceptions, sir.'

'I doubt it. Twisters, every one of them. So my errand was...what, Jeeves?'

'Bootless, sir.'

'Bootless? It doesn't sound right, but I suppose you know. Well, I wish the news you've just sprung could have broken before I presented myself *chez* Plank. I would have been spared a testing ordeal.'

'I can appreciate the nervous strain you must have undergone, sir. It is unfortunate that I was not able to arrive earlier.'

'How did you arrive at all? That's what's puzzling me. You can't have walked.'

'No, sir. I borrowed Miss Byng's car. I left it some little distance down the road and proceeded to the house on foot. Hearing voices, I approached the french window and listened, and was thus enabled to intervene at the crucial moment.'

'Very resourceful.'

'Thank you, sir.'

'I should like to express my gratitude. And when I say gratitude, I mean heartfelt gratitude.'

'Not at all, sir. It was a pleasure.'

'But for you, Plank would have had me in the local calaboose in a matter of minutes. Who is he, by the way? I got the impression that he was an explorer of sorts.'

'Yes, sir.'

'Pretty far-flung, I gathered.'

'Extremely, sir. He has recently returned from an expedition into the interior of Brazil. He inherited the house where he resides from a deceased godfather. He breeds cocker spaniels, suffers somewhat from malaria and eats only non-fattening protein bread.'

'You seem to have got him taped all right.'

'I made inquiries at the post office, sir. The person behind the counter was most informative. I also learned that Major Plank is an enthusiast on Rugby football and is hoping to make Hockley-cum-Meston invincible on the field.'

'Yes, so he was telling me. You aren't a prop forward, are you, Jeeves?'

'No, sir. Indeed, I do not know what the term signifies.'

'I don't, either, except that it's something a team has to have if it's hoping to do down the opposition at Rugby football. Plank, I believe, has searched high and low for one, but his errand has been bootless.

Rather sad, when you come to think of it. All that money, all those cocker spaniels, all that protein bread, but no prop forward. Still, that's life.'

'Yes indeed, sir.'

I slid behind the steering wheel, and told him to hop in.

'But I was forgetting. You've got Stiffy's car. Then I'll be driving on. The sooner I get this statuette thing back into her custody, the better.'

He didn't shake his head, because he never shakes his head, but he raised the south-east corner of a warning eyebrow.

'If you will pardon the suggestion, sir, I think it would be more advisable for me to take the object to Miss Byng. It would scarcely be prudent for you to enter the environs of Totleigh Towers with it on your person. You might encounter his lordship . . . I should say Mr. Spode.'

I well-I'll-be-dashed. He had surprised me.

'Surely you aren't suggesting that he would frisk me?'

'I think it highly possible, sir. In the conversation which I overheard, Mr. Spode gave me the impression of being prepared to stop at nothing. If you will give me the object, I will see that Miss Byng restores it to the collection room at the earliest possible moment.'

I mused, but not for long. I was only too pleased to get rid of the beastly thing.

'Very well, if you say so. Here you are. Though I think you're wronging Spode.'

'I think not, sir.'

And blow me tight if he wasn't right. Scarcely had I steered the car into the stable yard, when a solid body darkened the horizon, and there was Spode, looking like Chief Inspector Witherspoon about to make a pinch.

'Wooster!' he said.

'Speaking,' I said.

'Get out of that car,' he said. 'I'm going to search it.'

12

I was conscious of a thrill of thankfulness for Jeeves's prescience, if prescience is the word I want. I mean that uncanny knack he has of peering into the future and forming his plans and schemes well ahead of time. But for his thoughtful diagnosis of the perils that lay before me, I should at this juncture have been deep in the mulligatawny and no hope of striking for the shore. As it was, I was able to be nonchalant, insouciant and debonair. I was like the fellow I once heard Jeeves speak of who was armed so strong in honesty that somebody's threats passed by him as the idle wind, which he respected not. I think if Spode had been about three feet shorter and not so wide across the shoulders, I would have laughed a mocking laugh and quite possibly have flicked my cambric handkerchief in his face.

He was eyeing me piercingly, little knowing what an ass he was going to feel before yonder sun had set.

'I have just searched your room.'

'You have? You surprise me. Looking for something, were you?'

'You know what I'm looking for. That amber statuette you said your uncle would be so glad to have.'

'Oh, that? I understood it was in the collection room.'

'Who told you that?'

'A usually well-informed source.'

'Well, it is no longer in the collection room. Somebody has removed it.'

'Most extraordinary.'

'And when I say "somebody", I mean a slimy sneak thief of the name of Wooster. The thing isn't in your bedroom, so if it is not in your car, you must have it on you. Turn out your pockets.'

I humoured his request, largely influenced by the fact that there was so much of him. A Singer midget would have found me far less obliging. The contents having been placed before him, he snorted in a disappointed way, as if he had hoped for better things, and dived into the car, opening drawers and looking under cushions. And Stiffy, coming along at this moment, drank in his vast trouser seat with a curious eye.

'What goes on?' she asked.

This time I did laugh that mocking laugh. It seemed to be indicated.

'You know that black eyesore thing that was on the dinner table? Apparently it's disappeared, and Spode has got the extraordinary idea that I've pinched it and am holding it . . . what's the word . . . Not incognito . . . Incommunicado, that's it. He thinks I'm holding it incommunicado.'

'He does?'

'So he says.'

'Man must be an ass.'

Spode wheeled around, flushed with his excesses. I was pleased to see that while looking under the seat he had got a bit of oil on his nose. He eyed Stiffy bleakly.

'Did you call me an ass?'

'Certainly I did. I was taught by a long series of governesses always to speak the truth. The idea of accusing Bertie of taking that statuette.'

'It does sound silly,' I agreed. 'Bizarre is perhaps the word.'

'The thing's in Uncle Watkyn's collection room.'

'It is not in the collection room.'

'Who says so?'

'I say so.'

'Well, I say it is. Go and look, if you don't believe me. Stop that, Bartholomew, you blighted dog!' bellowed Stiffy, abruptly changing the subject, and she hastened off on winged feet to confer with the hound, who had found something in, I presumed, the last stages of decay and was rolling on it. I could follow her train of thought. Scotties at their best are niffy. Add to their natural bouquet the aroma of a dead rat or whatever it was, and you have a mixture too rich for the human nostril. There was a momentary altercation, and Bartholomew, cursing a good deal as was natural, was hauled off tubwards.

A minute or two later Spode returned with most of the stuffing removed from his person.

'I seem to have done you an injustice, Wooster,' he said, and I was amazed that he had it in him to speak so meekly.

The Woosters are always magnanimous. We do not crush the vanquished beneath the iron heel.

'Oh, was the thing there all right?'

'Er – yes. Yes, it was.'

'Ah well, we all make mistakes.'

'I could have sworn it had gone.'

'But wasn't the door locked?'

'Yes.'

'Reminds you of one of those mystery stories, doesn't it, where there's a locked room with no windows, and blowed if one fine morning you don't find a millionaire inside with a dagger of Oriental design sticking in his wishbone. You've got some oil on your nose.'

'Oh, have I?' he said, feeling.

'Now you've got it on your cheek. I'd go and join Bartholomew in the bath tub if I were you.'

'I will. Thank you, Wooster.'

'Not at all, Spode, or rather, Sidcup. Don't spare the soap.'

I suppose there's nothing that braces one more thoroughly than the spectacle of the forces of darkness stubbing their toe, and the heart was light as I made my way to the house. What with this and what with that, it was as though a great weight had rolled off me. Birds sang, insects buzzed, and I felt that what they were trying to say was 'All is well. Bertram has come through.'

But a thing I've often noticed is that when I've got something off my mind, it pretty nearly always happens that Fate sidles up and shoves on something else, as if curious to see how much the traffic will bear. It went into its act on the present occasion. Feeling that I needed something else to worry about, it spat on its hands and got down to it, allowing Madeline Bassett to corner me as I was passing through the hall.

Even if she had been her normal soupy self, she would have been the last person I wanted to have a word with, but this she was far from being. Something had happened to remove the droopiness, and her eyes had a gleam in them which filled me with a nameless fear. She was obviously all steamed up for some reason, and it was plain that what she was about to say was not going to make the last of the Woosters clap his hands in glee and start chanting hosannas like the Cherubim and Seraphim, if I've got the names right. A moment later she revealed what it was that was eating her, dishing it out without what I believe is called preamble.

'I am furious with Augustus!' she said, and my heart stood still. It was as if the Totleigh Towers spectre, if there was one, had laid an icy hand on it.

'Why, what's happened?'

'He was very rude to Roderick.'

This seemed incredible. Nobody but an all-in wrestling champion would be rude to a fellow as big as Spode.

'Surely not?'

'I mean he was very rude *about* Roderick. He said he was sick and tired of seeing him clumping about the place as if it belonged to him, and hadn't he got a home of his own, and if Daddy had an ounce more sense than a billiard ball he would charge him rent. He was most offensive.'

My h. stood stiller. It is not stretching the facts to say that I was appalled and all of a doodah. It just showed, I was telling myself, what a vegetarian diet can do to a chap, changing him in a flash from a soft boiled to a hard boiled egg. I have no doubt the poet Shelley's circle noticed the same thing with the poet Shelley.

I tried to pour oil on the troubled w's.

'Probably just kidding, don't you think?'

'No, I don't.'

'He didn't say it with a twinkle in his eye?'

'No.'

'Nor with a light laugh?'

'No.'

'You might not have noticed it. Very easy to miss, these light laughs.'

'He meant every word he said.'

'Then it was probably just a momentary spasm of what-d'you-call-it. Irritability. We all have them.'

She ground a tooth or two. At least, it looked as if that was what she was doing.

'It was nothing of the kind. He was harsh and bitter, and he has been like that for a long time. I noticed it first at Brinkley. One morning we had walked in the meadows and the grass was all covered with little wreaths of mist, and I said Didn't he sometimes feel that they were the elves' bridal veils, and he said sharply, "No, never," adding that he had never heard such a silly idea in his life.'

Well, of course, he was perfectly correct, but it was no good pointing that out to a girl like Madeline Bassett.

'And that evening we were watching the sunset, and I said sunsets always made me think of the Blessed Damozel leaning out from the gold bar of heaven, and he said "Who?" and I said "The Blessed Damozel," and he said, "Never heard of her". And he said that sunsets made him sick and so did the Blessed Damozel and he had a pain in his inside.'

I saw that the time had come to be a *raisonneur*.

'This was at Brinkley?'

'Yes.'

'I see. After you had made him become a vegetarian. Are you sure,' I said, raisonneuring like nobody's business, 'that you were altogether wise in confining him to spinach and what not? Many a proud spirit rebels when warned off the proteins. And I don't know if you know it, but medical research has established that the ideal diet is one in which animal and vegetable foods are balanced. It's something to do with the something acids required by the body.'

I won't say she actually snorted, but the sound she uttered was certainly on the borderline of the snort.

'What nonsense!'

'It's what doctors say.'

'Which doctors?'

'Well-known Harley Street physicians.'

'I don't believe it. Thousands of people are vegetarians and enjoy perfect health.'

'Bodily health, yes,' I said, cleverly seizing on the debating point. 'But what of the soul? If you suddenly steer a fellow off the steaks and chops, it does something to his soul. My Aunt Agatha once made my Uncle Percy be a vegetarian, and his whole nature became soured. Not,' I was forced to admit, 'that it wasn't fairly soured already, as anyone's would be who was in constant contact with my Aunt Agatha. I bet you'll find that that's all that's wrong with Gussie. He simply wants a mutton chop or two under his belt.'

'Well, he's not going to have them. And if he continues to behave like a sulky child, I shall know what to do about it.'

I remember Stinker Pinker telling me once that toward the end of his time at Oxford he was down in Bethnal Green spreading the light, and a costermonger kicked him in the stomach. He said it gave him a strange, confused, dreamlike feeling, and that's what these ominous words of M. Bassett's gave me now. She had spoken them from between teeth which, if not actually clenched, were the next thing to it, and it was as if the substantial boot of a vendor of blood oranges and bananas had caught me squarely in the solar plexus.

'Er – what will you do about it?'

'Never mind.'

I put out a cautious feeler.

'Suppose . . . not that it's likely to happen, of course . . . but suppose Gussie, maddened by abstinence, were to go off and tuck into . . . well, to take an instance at random, cold steak and kidney pie, what would be the upshot?'

I had never supposed that she had it in her to give anyone a piercing look, but that is what she gave me now. I don't think even Aunt Agatha's eyes have bored more deeply into me.

'Are you telling me, Bertie, that Augustus has been eating steak and kidney pie?'

'Good heavens, no. It was just a thingummy.'

'I don't understand you.'

'What do they call questions that aren't really questions? Begins with an h. Hypothetical, that's the word. It was just a hypothetical question.'

'Oh? Well, the answer to it is that if I found that Augustus had been eating the flesh of animals slain in anger, I would have nothing more to do with him,' she said, and she biffed off, leaving me a spent force and a mere shell of my former self.

13

The following day dawned bright and fair. At least I suppose it did. I didn't see it dawning myself, having dropped off into a troubled slumber some hours before it got its nose down to it, but when the mists of sleep cleared and I was able to attend to what was going on, sunshine was seeping through the window and the ear detected the chirping of about seven hundred and fifty birds, not one of whom, unlike me, appeared to have a damn thing on his or her mind. As carefree a bunch as I've ever struck, and it gave me the pip to listen to them, for melancholy had marked me for her own, as the fellow said, and all this buck and heartiness simply stepped up the gloom in which my yesterday's chat with Madeline Bassett had plunged me.

As may well be imagined, her obiter dicta, as I believe they're called, had got right in amongst me. This, it was plain, was no mere lovers' tiff, to be cleaned up with a couple of tears and a kiss or two, but a real Class A rift which, if prompt steps were not taken through the proper channels, would put the lute right out of business and make it as mute as a drum with a hole in it. And the problem of how those steps were to be taken defeated me. Two iron wills had clashed. On the one hand we had Madeline's strong anti-flesh-food bias, on the other Gussie's firm determination to get all the cuts off the joint that were coming to him. What, I asked myself, would the harvest be, and I was still shuddering at the thought of what the future might hold, when Jeeves trickled in with the morning cup of tea.

'Eh?' I said absently, as he put it on the table. Usually I spring at the refreshing fluid like a seal going after a slice of fish. Preoccupied, if you know what I mean. Or distrait, if you care to put it that way.

'I was saying that we are fortunate in having a fine day for the school treat, sir.'

I sat up with a jerk, upsetting the cuppa as deftly as if I'd been the Rev. H.P. Pinker.

'Is it today?'

'This afternoon, sir.'

I groaned one of those hollow ones.

'It needed but this, Jeeves.'

'Sir?'

'The last straw. I'd enough on my mind already.'

'There is something disturbing you, sir?'

'You're right there is. Hell's foundations are quivering. What do you call it when a couple of nations start off by being all palsy-walsy and then begin calling each other ticks and bounders?'

'Relations have deteriorated would be the customary phrase, sir.'

'Well, relations have deteriorated between Miss Bassett and Gussie. He, as we know, was already disgruntled, and now she's disgruntled, too. She has taken exception to a derogatory crack he made about the sunset. She thinks highly of sunsets, and he told her they made him sick. Can you believe this?'

'Quite readily, sir. Mr. Fink-Nottle was commenting to me on the sunset yesterday evening. He said it looked so like a slice of underdone beef that it tortured him to see it. One can appreciate his feelings.'

'I dare say, but I wish he'd keep them to himself. He also appears to have spoken disrespectfully of the Blessed Damozel. Who's the Blessed Damozel, Jeeves? I don't seem to have heard of her.'

'The heroine of a poem by the late Dante Gabriel Rossetti, sir. She leaned out from the gold bar of Heaven.'

'Yes, I gathered that. That much was specified.'

'Her eyes were deeper than the depths of waters stilled at even. She had three lilies in her hand, and the stars in her hair were seven.'

'Oh, were they? Well, be that as it may, Gussie said she made him sick, too, and Miss Bassett's as sore as a sunburned neck.'

'Most disturbing, sir.'

'Disturbing is the word. If things go on the way they are, no bookie would give odds of less than a hundred to eight on this betrothal lasting another week. I've seen betrothals in my time, many of them, but never one that looked more likely to come apart at the seams than that of Augustus Fink-Nottle and Madeline, daughter of Sir Watkyn and the late Lady Bassett. The suspense is awful. Who was the chap I remember reading about somewhere, who had a sword hanging over him attached to a single hair?'

'Damocles, sir. It is an old Greek legend.'

'Well, I know just how he felt. And with this on my mind, I'm expected to attend a ruddy school treat. I won't go.'

'Your absence may cause remark, sir.'

'I don't care. They won't get a smell of me. I'm oiling out, and let them make of it what they will.'

Apart from anything else, I was remembering the story I had heard
Pongo Twistleton tell one night at the Drones, illustrative of how
unbridled passions are apt to become at these binges. Pongo got mixed
up once in a school treat down in Somersetshire, and his description
of how, in order to promote a game called 'Is Mr. Smith at Home?'
he had had to put his head in a sack and allow the younger generation
to prod him with sticks had held the smoking-room spellbound. At a
place like Totleigh, where even on normal days human life was not
safe, still worse excesses were to be expected. The glimpse or two I
had had of the local Dead End kids had told me how tough a bunch
they were and how sedulously they should be avoided by the man who
knew what was good for him.

'I shall nip over to Brinkley in the car and have lunch with Uncle
Tom. You at my side, I hope?'

'Impossible, I fear, sir. I have promised to assist Mr. Butterfield in
the tea tent.'

'Then you can tell me all about it.'

'Very good, sir.'

'If you survive.'

'Precisely, sir.'

It was a nice easy drive to Brinkley, and I got there well in advance
of the luncheon hour. Aunt Dahlia wasn't there, having, as foreshadowed, popped up to London for the day, and Uncle Tom and I sat
down alone to a repast in Anatole's best vein. Over the *Suprême de
Foie Gras au Champagne* and the *Neige aux Perles des Alpes* I placed
him in possession of the facts relating to the black amber statuette
thing, and his relief at learning that Pop Bassett hadn't got a thousand-quid *objet d'art* for a fiver was so profound and the things he
said about Pop B. so pleasing to the ear that by the time I started
back my dark mood had become sensibly lightened and optimism had
returned to its throne.

After all, I reminded myself, it wasn't as if Gussie was going to be
indefinitely under Madeline's eye. In due season he would buzz back
to London and there would be able to tuck into the beefs and muttons
till his ribs squeaked, confident that not a word of his activities would
reach her. The effect of this would be to refill him with sweetness
and light, causing him to write her loving letters which would carry
him along till she emerged from this vegetarian phase and took up
stamp collecting or something. I know the other sex and their sudden
enthusiasms. They get these crazes and wallow in them for awhile,
but they soon become fed up and turn to other things. My Aunt
Agatha once went in for politics, but it only took a few meetings at

which she got the bird from hecklers to convince her that the cagey thing to do was to stay at home and attend to her fancy needlework, giving the whole enterprise a miss.

It was getting on for what is called the quiet evenfall when I anchored at Totleigh Towers. I did my usual sneak to my room, and I had been there a few minutes when Jeeves came in.

'I saw you arrive, sir,' he said, 'and I thought you might be in need of refreshment.'

I assured him that his intuition had not led him astray, and he said he would bring me a whisky-and-s. immediately.

'I trust you found Mr. Travers in good health, sir.'

I was able to reassure him there.

'He was a bit low when I blew in, but on receipt of my news about the what-not blossomed like a flower. It would have done you good to have heard what he had to say about Pop Bassett. And talking of Pop Bassett, how did the school treat go off?'

'I think the juvenile element enjoyed the festivities, sir.'

'How about you?'

'Sir?'

'You were all right? They didn't put your head in a sack and prod you with sticks?'

'No, sir. My share in the afternoon's events was confined to assisting in the tea tent.'

'You speak lightly, Jeeves, but I've known some dark work to take place in school treat tea tents.'

'It is odd that you should say that, sir, for it was while partaking of tea that a lad threw a hard-boiled egg at Sir Watkyn.'

'And hit him?'

'On the left cheek-bone, sir. It was most unfortunate.'

I could not subscribe to this.

'I don't know why you say "unfortunate". Best thing that could have happened, in my opinion. The very first time I set eyes on Pop Bassett, in the picturesque environment of Bosher Street police court, I remember saying to myself that there sat a man to whom it would do all the good in the world to have hard-boiled eggs thrown at him. One of my crowd on that occasion, a lady accused of being drunk and disorderly and resisting the police, did on receipt of her sentence, throw her boot at him, but with a poor aim, succeeding only in beaning the magistrate's clerk. What's the boy's name?'

'I could not say, sir. His actions were cloaked in anonymity.'

'A pity. I would have liked to reward him by sending camels bearing apes, ivory and peacocks to his address. Did you see anything of Gussie in the course of the afternoon?'

'Yes, sir. Mr. Fink-Nottle, at Miss Bassett's insistence, played a large part in the proceedings and was, I am sorry to say, somewhat roughly handled by the younger revellers. Among other vicissitudes that he underwent, a child entangled its all-day sucker in his hair.'

'That must have annoyed him. He's fussy about his hair.'

'Yes, sir, he was visibly incensed. He detached the sweetmeat and threw it from him with a good deal of force, and by ill luck it struck Miss Byng's dog on the nose. Affronted by what he presumably mistook for an unprovoked assault, the animal bit Mr. Fink-Nottle in the leg.'

'Poor old Gussie!'

'Yes, sir.'

'Still, into each life some rain must fall.'

'Precisely, sir. I will go and bring your whisky-and-soda.'

He had scarcely gone, when Gussie blew in, limping a little but otherwise showing no signs of what Jeeves had called the vicissitudes he had undergone. He seemed, indeed, above rather than below his usual form, and I remember the phrase 'the bulldog breed' passed through my mind. If Gussie was a sample of young England's stamina and fortitude, it seemed to me that the country's future was secure. It is not every nation that can produce sons capable of grinning, as he was doing, so shortly after being bitten by Aberdeen terriers.

'Oh, there you are, Bertie,' he said. 'Jeeves told me you were back. I looked in to borrow some cigarettes.'

'Go ahead.'

'Thanks,' he said, filling his case. 'I'm taking Emerald Stoker for a walk.'

'You're *what*?'

'Or a row on the river. Whichever she prefers.'

'But, Gussie –'

'Oh, before I forget. Pinker is looking for you. He says he wants to see you about something important.'

'Never mind about Stinker. You can't take Emerald Stoker for walks.'

'Can't I? Watch me.'

'But –'

'Sorry, no time to talk now. I don't want to keep her waiting. So long, I must be off.'

He left me plunged in thought, and not agreeable thought either. I think I have made it clear to the meanest i. that my whole future depended on Augustus Fink-Nottle sticking to the straight and narrow path and not blotting his copybook, and I could not but feel that by taking Emerald Stoker for walks he was skidding off the straight and narrow path and blotting his c. in no uncertain manner. That, at least, was, I was pretty sure, how an idealistic beazel like Madeline Bassett, already rendered hot under the collar by his subversive views on sunsets and Blessed Damozels, would regard it. It is not too much to say that when Jeeves returned with the whisky-and-s., he found me all of a twitter and shaking on my stem.

I would have liked to put him abreast of this latest development, but, as I say, there are things we don't discuss, so I merely drank deep of the flowing bowl and told him that Gussie had just been a pleasant visitor.

'He tells me Stinker Pinker wants to see me about something.'

'No doubt with reference to the episode of Sir Watkyn and the hard-boiled egg, sir.'

'Don't tell me it was Stinker who threw it.'

'No, sir, the miscreant is believed to have been a lad in his early teens. But the young fellow's impulsive action has led to unfortunate consequences. It has caused Sir Watkyn to entertain doubts as to the wisdom of entrusting a vicarage to a curate incapable of maintaining order at a school treat. Miss Byng, while confiding this information to me, appeared greatly distressed. She had supposed – I quote her verbatim – that the thing was in the bag, and she is naturally much disturbed.'

I drained my glass and lit a moody gasper. If Totleigh Towers wanted to turn me into a cynic, it was going the right way about it.

'There's a curse on this house, Jeeves. Broken blossoms and shattered hopes wherever you look. It seems to be something in the air. The sooner we're out of here, the better. I wonder if we couldn't –'

I had been about to add 'make our getaway tonight', but at this moment the door flew open and Spode came bounding in, wiping the words from my lips and causing me to raise an eyebrow or two. I resented this habit he was developing of popping up out of a trap at me every other minute like a Demon King in pantomime, and only the fact that I couldn't think of anything restrained me from saying something pretty stinging. As it was, I wore the mask and spoke with the suavity of the perfect host.

'Ah, Spode. Come on in and take a few chairs,' I said, and was on the point of telling him that we Woosters kept open house, when he interrupted me with the uncouth abruptness so characteristic of these human gorillas. Roderick Spode may have had his merits, though I had never been able to spot them, but his warmest admirer couldn't have called him couth.

14

'Have you seen Fink-Nottle?' he said.

I didn't like the way he spoke or the way he was looking. The lips, I noted, were twitching, and the eyes glittered with what I believe is called a baleful light. It seemed pretty plain to me that it was in no friendly spirit that he was seeking Gussie, so I watered down the truth a bit, as the prudent man does on these occasions.

'I'm sorry, no. I've only just got back from my uncle's place over Worcestershire way. Some urgent family business came up and I had to go and attend to it, so unfortunately missed the school treat. A great disappointment. You haven't seen Gussie, have you, Jeeves?'

He made no reply, possibly because he wasn't there. He generally slides discreetly off when the young master is entertaining the quality, and you never see him go. He just evaporates.

'Was it something important you wanted to see him about?'

'I want to break his neck.'

My eyebrows, which had returned to normal, rose again. I also, if I remember rightly, pursed my lips.

'Well, really, Spode! Is this not becoming a bit thick? It's not so long ago that you were turning over in your mind the idea of breaking mine. I think you should watch yourself in this matter of neck-breaking and check the urge before it gets too strong a grip on you. No doubt you say to yourself that you can take it or leave it alone, but isn't there the danger of the thing becoming habit-forming? Why do you want to break Gussie's neck?'

He ground his teeth, at least that's what I think he did to them, and was silent for a space. Then, though there wasn't anyone within earshot but me, he lowered his voice.

'I can speak frankly to you, Wooster, because you, too, love her.'

'Eh? Who?' I said. It should have been 'whom', I suppose, but that didn't occur to me at the time.

'Madeline, of course.'

'Oh, Madeline?'

'As I told you, I have always loved her, and her happiness is very dear to me. It is everything to me. To give her a moment's pleasure I would cut myself in pieces.'

I couldn't follow him there, but before I could go into the question of whether girls enjoy seeing people cut themselves in pieces he had resumed.

'It was a great shock to me when she became engaged to this man Fink-Nottle, but I accepted the situation because I thought that that was where her happiness lay. Though stunned, I kept silent.'

'Very white.'

'I said nothing that would give her a suspicion of how I felt.'

'Very pukka.'

'It was enough for me that she should be happy. Nothing else mattered. But when Fink-Nottle turns out to be a libertine –'

'Who, Gussie?' I said, surprised. 'The last chap I'd have attached such a label to. Pure as the driven s., I'd have thought, if not purer. What makes you think Gussie's a libertine?'

'The fact that less than ten minutes ago I saw him kissing the cook,' said Spode through the teeth which I'm pretty sure he was grinding, and he dived out of the door and was gone.

How long I remained motionless, like a ventriloquist's dummy whose ventriloquist has gone off to the local and left it sitting, I cannot say. Probably not so very long, for when life returned to the rigid limbs and I legged it for the open spaces to try to find Gussie and warn him of this V-shaped depression which was coming his way, Spode was still in sight. He was disappearing in a nor'-nor'-easterly direction, so, not wanting to hobnob with him again while he was in this what you might call difficult mood, I pushed off sou'-sou'-west, and found that I couldn't have set my course more shrewdly. There was a sort of yew alley or rhododendron walk or some such thing confronting me, and as I entered it I saw Gussie. He was standing in a kind of trance, and his fatheadedness in standing when he ought to have been running like a rabbit smote me like a blow and lent an extra emphasis to the 'Hoy!' with which I accosted him.

He turned, and as I approached him I noted that he seemed even more braced than when last seen. The eyes behind the horn-rimmed spectacles gleamed with a brighter light, and a smile wreathed his lips. He looked like a fish that's just learned that its rich uncle in Australia has pegged out and left it a packet.

'Ah, Bertie,' he said, 'we decided to go for a walk, not a row. We thought it might be a little chilly on the water. What a beautiful evening, Bertie, is it not?'

I couldn't see eye to eye with him there.

'It strikes you as that, does it? It doesn't me.'

He seemed surprised.

'In what respect do you find it not up to sample?'

'I'll tell you in what respect I find it not up to sample. What's all this I hear about you and Emerald Stoker? Did you kiss her?'

The Soul's Awakening expression on his face became intensified. Before my revolted eyes Augustus Fink-Nottle definitely smirked.

'Yes, Bertie, I did, and I'll do it again if it's the last thing I do. What a girl, Bertie! So kind, so sympathetic. She's my idea of a thoroughly womanly woman, and you don't see many of them around these days. I hadn't time when I was in your room to tell you about what happened at the school treat.'

'Jeeves told me. He said Bartholomew bit you.'

'And how right he was. The bounder bit me to the bone. And do you know what Emerald Stoker did? Not only did she coo over me like a mother comforting a favourite child, but she bathed and bandaged my lacerated leg. She was a ministering angel, the nearest thing to Florence Nightingale you could hope to find. It was shortly after she had done the swabbing and bandaging that I kissed her.'

'Well, you shouldn't have kissed her.'

Again he showed surprise. He had thought it, he said, a pretty sound idea.

'But you're engaged to Madeline.'

I had hoped with these words to start his conscience working on all twelve cylinders, but something seemed to have gone wrong with the machinery, for he remained as calm and unmoved as the fish on ice he so closely resembled.

'Ah, Madeline,' he said. 'I was about to touch on Madeline. Shall I tell you what's wrong with Madeline Bassett? No heart. That's where she slips up. Lovely to look at, but nothing *here*,' he said, tapping the left side of his chest. 'Do you know how she reacted to that serious flesh wound of mine? She espoused Bartholomew's cause. She said the whole thing was my fault. She accused me of having teased the little blister. In short, she behaved like a louse. How different from Emerald Stoker. Do you know what Emerald Stoker did?'

'You told me.'

'I mean in addition to binding up my wounds. She went straight off to the kitchen and cut me a package of sandwiches. I have them here,' said Gussie, exhibiting a large parcel and eyeing it reverently. 'Ham,' he added in a voice that throbbed with emotion. 'She made them for me with her own hands, and I think it was her thoughtfulness even more than her divine sympathy that showed me that she was the only girl in the world for me. The scales fell from my eyes, and I saw that what I had once felt for Madeline had been just a boyish infatuation. What I feel for Emerald Stoker is the real thing. In my opinion she stands alone, and I shall be glad if you will stop going about the place saying that she looks like a Pekinese.'

'But, Gussie –'

He silenced me with an imperious wave of the ham sandwiches.

'It's no good your saying "But, Gussie". The trouble with you, Bertie, is that you haven't got it in you to understand true love. You're a mere butterfly flitting from flower to flower and sipping, like Freddie Widgeon and the rest of the halfwits of whom the Drones Club is far too full. A girl to you is just the plaything of an idle hour, and anything in the nature of a grand passion is beyond you. I'm different. I have depth. I'm a marrying man.'

'But you can't marry Emerald Stoker.'

'Why not? We're twin souls.'

I thought for a moment of giving him a word-portrait of old Stoker, to show him the sort of father-in-law he would be getting if he carried through the project he had in mind, but I let it go. Reason told me that a fellow who for months had been expecting to draw Pop Bassett as a father-in-law was not going to be swayed by an argument like that. However frank my description of him, Stoker could scarcely seem anything but a change for the better.

I stood there at a loss, and was still standing there at a loss, when I heard my name called and looking behind me saw Stinker and Stiffy. They were waving hands and things, and I gathered that they had come to thresh out with me the matter of Sir Watkyn Bassett and the hard-boiled egg.

The last thing I would have wished at this crucial point in my affairs was an interruption, for all my faculties should have been concentrated on reasoning with Gussie and trying to make him see the light, but it has often been said of Bertram Wooster that when a buddy in distress is drawn to his attention he forgets self. No matter what his commitments elsewhere, the distressed buddy has only to beckon and he is with him. With a brief word to Gussie that I would be back at an early date to resume our discussion, I hurried to where Stiffy and Stinker stood.

'Talk quick,' I said. 'I'm in conference. Too long to tell you all about it, but a serious situation has arisen. As, according to Jeeves, one has with you. From what he told me I gathered that the odds against Stinker clicking as regards that vicarage have lengthened. More letting-I-dare-not-wait-upon-I-would-ness on Pop Bassett's part, he gave me to understand. Too bad.'

'Of course, one can see it from Sir Watkyn's point of view,' said Stinker, who, if he has a fault besides bumping into furniture and upsetting it, is always far too tolerant in his attitude toward the dregs of humanity. 'He thinks that if I'd drilled the distinction between right and wrong more vigorously into the minds of the Infants Bible Class, the thing wouldn't have happened.'

'I don't see why not,' said Stiffy.

Nor did I. In my opinion, no amount of Sunday afternoon instruction would have been sufficient to teach a growing boy not to throw hard-boiled eggs at Sir Watkyn Bassett.

'But there's nothing I can do about it, is there?' I said.

'You bet there is,' said Stiffy. 'We haven't lost all hope of sweetening him. The great thing is to let his nervous system gradually recover its poise, and what we came to see you about, Bertie, was to tell you on no account to go near him till he's had a chance to simmer down. Don't seek him out. Leave him alone. The sight of you does something to him.'

'No more than the sight of him does to me,' I riposted warmly. I resented the suggestion that I had nothing better to do with my time than fraternize with ex-magistrates. 'Certainly I'll avoid his society. It'll be a pleasure. Is that all?'

'That's all.'

'Then I'll be getting back to Gussie,' I said, and was starting to move off, when Stiffy uttered a sharp squeak.

'Gussie! That reminds me. There's something I wanted to tell him, something of vital concern to him, and I can't think how it slipped my mind. Gussie,' she called, and Gussie, seeming to wake abruptly from a daydream, blinked and came over. 'What are you doing hanging about here, Gussie?'

'Who, me? I was discussing something with Bertie, and he said he'd be back, when at liberty, to go into it further.'

'Well, let me tell you that you've no time for discussing things with Bertie.'

'Eh?'

'Or for saying "Eh?" I met Roderick just now, and he asked me if I knew where you were, because he wants to tear you limb from limb owing to his having seen you kiss the cook.'

Gussie's jaw fell with a dull thud.

'You never told me that,' he said to me, and one spotted the note of reproach in his voice.

'No, sorry, I forgot to mention it. But it's true. You'd better start coping. Run like a hare, is my advice.'

He took it. Standing not on the order of his going, as the fellow said, he dashed off as if shot from a gun, and was making excellent time when he was brought up short by colliding with Spode, who had at that moment entered left centre.

15

It's always disconcerting to have even as small a chap as Gussie take you squarely in the midriff, as I myself can testify, having had the same experience down in Washington Square during a visit to New York. Washington Square is bountifully supplied with sad-eyed Italian kids who whizz to and fro on roller skates, and one of them, proceeding on his way with lowered head, rammed me in the neighbourhood of the third waistcoat button at a high rate of m.p.h. It gave me a strange Where-am-I feeling, and I imagine Spode's sensations were somewhat similar. His breath escaped him in a sharp 'Oof!' and he swayed like some forest tree beneath the woodman's axe. But unfortunately Gussie had paused to sway, too, and this gave him time to steady himself on even keel and regroup his forces. Reaching out a hamlike hand, he attached it to the scruff of Gussie's neck and said 'Ha!'

'Ha!' is one of those things it's never easy to find the right reply to – it resembles 'You!' in that respect – but Gussie was saved the necessity of searching for words by the fact that he was being shaken like a cocktail in a manner that precluded speech, if precluded is the word I want. His spectacles fell off and came to rest near where I was standing. I picked them up with a view to returning them to him when he had need of them, which I could see would not be immediately.

As this Fink-Nottle was a boyhood friend, with whom, as I have said, I had frequently shared my last bar of milk chocolate, and as it was plain that if someone didn't intervene pretty soon he was in danger of having all his internal organs shaken into a sort of macédoine or hash, the thought of taking some steps to put an end to this distressing scene naturally crossed my mind. The problem presenting several points of interest was, of course, what steps to take. My tonnage was quite insufficient to enable me to engage Spode in hand-to-hand conflict, and I toyed with the idea of striking him on the back of the head with a log of wood. But this project was rendered null and void by the fact that there were no logs of wood present. These yew alleys or rhododendron walks provide twigs and fallen leaves, but nothing in the shape of logs capable of being used as clubs. And I had just decided that something might be accomplished by leaping on Spode's back and twining my arms around his neck, when I heard Stiffy cry 'Harold!'

One gathered what she was driving at. Gussie was no particular buddy of hers, but she was a tender-hearted young prune and one always likes to save a fellow creature's life, if possible. She was calling on Stinker to get into the act and save Gussie's. And a quick look at him showed me that he was at a loss to know how to proceed. He stood there passing a finger thoughtfully over his chin, like a cat in an adage.

I knew what was stopping him getting into action. It was not . . . it's on the tip of my tongue . . . begins with a p . . . I've heard Jeeves use the word . . . pusillanimity, that's it, meaning broadly that a fellow is suffering from a pronounced case of cold feet . . . it was not, as I was saying when I interrupted myself, pusillanimity that held him back. Under normal conditions lions could have taken his correspondence course, and had he encountered Spode on the football field, he would have had no hesitation in springing at his neck and twisting it into a lovers' knot. The trouble was that he was a curate, and the brass hats of the Church look askance at curates who swat the parishioners. Sock your flock, and you're sunk. So now he shrank from intervening, and when he did intervene, it was merely with the soft word that's supposed to turn away wrath.

'I say, you know, what?' he said.

I could have told him he was approaching the thing from the wrong angle. When a gorilla like Spode is letting his angry passions rise, there is little or no percentage in the mild remonstrance. Seeming to realize this, he advanced to where the blighter was now, or so it appeared, trying to strangle Gussie and laid a hand on his shoulder. Then, seeing that this, too, achieved no solid results, he pulled. There was a rending sound, and the clutching hand relaxed its grip.

I don't know if you've ever tried detaching a snow leopard of the Himalayas from its prey – probably not, as most people don't find themselves out that way much – but if you did, you would feel fairly safe in budgeting for a show of annoyance on the animal's part. It was the same with Spode. Incensed at what I suppose seemed to him this unwarrantable interference with his aims and objects, he hit Stinker on the nose, and all the doubts that had been bothering that man of God vanished in a flash.

I should imagine that if there's one thing that makes a fellow forget that he's in holy orders, it's a crisp punch on the beezer. A moment before, Stinker had been all concern about the disapproval of his superiors in the cloth, but now, as I read his mind, he was saying to himself 'To hell with my superiors in the cloth,' or however a curate would put it, 'Let them eat cake.'

It was a superb spectacle while it lasted, and I was able to understand what people meant when they spoke of the Church Militant. A good deal to my regret it did not last long. Spode was full of the will to win, but Stinker had the science. It was not for nothing that he had added a Boxing Blue to his Football Blue when at the old Alma Mater. There was a brief mix-up, and the next thing one observed was Spode on the ground, looking like a corpse which had been in the water several days. His left eye was swelling visibly, and a referee could have counted a hundred over him without eliciting a response.

Stiffy, with a brief 'At-a-boy!', led Stinker off, no doubt to bathe his nose and staunch the vital flow, which was considerable, and I handed Gussie his glasses. He stood twiddling them in a sort of trance, and I made a suggestion which I felt was in his best interests.

'Not presuming to dictate, Gussie, but wouldn't it be wise to remove yourself before Spode comes to? From what I know of him, I think he's one of those fellows who wake up cross.'

I have seldom seen anyone move quicker. We were out of the yew alley, if it was a yew alley, or the rhododendron walk, if that's what it was, almost before the words had left my lips. We continued to set a good pace, but eventually we slowed up a bit, and he was able to comment on the recent scene.

'That was a ghastly experience, Bertie,' he said.

'Can't have been at all pleasant,' I agreed.

'My whole past life seemed to flash before me.'

'That's odd. You weren't drowning.'

'No, but the principle's the same. I can tell you I was thankful when Pinker made his presence felt. What a splendid chap he is.'

'One of the best.'

'That's what today's Church needs, more curates capable of hauling off and letting fellows like Spode have it where it does most good. One feels so safe when he's around.'

I put a point which seemed to have escaped his notice.

'But he won't always be around. He has Infants Bible Classes and Mothers Meetings and all that sort of thing to occupy his time. And don't forget that Spode, though crushed to earth, will rise again.'

His jaw sagged a bit.

'I never thought of that.'

'If you take my advice, you'll clear out and go underground for a while. Stiffy would lend you her car.'

'I believe you're right,' he said, adding something about out of the mouths of babes and sucklings which I thought a bit offensive. 'I'll leave this evening.'

'Without saying goodbye.'

'Of course without saying goodbye. No, don't go that way. Keep bearing to the left. I want to go to the kitchen garden. I told Em I'd meet her there.'

'You told *who*?'

'Emerald Stoker. Who did you think I meant? She had to go to the kitchen garden and gather beans and things for tonight's dinner.'

And there, sure enough, she was with a large basin in her hands, busy about her domestic duties.

'Here's Bertie, Em,' said Gussie, and she whisked round, spilling a bean or two.

I was disturbed to see how every freckle on her face lit up as she looked at him, as if she were gazing on some lovely sight, which was far from being the case. In me she didn't seem much interested. A brief 'Hullo, Bertie' appeared to cover it as far as I was concerned, her whole attention being earmarked for Gussie. She was staring at him as a mother might have stared at a loved child who had shown up at the home after a clash with one of the neighbourhood children. Until then I had been too agitated to notice how dishevelled his encounter with Spode had left him, but I now saw that his general appearance was that of something that has been passed through a wringer.

'What . . . *what* have you been doing to yourself?' she ejaculated, if that's the word. 'You look like a devastated area.'

'Inevitable in the circs,' I said. 'He's been having a spot of unpleasantness with Spode.'

'Is that the man you were telling me about? The human gorilla?'

'That's the one.'

'What happened?'

'Spode tried to shake the stuffing out of him.'

'You poor precious lambkin,' said Emerald, addressing Gussie, not me. 'Gosh, I wish I had him here for a minute. I'd teach him!'

And by what I have always thought an odd coincidence her wish was granted. A crashing sound like that made by a herd of hippopotami going through the reeds on a river bank attracted my notice and I beheld Spode approaching at a rate of knots with the obvious intention of resuming at as early a date as possible his investigations into the colour of Gussie's insides which Stinker's intervention had compelled him to file under the head of unfinished business. In predicting that this menace, though crushed to earth, would rise again, I had been perfectly correct.

There seemed to me a strong resemblance in the newcomer's manner to that of those Assyrians who, so we learn from sources close to them, came down like a wolf on the fold with their cohorts all gleaming with purple and gold. He could have walked straight into their camp, and they would have laid down the red carpet for him, recognizing him instantly as one of the boys.

But where the Assyrians had had the bulge on him was that they weren't going to find in the fold a motherly young woman with strong wrists and a basin in her hands. This basin appeared to be constructed of some thickish form of china, and as Spode grabbed Gussie and started to go into the old shaking routine it descended on the back of his head with what some call a dull and others a sickening thud. It broke into several fragments, but by that time its mission had been accomplished. His powers of resistance sapped, no doubt, by his recent encounter with the Rev. H.P. Pinker, Spode fell to earth he knew not where and lay there looking peaceful. I remember thinking at the time that this was not his lucky day, and it just showed, I thought, that it's always a mistake to be a louse in human shape, as he had been from birth, because sooner or later retribution is bound to overtake you. As I recall Jeeves putting it once, the mills of God grind slowly, but they grind exceeding small, or words to that effect.

For a space Emerald Stoker stood surveying her handiwork with a satisfied smile on her face, and I didn't blame her for looking a bit smug, for she had unquestionably fought the good fight. Then suddenly, with a quick 'Oh, golly!' she was off like a nymph surprised while bathing, and a moment later I understood what had caused this mobility. She had seen Madeline Bassett approaching, and no cook likes to have to explain to her employer why she has been bonneting her employer's guests with china basins.

As Madeline's eyes fell on the remains, they widened to the size of golf balls and she looked at Gussie as if he had been a mass murderer she wasn't very fond of.

'What have you been doing to Roderick?' she demanded.

'Eh?' said Gussie.

'I said, What have you done to Roderick?'

Gussie adjusted his spectacles and shrugged a shoulder.

'Oh, that? I merely chastised him. The fellow had only himself to blame. He asked for it, and I had to teach him a lesson.'

'You brute!'

'Not at all. He had the option of withdrawing. He must have foreseen what would happen when he saw me remove my glasses. When I remove my glasses, those who know what's good for them take to the hills.'

'I hate you, I hate you!' cried Madeline, a thing I didn't know anyone ever said except in the second act of a musical comedy.

'You do?' said Gussie.

'Yes, I do. I loathe you.'

'Then in that case,' said Gussie, 'I shall now eat a ham sandwich.'

And this he proceeded to do with a sort of wolfish gusto that sent cold shivers down my spine, and Madeline shrieked sharply.

'This is the end!' she said, another thing you don't often hear.

When things between two once loving hearts have hotted up to this extent, it is always the prudent course for the innocent bystander to edge away, and this I did. I started back to the house, and in the drive I met Jeeves. He was at the wheel of Stiffy's car. Beside him, looking like a Scotch elder rebuking sin, was the dog Bartholomew.

'Good evening, sir,' he said. 'I have been taking this little fellow to the veterinary surgeon. Miss Byng was uneasy because he bit Mr. Fink-Nottle. She was afraid he might have caught something. I am glad to say the surgeon has given him a clean bill of health.'

'Jeeves,' I said, 'I have a tale of horror to relate.'

'Indeed, sir?'

'The lute is mute,' I said, and as briefly as possible put him in possession of the facts. When I had finished, he agreed that it was most disturbing.

'But I fear there is nothing to be done, sir.'

I reeled. I have grown so accustomed to seeing Jeeves solve every problem, however sticky, that this frank confession of his inability to deliver the goods unmanned me.

'You're baffled?'

'Yes, sir.'

'At a loss?'

'Precisely, sir. Possibly at some future date a means of adjusting matters will occur to me, but at the moment, I regret to say, I can think of nothing. I am sorry, sir.'

I shrugged the shoulders. The iron had entered into my soul, but the upper lip was stiff.

'It's all right, Jeeves. Not your fault if a thing like this lays you a stymie. Drive on, Jeeves,' I said, and he drove on. The dog Bartholomew gave me an unpleasantly superior look as they moved off, as if asking me if I were saved.

I pushed along to my room, the only spot in this joint of terror where anything in the nature of peace and quiet was to be had, not that even there one got much of it. The fierce rush of life at Totleigh Towers had got me down, and I wanted to be alone.

I suppose I must have sat there for more than half an hour, trying to think what was to be done for the best, and then out of what I have heard Jeeves describe as the welter of emotions one coherent thought emerged, and that was that if I didn't shortly get a snifter, I would expire in my tracks. It was now the cocktail hour, and I knew that, whatever his faults, Sir Watkyn Bassett provided aperitifs for his guests. True, I had promised Stiffy that I would avoid his society, but I had not anticipated then that this emergency would arise. It was a straight choice between betraying her trust and perishing where I sat, and I decided on the former alternative.

I found Pop Bassett in the drawing-room with a well-laden tray at his elbow and hurried forward, licking my lips. To say that he looked glad to see me would be overstating it, but he offered me a life-saver and I accepted it gratefully. An awkward silence of about twenty minutes followed, and then, just as I had finished my second and was fishing for the olive, Stiffy entered. She gave me a quick reproachful look, and I could see that her trust in Bertram's promises would never be the same again, but it was to Pop Bassett that she directed her attention.

'Hullo, Uncle Watkyn.'

'Good evening, my dear.'

'Having a spot before dinner?'

'I am.'

'You think you are,' said Stiffy, 'but you aren't, and I'll tell you why. There isn't going to be any dinner. The cook's eloped with Gussie Fink-Nottle.'

16

I wonder if you have ever noticed a rather peculiar thing, viz. how differently the same news item can affect two different people? I mean, you tell something to Jones and Brown, let us say, and while Jones sits plunged in gloom and looking licked to a splinter, Brown gives three rousing cheers and goes into a buck-and-wing dance. And the same thing is true of Smith and Robinson. Often struck me as curious, that has.

It was so now. Listening to the recent heated exchanges between Madeline Bassett and Gussie hadn't left me what you might call optimistic, but the heart bowed down with weight of woe to weakest hope will cling, as the fellow said, and I had tried to tell myself that their mutual love, though admittedly having taken it on the chin at the moment, might eventually get cracking again, causing all to be forgotten and forgiven. I mean to say, remorse has frequently been known to set in after a dust-up between a couple of troth-plighters, with all that Sorry-I-was-cross and Can-you-ever-forgive-me stuff, and love, after being down in the cellar for a time with no takers, perks up and carries on again as good as new. Oh, blessings on the falling-out that all the more endears is the way I heard Jeeves put it once.

But at Stiffy's words this hope collapsed as if it had been struck on the back of the head with a china basin containing beans, and I sank forward in my chair, the face buried in the hands. It is always my policy to look on the bright side, but in order to do this you have to have a bright side to look on, and under existing conditions there wasn't one. This, as Madeline Bassett would have said, was the end. I had come to this house as a raisonneur to bring the young folks together, but however much of a raisonneur you are, you can't bring young folks together if one of them elopes with somebody else. You are not merely hampered, but shackled. So now, as I say, I sank forward in my chair, the f. buried in the h.

To Pop Bassett, on the other hand, this bit of front page news had plainly come as rare and refreshing fruit. My face being buried as stated, I couldn't see if he went into a buck-and-wing dance, but I should think it highly probable that he did a step or two, for when he spoke you could tell from the timbre of his voice that he was feeling about as pepped up as a man can feel without bursting.

One could understand his fizziness, of course. Of all the prospective sons-in-law in existence, Gussie, with the possible exception of Bertram Wooster, was the one he would have chosen last. He had viewed him with concern from the start, and if he had been living back in the days when fathers called the shots in the matter of their daughters' marriages, would have forbidden the banns without a second thought.

Gussie once told me that when he, Gussie, was introduced to him, Bassett, as the fellow who was to marry his, Bassett's, offspring, he, Bassett, had stared at him with his jaw dropping and then in a sort of strangled voice had said '*What!*' Incredulously, if you see what I mean, as if he were hoping that they were just playing a jolly practical joke on him and that in due course the real chap would jump out from behind a chair and say 'April fool!' And when he, Bassett, at last got on to it that there was no deception and that Gussie was really what he had drawn, he went off into a corner and sat there motionless, refusing to speak when spoken to.

Little wonder, then, that Stiffy's announcement had bucked him up like a dose of Doctor Somebody's Tonic Swamp Juice, which acts directly on the red corpuscles and imparts a gentle glow.

'Eloped?' he gurgled.

'That's right.'

'With the cook?'

'With none other. That's why I said there wasn't going to be any dinner. We shall have to make do with hard-boiled eggs, if there are any left over from the treat.'

The mention of hard-boiled eggs made Pop Bassett wince for a moment, and one could see that his thoughts had flitted back to the tea tent, but he was far too happy to allow sad memories to trouble him for long. With a wave of the hand he dismissed dinner as something that didn't matter one way or the other. The Bassetts, the wave suggested, could rough it if they had to.

'Are you sure of your facts, my dear?'

'I met them as they were starting off. Gussie said he hoped I wouldn't mind him borrowing my car.'

'You reassured him, I trust?'

'Oh, yes. I said "That's all right, Gussie. Help yourself." '

'Good girl. Good girl. An excellent response. Then they have really gone?'

'With the wind.'

'And they plan to get married?'

'As soon as Gussie can get a special licence. You have to apply to the Archbishop of Canterbury, and I'm told he stings you for quite a bit.'

'Money well spent.'

'That's how Gussie feels. He told me he was dropping the cook at Bertie's aunt's place and then going on to London to confer with the Archbish. He's full of zeal.'

This extraordinary statement that Gussie was landing Emerald Stoker on Aunt Dahlia brought my head up with a jerk. I found myself speculating on how the old flesh-and-blood was going to take the intrusion, and it gave me rather an awed feeling to think how deep Gussie's love for his Em must be, to make him face such fearful risks. The aged relative has a strong personality and finds no difficulty, when displeased, in reducing the object of her displeasure to a spot of grease in a matter of minutes. I am told that sportsmen whom in her hunting days she had occasion to rebuke for riding over hounds were never the same again and for months would go about in a sort of stupor, starting at sudden noises.

My head being now up, I was able to see Pop Bassett, and I found that he was regarding me with an eye so benevolent that I could hardly believe that this was the same ex-magistrate with whom I had so recently been hobnobbing, if you can call it hobnobbing when a couple of fellows sit in a couple of chairs for twenty minutes without saying a word to each other. It was plain that joy had made him the friend of all the world, even to the extent of allowing him to look at Bertram without a shudder. He was more like something out of Dickens than anything human.

'Your glass is empty, Mr. Wooster,' he cried buoyantly, 'may I refill it?'

I said he might. I had had two, which is generally my limit, but with my aplomb shattered as it was I felt that a third wouldn't hurt. Indeed, I would have been willing to go even more deeply into the thing. I once read about a man who used to drink twenty-six martinis before dinner, and the conviction was beginning to steal over me that he had had the right idea.

'Roderick tells me,' he proceeded, as sunny as if a crack of his had been greeted with laughter in court, 'that the reason you were unable to be with us at the school treat this afternoon was that urgent family business called you to Brinkley Court. I trust everything turned out satisfactorily?'

'Oh yes, thanks.'

'We all missed you, but business before pleasure, of course. How was your uncle? You found him well, I hope?'

'Yes, he was fine.'

'And your aunt?'

'She had gone to London.'

'Indeed? You must have been sorry not to have seen her. I know few women I admire more. So hospitable. So breezy. I have seldom enjoyed anything more than my recent visit to her house.'

I think his exuberance would have led him to continue in the same strain indefinitely, but at this point Stiffy came out of the thoughtful silence into which she had fallen. She had been standing there regarding him with a speculative eye, as if debating within herself whether or not to start something, and now she gave the impression that her mind was made up.

'I'm glad to see you so cheerful, Uncle Watkyn. I was afraid my news might have upset you.'

'Upset me!' said Pop Bassett incredulously. 'Whatever put that idea in your head?'

'Well, you're short one son-in-law.'

'It is precisely that that has made this the happiest day of my life.'

'Then you can make it the happiest of mine,' said Stiffy, striking while the iron was h. 'By giving Harold that vicarage.'

Most of my attention, as you may well imagine, being concentrated on contemplating the soup in which I was immersed, I cannot say whether or not Pop Bassett hesitated, but if he did, it was only for an instant. No doubt for a second or two the vision of that hard-boiled egg rose before him and he was conscious again of the resentment he had been feeling at Stinker's failure to keep a firm hand on the junior members of his flock, but the thought that Augustus Fink-Nottle was not to be his son-in-law drove the young cleric's shortcomings from his mind. Filled with the milk of human kindness so nearly to the brim that you could almost hear it sloshing about inside him, he was in no shape to deny anyone anything. I really believe that if at this point in the proceedings I had tried to touch him for a fiver, he would have parted without a cry.

'Of course, of course, of course, of course,' he said, carolling like one of Jeeves's larks on the wing. 'I am sure that Pinker will make an excellent vicar.'

'The best,' said Stiffy. 'He's wasted as a curate. No scope. Running under wraps. Unleash him as a vicar, and he'll be the talk of the Established Church. He's as hot as a pistol.'

'I have always had the highest opinion of Harold Pinker.'

'I'm not surprised. All the nibs feel the same. They know he's got what it takes. Very sound on doctrine, and can preach like a streak.'

'Yes, I enjoy his sermons. Manly and straightforward.'

'That's because he's one of these healthy outdoor open air men. Muscular Christianity, that's his dish. He used to play football for England.'

'Indeed?'

'He was what's called a prop forward.'

'Really?'

At the words 'prop forward' I had, of course, started visibly. I hadn't known that that's what Stinker was, and I was thinking how ironical life could be. I mean to say, there was Plank searching high and low for a forward of this nature, saying to himself that he would pretty soon have to give up the hopeless quest, and here was I in a position to fill the bill for him, but owing to the strained condition of our relations unable to put him on to this good thing. Very sad, I felt, and the thought occurred to me, as it had often done before, that one ought to be kind even to the very humblest, because you never know when they may not come in useful.

'Then may I tell Harold that the balloon's going up?' said Stiffy.

'I beg your pardon?'

'I mean it's official about this vicarage?'

'Certainly, certainly, certainly.'

'Oh, Uncle Watkyn! How can I thank you?'

'Quite all right, my dear,' said Pop Bassett, more Dickensy than ever. 'And now,' he went on, parting from his moorings and making for the door, 'you will excuse me, Stephanie, and you, Mr. Wooster. I must go to Madeline and –'

'Congratulate her?'

'I was about to say dry her tears.'

'If any.'

'You think she will not be in a state of dejection?'

'Would any girl be, who's been saved by a miracle from having to marry Gussie Fink-Nottle?'

'True. Very true,' said Pop Bassett, and he was out of the room like one of those wing threequarters who, even if they can't learn to give the reverse pass, are fast.

If there had been any uncertainty as to whether Sir Watkyn Bassett had done a buck-and-wing dance, there was none about Stiffy doing one now. She pirouetted freely, and the dullest eye could discern that it was only the fact that she hadn't one on that kept her from strewing roses from her hat. I had seldom seen a young shrimp so above herself. And I, having Stinker's best interests at heart, packed all my troubles in the old kitbag for the time being and rejoiced with her. If there's one thing Bertram Wooster is and always has been nippy at, it's forgetting his personal worries when a pal is celebrating some stroke of good fortune.

For some time Stiffy monopolized the conversation, not letting me get a word in edgeways. Women are singularly gifted in this respect. The frailest of them has the lung power of a gramophone record and the flow of speech of a Regimental Sergeant Major. I have known my Aunt Agatha to go on calling me names long after you would have supposed that both breath and inventiveness would have given out.

Her theme was the stupendous bit of good luck which was about to befall Stinker's new parishioners, for they would be getting not only the perfect vicar, a saintly character who would do the square thing by their souls, but in addition the sort of vicar's wife you dream about. It was only when she paused after drawing a picture of herself doling out soup to the deserving poor and asking in a gentle voice after their rheumatism that I was able to rise to a point of order. In the midst of all the joyfulness and back-slapping a sobering thought had occurred to me.

'I agree with you,' I said, 'that this would appear to be the happy ending, and I can quite see how you have arrived at the conclusion that it's the maddest merriest day of all the glad new year, but there's something you ought to give a thought to, and it seems to me you're overlooking it.'

'What's that? I didn't think I'd missed anything.'

'This promise of Pop Bassett's to give you the vicarage.'

'All in order, surely? What's your kick?'

'I was only thinking that, if I were you, I'd get it in writing.'

This stopped her as if she had bumped into a prop forward. The ecstatic animation faded from her face, to be replaced by the anxious look and the quick chewing of the lower lip. It was plain that I had given her food for thought.

'You don't think Uncle Watkyn would double-cross us?'

'There are no limits to what your foul Uncle Watkyn can do, if the mood takes him,' I responded gravely. 'I wouldn't trust him an inch. Where's Stinker?'

'Out on the lawn, I think.'

'Then get hold of him and bring him here and have Pop Bassett embody the thing in the form of a letter.'

'I suppose you know you're making my flesh creep?'

'Merely pointing out the road to safety.'

She mused awhile, and the lower lip got a bit more chewing done to it.

'All right,' she said at length. 'I'll fetch Harold.'

'And it wouldn't hurt to bring a couple of lawyers, too,' I said as she whizzed past me.

It was about five minutes later, as I was falling into a reverie and brooding once more on the extreme stickiness of my affairs, that Jeeves came in and told me I was wanted on the telephone.

17

I paled beneath my tan.

'Who is it, Jeeves?'

'Mrs. Travers, sir.'

Precisely what I had feared. It was, as I have indicated, an easy drive from Totleigh Towers to Brinkley Court and in his exhilarated state Gussie would no doubt have kept a firm foot on the accelerator and given the machine all the gas at his disposal. I presumed that he and girl friend must have just arrived, and that this telephone call was Aunt Dahlia what-the-helling. Knowing how keenly the old bean resented being the recipient of anything in the nature of funny business, into which category Gussie's butting in uninvited with his Em in attendance would unquestionably fall, I braced myself for the coming storm with as much fortitude as I could muster.

You might say, of course, that his rash act was no fault of mine and had nothing to do with me, but it's practically routine for aunts to blame nephews for everything that happens. It seems to be what nephews are for. It was only by an oversight, I have always felt, that my Aunt Agatha omitted to hold me responsible a year or two ago when her son, young Thos, nearly got sacked from the scholastic institution which he attends for breaking out at night in order to go and shy for coconuts at the local amusement park.

'How did she seem, Jeeves?'

'Sir?'

'Did she give you the impression that she was splitting a gusset?'

'Not particularly, sir. Mrs. Travers's voice is always robust. Would there be any reason why she should be splitting the gusset to which you refer?'

'You bet there would. No time to tell you now, but the skies are darkening and the air is full of V-shaped depressions off the coast of Iceland.'

'I am sorry, sir.'

'Nor are you the only one. Who was the fellow – or fellows, for I believe there was more than one – who went into the burning fiery furnace?'

'Shadrach, Meshach and Abednego, sir.'

'That's right. The names were on the tip of my tongue. I read about them when I won my Scripture Knowledge prize at school. Well, I know just how they must have felt. Aunt Dahlia?' I said, for I had now reached the instrument.

I had been expecting to have my ear scorched with well-chosen words, but to my surprise she seemed in merry mood. There was no suggestion of recrimination in her voice.

'Hullo there, you young menace to western civilization,' she boomed. 'How are you? Still ticking over?'

'To a certain extent. And you?'

'I'm fine. Did I interrupt you in the middle of your tenth cocktail?'

'My third,' I corrected. 'I usually stay steady at two, but Pop Bassett insisted on replenishing my glass. He's a bit above himself at the moment and very much the master of the revels. I wouldn't put it past him to have an ox roasted whole in the market place, if he can find an ox.'

'Stinko, is he?'

'Not perhaps stinko, but certainly effervescent.'

'Well, if you can suspend your drunken orgy for a minute or two, I'll tell you the news from home. I got back from London a quarter of an hour ago, and what do you think I found waiting on the mat? That newt-collecting freak Spink-Bottle, accompanied by a girl who looks like a Pekinese with freckles.'

I drew a deep breath and embarked on my speech for the defence. If Bertram was to be put in the right light, now was the moment. True, her manner so far had been affable and she had given no sign of being about to go off with a bang, but one couldn't be sure that that wasn't because she was just biding her time. It's never safe to dismiss aunts lightly at times like this.

'Yes,' I said, 'I heard he was on his way, complete with freckled human Pekinese. I am sorry, Aunt Dahlia, that you should have been subjected to this unwarrantable intrusion, and I would like to make it abundantly clear that it was not the outcome of any advice or encouragement from me. I was in total ignorance of his intentions. Had he confided in me his purpose of inflicting his presence on you, I should have –'

Here I paused, for she had asked me rather brusquely to put a sock in it.

'Stop babbling, you ghastly young gas-bag. What's all this silver-tongued-orator stuff about?'

'I was merely expressing my regret that you should have been subjected –'

'Well, don't. There's no need to apologize. I couldn't be more pleased. I admit that I'm always happier when I don't have Spink-Bottle breathing down the back of my neck and taking up space in the house which I require for other purposes, but the girl was as welcome as manna in the wilderness.'

Having won that prize for Scripture Knowledge I was speaking of, I had no difficulty in grasping her allusion. She was referring to an incident which occurred when the children of Israel were crossing some desert or other and were sorely in need of refreshment, rations being on the slender side. And they were just saying to one another how well a spot of manna would go down and regretting that there was none in the quartermaster's stores, when blowed if a whole wad of the stuff didn't descend from the skies, just making their day.

Her words had of course surprised me somewhat, and I asked her why Emerald Stoker had been as welcome as manna in the w.

'Because her arrival brought sunshine into a stricken home. There couldn't have been a smoother piece of timing. You didn't see Anatole when you were over here this afternoon, did you?'

'No. Why?'

'I was wondering if you had noticed anything wrong with him. Shortly after you left he developed a *mal au foie* or whatever he called it and took to his bed.'

'I'm sorry.'

'So was Tom. He was looking forward gloomily to a dinner cooked by the kitchen maid, who, though a girl of many sterling merits, always adopts the scorched earth policy when preparing a meal, and you know what his digestion's like. Conditions looked dark, and then Spink-Bottle suddenly revealed that this Pekinese of his was an experienced chef, and she's taken over. Who is she? Do you know anything about her?'

I was, of course, able to supply the desired information.

'She's the daughter of a well-to-do American millionaire called Stoker, who, I imagine, will be full of strange oaths when he hears she's married Gussie, the latter being, as you will concede, not everybody's cup of tea.'

'So he isn't going to marry Madeline Bassett?'

'No, the fixture has been scratched.'

'That's definite, is it?'

'Yes.'

'You can't have been much success as a raisonneur.'

'No.'

'Well, I think she'll make Spink-Bottle a good wife. Seems a very nice girl.'

'Few better.'

'But this leaves you in rather a spot, doesn't it? If Madeline Bassett is now at large, won't she expect you to fill in?'

'That, aged relative, is the fear that haunts me.'

'Has Jeeves nothing to suggest?'

'He says he hasn't. But I've known him on previous occasions to be temporarily baffled and then suddenly to wave his magic wand and fix everything up. So I haven't entirely lost hope.'

'No, I expect you'll wriggle out of it somehow, as you always do. I wish I had a fiver for every time you've been within a step of the altar rails and have managed to escape unscathed. I remember you telling me once that you had faith in your star.'

'Quite. Still, it's no good trying to pretend that peril doesn't loom. It looms like the dickens. The corner in which I find myself is tight.'

'And you would like to get that way, too, I suppose? All right, you can get back to your orgy when I've told you why I rang you up.'

'Haven't you?' I said, surprised.

'Certainly not. You don't catch me wasting time and money chatting with you about your amours. Here is the nub. You know that black amber thing of Bassett's?'

'The statuette? Of course.'

'I want to buy it for Tom. I've come into a bit of money. The reason I went to London today was to see my lawyer about a legacy someone's left me. Old school friend, if that's of any interest to you. It works out at about a couple of thousand quid, and I want you to get that statuette for me.'

'It's going to be pretty hard to get away with it.'

'Oh, you'll manage. Go as high as fifteen hundred pounds, if you have to. I suppose you couldn't just slip it in your pocket? It would save a lot of overhead. But probably that's asking too much of you, so tackle Bassett and get him to sell it.'

'Well, I'll do my best. I know how much Uncle Tom covets that statuette. Rely on me, Aunt Dahlia.'

'That's my boy.'

I returned to the drawing-room in somewhat pensive mood, for my relations with Pop Bassett were such that it was going to be embarrassing trying to do business with him, but I was relieved that the aged relative had dismissed the idea of purloining the thing. Surprised, too, as well as relieved, because the stern lesson association with her over the years has taught me is that when she wants to do a loved husband a good turn, she is seldom fussy about the methods employed to that end. It was she who had initiated, if that's the word I want, the theft of the cow-creamer, and you would have thought she would have wanted to save money on the current deal. Her view has always been that if a collector pinches something from another collector, it doesn't count as stealing, and of course there may be something in it. Pop Bassett, when at Brinkley, would unquestionably have looted Uncle Tom's collection, had he not been closely watched. These collectors have about as much conscience as the smash-and-grab fellows for whom the police are always spreading dragnets.

I was musing along these lines and trying to think what would be the best way of approaching Pop, handicapped as I would be by the fact that he shuddered like a jelly in a high wind every time he saw me and preferred when in my presence to sit and stare before him without uttering, when the door opened, and Spode came in.

18

The first thing that impressed itself on the senses was that he had about as spectacular a black eye as you could meet with in a month of Sundays, and I found myself at a momentary loss to decide how it was best to react to it. I mean, some fellows with bunged-up eyes want sympathy, others prefer that you pretend that you've noticed nothing unusual in their appearance. I came to the conclusion that it was wisest to greet him with a careless 'Ah, Spode,' and I did so, though I suppose, looking back, that 'Ah, Sidcup' would have been more suitable, and it was as I spoke that I became aware that he was glaring at me in a sinister manner with the eye that wasn't closed. I have spoken of these eyes of his as being capable of opening an oyster at sixty paces, and even when only one of them was functioning the impact of his gaze was disquieting. I have known my Aunt Agatha's gaze to affect me in the same way.

'I was looking for you, Wooster,' he said.

He uttered the words in the unpleasant rasping voice which had once kept his followers on the jump. Before succeeding to his new title he had been one of those Dictators who were fairly common at one time in the metropolis, and had gone about with a mob of underlings wearing black shorts and shouting 'Heil, Spode!' or words along those general lines. He gave it up when he became Lord Sidcup, but he was still apt to address all and sundry as if he were ticking off some erring member of his entourage whose shorts had got a patch on them.

'Oh, were you?' I said.

'I was.' He paused for a moment, continuing to give me the eye, then he said 'So!'

'So!' is another of those things, like 'You!' and 'Ha!', which it's never easy to find the right answer to. Nothing in the way of a come-back suggested itself to me, so I merely lit a cigarette in what I intended to be a nonchalant manner, though I may have missed it by a considerable margin, and he proceeded.

'So I was right!'

'Eh?'

'In my suspicions.'

'Eh?'

'They have been confirmed.'

'Eh?'

'Stop saying "Eh?", you miserable worm, and listen to me.'

I humoured him. You might have supposed that having so recently seen him knocked base over apex by the Rev. H.P. Pinker and subsequently laid out cold by Emerald Stoker and her basin of beans I would have regarded him with contempt as pretty small-time stuff and rebuked him sharply for calling me a miserable worm, but the idea never so much as crossed my mind. He had suffered reverses, true, but they had left him with his spirit unbroken and the muscles of his brawny arms just as much like iron bands as they had always been, and the way I looked at it was that if he wanted me to go easy on the word 'Eh?' he had only to say so.

Continuing to pierce me with the eye that was still on duty, he said:

'I happened to be passing through the hall just now.'

'Oh?'

'I heard you talking on the telephone.'

'Oh?'

'You were speaking to your aunt.'

'Oh?'

'Don't keep saying "Oh?", blast you.'

Well, these restrictions were making it a bit hard for me to hold up my end of the conversation, but there seemed nothing to be done about it. I maintained a rather dignified silence, and he resumed his remarks.

'Your aunt was urging you to steal Sir Watkyn's amber statuette.'

'She wasn't!'

'Pardon me. I thought you would try to deny the charge, so I took the precaution of jotting down your actual words. The statuette was mentioned and you said "It's going to be pretty hard to get away with it." She then presumably urged you to spare no effort, for you said "Well, I'll do my best. I know how much Uncle Tom covets that statuette. Rely on me, Aunt Dahlia." What the devil are you gargling about?'

'Not gargling,' I corrected. 'Laughing lightly. Because you've got the whole thing wrong, though I must say the way you've managed to record the dialogue does you a good deal of credit. Do you use shorthand?'

'How do you mean I've got it wrong?'

'Aunt Dahlia was asking me to try to buy the thing from Sir Watkyn.'

He snorted and said 'Ha!' and I thought it a bit unjust that he should say 'Ha!' if I wasn't allowed to say 'Eh?' and 'Oh?' There should always be a certain give and take in these matters, or where are you?

'Do you expect me to believe that?'

'Don't you believe it?'

'No, I don't. I'm not an ass.'

This, of course, was a debatable point, as I once heard Jeeves describe it, but I didn't press it.

'I know that aunt of yours,' he proceeded. 'She would steal the filling out of your back teeth if she thought she could do it without detection.' He paused for a moment, and I knew that he was thinking of the cow-creamer. He had always – and, I must admit, not without reason – suspected the old flesh-and-blood of being the motive force behind its disappearance, and I imagine it had been a nasty knock to him that nothing could be proved. 'Well, I strongly advise you, Wooster, not to let her make a catspaw of you this time, because if you're caught, as you certainly will be, you'll be for it. Don't think that Sir Watkyn will hush the thing up to avoid a scandal. You'll go to prison, that's where you'll go. He dislikes you intensely, and nothing would please him more than to be able to give you a long stretch without the option.'

I thought this showed a vindictive spirit in the old wart hog and one that I deplored, but I felt it would be injudicious to say so. I merely nodded understandingly. I was thankful that there was no danger of this contingency, as Jeeves would have called it, arising. Strong in the knowledge that nothing would induce me to pinch their ruddy statuette, I was able to remain calm and nonchalant, or as calm and nonchalant as you can be when a fellow eight foot six in height with one eye bunged up and the other behaving like an oxyacetylene blowpipe is glaring at you.

'Yes, sir,' said Spode, 'it'll be chokey for you.'

And he was going on to say that he would derive great pleasure from coming on visiting days and making faces at me through the bars, when Pop Bassett returned.

But a very different Bassett from the fizzy rejoicer who had exited so short a while before. Then he had been all buck and beans, as any father would have been whose daughter was not going to marry Gussie Fink-Nottle. Now his face was drawn and his general demeanour that of an incautious luncher who discovers when there is no time to draw back that he has swallowed a rather too elderly oyster.

'Madeline tells me,' he began. Then he saw Spode's eye, and broke off. It was the sort of eye which, even if you have a lot on your mind, you can't help noticing. 'Good gracious, Roderick,' he said, 'did you have a fall?'

'Fall, my foot,' said Spode, 'I was socked by a curate.'

'Good heavens! What curate?'

'There's only one in these parts, isn't there?'

'You mean you were assaulted by Mr. Pinker? You astound me, Roderick.'

Spode spoke with genuine feeling.

'Not half as much as he astounded *me*. He was more or less of a revelation to me, I don't mind telling you, because I didn't know curates had left hooks like that. He's got a knack of feinting you off balance and then coming in with a sort of corkscrew punch which it's impossible not to admire. I must get him to teach it to me some time.'

'You speak as though you bore him no animosity.'

'Of course I don't. A very pleasant little scrap with no ill feeling on either side. I've nothing against Pinker. The one I've got it in for is the cook. She beaned me with a china basin. From behind, of all unsporting things. If you'll excuse me, I'll go and have a word with that cook.'

He was so obviously looking forward to telling Emerald Stoker what he thought of her that it gave me quite a pang to have to break it to him that his errand would be bootless.

'You can't,' I pointed out. 'She is no longer with us.'

'Don't be an ass. She's in the kitchen, isn't she?'

'I'm sorry, no. She's eloped with Gussie Fink-Nottle. A wedding has been arranged and will take place as soon as the Archbish of Canterbury lets him have a special licence.'

Spode reeled. He had only one eye to stare at me with, but he got all the mileage out of it that was possible.

'Is that true?'

'Absolutely.'

'Well, that makes up for everything. If Madeline's back in circulation . . . Thank you for telling me, Wooster, old chap.'

'Don't mention it, Spode, old man, or, rather, Lord Sidcup, old man.'

For the first time Pop Bassett appeared to become aware that the slight, distinguished-looking young fellow standing on one leg by the sofa was Bertram.

'Mr. Wooster,' he said. Then he stopped, swallowed once or twice and groped his way to the table where the drinks were. His manner was feverish. Having passed a liberal snootful down the hatch, he was able to resume. 'I have just seen Madeline.'

'Oh, yes?' I said courteously. 'How is she?'

'Off her head, in my opinion. She says she is going to marry you.'

Well, I had more or less steeled myself to something along these lines, so except for quivering like a stricken blancmange and letting my lower jaw fall perhaps six inches I betrayed no sign of discompo-sure, in which respect I differed radically from Spode, who reeled for the second time and uttered a cry like that of a cinnamon bear that has stubbed its toe on a passing rock.

'You're joking!'

Pop Bassett shook his head regretfully. His face was haggard.

'I wish I were, Roderick. I am not surprised that you are upset. I feel the same myself. I am distraught. I can see no light on the horizon. When she told me, it was as if I had been struck by a thunderbolt.'

Spode was staring at me, aghast. Even now, it seemed, he was unable to take in the full horror of the situation. There was incredulity in his one good eye.

'But she can't marry *that*!'

'She seems resolved to.'

'But he's worse than that fishfaced blighter.'

'I agree with you. Far worse. No comparison.'

'I'll go and talk to her,' said Spode, and left us before I could express my resentment at being called *that*.

It was perhaps fortunate that only half a minute later Stiffy and Stinker entered, for if I had been left alone with Pop Bassett, I would have been hard put to it to hit on a topic of conversation calculated to interest, elevate and amuse.

19

Stinker's nose, as was only to be expected, had swollen a good deal since last heard from, but he seemed in excellent spirits, and Stiffy couldn't have been merrier and brighter. Both were obviously thinking in terms of the happy ending, and my heart bled freely for the unfortunate young slobs. I had observed Pop Bassett closely while Spode was telling him about Stinker's left hook, and what I had read on his countenance had not been encouraging.

These patrons of livings with vicarages to bestow always hold rather rigid views as regards the qualifications they demand from the curates they are thinking of promoting to fields of higher activity, and left hooks, however adroit, are not among them. If Pop Bassett had been a fight promoter on the look-out for talent and Stinker a promising novice anxious to be put on his next programme for a six-round preliminary bout, he would no doubt have gazed on him with a kindly eye. As it was, the eye he was now directing at him was as cold and bleak as if an old crony had been standing before him in the dock, charged with having moved pigs without a permit or failed to abate a smoky chimney. I could see trouble looming, and I wouldn't have risked a bet on the happy e. even at the most liberal odds.

The stickiness of the atmosphere, so patent to my keener sense, had not communicated itself to Stiffy. No voice was whispering in her ear that she was about to be let down with a thud which would jar her to the back teeth. She was all smiles and viv-whatever-the-word-is, plainly convinced that the signing on the dotted line was now a mere formality.

'Here we are, Uncle Watkyn,' she said, beaming freely.

'So I see.'

'I've brought Harold.'

'So I perceive.'

'We've talked it over, and we think we ought to have the thing embodied in the form of a letter.'

Pop Bassett's eye grew colder and bleaker, and the feeling I had that we were all back in Bosher Street police court deepened. Nothing, it seemed to me, was needed to complete the illusion except a magistrate's clerk with a cold in the head, a fug you could cut with a knife and a few young barristers hanging about hoping for dock briefs.

'I fear I do not understand you,' he said.

'Oh, come, Uncle Watkyn, you know you're brighter than that. I'm talking about Harold's vicarage.'

'I was not aware that Mr. Pinker had a vicarage.'

'The one you're going to give him, I mean.'

'Oh?' said Pop Bassett, and I have seldom heard an 'Oh?' that had a nastier sound. 'I have just seen Roderick,' he added, getting down to the *res*.

At the mention of Spode's name Stiffy giggled, and I could have told her it was a mistake. There is a time for girlish frivolity, and a time when it is misplaced. It had not escaped my notice that Pop Bassett had begun to swell like one of those curious circular fish you catch down in Florida, and in addition to this he was rumbling as I imagine volcanoes do before starting in on the neighbouring house-holders and making them wish they had settled elsewhere.

But even now Stiffy seemed to have no sense of impending doom. She uttered another silvery laugh. I've noticed this slowness in getting hep to atmospheric conditions in other girls. The young of the gentler sex never appear to realize that there are moments when the last thing required by their audience is the silvery laugh.

'I'll bet he had a shiner.'

'I beg your pardon?'

'Was his eye black?'

'It was.'

'I thought it would be. Harold's strength is as the strength of ten, because his heart is pure. Well, how about that embodying letter? I have a fountain pen. Let's get the show on the road.'

I was expecting Pop Bassett to give an impersonation of a bomb falling on an ammunition dump, but he didn't. Instead, he continued to exhibit that sort of chilly stiffness which you see in magistrates when they're fining people five quid for boyish peccadilloes.

'You appear to be under a misapprehension, Stephanie,' he said in the metallic voice he had once used when addressing the prisoner Wooster. 'I have no intention of entrusting Mr. Pinker with a vicarage.'

Stiffy took it big. She shook from wind-swept-hair-do to shoe-sole, and if she hadn't clutched at Stinker's arm might have taken a toss. One could understand her emotion. She had been coasting along, confident that she had it made, and suddenly out of a blue and smiling sky these words of doom. No doubt it was the suddenness and unexpectedness of the wallop that unmanned her, if you can call it unmanning when it happens to a girl. I suppose she was feeling very much as Spode had felt when Emerald Stoker's basin had connected with his occiput. Her eyes bulged, and her voice came out in a passionate squeak.

'But, Uncle Watkyn! You promised!'

I could have told her she was wasting her breath trying to appeal to the old buzzard's better feelings, because magistrates, even when ex, don't have any. The tremolo in her voice might have been expected to melt what is usually called a heart of stone, but it had no more effect on Pop Bassett than the chirping of the household canary.

'Provisionally only,' he said. 'I was not aware, when I did so, that Mr. Pinker had brutally assaulted Roderick.'

At these words Stinker, who had been listening to the exchanges in a rigid sort of way, creating the illusion that he had been stuffed by a good taxidermist, came suddenly to life, though as all he did was make a sound like the last drops of water going out of a bath tub, it was hardly worth the trouble and expense. He succeeded, however, in attracting Pop Bassett's attention, and the latter gave him the eye.

'Yes, Mr. Pinker?'

It was a moment or two before Stinker followed up the gurgling noise with speech. And even then it wasn't much in the way of speech. He said:

'I – er – He – er –'

'Proceed, Mr. Pinker.'

'It was – I mean it wasn't –'

'If you could make yourself a little plainer, Mr. Pinker, it would be of great assistance to our investigations into the matter under discussion. I must confess to finding you far from lucid.'

It was the type of crack he had been accustomed in the old Bosher Street days to seeing in print with 'laughter' after it in brackets, but on this occasion it fell flatter than a Dover sole. It didn't get a snicker out of me, nor out of Stinker, who merely knocked over a small china ornament and turned a deeper vermilion, while Stiffy came back at him in great shape.

'There's no need to talk like a magistrate, Uncle Watkyn.'

'I beg your pardon?'

'In fact, it would be better if you stopped talking at all and let me explain. What Harold's trying to tell you is that he didn't brutally assault Roderick, Roderick brutally assaulted him.'

'Indeed? That was not the way I heard the story.'

'Well, it's the way it happened.'

'I am perfectly willing to hear your version of the deplorable incident.'

'All right, then. Here it comes. Harold was cooing to Roderick like a turtle dove, and Roderick suddenly hauled off and plugged him squarely on the beezer. If you don't believe me, take a look at it. The poor angel spouted blood like a Versailles fountain. Well, what would you have expected Harold to do? Turn the other nose?'

'I would have expected him to remember his position as a clerk in holy orders. He should have complained to me, and I would have seen to it that Roderick made ample apology.'

A sound like the shot heard round the world rang through the room. It was Sniffy snorting.

'Apology!' she cried, having got the snort out of her system. 'What's the good of apologies? Harold took the only possible course. He sailed in and laid Roderick out cold, as anyone would have done in his place.'

'Anyone who had not his cloth to think of.'

'For goodness' sake, Uncle Watkyn, a fellow can't be thinking of cloth all the time. It was an emergency. Roderick was murdering Gussie Fink-Nottle.'

'And Mr. Pinker *stopped* him? Great heavens!'

There was a pause while Pop Bassett struggled with his feelings. Then Stiffy, as Stinker had done with Spode, had a shot at the honeyed word. She had spoken of Stinker cooing to Spode like a turtle dove, and if memory served me aright that was just how he had cooed, and it was of a cooing turtle dove that she now reminded me. Like most girls, she can always get a melting note into her voice if she thinks there's any percentage to be derived from it.

'It's not like you, Uncle Watkyn, to go back on your solemn promise.'

I could have corrected her there. I would have thought it was just like him.

'I can't believe it's really you who's doing this cruel thing to me. It's so unlike you. You have always been so kind to me. You have made me love and respect you. I have come to look on you as a second father. Don't louse the whole thing up now.'

A powerful plea, which with any other man would undoubtedly have brought home the bacon. With Pop Bassett it didn't get to first base. He had been looking like a man with no bowels – of compassion, I mean of course – and he went on looking like one.

'If by that peculiar expression you intend to imply that you are expecting me to change my mind and give Mr. Pinker this vicarage,

I must disappoint you. I shall do no such thing. I consider that he has shown himself unfit to be a vicar, and I am surprised that after what has occurred he can reconcile it with his conscience to continue his duties as a curate.'

Strong stuff, of course, and it drew from Stinker what may have been a hollow groan or may have been a hiccup. I myself looked coldly at the old egg and I rather think I curled my lip, though I should say it was very doubtful if he noticed my scorn, for his attention was earmarked for Stiffy. She had turned almost as scarlet as Stinker, and I heard a distinct click as her front teeth met. It was through these teeth (clenched) that she spoke.

'So that's how you feel about it?'

'It is.'

'Your decision is final?'

'Quite final.'

'Nothing will move you?'

'Nothing.'

'I see,' said Stiffy, having chewed the lower lip for a space in silence. 'Well, you'll be sorry.'

'I disagree with you.'

'You will. Just wait. Bitter remorse is coming to you, Uncle Watkyn. Never underestimate the power of a woman,' said Stiffy, and with a choking sob – though there again it may have been a hiccup – she rushed from the room.

She had scarcely left us when Butterfield entered, and Pop Bassett eyed him with the ill-concealed petulance with which men of testy habit eye butlers who butt in at the wrong moment.

'Yes, Butterfield? What is it, what is it?'

'Constable Oates desires a word with you, sir.'

'Who?'

'Police Constable Oates, sir.'

'What does he want?'

'I gather that he has a clue to the identity of the boy who threw a hard-boiled egg at you, sir.'

The words acted on Pop Bassett as I'm told the sound of bugles acts on war-horses, not that I've ever seen a war-horse. His whole demeanour changed in a flash. His face lit up, and there came into it the sort of look you see on the faces of bloodhounds when they settle down to the trail. He didn't actually say 'Whoopee!' but that was probably because the expression was not familiar to him. He was out of the room in a matter of seconds, Butterfield lying some lengths behind, and Stinker, who had been replacing a framed photograph which he had knocked off a neighbouring table, addressed me in what you might call a hushed voice.

'I say, Bertie, what do you think Stiffy meant when she said that?'

I, too, had been speculating as to what the young pipsqueak had had in mind. A sinister thing to say, it seemed to me. Those words 'Just wait' had had an ominous ring. I weighed his question gravely.

'Difficult to decide,' I said, 'it may be one thing, or it may be another.'

'She has such an impulsive nature.'

'Very impulsive.'

'It makes me uneasy.'

'Why you? Pop B's the one who ought to be feeling uneasy. Knowing her as I do, if I were in his place –'

The sentence I had begun would, if it had come to fruition, have concluded with the words 'I'd pack a few necessaries in a suitcase and go to Australia,' but as I was about to utter them I chanced to glance out of the window and they froze on my lips.

The window looked on the drive, and from where I was standing I got a good view of the front steps, and when I saw what was coming up those front steps, my heart leaped from its base.

It was Plank. There was no mistaking that square, tanned face and that purposeful walk of his. And when I reflected that in about a couple of ticks Butterfield would be showing him into the drawing-room where I stood and we would meet once more, I confess that I was momentarily at a loss to know how to proceed.

My first thought was to wait till he had got through the front door and then nip out of the window, which was conveniently open. That, I felt, was what Napoleon would have done. And I was just about to get the show on the road, as Stiffy would have said, when I saw the dog Bartholomew coming sauntering along, and I knew that I would be compelled to revise my strategy from the bottom up. You can't go climbing out of windows under the eyes of an Aberdeen terrier so prone as Bartholomew was always to think the worst. In due season, no doubt, he would learn that what he had taken for a burglar escaping with the swag had been in reality a harmless guest of the house and would be all apologies, but by that time my lower slopes would be as full of holes as a Swiss cheese.

Falling back on my second line of defence, I slid behind the sofa with a muttered, 'Not a word to a soul, Stinker. Chap I don't want to meet,' and was nestling there like a turtle in its shell, when the door opened.

20

It's pretty generally recognized at the Drones Club and elsewhere that Bertram Wooster is a man who knows how to keep the chin up and the upper lip stiff, no matter how rough the going may be. Beneath the bludgeonings of Fate, his head is bloody but unbowed, as the fellow said. In a word, he can take it.

But I must admit that as I crouched in my haven of refuge I found myself chafing not a little. Life at Totleigh Towers, as I mentioned earlier, had got me down. There seemed no way of staying put in the darned house. One was either soaring like an eagle on to the top of chests or whizzing down behind sofas like a diving duck, and apart from the hustle and bustle of it all that sort of thing wounds the spirit and does no good to the trouser crease. And so, as I say, I chafed.

I was becoming increasingly bitter about this man Plank and the tendency he seemed to be developing of haunting me like a family spectre. I couldn't imagine what he was doing here. Whatever the faults of Totleigh Towers, I had supposed that, when there, one would at least be free from his society. He had an excellent home in Hockley-cum-Meston, and one sought in vain for an explanation of why the hell he didn't stay in it.

My disapproval extended to the personnel of the various native tribes he had encountered in the course of his explorations. On his own showing, he had for years been horning in uninvited on the aborigines of Brazil, the Congo and elsewhere, and not one of them apparently had had the enterprise to get after him with a spear or to say it with poisoned darts from the family blowpipe. And these were fellows who called themselves savages. Savages, forsooth! The savages in the books I used to read in my childhood would have had him in the Obituary column before he could say 'What ho', but with the ones you get nowadays it's all slackness and laissez-faire. Can't be bothered. Leave it to somebody else. Let George do it. One sometimes wonders what the world's coming to.

From where I sat my range of vision was necessarily a bit restricted, but I was able to see a pair of Empire-building brogue shoes, so I assumed that when the door had opened it was Butterfield showing him in, and this surmise was confirmed a moment later when he spoke. His was a voice which, once heard, lingers in the memory.

'Afternoon,' he said.

'Good afternoon,' said Stinker.

'Warm day.'

'Very warm.'

'What's been going on here? What are all those tents and swings and things in the park?'

Stinker explained that the annual school treat had only just concluded, and Plank expressed his gratification at having missed it. School treats, he said, were dashed dangerous things, always to be avoided by the shrewd, as they were only too apt to include competitions for bonny babies.

'Did you have a competition for bonny babies?'

'Yes, we did, as a matter of fact. The mothers always insist on it.'

'The mothers are the ones you want to watch out for,' said Plank. 'I'm not saying the little beasts aren't bad enough themselves, dribbling out of the side of their mouths at you and all that sort of thing, but it's the mothers who constitute the really grave peril. Look,' he said, and I think he must at this point have pulled up a trouser leg. 'See that scar on my calf? That's what I got in Peru once for being fool enough to let myself be talked into judging a competition for bonny babies. The mother of one of the Honourably Mentioneds spiked me in the leg with a native dagger as I was stepping down from the judge's stand after making my speech. Hurt like sin, I can assure you, and still gives me a twinge when the weather's wet. Fellow I know is fond of saying that the hand that rocks the cradle rules the world. Whether this is so or not I couldn't tell you, but it certainly knows how to handle a Peruvian dagger.'

I found myself revising to some extent the rather austere opinion I had formed of the slackness and lack of ginger of the modern native. The males might have lost their grip in recent years, but the female element, it seemed, still had the right stuff in them, though of course where somebody like Plank is concerned, a stab in the fleshy part of the leg is only a step in the right direction, merely scratching the surface as you might say.

Plank continued chatty. 'You live in these parts?' he said.

'Yes, I live in the village.'

'Totleigh?'

'Yes.'

'Don't run a Rugger club in Totleigh, do you?'

Stinker replied in the negative. The Totleigh-in-the-Wold athletes, he said, preferred the Association code, and Plank, probably shuddering, said 'Good God!'

'You ever played Rugger?'

'A little.'

'You should take it up seriously. No finer sport. I'm trying to make the Hockley-cum-Meston team the talk of Gloucestershire. I coach the boys daily, and they're coming along very nicely, very nicely indeed. What I need is a good prop forward.'

What he got was Pop Bassett, who came bustling in at this moment. He Good-afternoon-Plank-ed, and Plank responded in suitable terms.

'Very nice of you to look me up, Plank,' said Pop. 'Will you have something to drink?'

'Ah,' said Plank, and you could see that he meant it.

'I would ask you to stay to dinner, but unfortunately one of my guests has eloped with the cook.'

'Dashed sensible of him, if he was going to elope with anyone. Very hard to find these days, cooks.'

'It has of course completely disorganized our domestic arrangements. Neither my daughter nor my niece is capable of preparing even the simplest meal.'

'You'll have to go to the pub.'

'It seems the only solution.'

'If you were in West Africa, you could drop in and take pot luck with a native chief.'

'I am not in West Africa,' said Pop Bassett, speaking, I thought, a little testily, and I could understand him feeling a bit miffed. It's always annoying when you're up against it and people tell you what a jolly time you could be having if you weren't and how topping everything would be if you were somewhere where you aren't.

'I dined out a good deal in West Africa,' said Plank. 'Capital dinners some of those fellows used to give me, I remember, though there was always the drawback that you could never be sure the main dish wasn't one of their wives' relations, broiled over a slow fire and disguised in some native sauce. Took the edge off your appetite, unless you were feeling particularly peckish.'

'So I would be disposed to imagine.'

'All a matter of taste, of course.'

'Quite. Was there something you particularly wished to see me about, Plank?'

'No, nothing that I can think of.'

'Then if you will excuse me, I will be getting back to Madeline.'

'Who's Madeline?'

'My daughter. Your arrival interrupted me in a serious talk I was having with her.'

'Something wrong with the girl?'

'Something extremely wrong. She is contemplating making a disastrous marriage.'

'All marriages are disastrous,' said Plank, who gave one the impression, reading between the lines, that he was a bachelor. 'They lead to bonny babies, and bonny babies lead to bonny baby competitions. I was telling this gentleman here of an experience I had in Peru and showing him the scar on my leg, the direct result of being ass enough to judge one of these competitions. Would you care to see the scar on my leg?'

'Some other time, perhaps.'

'Any time that suits you. Why is this marriage you say she's contemplating so disastrous?'

'Because Mr. Wooster is not a suitable husband for her.'

'Who's Mr. Wooster?'

'The man she wishes to marry. A typical young wastrel of the type so common nowadays.'

'I used to know a fellow called Wooster, but I don't suppose it can be the same chap, because my Wooster was eaten by a crocodile on the Zambesi the other day, which rather rules him out. All right, Bassett, you pop back to the girl and tell her from me that if she's going to start marrying every Tom, Dick and Harry she comes across, she ought to have her head examined. If she'd seen as many native chiefs' wives as I have, she wouldn't be wanting to make such an ass of herself. Dickens of a life they lead, those women. Nothing to do but grind maize meal and have bonny babies. Right ho, Bassett, don't let me keep you.'

There came the sound of a closing door as Pop Bassett sped on his way, and Plank turned his attention to Stinker. He said:

'I didn't tell that old ass, because I didn't want him sticking around in here talking his head off, but as a matter of fact I did come about something special. Do you happen to know where I can find a chap called Pinker?'

'My name's Pinker.'

'Are you sure? I thought Bassett said it was Wooster.'

'No, Wooster's the one who's going to marry Sir Watkyn's daughter.'

'So he is. It all comes back to me now. I wonder if you can be the fellow I want. The Pinker I'm after is a curate.'

'I'm a curate.'

'You are? Yes, by Jove, you're perfectly right. I see your collar buttons at the back. You're not H. P. Pinker by any chance?'

'Yes.'

'Prop forward for Oxford and England a few years ago?'

'Yes.'

'Well, would you be interested in becoming a vicar?'

There was a crashing sound, and I knew that Stinker in his emotion must have upset his customary table. After a while he said in a husky voice that the one thing he wanted was to get his hooks on a vicarage or words to that effect, and Plank said he was glad to hear it.

'My chap at Hockley-cum-Meston is downing tools now that his ninetieth birthday is approaching, and I've been scouring the countryside for a spare. Extraordinarily difficult the quest has been, because what I wanted was a vicar who was a good prop forward, and it isn't often you find a parson who knows one end of a football from the other. I've never seen you play, I'm sorry to say, because I've been abroad so much, but with your record you must obviously be outstanding. So you can take up your duties as soon as old Bellamy goes into storage. When I get home, I'll embody the thing in the form of a letter.'

Stinker said he didn't know how to thank him, and Plank said that was all right, no need of any thanks.

'I'm the one who ought to be grateful. We're all right at half-back and three-quarters, but we lost to Upper Bleaching last year simply because our prop forward proved a broken reed. This year we'll show 'em. Amazing bit of luck finding you, and I could never have done it if it hadn't been for a friend of mine, a Chief Inspector Witherspoon of Scotland Yard. He phoned me just now and told me you were to be found at Totleigh-in-the-Wold. He said if I called at Totleigh Towers, they would give me your address. Extraordinary how these Scotland Yard fellows nose things out. The result of years of practise, I suppose. What was that noise?'

Stinker said he had heard nothing.

'Sort of gasping noise. Seemed to come from behind that sofa. Take a look.'

I was aware for a moment of Stinker's face peering down at me; then he turned away.

'There's nothing behind the sofa,' he said, very decently imperilling his immortal soul by falsifying the facts on behalf of a pal.

'Thought it might be a dog being sick,' said Plank.

And I suppose it had sounded rather like that. The revelation of Jeeves's black treachery had shaken me to my foundations, causing me to forget that in the existing circs silence was golden. A silly thing to do, of course, to gasp like that, but, dash it, if for years you have nursed a gentleman's personal gentleman in your bosom and out of a blue sky you find that he has deliberately sicked Brazilian explorers on to you, I maintain that you're fully entitled to behave like a dog in the throes of nausea. I could make nothing of his scurvy conduct, and was so stunned that for a minute or two I lost the thread of the conversation. When the mists cleared, Plank was speaking, and the subject had been changed.

'I wonder how Bassett is getting on with that daughter of his. Do you know anything of this chap Wooster?'

'He's one of my best friends.'

'Bassett doesn't seem too fond of him.'

'No.'

'Ah well, we all have our likes and dislikes. Which of the two girls is this Madeline he was speaking of? I've never met them, but I've seen them around. Is she the little squirt with the large blue eyes?'

I should imagine Stinker didn't care overmuch for hearing his loved one described as a little squirt, though reason must have told him that that was precisely what she was, but he replied without heat.

'No, that's Sir Watkyn's niece, Stephanie Byng.'

'Byng? Now why does that name seem to ring a bell? Oh yes, of course. Old Johnny Byng, who was with me on one of my expeditions. Red-haired fellow, haven't seen him for years. He was bitten by a puma, poor chap, and they tell me he still hesitates in a rather noticeable manner before sitting down. Stephanie Byng, eh? You know her, of course?'

'Very well.'

'Nice girl?'

'That's how she seems to me, and if you don't mind, I'll be going and telling her the good news.'

'What good news?'

'About the vicarage.'

'Oh, ah, yes. You think she'll be interested?'

'I'm sure she will. We're going to be married.'

'Good God! No chance of getting out of it?'

'I don't want to get out of it.'

'Amazing! I once hitch-hiked all the way from Johannesburg to Cape Town to avoid getting married, and here you are seeming quite pleased at the prospect. Oh well, no accounting for tastes. All right, you run along. And I suppose I'd better have a word with Bassett before I leave. Fellow bores me stiff, but one has to be civil.'

The door closed and silence fell, and after waiting a few minutes, just in case, I felt it was safe to surface. And I had just done so and was limbering up the limbs, which had become somewhat cramped, when the door opened and Jeeves came in carrying a tray.

21

'Good evening, sir,' he said. 'Would you care for an appetizer? I was obliging Mr. Butterfield by bringing them. He is engaged at the moment in listening at the door of the room where Sir Watkyn is in conference with Miss Bassett. He tells me he is compiling his Memoirs, never misses an opportunity of gathering suitable material.'

I gave the man one of my looks. My face was cold and hard, like a School Treat egg. I can't remember a time when I've been fuller of righteous indignation.

'What I want, Jeeves, is not a slab of wet bread with a dead sardine on it –'

'Anchovy, sir.'

'Or anchovy. I am in no mood to split straws. I require an explanation, and a categorical one, at that.'

'Sir?'

'You can't evade the issue by saying "Sir?". Answer me this, Jeeves, with a simple Yes or No. Why did you tell Plank to come to Totleigh Towers?'

I thought the query would crumple him up like a damp sock, but he didn't so much as shuffle a foot.

'My heart was melted by Miss Byng's tale of her misfortunes, sir. I chanced to encounter the young lady and found her in a state of considerable despondency as the result of Sir Watkyn's refusal to bestow a vicarage on Mr. Pinker. I perceived immediately that it was within my power to alleviate her distress. I had learned at the post office at Hockley-cum-Meston that the incumbent there was retiring shortly, and being cognizant of Major Plank's desire to strengthen the Hockley-cum-Meston forward line, I felt that it would be an excellent idea to place him in communication with Mr. Pinker. In order to be in a position to marry Miss Byng, Mr. Pinker requires a vicarage, and in order to compete successfully with rival villages in the football arena Major Plank is in need of a vicar with Mr. Pinker's wide experience as a prop forward. Their interests appeared to me to be identical.'

'Well, it worked all right. Stinker has clicked.'

'He is to succeed Mr. Bellamy as incumbent at Hockley-cum-Meston?'

'As soon as Bellamy calls it a day.'

'I am very happy to hear it, sir.'

I didn't reply for a while, being obliged to attend to a sudden touch of cramp.

This ironed out, I said, still icy:

'You may be happy, but I haven't been for the last quarter of an hour or so, nestling behind the sofa and expecting Plank at any moment to unmask me. It didn't occur to you to envisage what would happen if he met me?'

'I was sure that your keen intelligence would enable you to find a means of avoiding him, sir, as indeed it did. You concealed yourself behind the sofa?'

'On all fours.'

'A very shrewd manoeuvre on your part, if I may say so, sir. It showed a resource and swiftness of thought which it would be difficult to overpraise.'

My iciness melted. It is not too much to say that I was mollified. It's not often that I'm given the old oil in this fashion, most of my circle, notably my Aunt Agatha, being more prone to the slam than the rave. And it was only after I had been savouring that 'keen intelligence' gag, if savouring is the word I want, for some moments that I suddenly remembered that marriage with Madeline Bassett loomed ahead, and I gave a start so visible that he asked me if I was feeling unwell.

I shook the loaf.

'Physically, no, Jeeves. Spiritually, yes.'

'I do not quite understand you, sir.'

'Well, here is the news, and this is Bertram Wooster reading it. I'm going to be married.'

'Indeed, sir?'

'Yes, Jeeves, married. The banns are as good as up.'

'Would it be taking a liberty if I were to ask –'

'Who to? You don't need to ask. Gussie Fink-Nottle has eloped with Emerald Stoker, thus creating a . . . what is it?'

'Would vacuum be the word you are seeking, sir?'

'That's right. A vacuum which I shall have to fill. Unless you can think of some way of getting me out of it.'

'I will devote considerable thought to the matter, sir.'

'Thank you, Jeeves,' I said, and would have spoken further, but at this moment I saw the door opening and speechlessness supervened. But it wasn't, as I had feared, Plank, it was only Stiffy.

'Hullo, you two,' she said. 'I'm looking for Harold.'

I could see at a g. that Jeeves had been right in describing her demeanour as despondent. The brow was clouded and the general appearance that of an overwrought soul. I was glad to be in a position to inject a little sunshine into her life. Pigeon-holing my own troubles for future reference, I said:

'He's looking for you. He has a strange story to relate. You know about Plank?'

'What about him?'

'I'll tell you what about him. Plank to you hitherto has been merely a shadowy figure who hangs out at Hockley-cum-Meston and sells black amber statuettes to people, but he has another side to him.'

She betrayed a certain impatience.

'If you think I'm interested in Plank –'

'Aren't you?'

'No, I'm not.'

'You will be. He has, as I was saying, another side to him. He is a landed proprietor with vicarages in his gift, and to cut a long story down to a short-short, as one always likes to do when possible, he has just given one to Stinker.'

I had been right in supposing that the information would have a marked effect on her dark mood. I have never actually seen a corpse spring from its bier and start being the life and soul of the party, but I should imagine that its deportment would closely resemble that of this young Byng as the impact of my words came home to her. A sudden light shot into her eyes, which, as Plank had correctly said, were large and blue, and an ecstatic 'Well, Lord love a duck!' escaped her. Then doubts seemed to creep in, for the eyes clouded over again.

'Is this true?'

'Absolutely official.'

'You aren't pulling my leg?'

I drew myself up rather haughtily.

'I wouldn't dream of pulling your leg. Do you think Bertram Wooster is the sort of chap who thinks it funny to raise people's hopes, only to . . . what, Jeeves?'

'Dash them to the ground, sir.'

'Thank you, Jeeves.'

'Not at all, sir.'

'You may take this information as coming straight from the mouth of the stable cat. I was present when the deal went through. Behind the sofa, but present.'

She still seemed at a loss.

'But I don't understand. Plank has never met Harold.'

'Jeeves brought them together.'

'Did you, Jeeves?'

'Yes, miss.'

' 'At-a-boy!'

'Thank you, miss.'

'And he's really given Harold a vicarage?'

'The vicarage of Hockley-cum-Meston. He's embodying it in the form of a letter tonight. At the moment there's a vicar still vicking, but he's infirm and old and wants to turn it up as soon as they can put on an understudy. The way things look, I should imagine that we shall be able to unleash Stinker on the Hockley-cum-Meston souls in the course of the next few days.'

My simple words and earnest manner had resolved the last of her doubts. The misgivings she may have had as to whether this was the real ginger vanished. Her eyes shone more like twin stars than anything, and she uttered animal cries and danced a few dance steps. Presently she paused, and put a question.

'What's Plank like?'

'How do you mean, what's he like?'

'He hasn't a beard, has he?'

'No, no beard.'

'That's good, because I want to kiss him, and if he had a beard, it would give me pause.'

'Dismiss the notion,' I urged, for Plank's psychology was an open book to me. The whole trend of that confirmed bachelor's conversation had left me with the impression that he would find it infinitely preferable to be spiked in the leg with a native dagger than to have popsies covering his upturned face with kisses. 'He'd have a fit.'

'Well, I must kiss somebody. Shall I kiss you, Jeeves?'

'No, thank you, miss.'

'You, Bertie?'

'I'd rather you didn't.'

'Then I've a good mind to go and kiss Uncle Watkyn, louse of the first water though he has recently shown himself.'

'How do you mean, recently?'

'And having kissed him I shall tell him the news and taunt him vigorously with having let a good thing get away from him. I shall tell him that when he declined to avail himself of Harold's services he was like the Indian.'

I did not get her drift.

'What Indian?'

'The base one my governesses used to make me read about, the poor simp whose hand . . . How does it go, Jeeves?'

'Threw a pearl away richer than all his tribe, miss.'

'That's right. And I shall tell him I hope the vicar he does get will be a weed of a man who has a chronic cold in the head and bleats. Oh, by the way, talking of Uncle Watkyn reminds me. I shan't have any use for this now.'

And so speaking she produced the black amber eyesore from the recesses of her costume like a conjuror taking a rabbit out of a hat.

22

It was as if she had suddenly exhibited a snake of the lowest order. I gazed at the thing, appalled. It needed but this to put the frosting on the cake.

'Where did you get that?' I asked in a voice that was low and trembled.

'I pinched it.'

'What on earth did you do that for?'

'Perfectly simple. The idea was to go to Uncle Watkyn and tell him he wouldn't get it back unless he did the square thing by Harold. Power politics, don't they call it, Jeeves?'

'Or blackmail, miss.'

'Yes, or blackmail, I suppose. But you can't be too nice in your methods when you're dealing with the Uncle Watkyns of this world. But now that Plank has eased the situation and made our paths straight, of course I shan't need it, and I suppose the shrewd thing is to return it to store before its absence is noted. Go and put it in the collection room, Bertie. Here's the key.'

I recoiled as if she had offered me the dog Bartholomew. Priding myself as I do on being a preux chevalier, I like to oblige the delicately nurtured when it's feasible, but there are moments when only a *nolle prosequi* will serve, and I recognized this as one of them. The thought of making the perilous passage she was suggesting gave me goose pimples.

'I'm not going near the ruddy collection room. With my luck, I'd find your Uncle Watkyn there, arm in arm with Spode, and it wouldn't be too easy to explain what I was doing there and how I'd got in. Besides, I can't go roaming about the place with Plank on the premises.'

She laughed one of those silvery ones, a practice to which, as I have indicated, she was far too much addicted.

'Jeeves told me about you and Plank. Very funny.'

'I'm glad you think so. We personally were not amused.'

Jeeves, as always, found the way.

'If you will give the object to me, miss, I will see that it is restored to its place.'

'Thank you, Jeeves. Well, good-bye all. I'm off to find Harold,' said Stiffy, and she withdrew, dancing on the tips of her toes.

I shrugged a shoulder.

'Women, Jeeves!'

'Yes, sir.'

'What a sex!'

'Yes, sir.'

'Do you remember something I said to you about Stiffy on our previous visit to Totleigh Towers?'

'Not at the moment, no, sir.'

'It was on the occasion when she landed me with Police Constable Oates's helmet just as my room was about to be searched by Pop Bassett and his minions. Dipping into the future, I pointed out that Stiffy, who is pure padded cell from the foundations up, was planning to marry the Rev. H.P. Pinker, himself as pronounced a goop as ever preached about the Hivites and Hittites, and I speculated, if you recall, as to what their offspring, if any, would be like.'

'Ah yes, sir, I recollect now.'

'Would they, I asked myself, inherit the combined loopiness of two such parents?'

'Yes, sir, you were particularly concerned, I recall, for the well-being of the nurses, governesses, private schoolmasters and public school-masters who would assume the charge of them.'

'Little knowing that they were coming up against something hotter than mustard. Exactly. The thought still weighs heavy upon me. However, we haven't leisure to go into the subject now. You'd better take that ghastly object back where it belongs without delay.'

'Yes, sir. If it were done when 'twere done, then 'twere well it were done quickly,' he said, making for the door, and I thought, as I had so often thought before, how neatly he put these things.

It seemed to me that the time had now come to adopt the strategy which I had had in mind right at the beginning – viz. to make my getaway via the window. With Plank at large in the house and likely at any moment to come winging back to where the drinks were, safety could be obtained only by making for some distant yew alley or rhododendron walk and remaining ensconced there till he had blown over. I hastened to the window, accordingly, and picture my chagrin and dismay on finding that Bartholomew, instead of continuing his stroll, had decided to take a siesta on the grass immediately below. I had actually got one leg over the sill before he was drawn to my attention. In another half jiffy I should have dropped on him as the gentle rain from heaven upon the spot beneath.

I had no difficulty in recognizing the situation as what the French call an *impasse*, and as I stood pondering what to do for the best, footsteps sounded without, and feeling that 'twere well it were done quickly I made for the sofa once more, lowering my previous record by perhaps a split second.

I was surprised, as I lay nestling in my little nook, by the complete absence of dialogue that ensued. Hitherto, all my visitors had started chatting from the moment of their entry, and it struck me as odd that I should now be entertaining a couple of deaf mutes. Peeping cautiously out, however, I found that I had been mistaken in supposing that I had with me a brace of guests. It was Madeline alone who had blown in. She was heading for the piano, and something told me that it was her intention to sing old folk songs, a pastime to which, as I have indicated, she devoted not a little of her leisure. She was particularly given to indulgence in this nuisance when her soul had been undergoing an upheaval and required soothing, as of course it probably did at this juncture.

My fears were realized. She sang two in rapid succession, and the thought that this sort of thing would be a permanent feature of our married life chilled me to the core. I've always been what you might call allergic to old folk songs, and the older they are, the more I dislike them.

Fortunately, before she could start on a third she was interrupted. Clumping footsteps sounded, the door handle turned, heavy breathing made itself heard, and a voice said 'Madeline!' Spode's voice, husky with emotion.

'Madeline,' he said, 'I've been looking for you everywhere.'

'Oh, Roderick! How is your eye?'

'Never mind my eye,' said Spode. 'I didn't come here to talk about eyes.'

'They say a piece of beefsteak reduces the swelling.'

'Nor about beefsteaks. Sir Watkyn has told me the awful news about you and Wooster. Is it true you're going to marry him?'

'Yes, Roderick, it is true.'

'But you can't love a half-baked, half-witted ass like Wooster,' said Spode, and I thought the remark extremely offensive. Pick your words more carefully, Spode, I might have said, rising and confronting him. However, for one reason and another I didn't, but continued to nestle and I heard Madeline sigh, unless it was the draught under the sofa.

'No, Roderick, I do not love him. He does not appeal to the essential me. But I feel it is my duty to make him happy.'

'Tchah!' said Spode, or something that sounded like that. 'Why on earth do you want to go about making worms like Wooster happy?'

'He loves me, Roderick. You must have seen that dumb, worshipping look in his eyes as he gazes at me.'

'I've something better to do than peer into Wooster's eyes. Though I can well imagine they look dumb. We've got to have this thing out, Madeline.'

'I don't understand you, Roderick.'

'You will.'

'Ouch!'

I think on the cue 'You will' he must have grabbed her by the wrist, for the word 'Ouch!' had come through strong and clear, and this suspicion was confirmed when she said he was hurting her.

'I'm sorry, sorry,' said Spode. 'But I refuse to allow you to ruin your life. You can't marry this man Wooster. I'm the one you're going to marry.'

I was with him heart and soul, as the expression is. Nothing would ever make me really fond of Roderick Spode, but I liked the way he was talking. A little more of this, I felt, and Bertram would be released from his honourable obligations. I wished he had thought of taking this firm line earlier.

'I've loved you since you were so high.'

Not being able to see him, I couldn't ascertain how high that was, but I presumed he must have been holding his hand not far from the floor. A couple of feet, would you say? About that, I suppose.

Madeline was plainly moved. I heard her gurgle.

'I know, Roderick, I know.'

'You guessed my secret?'

'Yes, Roderick. How sad life is!'

Spode declined to string along with her in this view.

'Not a bit of it. Life's fine. At least, it will be if you give this blighter Wooster the push and marry me.'

'I have always been devoted to you, Roderick.'

'Well, then?'

'Give me time to think.'

'Carry on. Take all the time you need.'

'I don't want to break Bertie's heart.'

'Why not? Do him good.'

'He loves me so dearly.'

'Nonsense. I don't suppose he has ever loved anything in his life except a dry martini.'

'How can you say that? Did he not come here because he found it impossible to stay away from me?'

'No, he jolly well didn't. Don't let him fool you on that point. He came here to pinch that black amber statuette of your father's.'

'What!'

'That's what. In addition to being half-witted, he's a low thief.'

'It can't be true!'

'Of course it's true. His uncle wants the thing for his collection. I heard him plotting with his aunt on the telephone not half an hour ago. "It's going to be pretty hard to get away with it," he was saying, "but I'll do my best. I know how much Uncle Tom covets that statuette." He's always stealing things. The very first time I met him, in an antique shop in the Brompton Road, he as near as a toucher got away with your father's umbrella.'

A monstrous charge, and one which I can readily refute. He and Pop Bassett and I were, I concede, in the antique shop in the Brompton Road to which he had alluded, but the umbrella sequence was purely one of those laughable misunderstandings. Pop Bassett had left the blunt instrument propped against a seventeenth-century chair, and what caused me to take it up was the primeval instinct which makes a man without an umbrella, as I happened to be that morning, reach out unconsciously for the nearest one in sight, like a flower turning to the sun. The whole thing could have been explained in two words, but they hadn't let me say even one, and the slur had been allowed to rest on me.

'You shock me, Roderick!' said Madeline.

'Yes, I thought it would make you sit up.'

'If this is really so, if Bertie is really a thief —'

'Well?'

'Naturally I will have nothing more to do with him. But I can't believe it.'

'I'll go and fetch Sir Watkyn,' said Spode. 'Perhaps you'll believe him.'

For several minutes after he had clumped out, Madeline must have stood in a reverie, for I didn't hear a sound out of her. Then the door opened, and the next thing that came across was a cough which I had no difficulty in recognizing.

23

It was that soft cough of Jeeves's which always reminds me of a very old sheep clearing its throat on a distant mountain top. He coughed it at me, if you remember, on the occasion when I first swam into his ken wearing the Alpine hat. It generally signifies disapproval, but I've known it to occur also when he's about to touch on a topic of a delicate nature. And when he spoke, I knew that that was what he was going to do now, for there was a sort of hushed note in his voice.

'I wonder if I might have a moment of your time, miss?'

'Of course, Jeeves.'

'It is with reference to Mr. Wooster.'

'Oh, yes?'

'I must begin by saying that I chanced to be passing the door when Lord Sidcup was speaking to you and inadvertently overheard his lordship's observations on the subject of Mr. Wooster. His lordship has a carrying voice. And I find myself in a somewhat equivocal position, torn between loyalty to my employer and a natural desire to do my duty as a citizen.'

'I don't understand you, Jeeves,' said Madeline, which made two of us.

He coughed again.

'I am anxious not to take a liberty, miss, but if I may speak frankly –'

'Please do.'

'Thank you, miss. His lordship's words seemed to confirm a rumour which is circulating in the servants' hall that you are contemplating a matrimonial union with Mr. Wooster. Would it be indiscreet of me if I were to inquire if this is so?'

'Yes, Jeeves, it is quite true.'

'If you will pardon me for saying so, I think you are making a mistake.'

Well spoken, Jeeves, you are on the right lines, I was saying to myself, and I hoped he was going to rub it in. I waited anxiously for Madeline's reply, a little afraid that she would draw herself to her full height and dismiss him from her presence. But she didn't. She merely said again that she didn't understand him.

'If I might explain, miss. I am loath to criticize my employer, but I feel that you should know that he is a kleptomaniac.'

'What!'

'Yes, miss. I had hoped to be able to preserve his little secret, as I have always done hitherto, but he has now gone to lengths which I cannot countenance. In going through his effects this afternoon I discovered this small black figure, concealed beneath his underwear.'

I heard Madeline utter a sound like a dying soda-water syphon.

'But that belongs to my father!'

'If I may say so, nothing belongs to anyone if Mr. Wooster takes a fancy to it.'

'Then Lord Sidcup was right?'

'Precisely, miss.'

'He said Mr. Wooster tried to steal my father's umbrella.'

'I heard him, and the charge was well founded. Umbrellas, jewellery, statuettes, they are all grist to Mr. Wooster's mill. I do not think he can help it. It is a form of mental illness. But whether a jury would take that view, I cannot say.'

Madeline went into the soda-syphon routine once more.

'You mean he might be sent to prison?'

'It is a contingency that seems to me far from remote.'

Again I felt that he was on the right lines. His trained senses told him that if there's one thing that puts a girl off marrying a chap, it is the thought that the honeymoon may be spoiled at any moment by the arrival of Inspectors at the love nest, come to scoop him in for larceny. No young bride likes that sort of thing, and you can't blame her if she finds herself preferring to team up with someone like Spode, who, though a gorilla in fairly human shape, is known to keep strictly on the right side of the law. I could almost hear Madeline's thoughts turning in this direction, and I applauded Jeeves's sound grip on the psychology of the individual, as he calls it.

Of course, I could see that all this wasn't going to make my position in the Bassett home any too good, but there are times when only the surgeon's knife will serve. And I had the sustaining thought that if ever I got out from behind this sofa I could sneak off to where my car waited champing at the bit and drive off Londonwards without stopping to say goodbye and thanks for a delightful visit. This would obviate – is it obviate? – all unpleasantness.

Madeline continued shaken.

'Oh dear, Oh dear!' she said.

'Yes, miss.'

'This has come as a great shock.'

'I can readily appreciate it, miss.'

'Have you known of this long?'

'Ever since I entered Mr. Wooster's employment.'

'Oh dear, Oh dear! Well, thank you, Jeeves.'

'Not at all, miss.'

I think Jeeves must have shimmered off after this, for silence fell and nothing happened except that my nose began to tickle. I would have given ten quid to have been able to sneeze, but this of course was outside the range of practical politics. I just crouched there, thinking of this and that, and after quite a while the door opened once more, this time to admit something in the nature of a mob scene. I could see three pairs of shoes, and deduced that they were those of Spode, Pop Bassett and Plank. Spode, it will be recalled, had gone to fetch Pop, and Plank presumably had come along for the ride, hoping no doubt for something moist at journey's end.

Spode was the first to speak, and his voice rang with the triumph that comes into the voices of suitors who have caught a dangerous rival bending.

'Here we are,' he said. 'I've brought Sir Watkyn to support my statement that Wooster is a low sneak thief who goes about snapping up everything that isn't nailed down. You agree, Sir Watkyn?'

'Of course I do, Roderick. It's only a month or so ago that he and that aunt of his stole my cow-creamer.'

'What's a cow-creamer?' asked Plank.

'A silver cream jug, one of the gems of my collection.'

'They got away with it, did they?'

'They did.'

'Ah,' said Plank. 'Then in that case I think I'll have a whisky and soda.'

Pop Bassett was warming to his theme. His voice rose above the hissing of Plank's syphon.

'And it was only by the mercy of Providence that Wooster didn't make off with my umbrella that day in the Brompton Road. If that young man has one defect more marked than another, it is that he appears to be totally ignorant of the distinction between *meum* and *tuum*. He came up before me in my court once, I remember, charged with having stolen a policeman's helmet, and it is a lasting regret to me that I merely fined him five pounds.'

'Mistaken kindness,' said Spode.

'So I have always felt, Roderick. A sharper lesson might have done him all the good in the world.'

'Never does to let these fellows off lightly,' said Plank. 'I had a servant chap in Mozambique who used to help himself to my cigars, and I foolishly overlooked it because he assured me he had got religion and everything would be quite all right from now on. And it wasn't a week later that he skipped out, taking with him a box of Havanas and my false teeth, which he sold to one of the native chiefs in the neighbourhood. Cost me a case of trade gin and two strings of beads to get them back. Severity's the only thing. The iron hand. Anything else is mistaken for weakness.'

Madeline gave a sob, at least it sounded like a sob.

'But, Daddy.'

'Well?'

'I don't think Bertie can help himself.'

'My dear child, it is precisely his habit of helping himself to everything he can lay his hands on that we are criticizing.'

'I mean, he's a kleptomaniac.'

'Eh? Who told you that?'

'Jeeves.'

'That's odd. How did the subject come up?'

'He told me when he gave me this. He found it in Bertie's room. He was very worried about it.'

There was a spot of silence – of a stunned nature, I imagine. Then Pop Bassett said 'Good heavens!' and Spode said 'Good Lord!' and Plank said, 'Why, that's that little thingummy I sold you, Bassett, isn't it?' Madeline gave another sob, and my nose began to tickle again.

'Well, this is astounding!' said Pop. 'He found it in Wooster's room, you say?'

'Concealed beneath his underwear.'

Pop Bassett uttered a sound like the wind going out of a dying duck.

'How right you were, Roderick! You said his motive in coming here was to steal this. But how he got into the collection room I cannot understand.'

'These fellows have their methods.'

'Seems to be a great demand for that thing,' said Plank. 'There was a young slab of damnation with a criminal face round at my place only yesterday trying to sell it to me.'

'Wooster!'

'No, it wasn't Wooster. My fellow's name was Alpine Joe.'

'Wooster would naturally adopt a pseudonym.'

'I suppose he would. I never thought of that.'

'Well, after this –' said Pop Bassett.

'Yes, after this,' said Spode, 'you're certainly not going to marry the man, Madeline. He's worse than Fink-Nottle.'

'Who's Fink-Nottle?' asked Plank.

'The one who eloped with Stoker,' said Pop.

'Who's Stoker?' asked Plank. I don't think I've ever come across a fellow with a greater thirst for information.

'The cook.'

'Ah yes. I remember you telling me. Knew what he was doing, that chap. I'm strongly opposed to anyone marrying anybody, but if you're going to marry someone, you unquestionably save something from the wreck by marrying a woman who knows what to do with a joint of beef. There was a fellow I knew in the Federated Malay States who –'

It would probably have been a diverting anecdote, but Spode didn't let him get on with it any further. Addressing Madeline, he said:

'What you're going to do is marry me, and I don't want any argument. How about it, Madeline?'

'Yes, Roderick. I will be your wife.'

Spode uttered a whoop which made my nose tickle worse than ever.

'That's the stuff! That's how I like to hear you talk! Come on out into the garden. I have much to say to you.'

I imagine that at this juncture he must have folded her in his embrace and hustled her out, for I heard the door close. And as it did so Pop Bassett uttered a whoop somewhat similar in its intensity to the one that had proceeded from the Spode lips. He was patently boomps-a-daisy, and one could readily understand why. A father whose daughter, after nearly marrying Gussie Fink-Nottle and then nearly marrying me, sees the light and hooks on to a prosperous member of the British aristocracy is entitled to rejoice. I didn't like Spode and would have been glad at any time to see a Peruvian matron spike him in the leg with her dagger, but there was no denying that he was hot stuff matrimonially.

'Lady Sidcup!' said Pop, rolling the words round his tongue like vintage port.

'Who's Lady Sidcup?' asked Plank, anxious, as always, to keep abreast.

'My daughter will shortly be. One of the oldest titles in England. That was Lord Sidcup who has just left us.'

'I thought his name is Roderick.'

'His Christian name is Roderick.'

'Ah!' said Plank. 'Now I've got it. Now I have the whole picture. Your daughter was to have married someone called Fink-Nottle?'

'Yes.'

'Then she was to have married this chap Wooster or Alpine Joe, as the case may be?'

'Yes.'

'And now she's going to marry Lord Sidcup?'

'Yes.'

'Clear as crystal,' said Plank. 'I knew I should get it threshed out in time. Simply a matter of concentration and elimination. You approve of this marriage? As far,' he added, 'as one can approve of any marriage.'

'I most certainly do.'

'Then I think this calls for another whisky-and-soda.'

'I will join you,' said Pop Bassett.

It was at this point, unable to hold it back any longer, that I sneezed.

'I knew there was something behind that sofa,' said Plank, rounding it and subjecting me to the sort of look he had once given native chiefs who couldn't grasp the rules of Rugby football. 'Odd sounds came from that direction. Good God, it's Alpine Joe.'

'It's Wooster!'

'Who's Wooster? Oh, you told me, didn't you? What steps do you propose to take?'

'I have rung for Butterfield.'

'Who's Butterfield?'

'My butler.'

'What do you want a butler for?'

'To tell him to bring Oates.'

'Who's Oates?'

'Our local policeman. He is having a glass of whisky in the kitchen.'

'Whisky!' said Plank thoughtfully, and as if reminded of something went to the side table.

The door opened.

'Oh, Butterfield, will you tell Oates to come here.'

'Very good, Sir Watkyn.'

'Bit out of condition, that chap,' said Plank, eyeing Butterfield's retreating back. 'Wants a few games of Rugger to put him in shape. What are you going to do about this Alpine Joe fellow? You going to charge him?'

'I certainly am. No doubt he assumed that I would shrink from causing a scandal, but he was wrong. I shall let the law take its course.'

'Quite right. Soak him to the utmost limit. You're a Justice of the Peace, aren't you?'

'I am, and intend to give him twenty-eight days in the second division.'

'Or sixty? Nice round number, sixty. You couldn't make it six months, I suppose?'

'I fear not.'

'No, I imagine you have a regular tariff. Ah, well, twenty-eight days is better than nothing.'

'Police Constable Oates,' said Butterfield in the doorway.

24

I don't know why it is, but there's something about being hauled off to a police bin that makes you feel a bit silly. At least, that's how it always affects me. I mean, there you are, you and the arm of the Law, toddling along side by side, and you feel that in a sense he's your host and you ought to show an interest and try to draw him out. But it's so difficult to hit on anything in the nature of an exchange of ideas, and conversation never really flows. I remember at my private school, the one I won a prize for Scripture Knowledge at, the Rev. Aubrey Upjohn, the top brass, used to take us one by one for an educational walk on Sunday afternoons, and I always found it hard to sparkle when my turn came to step out at his side. It was the same on this occasion, when I accompanied Constable Oates to the village coop. It's no good my pretending the thing went with a swing, because it didn't.

Probably if I'd been one of the topnotchers, about to do a ten years stretch for burglary or arson or what not, it would have been different, but I was only one of the small fry who get twenty-eight days in the second division, and I couldn't help thinking the officer was looking down on me. Not actually sneering, perhaps, but aloof in his manner, as if feeling I wasn't much for a cop to get his teeth into.

And, of course, there was another thing. Speaking of my earlier visit to Totleigh Towers, I mentioned that when Pop Bassett immured me in my room, he stationed the local police force on the lawn below to see that I didn't nip out of the window. That local police force was this same Oates, and as it was raining like the dickens at the time, no doubt the episode had rankled. Only a very sunny constable can look with an indulgent eye on the fellow responsible for his getting the nastiest cold in the head of his career.

At any rate, he showed himself now a man of few words, though good at locking people up in cells. There was only one at the Totleigh-in-the-Wold emporium, and I had it all to myself, a cosy little apartment with a window, not barred but too small to get out of, a grille in the door, a plank bed and that rather powerful aroma of drunks and disorderlies which you always find in these homes from home. Whether it was superior or inferior to the one they had given me at Bosher Street, I was unable to decide. Not much in it either way, it seemed to me.

To say that when I turned in on the plank bed I fell into a dreamless sleep would be deceiving my public. I passed a somewhat restless night. I could have sworn, indeed, that I didn't drop off at all, but I suppose I must have done, because the next thing I knew sunlight was coming through the window and mine host was bringing me breakfast.

I got outside it with an appetite unusual with me at such an early hour, and at the conclusion of the meal I fished out an old envelope and did what I have sometimes done before when the bludgeonings of Fate were up and about to any extent – viz. make a list of Credits and Debits, as I believe Robinson Crusoe used to. The idea being to see whether I was ahead of or behind the game at moment of going to press.

The final score worked out as follows:

Credit	Debit
Not at all a bad breakfast, that. Coffee quite good. I was surprised.	Don't always be thinking of your stomach, you jailbird.
Who's a jailbird?	You're a jailbird.
Well, yes, I suppose I am, if you care to put it that way. But I am innocent. My hands are clean.	More than your face is.
Not looking my best, what?	You look like something the cat brought in.
A bath will put that right.	And you'll get one in prison.
You really think it'll come to that?	Well, you heard what Pop Bassett said.
I wonder what it's like, doing twenty-eight days? Hitherto, I've always just come for the night.	You'll hate it. It'll bore you stiff.
I don't know so much. They give you a cake of soap and a hymnbook, don't they?	What's the good of a cake of soap and a hymnbook?

I'll be able to whack up some sort
of indoor game with them. And
don't forget that I've not got to
marry Madeline Bassett. Let's
hear what you have to say to that.

And the Debit account didn't utter. I had baffled it.

Yes, I felt, as I hunted around in case there might be a crumb of
bread which I had overlooked, that amply compensated me for the
vicissitudes I was undergoing. And I had been musing along these
lines for a while, getting more and more reconciled to my lot, when
a silvery voice spoke, making me jump like a startled grasshopper. I
couldn't think where it was coming from at first, and speculated for
a moment on the possibility of it being my guardian angel, though I
had always thought of him, I don't know why, as being of the male
sex. Then I saw something not unlike a human face at the grille, and
a closer inspection told me that it was Stiffy.

I Hullo-there-ed cordially, and expressed some surprise at finding
her on the premises.

'I wouldn't have thought Oates would have let you in. It isn't
Visitors Day, is it?'

She explained that the zealous officer had gone up to the house to
see her Uncle Watkyn and that she had sneaked in when he had legged
it.

'Oh, Bertie,' she said, 'I wish I could slip you in a file.'

'What would I do with a file?'

'Saw through the bars, of course, ass.'

'There aren't any bars.'

'Oh, aren't there? That's a difficulty. We'll have to let it go, then.
Have you had breakfast?'

'Just finished.'

'Was it all right?'

'Fairly toothsome.'

'I'm glad to hear that, because I'm weighed down with remorse.'

'You are? Why?'

'Use the loaf. If I hadn't pinched that statuette thing, none of this
would have happened.'

'Oh, I wouldn't worry.'

'But I do worry. Shall I tell Uncle Watkyn that you're innocent,
because I was the guilty party? You ought to have your name cleared.'

I put the bee on this suggestion with the greatest promptitude.

'Certainly not. Don't dream of it.'

'But don't you want your name cleared?'

'Not at the expense of you taking the rap.'

'Uncle Watkyn wouldn't send me to chokey.'

'I dare say not, but Stinker would learn all and would be shocked to the core.'

'Coo! I didn't think of that.'

'Think of it now. He wouldn't be able to help asking himself if it was a prudent move for a vicar to link his lot with yours. Doubts, that's what he'd have, and qualms. It isn't as if you were going to be a gangster's moll. The gangster would be all for you swiping everything in sight and would encourage you with word and gesture, but it's different with Stinker. When he marries you, he'll want you to take charge of the parish funds. Apprise him of the facts, and he won't have an easy moment.'

'I see what you mean. Yes, you have a point there.'

'Picture his jumpiness if he found you near the Sunday offertory bag. No, secrecy and silence is the only course.'

She sighed a bit, as if her conscience was troubling her, but she saw the force of my reasoning.

'I suppose you're right, but I do hate the idea of you doing time.'

'There are compensations.'

'Such as?'

'I am saved from the scaffold.'

'The – ? Oh, I see what you mean. You get out of marrying Madeline.'

'Exactly, and, as I remember telling you once, I am implying nothing derogatory to Madeline when I say that the thought of being united to her in bonds of holy wedlock was one that gave your old friend shivers down the spine. The fact is in no way to her discredit. I should feel just the same about marrying many of the world's noblest women. There are certain females whom one respects, admires, reveres, but only from a distance, and it is to this group that Madeline belongs.'

And I was about to develop this theme, with possibly a reference to those folk songs, when a gruff voice interrupted our *tête-à-tête*, if you can call a thing a *tête-à-tête* when the two of you are on opposite sides of an iron grille. It was Constable Oates, returned from his excursion. Stiffy's presence displeased him, and he spoke austerely.

'What's all this?' he demanded.

'What's all what?' riposted Stiffy with spirit, and I remember thinking that she rather had him there.

'It's against regulations to talk to the prisoner, Miss.'

'Oates,' said Stiffy, 'you're an ass.'

This was profoundly true, but it seemed to annoy the officer. He resented the charge, and said so, and Stiffy said she didn't want any back chat from him.

'You road company rozzers make me sick. I was only trying to cheer him up.'

It seemed to me that the officer gave a bitter snort, and a moment later he revealed why he had done so.

'It's me that wants cheering up,' he said morosely, 'I've just seen Sir Watkyn and he says he isn't pressing the charge.'

'What!' I cried.

'What!' yipped Stiffy.

'That's what,' said the constable, and you could see that while there was sunshine above, there was none in his heart. I could sympathize with him, of course. Naturally nothing makes a member of the Force sicker than to have a criminal get away from him. He was in rather the same position as some crocodile on the Zambesi or some puma in Brazil would have been, if it had earmarked Plank for its lunch and seen him shin up a high tree.

'Shackling the police, that's what I call it,' he said, and I think he spat on the floor. I couldn't see him, of course, but I was aware of a spit-like sound.

Stiffy whooped, well pleased, and I whooped myself, if I remember correctly. For all the bold front I had been putting up, I had never in my heart really liked the idea of rotting for twenty-eight days in a dungeon cell. Prison is all right for a night, but you don't want to go overdoing the thing.

'Then what are we waiting for?' said Stiffy. 'Get a move on, officer. Fling wide those gates.'

Oates flung them, not attempting to conceal his chagrin and disappointment, and I passed with Stiffy into the great world outside the prison walls.

'Goodbye, Oates,' I said as we left, for one always likes to do the courteous thing. 'It's been nice meeting you. How are Mrs. Oates and the little ones?'

His only reply was a sound like a hippopotamus taking its foot out of the mud on a river bank, and I saw Stiffy frown, as though his manner offended her.

'You know,' she said, as we reached the open spaces, 'we really ought to do something about Oates, something that would teach him that we're not put into this world for pleasure alone. I can't suggest what offhand, but if we put our heads together, we could think of something. You ought to stay on, Bertie, and help me bring his ginger hairs in sorrow to the grave.'

I raised an eyebrow.

'As the guest of your Uncle Watkyn?'

'You could muck in with Harold. There's a spare room at that cottage place of his.'

'Sorry, no.'

'You won't stay on?'

'I will not. I intend to put as many miles as possible in as short a time as possible between Totleigh-in-the-Wold and myself. And it's no good your using that expression "lily-livered poltroon", because I am adamant.'

She made what I believe is called a *moue*. It's done by pushing the lips out and drawing them in again.

'I thought it wouldn't be any use asking you. No spirit, that's your trouble, no enterprise. I'll have to get Harold to do it.'

And as I stood shuddering at the picture her words conjured up, she pushed off, exhibiting dudgeon. And I was still speculating as to what tureen of soup she was planning to land the sainted Pinker in and hoping that he would have enough sense to stay out of it, when Jeeves drove up in the car, a welcome sight.

'Good morning, sir,' he said. 'I trust you slept well.'

'Fitfully, Jeeves. Those plank beds are not easy on the fleshy parts.'

'So I would be disposed to imagine, sir. And your disturbed night has left you ruffled, I am sorry to see. You are far from *soigné*.'

I could, I suppose, have said something about 'Way down upon the *soigné* river,' but I didn't. My mind was occupied with deeper thoughts. I was in pensive mood.

'You know, Jeeves,' I said, 'one lives and learns.'

'Sir?'

'I mean, this episode has been a bit of an eye-opener to me. It has taught me a lesson. I see now what a mistake one makes in labelling someone as a ruddy Gawd-help-us just because he normally behaves like a ruddy Gawd-help-us. Look closely, and we find humanity in the unlikeliest places.'

'A broadminded view, sir.'

'Take this Sir W. Bassett. In my haste, I have always pencilled him in as a hellhound without a single redeeming quality. But what do I find? He has this softer side to him. Having got Bertram out on a limb, he does not, as one would have expected, proceed to saw it off, but tempers justice with mercy, declining to press the charge. It has touched me a good deal to discover that under that forbidding exterior there lies a heart of gold. Why are you looking like a stuffed frog, Jeeves? Don't you agree with me?'

'Not altogether, sir, when you attribute Sir Watkyn's leniency to sheer goodness of heart. There were inducements.'

'I don't dig you, Jeeves.'

'I made it a condition that you be set at liberty, sir.'

My inability to dig him became intensified. He seemed to me to be talking through the back of his neck, the last thing you desire in a personal attendant.

'How do you mean, condition? Condition of what?'

'Of my entering his employment, sir. I should mention that during my visit to Brinkley Court Sir Watkyn very kindly expressed appreciation of the manner in which I performed my duties and made me an offer to leave your service and enter his. This offer, conditional upon your release, I have accepted.'

The police station at Totleigh-in-the-Wold is situated in the main street of that village, and from where we were standing I had a view of the establishments of a butcher, a baker, a grocer and a publican licensed to sell tobacco, ales and spirits. And as I heard these words, this butcher, this baker, this grocer and this publican seemed to pirouette before my eyes as if afflicted with St. Vitus dance.

'You're leaving me?' I gasped, scarcely able to b. my e.

The corner of his mouth twitched. He seemed to be about to smile, but of course thought better of it.

'Only temporarily, sir.'

Again I was unable to dig him.

'Temporarily?'

'I think it more than possible that after perhaps a week or so differences will arise between Sir Watkyn and myself, compelling me to resign my position. In that event, if you are not already suited, sir, I shall be most happy to return to your employment.'

I saw all. It was a ruse, and by no means the worst of them. His brain enlarged by constant helpings of fish, he had seen the way and found a formula acceptable to all parties. The mists cleared from before my eyes, and the butcher, the baker, the grocer and the publican licensed to sell tobacco, ales and spirits switched back again to what is called the status quo.

A rush of emotion filled me.

'Jeeves,' I said, and if my voice shook, what of it? We Woosters are but human, 'you stand alone. Others abide our question, but you don't, as the fellow said. I wish there was something I could do to repay you.'

He coughed that sheep-like cough of his.

'There does chance to be a favour it is within your power to bestow, sir.'

'Name it, Jeeves. Ask of me what you will, even unto half my kingdom.'

'If you could see your way to abandoning your Alpine hat, sir.'

I ought to have seen it coming. That cough should have told me. But I hadn't, and the shock was severe. For an instant I don't mind admitting that I reeled.

'You would go as far as that?' I said, chewing the lower lip.

'It was merely a suggestion, sir.'

I took the hat off and gazed at it. The morning sunlight played on it, and it had never looked so blue, its feather so pink.

'I suppose you know you're breaking my heart?'

'I am sorry, sir.'

I sighed. But, as I have said, the Woosters can take it.

'Very well, Jeeves. So be it.'

I gave him the hat. It made me feel like a father reluctantly throwing his child from the sledge to divert the attention of the pursuing wolf pack, as I believe happens all the time in Russia in the winter months, but what would you?

'You propose to burn this Alpine hat, Jeeves?'

'No, sir. To present it to Mr. Butterfield. He thinks it will be of assistance to him in his courtship.'

'His what?'

'Mr. Butterfield is courting a widowed lady in the village, sir.'

This surprised me.

'But surely he was a hundred and four last birthday?'

'He is well stricken in years, yes, sir, but nevertheless –'

'There's life in the old dog yet?'

'Precisely, sir.'

My heart melted. I ceased to think of self. It had just occurred to me that in the circumstances I would be unable to conclude my visit by tipping Butterfield. The hat would fill that gap.

'All right, Jeeves, give him the lid, and heaven speed his wooing. You might tell him that from me.'

'I will make a point of doing so. Thank you very much, sir.'

'Not at all, Jeeves.'

The P G Wodehouse Society (UK)

The P G Wodehouse Society (UK) was formed in 1997 and exists to promote the enjoyment of the works of the greatest humorist of the twentieth century.

The Society publishes a quarterly magazine, *Wooster Sauce*, which features articles, reviews, archive material and current news. It also publishes an occasional newsletter in the *By The Way* series which relates a single matter of Wodehousean interest. Members are rewarded in their second and subsequent years by receiving a specially produced text of a Wodehouse magazine story which has never been collected into one of his books.

A variety of Society events are arranged for members including regular meetings at a London club, a golf day, a cricket match, a Society dinner, and walks around Bertie Wooster's London. Meetings are also arranged in other parts of the country.

Membership enquiries

Membership of the Society is available to applicants from all parts of the world. The cost of a year's membership in 1999 was £15. Enquiries and requests for an application form should be addressed in writing to the Membership Secretary, Helen Murphy, at 16 Herbert Street, Plaistow, London E13 8BE, or write to the Editor of *Wooster Sauce*, Tony Ring, at 34 Longfield Road, Great Missenden, Bucks HP16 0EG.

You can visit their website at:
http://www.eclipse.co.uk/wodehouse

The Jeeves Omnibus
1
P. G. Wodehouse

'It beats me why a man of his genius is satisfied to hang around pressing my clothes and what not,' says Bertie. 'If I had Jeeves's brain, I should have a stab at being Prime Minister or something.'

Luckily for us, Bertie Wooster manages to retain Jeeves's services through all the vicissitudes of purple socks and purloined policeman's helmets, and here, gathered together, is the first omnibus of Jeeves novels and stories: *Thank You, Jeeves, The Code of the Woosters* and *The Inimitable Jeeves.*

The Jeeves Omnibus
2
P. G. Wodehouse

'To the best of my knowledge Jeeves has never encountered a charging rhinoceros, but should the contingency occur, I have no doubt that the animal, meeting his eye, would check itself in mid-stride, roll over and lie purring with its legs in the air.'

Jeeves may not always see eye to eye with Bertie on ties and fancy waistcoats, but he can always be relied on to whisk his young master spotlessly out of the soup (even if, for tactical reasons, he did drop him in it in the first place). The paragon of Gentlemen's Personal Gentlemen shimmers through these fat pages in much the same effortless way he did through the First Jeeves Omnibus.

This volume contains
Right Ho, Jeeves
Joy in the Morning
and *Carry on, Jeeves*

The Jeeves Omnibus
3
P. G. Wodehouse

'There are aspects of Jeeves's character which have
frequently caused coldness to arise between us. He is one of
those fellows who, if you give them a
thingummy, take a what-d'you-call-it.'
BERTRAM WOOSTER

This volume, containing *The Mating Season, Ring for Jeeves* and
Very Good, Jeeves, give bumper opportunities for both
thingummies and what-d'you-call-its in plots as devious and
situations as funny as any in Wodehouse.

The Jeeves Omnibus
5
P. G. Wodehouse

"He gave the hunting crop a twitch.
'My daughter has been here.'
'She did look in.'
'Ha!'
I knew what that 'ha!' meant. It was short for 'I shall now
thrash you within an inch of your life.' A moment later, he used
the longer version, as if in doubt as to whether he had made
himself clear."

Poor Bertie is in the soup again, and throughout this latest
omnibus it is only Jeeves who keeps him from being the fish
and the main course as well. In these delightful pages you will
encounter all the stalwarts who have made the Jeeves novels and
stories the very pinnacle of English humour, from Aunts
Agatha and Dahlia to Roderick Spode, Tuppy Glossop,
Madeline Bassett, Oofy Prosser and Anatole the Chef.

At the end even Augustus the cat has come to be much obliged
to Jeeves.

This volume contains
Much Obliged, Jeeves
Aunts Aren't Gentlemen
'Extricating Young Gussie'
'Jeeves Make an Omelette'
and *'Jeeves and the Greasy Bird'*

The Golf Omnibus
P. G. Wodehouse

'I attribute the insane arrogance of the later Roman emperors almost entirely to the fact that, never having played golf, they never knew that strangely chastening humility which is engendered by a topped chip-shot. If Cleopatra had been ousted in the first round of the Ladies Singles, we would have heard a lot less of her proud imperiousness.'

The Oldest Member's reverence for golf does not cramp his style in telling some of the funniest, tallest and most joyful stories in the whole Wodehouse canon. In this splendid Omnibus, introduced by Wodehouse himself, love and the links are inextricably intertwined, and the reader can click with Cuthbert, thrill to the feats of the Magic Plus Fours and even leap cleanly into The Purification of Rodney Spelvin.

To be published February 2000
What Ho!
The best of P. G. Wodehouse
Introduced by Stephen Fry

Published to mark the 25th anniversary of his death, this is the first major selection of P.G. Wodehouse's work to appear for a generation. Introduced by Stephen Fry, it also includes previously unpublished work.

We all know Jeeves and Wooster, but what is the best Jeeves story? What is your favourite story to feature Lord Emsworth and his unique pig, the Empress of Blandings? And how many readers of Wodehouse know the best of Ukridge, the Oldest Member, the Hollywood stories? This bumper anthology of stories, novel-extracts, working drafts, articles, letters and poems give a fresh angle on the twentieth century's greatest humorist as we enter a new century and a new millennium.

There are old favourites aplenty, but this selection provides the best overall celebration of side-splitting humour and sheer good nature available in the pages of any book. The anthology has been compiled with enthusiastic support from the various P.G. Wodehouse societies around the world.